RIDERS UPON THE STORM

RIDERS UPON THE STORM

PHILIP PAROTTI

CASEMATE

Philadelphia & Oxford

Published in the United States of America and Great Britain in 2023 by
CASEMATE PUBLISHERS
1950 Lawrence Road, Havertown, PA 19083, USA
and
The Old Music Hall, 106–108 Cowley Road, Oxford OX4 1JE, UK

Paperback Edition: ISBN 978-1-63624-244-6
Digital Edition: ISBN 978-1-63624-245-3

A CIP record for this book is available from the British Library

Printed and bound in the United Kingdom by CPI Group (UK) Ltd, Croydon, CR0 4YY

Typeset in India by Lapiz Digital Services, Chennai.

For a complete list of Casemate titles, please contact:

CASEMATE PUBLISHERS (US)
Telephone (610) 853-9131
Fax (610) 853-9146
Email: casemate@casematepublishers.com
www.casematepublishers.com

CASEMATE PUBLISHERS (UK)
Telephone (0)1226 734350
Email: casemate-uk@casematepublishers.co.uk
www.casematepublishers.co.uk

For Lisa, David, Angela, and Mike

Stand up and meet the war.

The Hun is at the gate!

Our world has passed away

In wantonness o'erthrown.

Rudyard Kipling, "For All We Have and Are"

1

The snows fell early that year, and not long after came the ice. By the middle of November, the ice breakers had ceased to plow up from Lake Michigan, the mouth of the harbor—indeed the entire south side of Lake Superior—had iced over, and the *Robert Duncan Fife*, made fast to her berth in Duluth, had laid up for the winter without her master knowing when in April, May, or even June she would once more be able to begin transporting her heavy cargoes of iron ore south to the mills around Gary and Detroit.

"So you intend to go ashore and head east?" the master was saying, speaking to his third mate, Ben Snow, who at the age of twenty-six still seemed to the master relatively young and whom he had been training to do the work for the previous three years, ever since Snow had joined the *Fife* fresh from his years at the Massachusetts Nautical School.

"Aye, Captain," Snow said. "Seems the right thing to do. Seems they might need me. Seems the right moment to go."

"Aye," the captain said, "there's a war on, no doubt about it. Wilson and the Congress declared one. Germans ain't got no cause to complain, not as I see it, not after sinking that *Lusitania* and killing all them folks. We ought to give 'em a lickin' for that, sure. Offered to go myself back in '98 as first mate on a ferry takin'

1

troops to Cuba, but she sank 'fore I could reach her, so it didn't come off. Spent that war right here, on the lakes, as second mate on the *Thomas G. Harding*. But that was merchant steamin'. You're talkin' Navy, ain't you?"

"Aye, Sir," Ben said, his tone remaining level.

"Ain't had no experience with the Navy myself," said the captain. "I've ridden Coast Guard cutters a time or two, as a passenger, but the Navy's a different kettle of fish. Blue water, those birds. From what I hear, a lot of them knows their business, but a few of 'em don't, so watch out for the ones that don't. Different out here, we're seamen pretty much. The paper pushers don't come out with us 'cept for occasional inspections, so we don't have much to do with 'em. Navy's different in that way. Lots of interplay between what goes on ashore and what goes on afloat. Mutual interference, if you sees what I mean. How'd you snag it?"

"I wrote a letter," Ben said, "to the Navy Department in Washington. They wrote back and set me up for an interview in New York City, on the 28th of November, with a Lieutenant Commander Howard, one of the district personnel officers at the Third Naval District."

Slowly, the master picked up the cracked pipe that rested on his desk, pressed some tobacco into it, struck a match, and lighted it, blowing a cloud of blue smoke into the air over his head. A few seconds passed, and then, a few more until finally the master looked up and said, "I don't like losin' you, Snow, but from the looks of the ice this year we're gonna be six months idle and laid up in berth, which will give you precious little to do, so I won't stand in your way. Maybe this thing will be over quick and you can get back to us without delay, but if things turn out different, you can count on me to recommend you to the owners when it does conclude. Meanwhile, I've written a letter which you can take along to show this Howard that you're gonna talk to. It attests to your skill with deck seamanship, navigation, and piloting, and it might come in useful. I hope it will back up what the man ought to see for himself if he has any sense."

At first, Ben wasn't quite sure what to say. He had expected more of an argument, a reluctance on the master's part to let him leave the Merchant Marine and shift his seagoing experience to the Navy. Relations between the Merchant Marine and the Navy were always friendly, but they were nevertheless competitive, each service taking pride in its own, each in a quiet way thinking that it was the better of the two.

"Thank you, Captain," Ben said. "I appreciate what you've taught me, and I appreciate your support."

"Don't." The master laughed. "Later, if them bullets start flyin', you might think better of me if I'd tried to hold you here and want to curse me for not doin' it. Jus' remember to keep your head down and hope them Germans never find the range."

"Aye, I'll do that, Sir," Ben said.

"Aye, Lad," the master said, standing and offering Ben his hand, the creases at the corners of his eyes pinching into a smile. "Now, off with you. Mind how you go, and good hunting."

At the foot of the brow, with the snow sweeping in from the lake and the temperature dropping, Ben tightened his scarf, hoisted his duffle bag onto his shoulder, and headed toward the station to catch his train for New York.

2

Benedict Jonson Snow—Ben to his friends, of whom he still retained one or two from the days of his schooling—knew the outline of New York City because, years before, he had been born and grown up there. His father, Bernard Snow, had immigrated from Manchester in the 1880s, established Snow's Marine Machine Works in one of the warehouses on the lower Manhattan side of the Hudson, and until the economic downturn at the beginning of the century, prospered. In the days when prosperity still remained well within his grasp, he had met and married Inger Jonson, the pretty blond daughter of a Swedish shipping family that had settled years earlier on the Heights in Brooklyn. Bernard Snow, preferring to live closer to the headquarters of his business, had then settled his wife in a comfortable three-bedroom apartment on East 89th Street, and there, some years later, Benedict—Ben, their only son—had been born. There he had grown up until, not long after he'd reached the age of eleven, his world had suddenly come apart.

Initially, it was the sudden, totally unexpected economic downturn, one that would only be felt throughout the remainder of the country later, that had thrown things awry. Almost overnight, from growing prosperity, his father's business had slipped into narrow straits. With Inger's family having died out before Ben was fully out of short pants and therefore being unable to help, Bernard had made arrangements for a sizable loan from a New Jersey bank that would have allowed Snow and Son Marine Machine Works to remain solvent. On the morning when Bernard and Inger were to conclude the arrangements, the water taxi they were riding on was struck and cut in half by a Panamanian freighter. Neither of his parents survived the collision.

For Ben, at the age of twelve, the shock was almost too much to bear. Prior to the accident, the home in which Ben had grown up had been one which took a serious, no-nonsense approach to life. While his parents had never been outwardly affectionate, gushing, they had nevertheless been loving, and while his upbringing had been strict, it had also been always mindful of his welfare. With their sudden death it was as if he'd slipped from his moorings, leaving him adrift. Within weeks, without recourse to surviving family anywhere, he was thrown back onto the unknown benevolence of a court-appointed guardian, T. Pierpont Dobbs, his parents' able but aloof lawyer.

Dobbs, a sixty-year-old bachelor with gray hair, a man who had never been married and who had never had children, took Ben into his home following the accident, and there Ben was more or less taken in hand by Dobbs' housekeeper, Mrs. Theodore, whose family had once played an important role in New York politics. To Mrs. Theodore's regret, her family's lights had dimmed considerably in the 1890s until they went out altogether before the turn of the century when the last of her surviving relatives died. Mrs. Theodore, Dobbs' senior by at least six years, proved amiable and clear sighted. At her urging, Dobbs, who considered himself totally unfit to guide Ben into and through his teens, called Ben in not long after he had moved into the house, sat him down in a chair across from his desk, and announced what he called a "man-to-man chat."

"I think," T. Pierpont Dobbs said, showing Ben the shadow of a smile, "that you might not like it here if you were to remain in residence on a permanent basis. No boys or girls your own age, if you see what I mean. All things dull and boring for a lad your age."

Recognizing that Dobbs expected a response, Ben nodded and said, "Yes Sir."

"Therefore," Dobbs continued, "if I am to do right by you and do right by your parents whom I greatly admired, I think it best that I enroll you in a school where you may thrive among boys your own age. Your mother, bless her, inherited enough from her own family so that she and your father set aside a competence for your education, so it will be upon that competence that your future will ride. Tomorrow, you and Mrs. Theodore will take the train to New London, and there you will be enrolled in St. Martin's School, which will give you your initial grounding, and a good school it is. I can tell you that because my brother and I were both students there before you were born. The Masters at St. Martin's will prep you thoroughly for places like Harvard, Yale, or Princeton, but once you pass out, I think it might be prudent to see you prepared for a practical career by means of which you may immediately begin to earn your living. Your father, never having attended a university himself, was not a great fan of those institutions. But at least twice in my dealings with him, he mentioned that he hoped to prepare you for a life at sea in which you might rise in time to command one of the great ships which his business so ably helped to equip. With that thought in mind, should your studies prove congenial, I intend to enter you eventually at the Massachusetts Nautical School, which will give you an able grounding in seamanship, sailing, and the engineering fundamentals that will support a future for you in the American Merchant Marine. Have you any objections to this plan?"

Knowing little about boarding schools, universities, or maritime academies and even less about what it might mean to command a ship, Ben could think of no objections. The next day, following a pleasant trip to New London with Mrs. Theodore, he was set down at St. Martin's and left there to thrive.

His first six months at St. Martin's had proved difficult. As a new boy, he had hurdles to leap and adjustments to make, but quick of wit and determined to make the best of what he had been left with, Ben leapt the hurdles and made the adjustments. Then, taking an interest in his studies and in the sports and means of recreation that St. Martin's offered, he did actually thrive. Early on and to his surprise, he showed a particular capacity to excel in mathematics, and later, joined to that expertise, he added what St. Martin's offered in the way of both chemistry and physics. Latin he did not find congenial, although he liked Virgil when he could read him in translation and Homer when *The Iliad* and *The Odyssey* finally presented themselves. Thus, reading became a pastime for him, a form of recreation other than soccer and baseball, in which he took part and played proficiently. Vacations he spent at the school, living temporarily with this or that master and his family, save for a week at Christmas when he returned to New York. Dobbs saw to it that he was kept busy visiting the city's plentiful supply of museums as well as a theater performance or two. But then it was back to school for another year until, not long after he finally popped out of St. Martin's at the age of eighteen, he popped almost as quickly right back into Massachusetts Nautical and began a professional preparation for the remainder of his life.

Ben's time at Massachusetts Nautical School turned out to be well spent. At nearly six feet in height and weighing well over 170 pounds, Ben sailed through his "Youngie" year, enduring whatever the upperclassmen threw his way with regard to hazing and professional questions which came, as he knew and accepted, as his introduction to the school. He resumed playing soccer and baseball, boxed, and dug into his studies. Later, cruising aboard the *Rockport*, the former USS *Ranger*, a U.S. Navy screw-driven gunboat that the State had purchased for use as the school's training ship, he learned both to sail—the ship having retained her three masts—and to steam—her plant supplying her with an ample means of propulsion. During his first summer cruise and the annual cruises which followed, he gradually turned himself into a competent junior officer. When he graduated at age twenty-two and passed the examination for a third mate's certificate in the Merchant Marine, Dobbs and the aging Mrs. Theodore looked on with some degree of pride.

"Of the competence left to you by your parents, nearly one thousand dollars remains," Dobbs said to Ben following the ceremony, handing him a check for the said amount. "My advice to you is to bank this as a cushion against the unforeseen. And I have something else for you as well. A client of mine owns shares in an ore carrier on the Great Lakes. The master of that vessel happens to be looking for a third mate, the previous holder of the position having passed his examinations for a second mate's certificate, advanced, and moved to a new billet elsewhere. The name of the ship is the *Robert Duncan Fife*, and she is home-ported at Duluth on Lake Superior. If you are amenable," Dobbs said with a smile, shaking Ben's hand, "I would like to stand you to a train ticket as a graduation gift and see you on your way."

Ben was amenable and so said; three hours later, after boarding a train in Buzzards Bay, he was on his way west to take up a life at sea.

So, when Benedict Snow stepped from the station on the morning of November 28, 1917, regardless of the snow which seemed to be filtering down onto the morning rush, he knew where he was and where he was going. Without hesitation, he picked up his duffle bag and went there, telling the cabbie to take him to Third Naval District Headquarters, 280 Broadway. Having gained entrance to the building by first showing Commander Howard's letter to the Marine sentry at the door and then showing it again to a yeoman inside who had mounted his watch behind a reception desk, he was told to wait and took up a spot on a row of benches which backed against the wall of the foyer. But on that particular morning, with naval officers and enlisted men moving to and from the doors in what seemed to be herds, he did not have to wait long before a stubby yeoman wearing pressed blues called his name and summoned him from his perch. Not five minutes passed before the yeoman had knocked twice upon the pane of a glazed glass door, opened it, announced "Mr. Snow to see you, Sir," and directed Ben inside.

The office as Ben saw it seemed spare and sparsely furnished. Three file cabinets stood upright against one wall, a coat tree with an officer's cap and greatcoat hanging from it stood beside them, and additional piles of files and papers seemed to be stacked on the deck beside those. To Ben's left he saw a desk, two straight-backed chairs placed in front of it, and a tall, gray-headed man wearing the gold braid on his sleeves of a lieutenant commander—a man who seemed so thin to Ben that he felt he might have mistaken him for a coach whip.

"Lieutenant Commander Howard, Sir?" Ben inquired. "I'm Benedict Snow, Sir, here for my 0900 appointment."

"Welcome, Mr. Snow," Howard said, his voice coming up from below like the echo from a tunnel. "Take a seat. We have much to discuss. I presume you had a good trip from Duluth. I'm afraid we can't match her for the extent of her ice and the bitterness of her cold, but as you probably noticed, New York is trying."

It wasn't much in the way of levity, but it was enough; the hint of a smile showing around Lieutenant Commander Howard's lips and eyes told Ben that his interview would not be hostile, that he hadn't arrived to be raked over some kind of naval furnace.

"Thank you, Sir," he said, taking the chair to which he'd been directed. "I had a good trip and a quick one."

"Get some sleep on the train, did you?"

"Yes Sir," Ben said.

"Good," Howard said, "because we have much to do, you and I, and if you don't mind, I think we ought to get right to it."

"Yes Sir," Ben repeated.

To Ben's surprise, Howard reached into a drawer and heaved a thick file onto the top of his desk, opened it, studied the first page, and then looked up with yet another hint of a smile.

"I think," Howard said, "that we may dispense with the usual preliminaries. As you can see from the thickness of your file, we already know a great deal about you, Mr. Snow. I won't say that our investigative people are exceptionally thorough, but since you first wrote to the Navy Department, they have been busy, and what they've collected seems thorough enough. We know about your antecedents in New York, the Snows and the Jonsons. It's a pity that Mr. Dobbs is no longer with us, but his firm felt no hesitation in letting us read their files on you, so we know all about your education both at St. Martin's and the Massachusetts Nautical School, and the owners of the *Robert Duncan Fife* were also gracious enough to let us read their files on you. I presume you have a letter for me from your former captain?"

"I do," Ben said, instantly producing the master's letter.

Very quickly, Howard took the letter, slit the envelope, and read it before looking up with a broader smile. "Exactly what we expected," he said. "We had some questions about whether or not you were fully qualified to do celestial navigation, but this entirely satisfies me on that point.

"Now, the question we must next answer is this: are you prepared at this time, Mr. Snow, to join the United States Naval Reserve and take a commission as a temporary naval officer in your country's service? Sorry that we can't offer you a regular commission, because in my view you are eminently qualified, but the Reserve is the next best thing, and at a later date, should you find that you wish to continue with the Navy, you can always apply to augment. So, what about it, Mr. Snow?"

"Yes Sir," Ben said. "A Reserve commission is what I'd hoped for."

"Good," Howard said, immediately pressing a button on his desk.

Even as Ben could hear the bell still ringing in the adjacent room, the door opened. Something resembling a specter entered, a tall ensign wearing a cocked hat, full dress, and equipped with a sword.

"Mr. Gill," Howard said, standing and indicating for Ben to stand, "our recruiting officer. He will administer your oath and have you sign a paper or two, and that will conclude the formalities."

Never once cracking a smile or changing his expression in any way from the august demeanor with which he had entered the room, Ensign Gill carried out his duties with enough formality to have impressed a president or a king, had Ben sign twice on dotted lines, did an abrupt about face, and returned to the adjoining office, closing the door behind him.

Ben didn't know whether to laugh or remain silent, but in the end, he remained silent and let Howard do the laughing. "Mr. Gill is very efficient," Howard said *sotto voce*. "He's a Yale man," as though that revelation covered all of the bases.

Ben allowed himself a mere trace of a smile.

"Right," Howard said, pulling onto his desk a second file and a blueprint. "Now, with that out of the way—and incidentally, Mr. Snow, you're being commissioned as a lieutenant junior grade rather than as an ensign based upon your extensive experience at sea—we can get down to some serious business. Do you know what a submarine chaser is?"

"If that is a class of ship, Sir, I can't say that I've ever seen one."

"A class of ship it is," Howard said, unrolling a blueprint and quickly taping down the corners to the top of his desk. "And this is a print of SC 65X, the very subchaser you'll be commanding by this evening. I ..."

"Pardon, Sir," Ben said, a note of alarm filtering into his voice. "Will there be no schooling by way of introduction to such things as naval procedure, discipline, expectations, that sort of thing?"

"None," Howard said, showing Ben an even broader smile. "We simply don't have time for it, Mr. Snow. There's a war on, as you know, and we need you now, right now, rather than tomorrow or next month. You already know enough about leadership and discipline from your previous duty, and if you will sit down and read a copy of Navy Regulations when you assume command of your ship, you will know as much as the other officers with whom you are to serve. Good enough?"

"Yes Sir," Ben said, not wishing to press the point, despite suddenly feeling a little weak in the knees.

"Right," Howard said, "now, the SC 65X. She was originally designed to be sold to the French, but having added one or two pieces of confidential equipment to her we declared her experimental, which explains the X designation, and decided to keep her to ourselves. So, with regard to vital statistics, here's what you need to know: SC 65X is 110 feet long, with a beam of fifteen feet five inches, and she displaces seventy-five tons. She carries three six-cylinder gasoline engines that turn three propellers with a fuel capacity of 2,500 gallons and has a cruising radius of around one thousand nautical miles. In a pinch, she can probably get up to 16 or 17 knots but normally cruises at 8–10 knots. She's built of wood, and from what we now know, she rolls but remains very seaworthy. With regard to her armament, she carries one 3″/23 caliber gun forward, capable of holing a submarine's conning tower, one Y-Gun amidships for throwing three-hundred-pound depth charges, two depth-charge racks on her stern, and will carry two 30-caliber Browning machine guns, one mounted on each wing of her bridge. In her magazines, she can carry at least a hundred rounds of three-inch ammunition and at least twelve additional depth charges. Have all that, do you?"

"Yes Sir," Ben said.

"Now, here's the pretty part." Howard said, leaning forward on his desk, a glint in his eye. "SC 65X also carries a C-Tube hydrophone, the new, confidential equipment I mentioned. It's a T-shaped instrument which is lowered and raised through the magazine. When the T is lowered down into the sea beneath the keel, rubber C-Tubes at each end of the head of the T can pick up the sounds of a submarine's propellers at a considerable distance. An operator sitting in the magazine and wearing earphones can hear those sounds very well and take a bearing on them from a dial attached to the long arm of the T. Then, when operating with at least one or two other chasers, the bearings taken on each vessel can be triangulated so as to cross on or very near the actual position of the submarine so that it can be attacked."

"Does this hydrophone pick up the sounds of other propellers, Sir?" Ben asked.

"Ah, very quick on the uptake." Howard laughed. "Yes it does. Which means that when listening for a sub, your boat and the others must be stopped, and if ships are in the area their propeller beats can also interfere. So, in pursuit of an attack, you will be stopping for listening periods, and then going forward toward the supposed location, stopping to listen again, and then going forward once more, hopefully to drop your ash cans and sink whatever U-boat you've detected and planned to attack. Clear enough?"

Ben found Lieutenant Commander Howard's swift explanation clear enough in theory but imagined that it would take a deal of training and practice to become effective. "Yes Sir," he said.

"Good," Howard said. "I'm not going to tell you that this device isn't primitive because it is, but Raytheon has developed it for us, and it is a light year beyond having to find German and Austrian U-boats on the surface before we can attack them. What you will mostly be doing is hunting for enemy submarines in an attempt to attack or hold them down, as well as escort duty. This little honey will put you far out beyond what either we, the French, the Italians, or the Royal Navy have previously had at their disposal for the hunt."

It was an advance that Ben had never dreamed of when he had given the matter any thought.

"Now," Howard continued, "take another look at the blueprint. Up forward you can see the crew's head and the forward crew's quarters. Moving back from those and beneath the 3″/23 you have the magazine and the listening room. Aft of those are the officer's quarters and above them the pilot house and the bridge. Astern of the officer's quarters is the engine room, with depth-charge stowage astern of that compartment, and moving on back, the after crew's quarters, the galley, and the lazaret for stowage. It's a neat package, but it is also cramped. You're going to have a crew of twenty-two men aboard including you and your exec, and if all of you aren't living armpit to armpit, you'll nevertheless be close. I won't say that it's going to be comfortable, but you'll have to make the best of it, and I know that you will."

As Ben studied the blueprint for details, Howard sat back in his chair, took out his pipe, filled and lighted it, and then after a puff or two once more focused his attention on Ben.

"You'll be taking a copy of that blueprint with you," he said, "so you will have plenty of time to familiarize yourself with the details once you reach your ship. Next point: once you leave here, go straight to Broadbent and Stevens Naval Tailors on Greenwich Ave. They'll be expecting you, and they'll be able to fix you up with a full kit of uniforms pretty much off the rack. Be damn sure that you get a greatcoat because you're going to need one where you're going."

"Will they advance those uniforms on credit?" Ben asked.

"No need," Howard said. "An initial uniform allowance has been credited to your account, so for most of what you'll want, you should be covered. And don't let them fob you off with inferior or synthetic material; demand wool because it will hold up over time, and it's best against the weather."

Ben made a mental note, knowing that his working khaki from the *Fife* would be interchangeable with whatever the Navy required.

"Got all that, with regard to the uniforms?" Howard said. "Any questions about them?"

"No Sir," Ben said.

"Right," Howard went on, "and be sure you change into one before you go to your ship."

"Understood," Ben said, although he couldn't imagine why Howard had chosen to emphasize the point.

"So," Howard said, "that brings us to the most important issue we have to discuss and one which is going to take some handling on your part."

Somehow, Ben had known it was coming. What *it* might be or what *it* might portend he didn't know, but understood that he was about to find out.

"The Navy, Mr. Snow, does not often make mistakes," Lieutenant Commander Howard said with a sigh, "but it's a human institution, so sometimes it does, and in the case of SC 65X, it has made a whopper. Whoever made this one made it well before I came to this office, so I'm pleased to say that I am not responsible, but I am most certainly responsible for correcting it. That's where you come in. You're the correction. With me so far?"

With a slight nod of his head and a wary smile, Ben said that he was.

"SC 65X came off the ways in September, down in Camden, and someone down there in the Fourth Naval District assigned her officers and her crew. In my humble opinion—and believe me, Sir, I do not like to think ill of a brother officer—but in my opinion, that man was either drunk or an idiot because the officer he assigned to command SC 65X has proved himself to be an utter disaster. The man's name—and I will not call him a captain because in my opinion he isn't fit to be a seaman recruit—but the man's name is Garrison, Willard Garrison, and apparently, before he wrangled his commission, he was raising swine in Arkansas somewhere in the vicinity of Magnolia. How he managed to talk someone into giving him a direct commission as a lieutenant, junior grade, is a mystery that I cannot solve, but I suspect that some kind of really offensive political corruption may have played a role. As far as any of us know, the man had never gone near the sea before he reported aboard, and since his arrival has never bothered to learn the first thing about it."

Ben had difficulty accepting what he was hearing. The odds against it were too high.

"Right now," Howard continued, "SC 65X is tied up in a nest over on the Section Piers at Staten Island. She came up from Camden last week, and given the little that man knows about the sea, I can't imagine how he even got her out of the Chesapeake and up here. Either his exec conned her or her quartermaster did because that's the only way the ship could have made the voyage. But that's just the beginning of the problem. Because I'm in charge of manning the subchasers, I went over to take a look at them when they arrived, and while the others are in fit condition, all of them being relatively new and untried, SC 65X looks like a virtual pigsty. It's barely two months old but it is filthy. The equipment isn't being maintained, neither below decks nor above, and I found the crew both surly and lazy. If I had the manpower to spare, I'd jerk the entire bunch off that vessel and set them to cleaning receiving barracks somewhere inland as a punishment. But the fact is that we don't have the manpower, not at the moment, so what I'm sending you over there to do is to relieve Garrison and whip that vessel into shape. She's got to be ready for operations in two or three weeks so you're going to have to act fast, and rest assured, I'm going to back you to the hilt with whatever measures you take. Judging from your record and what your previous master has had to say about you, I think you're the man for the job. Sorry about this, Mr. Snow, but we've got a war to win, and it's going to be up to men like you to win it. It's time to get cracking, if you see what I mean."

Ben saw. He didn't like what he saw. It was about the last thing that he'd expected when he'd made his decision to sign up and join the service, but realizing at once that there was nothing for it and that he would have to prevail and impose his will on the job to which he'd been assigned, he nodded his head and simply asked: "Right, Sir. When do I start?"

"Now." Howard said, standing up and shaking Ben's hand. "Uniforms first, and then get yourself straight over to Stanton Island and start getting that vessel into shape. Here are your orders," he said, handing Ben a packet, "and good luck to you, Lieutenant Snow."

3

By 1500 that afternoon, in service dress blue and with his greatcoat buttoned up to his chin against the snow which blew down from the Hudson across the Upper Bay, Ben found himself standing at the head of the Section Piers on Stanton Island, his eyes narrowing as he surveyed with disgust the small wooden chaser that was to be his home. SC 65X was tied up outboard in a nest of three submarine chasers, the other two looking pristine and clean, his looking old, filthy, and utterly devoid of attraction.

Oh Christ, he thought, wondering why he had ever let Dobbs talk him into taking to the sea in the first place, *how has it come to this?* But Ben knew the question was rhetorical. He knew exactly how things had arrived at this point in his life, and he wasn't disappointed. And he knew in his bones that if he'd had it all to do over again, he would have acted in precisely the way that had brought him to this final pass. He faced a challenge—about that he had no doubts—the first task being to get himself aboard and in command of SC 65X. There, he would have no choice other than to organize his command of things in response to the way they presented themselves. Picking up his duffle bag with one hand and the valise that Broadbent and Sevens had given him with the other, Ben threw back his shoulders, straightened himself up, and stepped forward down the pier, stopping on the inboard subchasers to salute the ensign and request permission from the officer of the deck to cross their ships.

Stepping at last onto the deck of SC 65X, Ben looked for the officer of the deck and found no one in sight. Twice he called out and no one answered. Glancing by chance up the deck of the chaser from which he'd just stepped, Ben spotted a sailor having a smoke, leaning against the side of the pilot house.

"They never set no watch, Sir," the man said, shaking his head in disbelief, his contempt for the SC 65X radiating from him like a glow. "They's all down below, probably sleepin' or drinkin' coffee."

"Right," Ben said, his jaw setting. "Thanks."

And with that, leaving his bags near the brow, Ben stepped up the starboard side of the chaser, found the hatch just forward of the pilot house that led down to Officer's Country, and descended into the confined space that served as the cramped wardroom and officer's bunk room. Ben's nose was instantly assaulted by an overpowering stench of alcohol; what smelled to him in every way like cheap, rot-gut Kentucky bourbon. The bunk to starboard was empty, although a grip carrying the label "Ensign Keel" seemed to be sitting in the middle of it, but the bunk to port contained a body—a sleeping, snoring body, a body still wearing scuffed shoes, a body clad in stained and filthy service dress blue, a body that was apparently responsible for the odor in the space. Looking it over with disgust, Ben stepped forward and said two words: "Get up."

The body didn't move, didn't even register a response.

"Get up!" Ben said again, louder, anger coloring his tone.

Still there was no response.

Stepping forward, Ben gave the man a nudge. When that brought no response, he put his hand on the man's shoulder and began to shake him, and after shaking him vigorously for a few seconds, he heard the man growl out a "What the fuck" in half-mumbled, half-swallowed words that indicated the individual still to be almost passed out. Even from two feet away, Ben's nose twitched, sensing the heavy alcoholic odor that the semi-comatose form had exhaled.

"Get up!" Ben once more ordered. "I'm here to relieve you."

That brought a kind of response which, as Ben heard the words, amounted "Get the fugg off my ship!" before the man once more relapsed and began to snore. With that, Ben decided that he'd had it, turned, and climbed back to the main deck where a sailor—wearing a uniform which looked like it had been thrown together out of a rag bag and with a cigarette dripping from his lip—looked Ben up and down and said with a sneer, "You want somethin' 'round here?"

Ben felt the hair on the back of his neck begin to rise with anger.

"Stand to attention and chuck that butt over the side!" Ben snapped. "You address me as *Sir*, sailor, and above decks, upon first sighting of an officer in the day, you salute! Now, let's have it!"

The firmness with which Ben charged his voice shook the man in front of him to his toes. Instantly, the butt went over the side, the man straightened up, and with his hand shaking he attempted an imperfect salute which Ben left quavering for a few seconds before he returned it.

"You have a chief petty officer aboard this vessel?" Ben asked.

"Yeah ... yes Sir," the sailor quickly corrected.

"Find him right now and send him to me in Officer's Country," Ben said. "Do you also have a bucket on this ship?"

"Yes Sir," the sailor said, and by this time he had almost started to vibrate where he so rigidly stood.

"Put it over the side, fill it from the slip, and bring it to me the minute you've found the chief," Ben ordered. "Dismissed!"

Less than a minute later, after the offending sailor had raced aft toward the after crew's quarters and the galley, Ben saw a chief petty officer buttoning his duffle coat emerge from the galley hatch and hasten toward him. Clearly, this particular chief was older than Ben had expected, a man who looked to be in at least his mid-thirties. Neither fat nor thin, the man had obviously started putting on the weight that came with middle age, but judging from his hands that looked dark with a residue of oil, bony, and strong, Ben imagined him to be the vessel's chief engineer and also imagined him to have the mechanical capability to be reliable.

Without going to the extreme of bracing up like a Nautical School cadet, the man nevertheless came to attention when he stood in Ben's presence, saluted, and reported himself.

"Chief Petty Officer Pack, Sir," he said, showing Ben a straight face without guile.

"Chief," Ben said, returning the man's salute. "There's going to be a change of command on this ship in about twenty minutes. Get your men on their feet. Get them into dress blues with duffle coats, and assemble them on the fantail. Where's the executive officer?"

"Ashore, Sir," Pack answered. "Three-day school, ordered by District Headquarters. Due back tomorrow."

"Right," Ben said. "We won't be waiting for him, so see to the men."

With a crisp "Aye, aye," Pack once more saluted and turned on his heel, the sailor with the bucket passing him amidships as he hurried by.

"Sir," the sailor said, holding out the bucket to Ben while saluting with the other hand, his Adam's apple bouncing up and down beneath his scarf.

"Bring that with you, and follow me," Ben ordered, turning and descending again into forward officer's quarters.

Once more below and standing on deck beside the bunk where the officer he took to be Garrison was passed out, Ben spoke sharply but clearly. "Get up, Mr. Garrison. We have a change of command to attend to!"

Garrison, barely moving where he lay, uttered something waspish on the order of "Fugg off!" With that, Ben reached for the bucket, told the sailor who handed it to him to stand back, and pitched everything which the bucket contained straight over Garrison's head.

Garrison roared with outrage and came flailing from the bunk, throwing haymakers in every direction. Ben, prepared for that response, simply sidestepped smartly, planted his right foot, and landed the hardest punch he could throw straight into Garrison's midsection, causing the man to double up and begin vomiting. Ben waited until the contents of the man's stomach had emptied and then pushed him back into a sitting position on the edge of his bunk.

"Your time here has ended," Ben said to Garrison. Then he turned to the sailor. "Fill this bucket with fresh water and bring it back here with some rags, and a clean mop. While you throw this officer's clothes into his valise and carry it out to the pier, he will clean up his own mess. Now, move!"

As the sailor shot up the ladder onto the main deck, Ben once more turned to Garrison, who continued to gasp and heave for air.

"You asked for that punch," Ben said, his eyes boring into the man, "and you had it coming for being drunk on duty and for the shit you've turned this ship into. You've made a mess of things on this vessel, and I don't thank you for having to come in here and clean it up for you. Get on your damn feet, clean up your own vomit, and be on the fantail in fifteen minutes for a change in command. If you aren't there, I promise you that I'll come back down here, drag you up, and toss you right into the bay in front of your entire crew. Now, start moving!"

At the top of the ladder, Ben met the sailor hurrying to return with fresh water and rags.

"Clear out Mr. Garrison's drawers, get all of his uniforms into a bag, and get his kit out to the pier. And then you stay there with it for security until he comes out to fetch his stuff," Ben ordered.

Fifteen minutes later, with the crew assembled on the fantail and with Garrison—unshaven, still staggering, and looking a sickly shade of gray—standing in front of them, Ben produced his orders

22

from the Naval District and read himself into command of SC 65X. Immediately upon announcing that he'd relieved Garrison, Chief Pack, acting on Ben's orders, escorted Garrison to the brow and across the two other subchasers moored inboard where, here and there, sailors and one officer had gathered to witness what seemed to be going on aboard number 65X. When Pack returned, and only then, did Ben give the crew the order to stand at parade rest so that he could speak his piece.

With as stern an expression as he could muster Ben surveyed the men before him, left them standing in silence for a few moments, and then began.

"I don't know what's been going on aboard this vessel since she came off the ways," Ben said, charging his voice with determination, "and I don't care. Starting right now, things are going to be different. Naval discipline, naval courtesy, and naval tradition are coming into effect right now. You may be new to the Navy, some of you, but without regard to time in service, you are all going to become sailors and first-rate professionals, and I mean to break any man among you who can't get with the program. Starting right now with no break for the evening meal, you are going to begin cleaning this ship from the top of the mast to the bottom of the bilges. If you don't get it spotless by midnight, you'll resume in a hurry when I break you out at 0500 in the morning. After the ship is clean, you're going to get clean at the bathhouse up at the head of the pier, and when I say you're to be clean, that includes your uniforms, which are a perfect disgrace."

For several seconds, while once more surveying the men in front of him, Ben let his words sink in. And then, he gave them a sharp command: "Attention on deck! Dismissed! Now, get to it! Chief Pack, if you will see me in my quarters in fifteen minutes, we have things to discuss."

And with that, Ben turned on his heel and strode away toward Officer's Country.

Although the space still stank of bourbon—bad bourbon, the kind of bourbon that Ben wouldn't have wanted to touch with tongs—the deck where Garrison had thrown up seemed fairly clean when Ben once more descended to it. Whether Garrison had taken a strain in cleaning up after himself from shame or through sheer despondency over what Ben had done to remove him didn't matter to Ben; the fact that the deck had been both wiped up and scrubbed with a cleaning and disinfecting agent was all that concerned him, almost making him think that if given half a chance, Garrison might, in time, have made a good deck seaman. How the man had ever become an officer remained the same mystery to Ben that it had been for Commander Howard. From somewhere, the mattress of what would become his bunk had been replaced, and there, as well, he found his duffle bag and the valise containing his uniforms waiting for him to stow. For the time being Ben ignored them and waited for Chief Pack to come to him.

Sitting in a chair beside the small table that folded down from the forward bulkhead, Ben knew that he would have liked to have been able to feel sorry for Garrison. The man's disgrace was total, and Ben had no doubt that Howard intended to dismiss him from the service and return him to whatever pig farm he'd originally managed. But given the condition of SC 65X as he found it and the attitude and morale of the crew that he'd inherited, Ben found that any sympathy he might have felt for Garrison had dissolved the minute he found him drunk and passed out in his bunk. Garrison was obviously a man who wanted to be a naval officer for whatever privileges he thought a commission carried but not for any of the responsibilities that went with it. Somewhere in the Navy, somewhere a sycophant might have been appreciated or even tolerated, he might have found a place. But within the confines of his own experience at sea and what he knew or imagined he knew about the Navy, Ben could not imagine such a place. Sooner or later Garrison would have been found out, and as far as Ben could imagine or fathom it, the finding out would have led to the same dismissal that the command of the Third Naval District was about to accord the man.

At the sound of a knock on the overhead hatch and the question "Permission to enter, Sir?" Chief Pack arrived.

With Ben's permission, Pack descended into the tiny wardroom, stood once more at attention, and presented himself. "Chief Petty Officer Pack, reporting as ordered, Sir?"

"Have a seat," Ben said, pushing the only other chair on the deck over toward where Pack stood, "and relax."

"Thank you, Sir," Pack responded, removing his hat and sitting down before Ben.

"All right, Chief," Ben said, showing the man a straight face. "Let's cut straight through the bullshit and get to brass tacks. This ship is a perfect mess. Why? And Garrison's gone, so let's have it in plain language."

"The man didn't know what he was doing," Pack said straightforwardly. "The job was totally beyond him, and because he didn't know the first thing about it he wouldn't let Mr. Keel or me or any of the others do our jobs either. I guess he was afraid we'd show him up somehow."

"Been in the Navy long, have you?" Ben asked.

"No Sir, only about seven months," Pack said. "I was a gasoline engine mechanic at Ford in Detroit 'fore all this started. When I signed up and swore in, they made me a chief machinist's mate direct, on the basis of my experience, and sent me here as chief engineer. They made Lithgow an MM1 for pretty much the same reason. He was a garage mechanic in Indiana, and Garcia—he's our third man in the black gang—an MM2; he worked as a mechanic at some copper mine in Santa Rita, New Mexico somewheres."

"Any others, while we're on the subject?" Ben asked.

"Pettigrew," Pack said, "MM3, worked in a garage in Chicago 'fore he joined up, and we got two oilers, Bates and Willis. Willis is from Odessa, oil field worker of some kind 'fore he signed, and Bates. Bates was a grease monkey in Philadelphia."

"And that's the lot?"

"Down in the engine room, yes Sir," Pack said.

"Garrison interfere down there, did he?"

"Never," Pack said. "Didn't know the first thing about engines or how to run 'em. Left us completely alone in that way, but he wouldn't order parts for us because he said we'd have to run on what the Navy give us off the ways; said we should have had everything we needed when they put us in commission, an' we didn't. If youse asks me, I'd say he was 'fraid of drawin' attention to hisself. We got some problems down there, even new as we is, and we ain't gonna fix any of 'em 'til we get the parts we need."

"Right," Ben said. "Get me up a list, and if we can't get them through the regular supply channels, I'll want to have another visit with you about them. Magnetos are sometimes hard to come by, and I'll have an idea or two about that for you."

At the mere mention of magnetos, Pack's eyes lighted up. "Almost same items as on Ford automobiles," Pack said quickly.

"And somewhat interchangeable, if I know the business," Ben said, "but mum's the word on that, and let's try the official channels before we take matters into our own hands. Now, what about some of the other so-called departments aboard?"

"Well, Sir," Pack said, "I leave 'em to the petty officers in charge."

"And you're right to do so," Ben said, "but all the same, you're the chief of the ship, you know what the score is, and I want to hear it now."

"Well, Sir," Pack said, looking down at the desktop before once more looking up and tightening his jaw, "O'Neal's the bosun, an' he knows his stuff. I don't know if them tugs have such things as mates, but he was pretty much the second man on a tug in Boston harbor. Boston Irish, I guess, an' a tough, good man."

"So how is it that the sailors on this ship look like a pack of rats?" Ben asked.

"Yes Sir," Pack said. "Well, I'd say that's the cap'n again, Sir. He sorta didn't care. Said workin' men ought to look like workin' men. Mr. Keel, him tried to sharpen 'em up once, and Garrison got all over him. Called him a ponce and didn't even want him talkin' to the crew. Said it was his responsibility, the cap'n's, and his alone."

Ben could have hardly imagined what he was hearing. Garrison was turning out to be an even worse fool than he could have foreseen. Howard hadn't known the half of it.

"So let's hear about the rest of them," Ben said.

"Well, Sir, Carson's the coxswain; he comes from Los Angeles. Apparently crewed some kind of yacht out there. Farris is your gunner, GM3. Montana man. Knows a lot about small arms and went to a school on the 3"/23 and the depth charges, but Garrison kept him from doing much work on 'em and I think they may need some. Crim is an EM2; he was an electrician in Baltimore 'fore all of this got going. Seems to know what he's doing and helps us out in the engine room whenever we need him. Technically, he's supposed to be one of my men, but given what he does, I pretty much lets him run his own shop. Townsend is the quartermaster, QM3; he don't know how to shoot the stars, but he got us up here by takin' bearings off the beach an plottin 'em. Then there's Grange; he's our supply man, SC4. An' we got seven seamen, all of 'em come to us late, straight out of some boot camp in Chicago, Great Lakes, I think. They know a lot of basics and would have had this ship looking spruce if the cap'n had let 'em, but he didn't, and 'cause the ole man wouldn't let O'Neal ramrod 'em, they sorta started suckin' up to the cap'n like they was a pack of puppies. Bad for them, and bad for the rest of us, if you see what I mean. Light, that kid you jerked up this afternoon, is one of 'em. Good to see him put in his place for a change."

So there it was—a crew somewhat divided against itself, mere seamen, captain's pets, pitted in nagging ways against the petty officers who were supposed to be appointed over them. Fortunately, as Ben knew, the six weeks the seamen had actually been aboard would not have allowed enough time for things to get totally out of hand, and with Garrison gone, those seamen were in for the comeuppance of their lives as Ben turned the petty officers loose to restore a proper element of leadership aboard.

"How, I'm wondering," Ben said, "did you manage to get this ship up here?"

"Well, Sir," Pack began again, "I was in the engine room for the most of it, and our show ran fine down there, but from what I heard it was kinda touch an' go on the bridge. The ole man stayed down in his cabin and almost never went up there. When he did go up, he apparently did a lot of yelling and screaming, but nevertheless, he more or less turned the ship completely over to Mr. Keel, Townsend, and Carson for the whole voyage. Townsend navigated in the way I told ya, Carson stayed in the pilot house on the wheel, an' Mr. Keel, he did what he could to keep us from colliding with the others, and the way he did that was to keep us pretty much out behind 'em. So from what I could understand, we sorta followed the herd, six chasers comin' up here together with us last into harbor and tied up outboard. We haven't gone to sea since, work goin' on aboard these others, all of 'em tryin' to get us ready to go somewhere in what is supposed to be two or three weeks from now."

The whole thing nearly gave Ben a headache. What he most wanted to know had to do with the man who would be his exec,

Ensign Keel. Had Keel had any previous experience at sea? From what Pack had said, from the way he described their trip from Camden to Staten Island, Keel appeared to be totally untrained and unprepared for the duty which they now faced. But Ben didn't intend to ask Pack about Keel. He would have to meet the man when he returned from whatever school he was attending and judge for himself, and then, if Keel was the kind of man that one or two of Pack's comments had suggested, Ben knew that he would have to take Keel in hand and somehow get him trained.

"All right, Chief," Ben said. "Here's what we're going to do. In the first place, I want disciplined, humane leadership from the petty officers on this ship, but if the seamen have been allowed to get out of hand and above themselves, that has to stop—and stop now. Next, this business of not maintaining the equipment because it is Navy issue and not supposed to get broken . . . well, that's the most ridiculous thing I've ever heard. I want every piece of equipment on this ship maintained and kept in top working condition, and if that means stripping down guns, radio equipment, engines, pumps, or whatever because they need work, it is to be done starting the minute we get this ship clean, done consistently, and parts ordered as needed. Like I said, if we have trouble getting parts through the standard supply channels, you and I and the concerned petty officers will put our heads together. The Germans will not care about how our supply channels work or don't work, so if we're to respond to whatever threats they throw in our way, I intend to have what we need in order to meet our commitments."

Chief Pack smiled. "I think the men will be pleased to hear that, Sir," he said. "One or two of 'em that have had problems with their gear have already helped themselves a time or two."

"I don't want them to make a habit of it," Ben said, "but we'll do what we need to do and let the devil take the hindermost. Now, get on out there, drop the word to our petty officers, and I'll begin inspecting what's going on at around 2000 tonight."

At 2000 that evening, Ben began to inspect his ship. Up forward, two seamen, Paxton and Treemont, working on the forward crew's head and the forward bunk room were starting to make progress. Accumulated crud seemed to be coming up, the sink and toilet had been scrubbed and disinfected, and the filthy linen had been changed. In the magazine, the gunner, Farris, had made progress in removing dirt and grime. There, too, Ben made an inspection of the C-Tube hydrophone, raised in port, and acquainted himself with how the dials worked and how, on the bridge, he would have to convert the bearings relative to the ship's axis that the listeners sent up to him into magnetic compass headings that he would relay to the other subchasers with which he worked. It was a minor calculation, one that might take a few seconds, but one which could also delay an attack by those few necessary seconds, and Ben resolved to school both himself and Keel to make the calculation quickly. Astern of the magazine, he looked into the radio room—Crim the electrician's tiny headquarters—where he found everything looking shipshape. From there, bypassing the wardroom and his own quarters, he climbed to the pilot house where he studied the layout of the helm, the speaking tubes, the bells for signaling changes in speed and direction to the engine room, and the table that had been erected for holding charts and maneuvering boards. Ben thought it a trim space, one which the quartermaster, Townsend, with the help of yet another seaman named Redfern, was laboring to clean, and when he'd finished, he made his exit onto the wing and climbed to the flying bridge. There, regardless of the wind and snow blowing almost straight in from the bay, he made as much of a close inspection of the equipment and its cleanliness as the atmosphere would afford.

Descending into the engine room which was both below and astern of the pilot house, Ben found Chief Pack and the black gang hard at work amid a space in which the strong odor of oil and lubricants pervaded. Between the big 220 hp gasoline engines—the middle engine centered aft with the other two six-cylinder engines staggered forward to port and starboard—the deck plates over the bilges showed themselves to be firmly in place and recently cleaned. The auxiliary two-cylinder engine for running the ship's electrical system and the air tanks for starting the entire power plant stood forward of the engines, and those, too, looked both clean and tidy.

"I'm guessing that the gasoline fumes can become bad down here," Ben said to Pack as the two of them stood together while Pack pointed out other fittings in the space.

"Aye, they can Captain," Pack said. "And they can be a danger, that's certain, so we're takin' great care not to set 'em off with a spark or somethin.'"

One by one, Pack called Garcia, Pettigrew, Bates, and Willis, the whole of his black gang, forward to introduce them to Ben, and with that done, the men swiftly returned to their work—work which they did with close attention under Pack's eye and work, Ben saw, that they seemed to enjoy.

"Steady as you go," Ben said, turning toward the ladder to make his ascent, "and keep them at it until midnight, Chief, so that we leave them with no doubt about what we expect from them from now on."

"Right, Sir," Pack said.

Astern of the engine room, Ben descended into the depth-charge stowage magazine. There he found two seamen, Scarlatti, a Chicago Italian, and Kaine, an Iowa farm boy, scrubbing the decks of a space that had obviously become filthy through downright neglect.

"Who's supervising your work?" Ben asked.

"Bosun," Kaine replied.

"Bosun, *Sir*," Ben said.

"Right, Sir. Bosun, Sir," Kaine responded, trying to show Ben a quick smile.

"When was the last time he looked in?" Ben asked.

"'Bout five minute, Sir," Scarlatti piped up. "He in da galley. Lotta work in dere."

"All right," Ben said, "carry on. Looks like you're getting it right."

Ben found the ship's bosun, O'Neal BM1, in the after crew's quarters which, adjoining the gallery in the next space aft, also served as the crew's mess. There, with O'Neal working right alongside them, even with the winter blowing fiercely above decks and a chill in the space, Ben also found Osborn, an Oklahoma ranch hand, Light, and Santos, the mess attendant and cook, working up a sweat, scrubbing everything in sight. From what Ben could see, the space with the galley included was about two-thirds the size of the engine room. By the time Ben got in there about half of it had been cleaned, but the half that remained, including the galley, looked to him like it had been allowed to deteriorate into deplorable shape. Food and grime were showing everywhere. The fact that Garrison had allowed men to go on living in this condition infuriated him, and he couldn't help wondering if Garrison had ever bothered to inspect the space.

"Boats," Ben said to the fair, muscular Irishman named O'Neal, "how the hell did you let this space get into this condition?"

"I was again' it, Sir," O'Neal said, standing up straight and looking Ben in the eye, "but himself came down here once, said it looked 'lived in,' and tole me to let it be. An' he wouldn't let Mr. Keel give the order to clean up nohow."

"You have cockroaches down here?" Ben asked.

"Aye, Sir, some. Picked 'em up in Camden 'fore we left there."

"All right," Ben said. "We've got two or three weeks before we leave here according to the word that has been handed down to me. For the sailor who catches and kills the most roaches, I'll be good for standing him three free beers in the first liberty port we visit after we go to sea. You make the count, you keep a jar of the dead bodies, and you be damn sure that they don't try to pull a fast one on you. Got me?"

"Aye Sir," O'Neal said with smile. "We'll eradicate 'em Sir, with no mistakes."

After a perfunctory look into the lazaret, a space that O'Neal and his cleaning crew would obviously not get to until the morning, Ben inspected the main deck, noting what would also have to be tackled on the morrow. Satisfied that the necessary work was proceeding, he retraced his steps, descended into Officer's Country, opened his duffle bag and valise, and prepared to begin stowing his gear. Upon opening the locker which was to be his own, he found as many as ten thoroughly pornographic photographs, Garrison's obvious property, still pinned to the inside of the door, photos which Light had either not dared to touch or which he hadn't even noticed. One by one, Ben stripped them from the door, chucked them into the scuttlebutt, and began stowing his gear.

4

Ben's second day aboard SC 65X dawned cold but clear, clear enough that O'Neal could turn some of the crew to both cleaning and doing maintenance above decks. After a so-so breakfast brought up to him from the galley by Santos—something Ben took at the fold-down table he was amused to call the wardroom mess—he called for Grange SC4, the ship's storekeeper. There, working side by side at the same table, they began to fill out the requisitions for both equipment and spare parts that Chief Pack had collected from the engine room mechanics and the ship's petty officers before they'd retired at midnight. Ben didn't expect the Navy to supply more than half of what he asked for, needed, and desperately wanted to make his ship whole, to give it the edge he believed it would need before it tried to contend with the seas; nevertheless, he knew that he had no choice but to try the supply chain first, making the best use of official procedure and channels before he turned to what he'd imagined all along that he would have to turn to—that thing the Navy called *midnight requisition* and which civilians knew as *theft*. Ben had never been in the Navy before, but about that operating rule he'd known all along. There was a war on, and if men and ships were to fight it they needed to have what they needed to have. According to the old rule that what was best for the ship was best for the Navy, whatever wasn't tied down, whatever could be scrounged, whatever could be *found* was thought to be fair game to support the war effort. Ben didn't want to have to resort to the procedure, but he knew from the start that if he was given no other choice, he would do what he had to in order to prepare his ship.

So throughout the morning Ben worked with Grange—a tiny bespeckled slip of a man, an intelligent man who had apparently been a bookkeeper and parts manager for the railroads some-where—until together they completed a stack of requisitions that measured at least three inches in height. Then, going ashore himself, Ben walked straight to the supply depot that tended to the Section Piers, found Lieutenant Spears, a blond, portly regular who handled the needs of the chasers, and presented him with his supply requests.

"You've got to be kidding." Spears said, shaking his head and showing Ben a grin of disbelief when Ben handed him the stack of requisitions.

"I'm not," Ben said, showing the man a straight face.

"Former yachtsman, are you?" Spears asked. "Ivy League graduate with money in your background?" The man's tone wasn't offensive, but it nevertheless indicated that he thought that Ben believed that parts, equipment, and everything else Ben had asked for came with a snap of the fingers.

"I'm former Merchant Marine," Ben said flatly. "Three years as third mate on an ore carrier on the Great Lakes. I wouldn't ask for this stuff if we didn't need it, if the Navy hadn't shorted the ship when they commissioned her. You may not have the stuff, Sir, but if you can't supply what we need, that means I've got to get it somewhere else, and that means I need to know what you can supply."

"OK," Spears said, changing his tone and speaking seriously. "I've got you. This will take a day or two, but I'll give you what I have, what I can, and leave the rest up to you. Expect a stake truck a couple of days from now, and be damn careful the other ships in your nest don't cop what I send you before you can get it aboard."

"I'll do it," Ben said. "Thanks for the advice. And thanks for the help. We'll take whatever you can send us."

Spears smiled. "We're short of everything ourselves," he said. "I'm sorry for it, but there it is. I suppose all wars begin this way, but the words 'beg, borrow, or steal' do come to mind," and laying a finger alongside his nose, Spears showed Ben an even broader grin.

Ben couldn't help but laugh. "That's rather what I imagined when I came over here," he said, "and really, Sir, thank you sincerely for whatever you can do for us."

By the time Ben returned to SC 65X, Farris, working in the cold beside Paxton and Treemont who served in his gun crew, had broken the breech on the 3″/23 and seemed hard at work greasing and maintaining the weapon. Topside, regardless of the bitter wind which had picked up, Townsend was up the mast, cleaning the crow's nest and some of the rigging while on the main deck. O'Neal had three seamen working up and down the ship, scrubbing down the main deck while one other and Santos finished cleaning the lazaret. Dropping into the after crew's quarters, Ben felt a degree of relief when he found the galley virtually gleaming.

"At 1700, I'll march them all up to the bathhouse for a good shower and to do their laundry," Chief Pack told Ben when Ben finally dropped down into the engine room for a word.

"Good," Ben said. "By the time you get them there, they'll need it, what with the accumulation of grime that they'll have built up. And after they've worked in this cold all day, a hot shower will be just the thing to bring them around. Now, change of subject. I've been to supply. We'll know in a couple of days what they can give us, and after that we'll do what we need to do to pick up essentials. I imagine a truck will come over from the supply depot, so as you bring things across, don't let the ships inboard siphon off anything intended for us."

"Pack of thieves, those chasers inboard," Pack said. "Caught one of their people trying to get away with a couple of our wrenches once we tied up."

"That's what I mean," Ben laughed. "Thieves everywhere, whereas our people are only good scroungers and alert opportunists."

"Right, Sir," Pack laughed.

"All right," Ben said. "Looks like you and O'Neil have things in hand, so I'm going below. I wish it weren't so, but I've got some reports to write for District Headquarters, and I've got some reading to do if I intend to master the Navy's regulations.

At 1700 that afternoon, at about the time that Pack started marching the crew toward the bathhouse at the head of the pier, Ensign Keel returned to the ship, dropped straight down into Officer's Country, took one wide-eyed look at Ben, and stuttered, "Si-Sir?" packing a multitude of questions into a single mangled word.

Ben stood, smiled, extended his hand, and said, "I'm Lieutenant Junior Grade Snow, your new commanding officer. You must be Mr. Keel."

Unable to control his reaction, Keel wobbled, and sagged down into the wardroom's chair, sighing and cutting loose under his breath with a single expression, "thank God!" Then, suddenly mindful that he'd crossed the line of what could be considered correct naval behavior, he instantly pulled himself together, leaped to his feet, came to attention, and began to bluster, "Yes Sir! Welcome aboard, Sir! Ensign Keel reporting back from school, Sir!"

Ben felt an urge to laugh, but he didn't. Instead, continuing to show the man the same easy smile, he tried to put him at ease.

"Relax, Mr. Keel. And take a seat. It's Terrance Reardon Keel, isn't it?"

"Yes Sir," Keel said, his body slowly relaxing as he removed his hat—exposing a shock of red hair parted in the middle—and sat back down across the table from Ben. "But I go by Terry, if that's of any help."

"Terry, it is," Ben said. "How was your school, and to what school were you sent, by the way?"

"Good school, Sir," Terry Keel said, an open expression now showing across his face, his blue eyes opening wide. "Coding and decoding. I'd suppose the procedure rudimentary, but it was interesting nevertheless, and I think it will be of use."

"I'm sure it will," Ben said, "and probably sooner than any of us have a right to expect. So, tell me a little about yourself. Where are you from? What's your background? That kind of thing."

"Excuse me, Sir," Keel said, "but is Mr. Garrison really gone, or is this just temporary?"

"Mr. Garrison is gone from the ship, and he is probably gone from the Navy as well," Ben said. "We held the change of command yesterday afternoon."

Once more Keel seemed to register relief.

"I gather that things didn't go too well under Mr. Garrison's command?" Ben said.

For a moment, Keel seemed to hesitate, but then, as though coming to a decision, he spoke, and spoke seriously. "No Sir," he said firmly. "They didn't. I've only been in the Navy a few months, but Captain Garrison was not what I expected in a commanding officer. I'm supposed to be the executive officer aboard, but he wouldn't so much as allow me to talk to the men, and when I tried to do something about upkeep, training, or discipline, he squelched me immediately. I was allowed to sleep in here but that was about all, so for most things it was like I didn't exist, like I was aboard on sufferance and had no genuine function."

"So," Ben said, "how did you spend your time?"

"I read Sir. Bowditch, Navy Regulations, technical manuals, everything Navy available, and the more I read, the more I could see that things were wrong."

"I shouldn't wonder," Ben said. "Well, Mr. Keel, all of that reading is going to come in very handy, I can assure you. Sounds to me like the one thing positive that Garrison accomplished is that without intending to he gave you the time to put yourself through a good post-graduate course in what you're going to have to know, and for that, I suppose we can thank him, but given the condition in which I found this ship and some of the crew, I'm not thanking him for anything else. Things are going to be very different around here from now on, and perhaps to your surprise, you're going to find that you're going to be in charge of any number of them."

"Yes Sir," Keel said, "that will be fine by me. I'll do my best."

"I'm sure you will," Ben said. "Now, back to my original question. Give me a little of your background."

"Well, Sir," Keel began, "I grew up in New Rochelle. My father is a coffee broker with offices in the City, my mother's a housewife, although she does committee work and that sort of thing, and I have two brothers, one of whom is still in school while my older brother is an officer in the Marines. One sister, married, with one child. I started in the public schools, but my parents sent me to Andover for prep, and then I went to Yale and graduated last year. I'd hoped to fly with the Yale Flying Club, but they formed and left for Florida before I could join them, so the Navy still took me in and put me through a two-month Naval Reserve officer's training course in Annapolis. Then, the next thing I knew, I was sent orders to SC 65X and went aboard in Camden. Mr. Garrison, probably because he wanted to get rid of me, sent me to firefighting school, a training session on the C-Tube hydrophone, and to this coding school. The rest of the time, like I say, I read and kept out of his way."

"I found him drunk when I came aboard," Ben said. "Did much of that go on?"

"That went on a lot," Keel said. "He was a nasty drunk, Garrison, but he was usually so drunk when he came back aboard that he passed out, and that cut the amount of time one had to endure the nastiness."

"Was there alcohol aboard ever?" Ben asked.

"Yes Sir. He kept a bottle in the drawer, and twice, when I caught Light and Osborn drinking in the lazaret, he told me to leave them be and mind my own business."

"As you know from reading Navy Regs," Ben said firmly, "U.S. Navy ships are dry, and that's the way that this one is to be, so get out the word that if I ever find liquor of any kind aboard this ship, the man who's responsible is going to be hanged by his heels."

Keel's grin spread wide. "I think that will come as a real revelation to one or two of them," he said.

"Let's hope," Ben said. "So, what do you know about ships and the sea? I trust you can pilot because you apparently got the ship up here from Camden. What about celestial navigation?"

"During the summers, I used to help crew the yacht of a family friend," Keel said. "We'd sail up and down the Sound, so I know how to take bearings and plot a course on a chart, but I've never once shot the stars or tried to work out a celestial fix."

"Not to worry," Ben said. "I'm a fair hand with a sextant and the calculations required, so we'll begin your practice as soon as we go to sea."

"What about gunnery? Know anything about the three-inch, or the depth charges?"

"Only what we were taught in the training course," Keel said. "I've never seen a gun fired or rolled a depth charge, but we did do dry runs, and I know how to set the pistols for both the depth charges and for the Y-Gun."

"All right," Ben said. "Have you been commuting to New Rochelle since you arrived here, or living aboard?"

"I've been commuting only on weekends, Sir. The rest of the time, I've tried to bunk aboard, turning in after Garrison passed out and getting up before he did so as to keep out of his way."

Ben shook his head. As far as Keel told it, he'd been living through a perfect hell.

"Well," Ben said, "starting from now, I'm going to need you here. Aside from our people in the engine room, I'm doubtful that the crew is prepared for very much at all, so beginning in the morning, we're going to start drilling: signals, man overboard, damage control, dry runs with the guns and the depth charges, breakdowns, loss of steering, navigation . . . you name it, and we're going to do it, and one of the first things I want to master is this crew getting to General Quarters and getting this ship ready to fight. Our aim will be two minutes flat, and we'll put a stopwatch on it to check. We've got a lot to do, Terry, and I'll be looking to you to keep things moving along because I don't mean to give these men a free minute during working hours. It looks to me like they've already had about two months of downtime in which they've barely lifted a finger. Your first job is to work up an in-port watch bill because we're going to have an officer of the deck standing watch on the brow from now on, and then, let's get cracking on a watch bill for sea. Until I get you qualified, I'll be on the bridge pretty much continuously, but because the Navy isn't allowing us a third officer—something we very much need—O'Neal is also to go on the watch bill as an officer of the deck. I think he has the experience, and we're going to need him to relieve us if the two of us don't intend to drop from pure exhaustion."

Regardless of the winter cold, which seemed to be intensifying, and the ice which had formed in the bay, crusting the surface of the sea with coatings that were soon broken up by tugs as they opened channels to facilitate traffic coming in from the Atlantic or preparing to go out, Lieutenant (j.g.) Ben Snow started his third day aboard the chaser by sounding the ship's General Quarters alarm in place of reveille and putting a stopwatch on the crew's response. As a professional exercise, it was Ben's first act in response to what Commander Howard had meant when he'd told Ben to get down to SC 65X and whip the vessel into shape. The result of that first exercise—one that both Ben and Terry expected—was as grossly disappointing as they'd anticipated. Fully eleven and a half minutes passed before the phone talkers reported all battle stations manned and ready, and even when the report was made, Light was still plodding forward up the starboard side toward his post as loader on the forward gun mount.

"You're all dead," Ben said, gathering the crew together on the fantail after he'd secured them from their stations. "If we'd been at sea with a Hun U-boat in sight, she would have blown us out of the water before most of you would have gotten out of your bunks, much less buttoned your trousers. You were eleven slow minutes reaching your battle stations. Even from a dead sleep, you'll have to do it in two. No more time to linger and think about things. We're going to sea soon and you've got to be ready, or you will wind up killing the lot of us, so get sharp, and do it fast."

Throughout the remainder of that day, Ben and Terry put the crew through one drill after another. In one instance, he called away a fire drill in the forward crew's quarters, and in the next, he had the damage control team shoring a bulkhead between the galley and the lazaret. Well before lunch, a man overboard drill was called, Terry checking to see that each man concerned carried the required equipment and knew what he was supposed to have, and in the next instance, Ben had them all rigging fenders in anticipation of a collision. Three times during the day, Ben put the gun crew through their paces on dry runs; in at least four instances, he had Farris man the depth charge crews standing ready to hoist their 300-pound charges onto the Y-Gun while yet another two men stood by the racks on the stern, ready to roll their ash cans on command.

At the same time, in the engine room, Chief Pack spent his day putting his machinist's mates through an unending series of casualty drills covering everything from the engines to the pumps as well as the electrical circuits. Sometimes they worked with the lights on; at other times, in order to prime them for emergencies, Pack turned the lights out and made them work in the dark or with only the assistance of battle lanterns.

"It's a pisser," Ben said to Pack, "but they'll have to be able to do these things with their eyes closed because, with smoke or electrical failure, they may have to."

"Aye, Sir," Pack said. "And they'll be ready when I finish with 'em, or we'll know the reason why."

Knocking off finally at 1600 that afternoon, Chief Pack assembled the crew around the mess table in after crew's quarters. Then, to their shock, Ben and Terry went down and began quizzing them orally, singling each man out by name and grilling him on what he'd done right during the day, what he'd done wrong, and what he was going to do to correct his errors. It was an experience that none of them had expected or ever been subjected to, and when it ended, and after the evening meal had been served, it produced precisely the effect that Ben had hoped for. Embarrassed in front of their shipmates by what this one or that one hadn't known or performed correctly, they began to break out manuals and directives in order to find out what they'd done wrong and correct their mistakes. They groused about it, they complained, but fearful about drawing even more of their new captain's ire, they did what they had to do in order to feel secure and free from danger. In the process, each of them learned more about his job, the equipment he was responsible for, and the anticipated functions of the ship.

"I won't tell you that it's the best way to lead," Ben said, as he and Terry sat over the little fold-down wardroom table and ate the last of the tuna fish and noodle concoction that Santos had carried up to them. "The best way is with a willing crew where mere suggestions and a relaxed hand can serve as their guides, but this bunch, although some of them do have the skills, has fallen into such a slough that putting a little fear into them isn't a bad idea. Best they know that we're going to bite when they fall short. Once they know that, they'll try to avoid it. Here and there, one will shirk, but most of them will bear down, get in step. Peer pressure should do the rest, particularly when they begin to realize that their survival depends as much on the man next to them as it does on themselves. Follow me, do you?"

"Yes Sir," Keel said.

"Right," Ben said. "Firm but fair. Let justice be your watchword, but if or when one of them steps out of line or comes up short, discipline is essential. And if we're hard on them now, it will be much better to ease up on them later when they've sorted themselves out and gotten into the right routine."

On the following morning when Ben once more sounded the alarm for General Quarters at 0600, the crew reported their battle stations manned and ready in six minutes. This time, Light was on station and cradling a three-inch round by the time the talker passed the word to the bridge.

"Well, it's a start," Ben said. "Six minutes is something we can work with, and work with it we will. I'm guessing that by the time we get out of here, we'll have it down to near three."

"I thought we were working toward two minutes?" Terry said to Ben, speaking so that Townsend wouldn't hear him where he stood ready at his battle station over the chart table.

"We are," Ben grinned, "but I'm guessing that it is going to take the sighting of a genuine U-boat and the fear that goes with it to finish the job."

Ben and Terry continued to drill the ship throughout the remainder of that day. The crew—having originally responded like a disorganized mob—began moving more smoothly, learning how to cut corners to reach the places they needed to go, and becoming more and more familiar with both their equipment and how to operate it. Little by little, Ben could see elements of teamwork beginning to grow. Here and there, this man or that learned to help his mate, learned that two of them working together eased whatever task they were trying to perform. At the same time, information about the ship and the task at hand began to pass back and forth between them in ways that they'd never thought to feed one another before. Ben wouldn't have called the process a fast one, but the speed with which it took place wasn't the object; the fact that they were doing it at all is what mattered to him, and then, too, he began to notice something else. Once more, the men were beginning to take an interest in their fellows' jobs as well as their own, offer suggestions, and, even better, offer help and assistance. In the process, they were all learning how to do more than one thing, more than the single skill that went with their rate or assignment. As Ben knew, that development would not manifest its value overnight, but the mere fact that it was underway seemed encouraging to him and something which could or would be of immense value to the ship when she finally got underway.

On Ben's fifth day aboard, as promised, a stake truck from the supply depot came down the pier, stopped inboard of the nest, and waited until Ben had sent Terry and Chief Pack out to inventory and take charge of what Lieutenant Spears had coughed up for them.

"Well, Sir," Pack said when Terry sent him back to report, "I can't say that the base hasn't done right by us because according to the storekeeper who brought that stuff over here, they give us what they had, and what they didn't have, they couldn't give us. Looks like we got about two-thirds of what we asked for, but I'm missin' a number of things that I gotta have, and them magnetos is one of 'em."

"I was afraid of that," Ben said. "All right, Chief. We've got to have those rascals, or we'll never get this ship anywhere for very long. I'm going to leave it to you, but Ford is going to have to supply us, and be sure that whoever goes out to garner that supply doesn't do it all in the same neighborhood."

"And you an' I don't know a thing about it," Pack said.

"I wish," Ben said, "but it will be my responsibility if the man gets caught, and you'd better warn him not to. Everything else, your people ought to be able to scrounge on the base somewhere, and as far as I'm concerned that's fair game, but what Ford is going to have to supply can't be covered up if it's caught. We know and the Navy knows there's a war on, but that probably won't cut any ice with a civilian court, and the police won't have a clue, so whoever goes is going to have to bear that in mind."

"I'll see to it," Pack said.

While Terry kept watch on the diminishing supplies in the stake truck, and the crew hauled the load over the inboard chasers and onto SC 65X, Ben checked off the items of the inventory as the consignment came aboard. He hadn't even reached the final items before Farris GM3 stood before him, red in the face, with an angry expression contorting his lips.

"Cap'n, Sir," the man said, practically sputtering. "Can I have a word, Sir?"

"Shoot," Ben said.

"Them two machine guns they sent us."

"Yes," Ben said. "What's the problem?"

"They're pieces of shit, Sir. They's corroded, filthy, and the sights are missin' from both of 'em. Like as not, they's cast offs. Hell, Sir, they might even be relics from the Spanish–American War!"

"All right," Ben said. "Where did you uncrate them? In the armory?"

"Yes Sir," Farris said, shaking his head with disgust.

"Right," Ben said, "I'll be down to look at them just as soon as I finish here."

Twenty minutes later, finished with the check off, Ben descended into the armory where Farris had uncrated the machine guns that the depot's armory had sent him. Farris had been right; the M1895 Brownings were relics, possibly from the Spanish–American War, the Boxer Rebellion, or the Philippine Insurrection, their barrels pitted with rust, the stocks scarred and chipped, and their breeches ungreased and coated with grime. On one of them, the trigger was missing.

"Cap'n," Farris fumed, "them things would jamb even 'fore we got out three rounds, and that's if I could take 'em down, clean 'em up, and git 'em workin' in the first place."

"You're right," Ben said. "They're worthless. They should have been surveyed to the junk heap ten years ago, if not earlier. Know where the armory is on the beach?"

"Yes Sir," Farris said.

"All right," Ben said. "You and Paxton get over there tonight. See if you can find a door or a window open, get inside, and find something better. If you do, we'll switch the guns in their cases. I'll have O'Neal put the wherry in the water for you so that you can come and go without the inboard chasers seeing you, and if you find what you're looking for, we'll move the guns that way. Don't get caught, mind, because if you do, all hell's liable to break loose, and we don't want that."

"Right Sir," Farris said, a broad grin stretching from ear to ear as he looked quickly left and right.

"So," Terry said, as the two of them finished what they had laughingly dubbed Santos' bowls of Philippine-Irish stew that had been sent up to them from the galley for their evening meal, "I understand that the machine guns we received didn't come up to scratch."

"Not by a long shot," Ben said.

"So what do we do?" Terry asked.

"Wait patiently until after midnight to see what develops," Ben said, raising an eyebrow.

"*Ah*," Terry said.

"I don't like doing it," Ben said, "and I wouldn't if I didn't have to, but for what we've received, we are going to be truly thankful, and for what we didn't, I've sent the troops out to forage."

"Any danger in that?" Terry wanted to know.

"Plenty," Ben said. "If the foragers are caught, I'll probably be canned. But you can rest easy because you don't know the first thing about it. Right?"

"Right," Terry said.

"Then let's call for Santos to take the empty bowls away, and get to work on what we're going to do about tomorrow's drills," Ben said.

Not long after midnight, with their work for the evening done and leaving Terry to turn in, Ben threw on his greatcoat, made his exit from Officer's Country, and climbed to the pilot house amid the beginnings of yet another snowfall. To his surprise the wind had ceased to blow; the snow seemed to be falling straight down in large flakes. The pilot house remained dark and cold, but for the next hour, in order to keep warm, Ben walked back and forth across the tiny space, waiting to see what, if anything would happen. Finally, nearing 0200, he saw Pack coming back aboard, and then, stepping onto the port side from the hatch into the pilot house, he stopped and had a word with the man.

"Any luck?" Ben asked.

"Five Ford magnetos," Pack said, "and a few other things."

"Enough said," Ben replied. "What about the others?"

"If they aren't back already," Pack said, "they'll be coming in, you can be sure."

And come in they did, one here, one there, until around 0300; each arriving aboard with the folds of his duffle coat bulging, each disappearing into the engine room with the speed of a ferret on the hunt. And it was at about that time that Ben felt a slight bump alongside, stepped across to the starboard side, and helped Farris and Paxton lift two machine gun crates onto the deck.

"You're going to have to work fast," Ben said. "Find what you were looking for?"

"New, pristine, and in perfect workin' condition," Farris said.

"Enough time to make the exchange?"

"I think so," Farris said. "Ain't a sentry in sight over there, an' we even found a window unlocked. Whoever runnin' that armory ain't got the brains of a twit. We could of stole the place blind."

"See that you don't," Ben said. "This exchange is enough."

Fifteen minutes later, Ben once more helped Farris and Paxton return the packing cases they'd rowed to the side of the ship, both of them now containing the antique Brownings, and then saw both men once more board the wherry and depart the ship, rowing silently through the falling snow to the deserted landing they'd used somewhere along the sea wall. To Ben's relief, they were back within the hour, undetected and grinning.

"No problems?" Ben asked.

"No problems," Farris answered. "Least not right now. Probably gonna be a scream or two when them relics is delivered to the *Momsom* in a day, a week, or a month, but she's a coastal minesweep, and why she'd need new machine guns don't make no sense. All she gonna do is shoot mines with 'em, if she finds mines, and she can do that with rifles. Call it what you want, Sir, but the Navy's better off our way."

Ben thought it was too and almost let the matter drop.

"Leave those things packed until we get underway to make it look like we haven't yet opened them," Ben said, taking a puff on his pipe. "We get an inspection of some kind, and someone might ask. If the guns are still crated, maybe whatever inspectors show up won't ask us to uncrate them."

As a result, the new Brownings went into the armory crated where Farris lashed them to the bulkhead with extra lines so that if or when an inspector did show up, he would see the heavy lashing as yet another excuse to leave them where they were.

On the following morning, Ben did not sound General Quarters at 0600, and he did not sound reveille an hour later. Instead, given the work the crew had done the night before, he let them sleep in, finally calling the first of the day's drills after lunch. In touring the ship's spaces while the drills for the day progressed, Ben took a degree of quiet satisfaction in finding a hoard of new spare parts in the engine room, noticed several tools that he had not seen on an earlier visit, spotted two coils of line that looked new in a forward storeroom, enough gray paint to cover the ship when the time came—paint that had not been on the supply depot's inventory—and two new pairs of binoculars in the pilot house.

Without saying a word about the ship's new acquisitions to anyone, Ben finally believed, if he could get the crew reasonably trained and ready, that SC 65X was prepared to go to sea and equipped to handle any material casualties that might develop once she went.

Meanwhile, outside the skin of the ship, the snow continued to fall, more and more ice continued to form in the surrounding waters of the harbor, and what seemed to be an extremely bitter winter continued to develop.

At the beginning of Ben's third week aboard, the inspection that he'd anticipated came to pass. The inspection that SC 65X endured proved to be a light one, conducted by one man only when Lieutenant Commander Howard stepped aboard one morning and asked for the captain.

"Things look a deal different here," Howard said, shaking hands with Ben following an exchange of salutes.

"I hope so, Sir," Ben said. "The crew has turned to, we've got her cleaned up a mite from the last time you saw her, and I've been drilling the men daily. We're down to four minutes in getting to General Quarters from a dead sleep, I've got at least five men, including Mr. Keel and myself, ready to read flashing light and semaphore, we're up on the signal flags, the gun crew looks efficient on dry runs, and our depth-charge people are well prepared and ready to go."

"Good," Howard said. "Let's take a run through so that I can see what you've accomplished. Where's Mr. Keel?"

"On the beach, Sir, at the supply depot, trying to talk Lieutenant Spears out of two or three more things our chief engineer would like to have."

"Magnetos, perhaps?" Howard said, lifting one eyebrow.

"If we can get some, I'm sure they'd come in handy with these engines," Ben said.

"Curiously," Howard said, raising one eyebrow, "I understand that the magnetos used on Ford automobiles can also be used on engines like yours. Had a talk with the district's chief engineer this week, and he told me about that."

"Really?" Ben said. "I'll have to inform Chief Pack."

"I think he might already know," Howard said flatly. "Suppose we start this inspection by having a look at your armory, Mr. Snow. I'd like to have a look at how you have your ammunition stowed."

"Right, Sir," Ben said, a sinking feeling stabbing at the pit of his stomach.

Once down into the armory with their heads bent to avoid hitting them on the overhead, Commander Howard looked over the ammunition storage closely, checked to see if the three-inch rounds had been wiped and clean so as not to foul the gun's breech, and finally settled his eyes on the machine gun crates.

"I see that your machine guns are still in their crates," Howard said.

"Yes Sir," Ben said. "I told our gunner to leave them crated until we received some definite orders so that we wouldn't expose them to the weather and the humidity."

"Yes, that's what I was thinking you'd probably done," Howard said. "Had a look at them, have you?"

"Yes Sir," Ben said. "Opened the crates and had a look at them when we brought them aboard."

"In good shape, were they?"

"New Brownings, Sir. Excellent condition," Ben said.

"So I've heard," Howard said, "from the armory," a remark which made Ben swallow hard, twice, and nearly break into a fit of coughing.

"Yes Sir," Ben managed to stammer.

"Things look shipshape down here," Howard said. "Let's go back up and take a look at the rest of your spaces."

An hour later, after sharing a cup of coffee with Ben in the vessel's tiny wardroom, Howard stood, picked up his cap, and turned to Ben.

"You've done exactly what I sent you over here to do," he said, speaking bluntly. "If it's of any interest, Garrison is gone, right out of the Navy, and for good. This is not for the crew's consumption, and you don't even need to tell Mr. Keel about it yet, but at the end of the week, you and the other chasers in the slip will be given orders to New London. You'll probably train up there for a couple of weeks; I'm guessing that you'll be working with a submarine for practice, and after that I think the entire lot of you are destined for overseas. Good hunting, Mr. Snow. If you do as well with what's coming as you've done with what's behind you, the Huns will have good reason to fear you."

5

On the night of December 20, 1917, Ben and SC 65X received orders. On the morning of the 21st, a Friday, after a hasty pre-sailing conference conducted on the fantail of an inboard subchaser whose commanding officer had seniority in the nest, Submarine Chaser Division AA—that was what the six chasers in the nest had been designated—sortied from the Stanton Island Section Piers and set a course for New London. For Ben, the word *sortie* suggested a determined and swift exit, the knife-edged bows of his chaser plowing through clear blue seas, white-capped bow waves curling back from both sides, the fresh wind causing the ensign to flutter in the breeze. SC 65X's exit from New York harbor defied that mental association in every way that Ben could imagine. Rather, after a yard tug came into the slip to break up the ice, SC 65X took in her lines and inched away from the pier, moving slowly and carefully so as not to damage her propellers on shards of shelved ice that looked to be two to three inches thick. Once beyond the pier, Ben then stopped all engines which had been going in reverse, gave Chief Pack and his men a few seconds to engage the forward gears, and began to move ahead slowly, following the tug out into the harbor where other tugs had been breaking up the ice. There, with the remainder of the chasers slowly emerging from the nest,

Ben fell in behind an even larger tug slowly towing two enormous garbage scows down through the narrows into the lower bay. All told, Division AA spent a full two hours and forty minutes working their way out to the open sea, none of it pleasant, all of it fraught with cakes of floating ice, all of it carrying a stench from the rotting garbage on the scows that, for a while, made their lives miserable and not a few of them sick to their stomachs.

When Ben finally did succeed in getting SC 65X to sea, the men really did become sick, the heavy seas running off the east coast of Long Island forcing them into a trough that rolled them 25 degrees to either side of their centerline. All the while as Ben and Terry stood their watch on the flying bridge, wrapped in double layers of heavy coats and foul weather gear, the spray whipped back from the bow and pelted them mercilessly, some of it freezing in the air before it reached them so that it felt like they were being consistently struck by sleet.

"It ain't pleasant, is it?" Ben said, showing his exec a smile.

"No Sir, it ain't," Terry said, turning swiftly and upchucking into the bucket that Ben had had the foresight to have a sailor lash to a stanchion behind the wind break.

"All right?" Ben asked when Terry recovered himself and after he'd wiped his mouth with his handkerchief.

"I guess I'm not as much of a sailor as I'd hoped," Terry said, his face going pale as he held onto the base of the pelorus in order to keep his feet.

"Given the amount of pitch and roll we're taking," Ben said in order to reassure him, "I'd bet money that every man aboard is sick right now, and if you want to know the truth, I don't feel so good myself. Things kicked up big time on the Lakes, and I've been through a lot of heavy weather, but there is something about this that puts it in a class by itself. Best to be up here, facing into it, because the men down below are going to be miserable."

An hour later, Ben sent Terry below to see how the chaser was riding and to inspect the vessel's watertight integrity.

"Well?" Ben asked when Terry returned.

"You called it right," Terry said to him. "They're sick, almost to a man. Pack and O'Neal aren't so bad but the rest of them have been barfing since we first came out, and it stinks to high heaven down there. I gave orders for them to start cleaning up, and they're doing that now. Somewhere about twelve feet back from the bow, below the crew's head, we've got a seep. Some of the caulking must have worked loose, but for the time being, it's no more than a trickle."

"That we'll have to have seen to in New London," Ben said, "so before you turn in tonight, make out a work order and we'll have it corrected as soon as we put in."

After the first four hours on deck, Ben sent Terry down for some kind of cold cut lunch, told him to send Santos up with a sandwich for his own meal, and called for O'Neil. When the big Irish bosun arrived on the bridge, Ben told him their course, told him to remain at their 8-knot cruising speed, and gave him the con.

"Captain often give you the deck on that tug of yours?" Ben asked. "Think you know the drill?"

"Sometimes," O'Neal said. "I know 'nough of it to keep us headed, Cap'n, and what I don't know, I guess you gonna teach me."

"That's the plan," Ben said. "You hold her steady on, and I'm going to drop down to the pilot house and see how Townsend is doing with the piloting. Give me a shout down the voice tube if anything out of the ordinary turns up or if you see something in the seas ahead, anything at all."

"Aye, Sir," O'Neal replied, his Sou'wester beginning to drip.

In the pilot house, Ben went straight to the chart table and took a look at the track that he had laid out the night before as soon as he'd heard that they would be relocating to New London, a voyage for which he's been designated lead navigator. Townsend, standing back to let Ben make his examination, had done his job; he'd taken visual fixes ever since leaving the lower harbor, the bearings that he'd taken plotted and annotated in pencil with a neat hand.

"You can see the lighthouses on Long Island without any problems?" Ben asked.

"Mostly, Sir," Townsend replied.

"Good job," Ben said. "Spotting the lighthouses at night will be a deal easier, but as long as you can see them standing, we're in good shape. We do seem to be drifting a mite, but considering the currents we're dealing with, that's what I'd expect. If we drift more than a quarter of a mile north of the track, call me at once. Otherwise, we're far enough off Long Island to remain safe. How are the windows holding? Getting any seawater in here from them?"

Ben was referring to the glass windows on the forward face of the pilot house; owing to their square shape, he couldn't bring himself to call them portholes. They were the one thing about the chaser's design that he didn't like. In a really heavy blow, he didn't think they'd hold together; he expected them to shatter.

"We got some seepage around 'em, Cap'n, but not much," the sailor said.

"I'm going to have Mr. Keel get up a work order for New London," Ben said. "I'm going to want those windows covered with copper screens; mesh screens will break up the force of the sea before it hits them full on, maybe keep them from shattering under a big blow." And then, Ben turned to the coxswain. "Any trouble holding her on course, Carson?"

"Some, Cap'n. This trough keeps her yawin', an' that ain't much fun, but I got her and can keep her within 5 degrees on either side of the course without too much trouble."

"Good," Ben said. "That's about what I expected. Hang in there, and when your watch ends, you can put Redfern on the wheel and then Scarlatti when it's time for his turn, but you keep them under instruction long enough to be sure that they know what they're doing."

Thus far, the voyage was running as Ben had expected it to run. The weather was lousy, but given the winter the East Coast had started to experience, he wasn't surprised. At 8 knots, they wouldn't make New London before morning, and by morning, Ben hoped the men would be through their seasickness, the most of them, and finding their sea legs. He would not have called it a great beginning by any means, but given the conditions through which they ran, it was a good one.

South of New London, south of the mouth of the Thames river, Division AA found the coast iced over, a clear indication that the Division would not be able to enter port until tugs broke up the ice on the following morning in order to open a channel for them. As a result, the Division anchored along the edge of the ice shelf and rode out the night uncomfortably, every man aboard sleeping fully dressed in uniform, duffle coats, watch caps, and scarves against the bitter cold that, on a vessel with totally inadequate heating, penetrated every space and even caused ice to form on some interior bulkheads.

In Officer's Country, where conditions were no better than in the rest of the ship, both Ben and Terry spent a restless night, cowering in their greatcoats beneath as many blankets as they'd been issued and sleeping in snatches. Ben had taken the evening watch himself, turned over and turned in around midnight, slept fitfully for three hours, and risen once more around 0300 in order to snatch a cup of coffee before he once more joined Terry on the bridge for the 0400–0800 watch. Terry, saying that he'd managed to grab at least five hours of something resembling sleep, was clearly the more rested of the two when he climbed to the bridge to relieve O'Neal, and O'Neal, professing to be half frozen and as hungry as a bear, dropped immediately into after crew's quarters for whatever relief the space might afford.

"Warmer back there," Terry joked. "A lot more body heat with less ice on the bulkheads."

"Right," Ben laughed. "The crew gets all the breaks. Which reminds me. Christmas is only two days away. No leave for anyone this year, so once we get in, I want you to go over on the beach and arrange Christmas dinner for them. If we tie up at the sub base, go to the EM Club and set them up for two dinner sittings. We'll split the crew into two sections, send one over around 1100, give them a couple of hours to eat and then send the second section over at 1300. If we don't tie up to the piers at the sub base but at somewhere lower down near the city, you're going to have to find them a place and cut a deal with the owner. Ship's recreation fund will pay for the meal, but keep it within reason. We'll spring for turkey, chicken fried steaks, or a good pot roast, but crepes suzette and flutes of champagne are not to be on anyone's menu, although they can each have one bottle of beer before they show up back here and go on duty."

"I can't be sure," Terry said, "but after being around Light and Kaine for more than a few weeks, I'm guessing that each of them would see a hamburger or a ham sandwich with a pickle as *haute cuisine*."

"Good guess," Ben said. "But lay it out for whoever is going to prepare the meal that we want them to have a good feed and that trouble will follow if it isn't up to standards."

"Right," Terry said.

By 0800 that morning, the tugs had broken up the ice enough for Division AA to enter port, and as Ben had suspected they might, they did not go all the way up the Thames to the sub base. Instead, they were directed to berths on Shaw's Neck near old Fort Trumbull, the object being to put them closer to the open sea for whatever practice exercises they would be conducting with a sub or subs coming downriver from the submarine base which was much farther north.

Using the remainder of the morning to clean ship and put things in order from the trip, and after seeing a repair crew come aboard to caulk the seep up forward, Ben waited until after lunch to grant liberty. Then, having set Condition 3 watches for their time in port, keeping one section aboard on duty, he released the other two sections for liberty ashore. Almost at once, O'Neal approached him carrying a jar of dead and desiccated cockroaches.

"How many?" Ben asked.

"Two hundred and thirteen," O'Neal said, "but I think we've still got one or two runnin' loose, Sir."

"And the winner is?" Ben asked.

"Light, Sir."

"Stands to reason," Ben laughed. "All right, Boats, here's a buck which will easily cover three draft beers and maybe a couple more, depending on where he drinks them. And tell him, 'good job.' He may not be able to do anything else well, but at least he can do one thing to our satisfaction."

"Right, Sir," O'Neal grinned. "The troops 'ave started callin' him 'Roach Man.'"

SC 65X, along with the rest of Division AA, remained tied up in port straight through Christmas. Ashore, Terry Keel managed to make an arrangement with a restaurant called The French Kitchen, which served the men individual Cornish hens for their Christmas dinner, something which appealed to all of them regardless of the fact that more than one of the men in the first sitting returned to the ship and reported to the second sitting, without ever before having seen a Cornish hen, that they were about to dine on something really new—pygmy turkeys.

According to the orders that Ben had received, Division AA, consisting of six subchasers, had been further subdivided into two three-chaser groups—Group AA1 and Group AA2. Because SC 65X would be working with the other two chasers in AA1, Ben and Terry joined the other four officers in the Group for Christmas dinner, giving each the opportunity to get to know every other officer and begin attuning himself to their various personalities. Lieutenant (j.g.) Horn, a graduate of Northwestern, commanded SC 56X, an Ichabod-looking ensign named Speck acting as his executive officer. Aboard SC 71X, senior Ensign Feller had taken command while a junior ensign, a former accountant named Hyde, backed him up. Of the six, Horn appeared to be at least three months senior to the others and had actually spent eight months on a destroyer before being given command of his chaser, so according to Navy procedure, at sea he would lead the Group and, when all six chasers operated together, the entire Division. Ben and Terry found that they liked him; Horn had an easy manner, spoke with an inviting degree of wit, laughed a lot, and told some good stories. Speck exhibited a very dry wit but didn't say much while both Feller and Hyde deferred to Horn. Neither of them sucked up nor exhibited anything of the sycophant about them, but they were nevertheless guarded about what they had to say and appeared to think before they ventured additions to the conversation.

Together, in a place called Olivia's Hut, the men shared an adequate serving of onion soup followed by prime rib and a slice of pumpkin pie, and owing to the tone of the place, they were each able to polish off the meal with a brandy before returning to their ships. As an initial gathering, both Ben and Terry found it congenial without being oppressive, open without broaching subjects that were best kept quiet.

"So," Terry asked, as the two of them once more walked aboard and dropped down the hatch into what passed for their wardroom, "what's on for tomorrow?"

"If the tugs can break us out," Ben said, seating himself on his chair, still wearing his greatcoat against the frigid chill in the space, "we'll be going out to exercise with a submarine—that's if the tugs can also break open a passage for the sub."

"And what do you think that will entail?" Terry asked.

Ben placed a sheet of paper on the table, drew an equilateral triangle on it, labeled the apex of the triangle "Sub," and at the bottom, along the baseline, he marked three dots, labeling the center one directly below the apex as SC 56X, the dot on the right-hand corner of the triangle SC 65X, and the dot on the left-hand corner of the triangle SC 71X.

"Here's the way I understand it," Ben said, drawing yet another line straight up from the dot representing 56X to the sub. "The line that I've just drawn is assumed to be our base course. 65X will be two thousand yards to starboard of 56X, while 71X will be stationed two thousand yards to port. We will move forward at perhaps 6 or 8 knots, stop, turn off our engines, lower the C-Tube hydrophone, listen, and when we pick up the sound of the sub's propellers, we'll read a bearing off the C-Tube's bearing dial. That bearing will be relative to the direction our ship is headed. We will then instantly convert that to a magnetic compass bearing and transmit our findings to Horn on 56X by means of that supposedly secret radio telephone that has given us the X designation for our hull number. Horn will then triangulate the bearings which the three chasers come up with, and that should show us the position of the submarine. As soon as Horn and the rest of us triangulate those bearings, we'll start engines and head for the sub's supposed position, perhaps stopping once more to take fresh bearings. Once we get in to somewhere around five hundred yards on the basis of what we consider a good contact, one or another of us, or at least two acting together, will rush in and launch an attack."

"And will that sub sit there and allow us to do that?" Terry laughed.

"Well, there's the catch," Ben said. "As long as he stays under, he can't outrun us. If he goes totally silent, stops his engines, and tries to sit on the bottom, he can also elude us. But if he gets antsy, comes to the surface, and pours on the steam, he can outrun us, and that, I suppose, is why we have the 3"/23, so that we can sink him or damage him before he can get beyond our range."

"Promises to be interesting, doesn't it?" Terry said, wrapping his scarf more closely around his chin.

"Interesting and probably frustrating," Ben said, "but you'll have to admit, there's a resemblance here to fishing, no matter how you look at it. I'd bet money that patience is the key."

On the day after Christmas, with SC 65X's crew back aboard and no worse for wear after their two days of liberty and what they remembered as a satisfying Christmas dinner ashore, two tugs broke a path down from the sub base in order to give the submarines with which the chasers were to practice a clear path to the sea. Then, one of those tugs returned and broke up the slip surrounding the chasers, allowing them to make a slow and careful exit to the upper reaches of the Sound.

To Ben and Terry, standing on the bridge, the wind seemed bitterly cold, pieces of sleet snapping down from the low-hanging clouds, flakes of snow occasionally falling when the winds died down, and rimes of ice forming on stanchions and handrails in a way that, even with thick gloves, made remaining upright difficult.

"Wouldn't you know?" Terry said, putting up one hand to shield his face against the sleet.

"When, I wonder," Ben said, "was the last time that New England had a winter like this?"

Group AA1 needed more than an hour to reach the area which had been designated for their exercise, but once there, Horn signaled an immediate change from their line astern formation. After quickly making a mental computation about where his assigned position would be, Ben ordered a change of speed, worked out on Horn's starboard beam, and finally settled 65X into her assigned slot with 56X two thousand yards distant, the entire formation steering east on a course of 090. Less than a minute after 71X slipped into her station four thousand yards north of 65X, Horn ordered all three chasers to stop, shut off their engines, lower their C-Tubes, and listen. Then, within two minutes, Crim, sitting in the magazine, holding the earphones connected to the C-Tube to his head, sent up a relative bearing which Ben and Terry both instantly converted to 075 magnetic and reported over the R/T phone to Horn. Just as quickly, Horn appeared to triangulate the bearing with whatever his sound device had picked up and with the bearing that 71X had reported. Seconds later, once more bringing the R/T into play, he reoriented a new base course and headed for the apparent position of the sub.

During the first hour that morning, the hunt actually seemed enjoyable, the chasers stopping twice to check their solutions to the supposed position of the sub before Horn ordered both 65X and 71X to make their attack. When they did, and on Ben's command, Farris threw out a single Mills bomb which exploded in the sea not more than a second after it sank over the submarine—a sound which alerted the practice sub that it had been attacked. At that point, after clearing off to a safe distance to starboard, the sub came to the surface, signaled the chasers that they had made a successful attack, gave them a BRAVO ZULU for a job well done, and dived once more to initiate the second exercise of the day.

"I don't want to accuse our brother submariners of gilding the lily," Ben said, "but that was too easy. I'm guessing they gave us a free ride to let us get a clear idea about things, and I'll bet they're going to start trying to elude us from here on out."

Ben had never considered himself to be a prophet, but in this particular case, his words proved true. Once the practice sub had served itself up to them like some kind of prize at a twenty-yard turkey shoot, it never did so again. Instead, deep beneath the crest of the whitecaps which continued to whip back against the chaser with gale force, the sub began to maneuver, turning, doubling back, going silent before starting up again and restarting the hunt, and four additional hours passed before the chasers in Group AA1 managed to get themselves into a position from which they felt justified in launching their second attack of the day. When the sub finally surfaced well out astern of them, they knew, all three of them, that they had botched the attack and not even come close.

"Good hunt," the sub signaled as all vessels together started back toward New London. "Good fun."

"This guy has a sense of humor," Terry laughed. "Fun for the sub, I'll bet, running rings around us, and I'll bet those guys are warm down there as well, what with all of them pressed together like sardines and with all the heat coming off their diesels."

"Right," Ben joked, "not real sailors at all. Perhaps we should send them a letter and let them know what they're missing."

"And I understand that they eat better than we do, too," Terry ventured.

"Probably," Ben said, "but I've got to give Santos credit. He's coming along. I hear we're having meatloaf tonight. Let's keep our fingers crossed. If he puts the right ingredients into it, we might even be able to taste it, once we thaw out."

Group AA1 spent two hours working back into New London that night, Group AA2 returning nearly an hour before them as a result of having a shorter distance to travel. The subs, to Ben and Terry's surprise, remained at sea, detailed, it seemed, for the next day's exercises before they returned to port and exchanged the exercise duty with a different pair.

"We're fully operational now," Ben said, as they finally tied up alongside the other chasers in their nest, "so from this moment on, we're going to eat with the crew, first sitting. It seems unlikely, but regardless of the fact that we're out there training and doing exercises, we also have to face the fact that at any time, an actual Hun U-boat could show up in the Sound, which means that we've got to keep this ship ready for action, both in port and while we're out. Santos will be relieved that he doesn't have to carry our food up to us, and we'll be better off because it will still be hot when we sit down to it."

Their first meal on the mess decks went pretty much as both Ben and Terry expected it to. The crew, somewhat in awe of having officers sitting with them, remained virtually silent unless directly spoken to, but by the time that they finally stood up, the men seemed to be loosening their tongues, talking over the day's events, telling a joke or two, and it was then that Ben felt sure that the arrangement would work out as he'd expected it to. And the meatloaf had proved a success, Ben and Terry stepping to the galley following the meal to commend Santos for a job well done.

The following day—a day in which the tugs once more had to break the chasers out of the ice before they could sortie—Group AA1

worked closer to port with the sub which had exercised with Group AA2 on the day before. This time, Horn led them into three attacks, two of which apparently proved successful, the sub surfacing after each to send them a BRAVO ZULU for each success.

"You think this skipper is as accomplished as the first one?" Terry asked Ben as they once more headed into port beneath the descending dusk.

"We had an easier day of it, that's certain," Ben said. "What's impossible to measure is how much of an effort he was putting into it. These guys don't have to worry about us killing them. The Huns and the Austrians are probably going to be a devil of a lot harder to deal with. They are going to have no doubts about the fact that we're trying to kill them, and we're going to have to be dead careful that they don't get a chance to kill us. Wholly different situation, if you see what I mean."

Terry saw and said so, and then he asked Ben yet another question. "Where do you suppose they'll send us?"

For a moment, as though thinking, Ben said nothing. Then, breathing carefully through the sleet, he turned his face from it and said, "According to Horn—and he didn't tell me much— apparently we're going down to Bermuda eventually. I gather that we'll spend another week or two there, working up, doing drills that we can't really do up here in this miserable weather, and then, I'm guessing we'll go overseas."

"And where, I wonder, might that take us?" Terry ventured.

"From what little I know," Ben said, "I think there are three possibilities, although there may be others that I don't know about. I've heard talk that we might go to Corfu; the Italians and the Royal Navy have something called a 'barrage' set up across the mouth of the Adriatic. They're using everything from anti-submarine nets on the fringes to trawlers and destroyers in an attempt to keep Hun and Austrian U-boats bottled up over there. A second possibility is that we could operate out of the Azores, patrolling between Brest and Gibraltar, and then, I guess they could send us to England to do escort or barrage duty in the Channel. I've never been to any of those places before, so for the time being, they look equally attractive, and if one or the other of them will take us away from the winter we're trying to endure up here, I'm ready to get started now."

"Amen," Terry said. "The last time I heard from the folks, they said that New Rochelle was having the worst winter they could remember."

For the two weeks that followed—all of them bitterly cold, all of them fraught with ice in harbor and boisterous seas in the Sound—SC 65X and the remainder of the chasers in the Division worked at their craft, learning as they went, perfecting the skills which, all of them hoped, would permit them to survive and put paid to the intensifying Hun U-boat campaign. News reaching them from England and from the Mediterranean suggested that both the Germans and the Austrians were stepping up their U-boat attacks and sinking more Allied merchant ships, not to mention more than a few warships, in ever growing numbers, and threatening the United Kingdom with something on the order of starvation. And for the Americans only then entering the war, that seemed hardly the least of it; already, U-boats had been sighted off Hatteras and the New Jersey coast, and rumor had it that American ships were being sunk in home waters before they could even start overseas. News of that kind proved sketchy. Intelligence reports, had they received any, might have revealed the truth, but thus far into their training, information that could be counted on had remained slim, so what the men knew or thought they knew they filed away mentally, stuck to the business at hand, and endured what the wicked weather threw their way.

Once during the two-week period, a tug pulled a sled out to operate with them, and then all six chasers participated in a gunnery practice, shooting up to thirty rounds at the massive target which the tug towed behind her at a considerable distance. Given the pitch and roll which SC 65X and the others were forced to endure during the exercise, the level of proficiency that Farris and his gunners were able to demonstrate set no records, but they did score hits, and near misses. While Ben wouldn't have called the practice a huge success, he didn't call it a failure.

"What would you think," Terry asked, "five hits or six?"

"I think," Ben said, "that if they'd been shooting at something as large as a U-boat, we might have been able to count four good ones and a near miss."

"So, enough to do damage?" Terry asked.

"I'd say so," Ben said. "I doubt that we could have sunk whatever it was that we were shooting at, but we would certainly have forced her down where we could depth charge her."

In the evenings, if shards of sleet weren't whipping across the piers like shotgun pellets, they went onto the beach for a beer, Ben, Terry, Horn, Speck, Feller, and Hyde trading small talk, stories, college reminiscences, snatches of news that one or another of them had picked up, and unclassified bits of Navy lore that had struck them as unusual. As a rule, they slid in together around a table at Olivia's Hut where a lounge off the main dining room catered to their needs, all of them supplied swiftly and deftly by a nondescript waiter who looked to Ben like he'd been employed by the business for sixty years. By that time, Feller and Hyde had emerged from their shells, and Feller, it seemed, showed a capacity for wit that resembled Horn's, something that added to the table and kept the men laughing, particularly when Horn and Feller ventured into an exchange.

"Very nice, all of this," Feller remarked as they walked back to their ships one evening with the snow settling on their shoulders. "The only thing missing—and I'm sorry to inform you boys that you are no substitutes—are the beautiful femmes that we so richly deserve to have clinging to our arms and waiting with bated breath to answer to our every need."

"Spoken like a true naval officer and a gentleman," Horn said.

"Ha," Terry laughed, "spoken like a true Irish storyteller, if you ask me. You ought to come over and compare notes with our boy, O'Neal. With the amount of imagination the two of you are demonstrating, it sounds like the three of you could build up a regular mountain of myth, fantasy, and wishful thinking."

"Now, now," Horn cautioned. "Let's not be skeptical. I'm sure that Odysseus didn't expect to meet the sirens when he first set out, but you can bet your bottom dollar that the *overseas* which we are all destined to visit will be filled with them; therefore, it is only right that we assume that the gardens of delight are merely waiting for us to arrive and present our credentials."

"My guess," Ben laughed, "is that you'd best see to the secure protection of those credentials if you meet any sirens over there, Greek, Italian, or British."

"Goes without saying," Horn laughed, "but what a wonderful thought to keep in mind."

In the middle of the following week, as the chasers exercised without a submarine, drilling their crews on everything from the procedures for abandoning ship to recovering a man who had gone overboard, they also received a message ordering them to test their Y-Guns and authorizing them to expend two depth charges each. The particular day upon which the depth-charge exercise was to take place kicked up a truly miserable sea, but with Terry down behind the deck house supervising Farris and his depth-charge team, the men managed to hoist the massive ashcans onto their mountings. Then, while the other two chasers stood off at a distance of two thousand yards, and with Terry once more on the bridge beside him, Ben took SC 65X up to full speed and ran her toward the wholly fictitious but designated spot where an enemy submarine was imagined to be lurking beneath the waves.

Carefully, Ben timed his approach so as to fire on the level crest of the nearest roller. There, within the one or two seconds during which the chaser remained on a relatively even keel, he gave the order. Farris fired the charge, and the two ashcans that they'd loaded onto the Y-Gun burst from their housings and went flying out into the air on both sides of the ship, Ben shouting down the voice tube for Chief Pack to pour on the power so that the tiny chaser would escape most of the concussion and not spring leaks when the charges reached their assigned depths and exploded.

Seconds passed, and then two or three more, and suddenly, well astern of the ship but to port and starboard, the seas simply erupted, flinging massive plumes of water and some mud two hundred feet into the sky, blotting out even what little light might have filtered through the low-hanging clouds astern.

"Jesus!" Terry exclaimed, as the crew on deck cut loose with a cheer.

For a moment, the upper reaches of the plume hung in the air; then, as the entire disturbed mass began to fall back down into the sea, they felt the vibrations as the outer waves of the concussion overtook them.

"Sobering, isn't it?" Ben said, surveying the turmoil they'd created. "Makes you wonder how a submarine can survive it, but apparently, they do."

"Whatever the case," Terry gasped, "I wouldn't want to be down there in one of them when one of those charges blows."

"No," Ben said. "I can't see anything positive about that at all, save for the fact that if it does do for the U-boat, it must be over in an instant."

"Yeah," Terry said, "if that's of any consolation. Somehow, I doubt that it is."

"No," Ben said, giving his head a slight shake, "and it doesn't seem to me to be a thing that hazard pay can be much of a compensation for."

Division AA and her chasers trained on for another week, the weather never giving them a break, the ice still surrounding their hulls each morning until the tugs broke them free. The seas in the Sound and beyond still kicked up so much pitch and roll that their physical efforts to compensate for the motion left them exhausted by the time they finally secured from the drills and returned to New London.

And then, very quickly one morning, stake trucks pulled up on the pier, and working parties from all six chasers were called away to begin taking on stores. At the same time, summoning all of his officers, twelve of them in total, Horn assembled them on the fantail of 56X and spoke to them briefly.

"We're leaving for Bermuda in the morning," he said, in flat, straightforward terms. "SC 65X is once more designated lead navigator, and we will travel in two lines abreast: Group AA1 in the lead with five-hundred-yard intervals between ships, Group AA2 to port, same intervals but two thousand yards off AA1's beam. Cruising speed is set at 10 knots. Silence on the R/T will be in effect; communication will be by flag hoist and flashing light or semaphore. A destroyer, the *Abel Gibson* will be leading us, and her commanding officer will be in tactical command. A tug, the *Buntaka*, will be stationed astern of the formation in case any engineering casualties develop and one or another of us requires a tow. With 730 miles to travel, I estimate that we should make landfall sometime on our fourth day out, possibly in the morning if we have a smooth voyage. Any questions?"

The various captains posed a few, but brief though Horn's coverage of their proposed operation had seemed to be, it had dealt with the high points and left little doubt about what the chasers would be doing. So, after a fifteen-minute exchange of questions and answers, the pre-sailing conference broke up and the officers returned to their ships.

Fetching each a mug of coffee from the galley, Ben led Terry up to the pilot house, and there, with the snow and sleet beating against the window screens that Ben had ordered installed, they considered what lay ahead of them.

"This is not going to be the picnic that our orders suggest," Ben said. "We've got enough of a storm right here to keep sensible ships in port, and my guess is that it's going to be a lot worse when we reach the open sea. And if the weather slacks off anywhere within three hundred miles of Bermuda, I'll be surprised. So, here's what we've got to do. First, we've got to make believers of this crew, and then we have to see to it that they lash down, tie down, or bolt down everything in sight until all loose equipment is so secure that not even a 40-degree roll will break it loose. After that, we've got to be sure that each of them has his keeper bars up around his bunk; I don't want anyone being thrown out or sliced open by a fall, because without a doctor or a pharmacist's mate aboard, one or the other of us will have to sew them up. Once at sea, they've got to be mindful about looking for leaks where caulking has worked loose, and all of them—and that means all—are going to have to be constantly looking after their equipment to be sure that it functions properly. If we ever get a star to shoot, I'll begin breaking you in on the sextant, but don't get your hopes up; I'm betting that this storm will bedevil us most of the way, so I only hope we can keep the rest of the formation in sight. Understand what I'm telling you?"

"Yes Sir," Terry said.

"All right," Ben said, "let's get to it, and if we can light enough of a fire under this crew of ours, I think they'll give us what we want."

On the fantail, Ben put out the word to the crew. Throughout the remainder of the day, the crew, sobered by what Ben had told them, turned to with a degree of determination that Ben and Terry found gratifying. And then, prior to the evening meal, Ben and Terry made an inspection of the vessel which turned up only occasional lapses of a minor kind—so few that when the two of them finally turned in that evening, Ben thought that SC 65X was fully and finally ready for sea, the real sea, the sea that had loomed in their imaginations since the day that all of them had come aboard.

6

If things had seemed bad in the Sound and off the coast of New London, six hours into the Atlantic proper took Division AA into a gale that showed every man on every chaser, not to mention the crews of the *Abel Gibson* and the *Buntaka*, weather that they had never seen before. With the seas raging down from the North Atlantic, Ben would have liked to have headed up into them. It would have been the seamanlike thing to do; it would have been what he would have done on the ore carrier on the Lakes. But with their course and destination set to the southeast, none of the ships in the formation had a choice. As a result, they were taking the ever-rising seas on their beam and on their port quarter, causing each chaser in the Division to roll like there could be no tomorrow at the same time that it found its stern being endlessly pushed to the south—an eventuality that so rapidly wore out the helmsmen that Ben took to having them relieved and rested at thirty-minute intervals. No man in the pilot house could have remained comfortably or even uncomfortably on his feet. Even before they'd left port, foreseeing what they might encounter, Ben had ordered O'Neil to rig both slings and harnesses from the overhead so that the men serving in the space could quickly buckle themselves into them and remain relatively upright and keep from being thrown to the deck by the gyrations of the chaser.

Ahead, as SC 65X plunged over the crest of a wave and nearly straight down into the trough, the seas continually buried her bow. When she once more labored to come up and climb the mountain that rose before her, the wind screens to the fore in the pilot house were pounded by green water that flew all the way back over the flying bridge. Ben and Terry did not try to go up to the flying bridge. Instead, they stood their watches in the pilot house, and O'Neal did the same, all of them seeking to avoid being swept overboard and doing what they could to maintain control over conditions that, in truth, allowed for little and almost no control.

Below decks, water sloshed everywhere. It wasn't that the caulking had worked loose, although it had in at least two places; secured as tightly as the hatches would allow, the water which continually washed across the main deck still managed to work itself in before the bilge pumps in the engine room could force it back out through the overboard discharges. Rather than brave their way forward, nearly every man sleeping in the forward crew's quarters had taken refuge in the after crew's quarters. There, throughout the time they remained fighting the gale, the men from up forward hot-bunked with the men going on watch, all of them sleeping in their clothes and duffle coats in an attempt to keep warm. As far as Ben could determine, even before they steamed into their first night underway, the voyage promised more misery than he had ever experienced at sea.

Although both Terry and O'Neal were able to catch some fitful sleep during their hours off watch, Ben did not go down, did not leave the bridge; instead, strapped into the small captain's chair that he'd had bolted to the deck on the starboard side of the pilot house, he remained largely awake, dozing only occasionally, mindful of both his charge and his responsibility.

Bitter though the gale was, miserable as the seas continued to be, he silently thanked a man he'd never met or ever expected to meet, a man named Albert Loring Swasey, the marine architect who'd designed the subchaser for the Navy. She was small, SC 65X, and she was built of wood, but she was seaworthy, and no matter what contortions the raging Atlantic forced her through, she always recovered—a lasting testament to Swasey's expertise and both the skill and attention to detail which the East Coast shipwrights had lavished on her when they'd constructed her and launched her at Camden.

Throughout the night and on into the first dawn underway, Ben remained firm in his place, and when a gray, gale-filled morning finally broke and he got his binoculars up, the only thing he could see appeared to be a slight smoke haze well up ahead of him, apparent stack gas from the *Abel Gibson*, but behind and to either side of him, he couldn't see a subchaser anywhere.

"Where are they?" Terry asked, a look of desperation on his face, when he finally came to the bridge that morning, carrying a thermos of hot coffee for Ben and two pieces of bread wrapped around several slices of bacon, a meal into which Ben immediately launched himself, having foregone anything the night before.

"Your guess is as good as mine," Ben said, his brow knitting beneath his watch cap. "They were still out there last night when you turned in, but I can't see a one of them this morning. The *Gibson* is showing some smoke up ahead, but she's worked much farther out in front of us than the op-order allowed for. While we may be making turns for 10 knots, I'm guessing that these seas have cut us down to seven or eight. I'd like to be able to shoot a fix, but as you can see for yourself, we couldn't find a star in this muck if our lives depended upon it. Right at the moment, it looks like dead reckoning all the way with no hope for anything better. The fact that we've still got the *Gibson* in sight is at least encouraging. But that's if her own navigator is any good because he sure as hell can't shoot stars either which means that all of us are steaming blind, if you see what I mean."

Keel saw. That didn't mean that he liked what he saw, but Terry was a reasonable fellow and accepted what he had no choice other than to accept.

"What if they don't catch up with us?" he asked. "You're the designated navigator for the trip, so if they don't have you to follow, what do they do?"

"I'd imagine," Ben said, "that they'll dead reckon the way we are, and if they are all still together back there somewhere behind us—and that seems doubtful—Horn told me that he can shoot the stars when he has to, so they'll have Horn to go by, if they can find him."

"And if they can't?" Terry said.

"That's an eventuality that I'd rather not consider," Ben said. "In a pinch, after this thing blows through and we reach where we're supposed to be going, we might have to go back out and look for some of them."

"Seems like the R/T might have come in handy in a case like this," Terry said.

"Seems that way, doesn't it," Ben observed.

"Then why didn't Horn use it?" Terry wanted to know.

"Can't say," Ben said. "But if I had to guess, I'd guess that he followed orders for radio silence and that if he'd broken them, the skipper of the *Gibson* might have raised hell, regardless of the conditions that have turned up."

"Regular Navy, that skipper?"

"I'd bet on it," Ben said.

For two more days, the seas pounded SC 65X with unremitting fury, but she held together, and when Chief Pack came to the pilot house to report the condition of his engines, he told Ben pretty much what Ben had expected to hear.

"Cap'n," Pack said, "don't know if you want to hear it or not, but if you don't mind me mentioning it, I'd say that we have Ford motors and some unhappy civilians on Stanton Island to thank for keeping us going. A couple of them magnetos have come in real handy."

"I thought they might," Ben said, with the merest trace of a smile. "I hear you about the civilians, but if, a few months or a year from now, they don't have to wake up in the morning and start speaking German, maybe they'll learn to forgive us."

"Yes Sir," Pack said, showing Ben a half-smile of his own. "It's a hard life if you don't weaken."

"You can bet on it," Ben said.

In the afternoon of their third long day at sea, as Ben remained in his chair wondering whether or not he was going to pass out from nothing more than blind fatigue, Townsend reported the barometer starting to rise, and within the next hour, with the seas diminishing and the temperature rising, Ben sensed that they had weathered everything that the gale had thrown at them and survived. The following morning, not long after first light, with warm mid-Atlantic air breezing back from the bow and with Terry and Townsend standing beside him to record the stopwatch, Ben shot morning stars; then, working on a chart table that had stabilized enough to remain fairly level, Ben began showing Terry how to make the necessary calculations to work out their position, and they did, showing SC 65X to be within twenty-six miles of His Majesty's Dockyard in Bermuda.

By 0942 that morning, SC 65X was tied up beside the USS *Mulgrew*, an antiquated armed cruiser which had last seen action in the Spanish–American War—a ship which had already been old in 1898 and which, now turned into a tender or what some called a mother ship for the chasers, was even older. No matter; fitted out like a partial tanker for the chasers' support, she carried all the spare parts, fuel, and equipment that any of them were ever likely to need during their deployment. Once Ben arrived and tied up, her carpenters and specialists instantly descended onto Ben's deck and went straight to work caulking seams that had worked loose and seeing to whatever other damage the chaser had suffered during her voyage. Although a lieutenant commander named Kettle commanded the *Mulgrew*, Ben went aboard and reported himself in to Commander Radford, the energetic but elderly three-striper who, one rank senior to Kettle, had been appointed to overall command of the chaser contingent and whatever operations they would eventually conduct wherever they were going.

Ben's welcome seemed warm, and when Radford stood upon Ben's entry into his cabin and asked how the voyage had gone, Ben told him at once that it had been the worst three-day trip that he had ever made at sea.

"And you all became separated in the storm?" Radford asked, a frown beginning to distort his face.

"Yes Sir," Ben said. "Without running lights and forbidden to break radio silence . . . well, Sir, by the second morning out, the only thing I could see was what appeared to be smoke on the horizon rising from where I imagined the *Gibson* to be steaming. Rain and spray obscured everything else."

"And you dead reckoned all the way?"

"Yes Sir," Ben said, "until this morning when I finally shot stars and worked a fix."

"All right," Commander Radford said. "Well done, Mister. Let's hope the rest of them make it, and if they don't we'll have to go look for them. In the meantime, see to your ship and whatever repairs you need to make, and we've a plenitude of spare parts aboard, so draw what you need. I want your chaser and the rest of them brought up to speed as quickly as possible. We're going to do two weeks' training here, and then we're setting off for the Azores, the whole lot of us as well as a contingent from Charleston. Steady as you go, now, and keep me informed."

Ben, Terry, and the crew of SC 65X were already hard at work putting the chaser in order when at 1300 that afternoon SC 56X and SC 71X finally limped in and tied up beside them, and then, yet three more hours passed before the leading chaser in Group AA2 arrived and still two more hours before the *Buntaka* towed the last two chasers into the harbor and nested them astern of AA1 alongside the *Mulgrew*.

"Well, at least we all made it," Horn said to Ben when the two of them finally met. "Hell of a blow, that. I hope to God we never see another like it."

"Same here," Ben said. "What's the damage?"

Horn screwed up his mouth and shook his head. "Minor on my boat," he said. "Window glass shattered in the pilot house, hot bearing in the engine room, and leaks from bad caulking. 71X will have to have one of her propellers straightened or replaced, and all of her pilot house glass has been shattered. AA1 is in fair shape, but AA2 is a mess. Two engines quit owing to faulty magnetos on both 61X and 64X, and 73X's auxiliary engine crapped out altogether, so they lost the electrical load, and that rascal's going to have to be replaced as well."

"I recommend copper screens on the pilot house windows," Ben said. "They won't rust, and they'll break up the force of the seas when they flip up over the bow and smash into 'em. I put screens on, and our windows remained intact."

"Good suggestion," Horn said. "I'll see to it. Any other ideas?"

"I gather that the *Mulgrew* has plenty of magnetos," Ben said. "From what Commander Radford told me when I checked in, that old hulk is carrying a load of spare parts for us, so I'd suggest that each chaser draw extras and keep them on hand."

"Right," Horn said. "Thanks for the tip. I guess I'd better get in there and see Radford. He'll be wondering where I've been."

No one went ashore on their first night in Bermuda. Instead, like a tired flight of swallows after a long migration, everyone aboard all six of the chasers, all save for the watch sections, crashed almost at once following the evening meal and slept the sleep of the dead. For the two days following, days in which the chaser crews and the *Mulgrew*'s accomplished ratings worked nearly around the clock cleaning, doing upkeep, and making repairs, Radford also declined to permit a liberty. But on the following Saturday morning, those men not on watch were turned loose, large liberty boats from the *Mulgrew* carrying them ashore. Once more on the firm ground of the beach—but after strong-minded lectures on how to behave in a foreign port—the sailors of the chasers gave themselves up to recreation and enjoyment in a climate that no longer pelted them with bitterly cold snow and ice. Some of them drank beer; some of them, to use the English expression, *chatted up* whatever women they could find; and some of them merely ate new foods and took carriage rides. Ben and Terry, once they got ashore, found bicycles to rent and rode around the island they were on, taking in the sights and enjoying the pastels with which the houses in Somerset Village had been painted.

Sunday, for those who went ashore, was pretty much given over to the same activities, each man soaking up the sun that warmed his back, each out for whatever larks the environment permitted. Not a few also indulged themselves by swimming from the beaches, the waters surrounding the shore offering a plethora of good opportunities. On Monday morning, according to the training orders Commander Radford's staff had distributed, the six chasers in Division AA returned to sea. This time, carrying inspectors which the staff had named "instructors," they began demonstrating what was supposed to be their proficiency with everything from damage control and engineering casualty repair to gunnery, navigation, and the intricacies of anti-submarine warfare, what they knew of it.

Commander Radford, as Ben intuited, turned out to be a hard taskmaster. Up before dawn, the Division sortied with the rising of the sun. For hour after hour, they worked on one problem after another, only returning to port as the sun set. Thereafter, the officers, summoned to the wardroom of the *Mulgrew*, sat for a critique of the exercises they'd been through that day until, finally, they were permitted to return to their chasers. There they set in motion whatever corrections or orders Radford had handed down before, at last, falling into their bunks for the few hours of rest that were to be allowed them.

Near the end of the period, behind yet another antiquated cruiser named the USS *Crandle*, twelve additional chasers, all of them coming from Charleston, steamed into the harbor, anchored five hundred yards from the *Mulgrew*, and at once turned their liberty crews loose, their sailors joining Division AA's on the beach. To Ben and Terry's relief, rivalries did not develop, the chaser personnel contenting themselves with comparing notes on what they'd been doing, seeing the sights, and drinking more of the island's beer.

For that last weekend, shore leave for the officers in both groups did not take place. Instead, Radford, who turned out to be senior to the commander leading the Charleston group, called for an officers' conference aboard the *Mulgrew*. For hours, the officers in both groups studied charts and went over the details of the operations orders that were to govern their activities for the following months.

Finally, Radford stood and spoke his piece to the two groups. "With training for the New London group completed here," he said, speaking firmly, "and with the Charleston group's training completed in Charleston, it's time to go. We have a war to win and a job to do. We have 2,140 miles to steam in order to reach Ponta Delgada in the Azores, so I anticipate that each group will refuel from her tender at least twice on the way over. If we are able to maintain a ten-knot speed, we should be able to make landfall in ten days, and once arrived, we will remain in port for six days' upkeep before the Charleston contingent departs for Gibraltar, Malta, Corfu, and duty on the Otranto Barrage at the mouth of the Adriatic. The New London group, upon its departure, will head north, putting into Brest in company with *Mulgrew* before moving on to Plymouth and probably Weymouth, where the Navy plans to establish a temporary base for us. Depending upon the weather, refueling in the Mid-Atlantic during the transit may prove difficult, so it will behoove all hands to take a particular strain to perform the evolution successfully. At the same time, from the moment we leave here, we must all consider ourselves to be in the war zone and at war. We have no idea where or when a Hun or Austrian U-boat might pop to the surface, and that means that we must be instantly ready for battle at any time during the day or night. The ready magazines are to be charged, and our depth charges are to be prepared for instant launch. Do I make myself clear?"

No one in *Mulgrew*'s wardroom had any doubts about Commander Radford's meaning.

"All right, gentlemen," Radford said, "return to your ships, prepare yourselves for war, and I wish each and every one of you good hunting."

The following Monday morning, the *Mulgrew* and the *Crandle*, with their chaser divisions acting as their screening escorts, sortied from Bermuda and set a course to the east. Throughout most of their first day in transit, the seas remained relatively calm. On their second day out, the swell picked up, running at what Ben judged to be a steady condition somewhere between a State 4 and a State 5 on the

84

Beaufort Scale—the scale that Massachusetts Nautical had taught him to follow during his training. As far as Ben was concerned, if things remained that way all the way to the Azores, he would come away from the voyage with a smile upon his face. The skies did not remain altogether clear, but given the amount of cloud that came and went, he had no trouble teaching Terry to shoot noon sun lines and, at least once each day, morning or night, and sometimes twice, they managed to find enough stars showing to shoot a fix.

Once more, the transit was made under conditions of radio silence. With Ben remaining on the bridge for much of the trip, he gave both Terry and O'Neal enough training so that he felt it safe to descend into after crew's quarters to take his meal sitting at the mess table, leaving them on their own to stand their watches without relying on his immediate supervision. And as the voyage progressed and the two became more attuned to what they were doing and more confident about doing it, Ben began slipping down to his bunk for occasional naps, some of them extending across three manageable hours; thus, although there seemed never a moment when he didn't feel fatigued, total exhaustion never troubled him.

Refueling, however, put him under a degree of stress that he wished it hadn't because Commander Radford had worked out a system which differed from standard refueling at sea in several ways, including one which struck Ben as dangerous. Normally, a minesweeper, a destroyer, or even a cruiser which intended to take on fuel ran up alongside a tanker, passed messenger lines, secured a hose cable somewhere to one of its exterior bulkheads, and stood by for a fueling hose to slide down where it could be thrust into a fueling trunk. With the chasers, things were to be different. What Commander Radford and Kettle had devised and what the Charleston group apparently also followed was a system in which a chaser—Ben's chaser when his turn came—would run up alongside the *Mulgrew*, take a heavy sea painter from somewhere forward on the tender, attach it to a cleat up forward on the chaser's bow, and then allow the forward motion of the *Mulgrew* to pull 65X in alongside while a gasoline hose was passed down to her. Ben's job, and an intense strain it proved to be, was to steer his chaser alongside while she was being pulled along without letting her move in so close that she collided with the mother ship. Both ships hung fenders from their sides to minimize any contact the two vessels did encounter, but Ben didn't find them reassuring and labored mightily to keep his vessel three to four feet away from the steel hull of the *Mulgrew*. Fortunately, once the hose was passed and fuel began to pump, the tanks filled swiftly. For Ben, they never filled swiftly enough; when he finally had his crew pass back the hose and threw off the big ship's sea painter so that he could break away, he found his face, head, and body bathed with sweat as a result of the tension that he'd been under while conning his chaser alongside.

"Nasty risk, isn't it?" Terry said to him after the first time they performed the evolution.

"Very," Ben said. "Catch a bad swell, and who knows what might happen? That rascal might come straight down on us and crush a gunnel or even stave in our side. Much better, I think, to refuel in port or pass that gasoline line down a fueling cable. But the *Mulgrew* isn't equipped with a rig for that which is why, I suppose, we're having to do it this way."

Three days from the Azores, with several hundred miles left to go, one of the Charleston's chasers reported sighting a submarine. Commander Radford instantly broke radio silence, came up on the R/T with a brief command, sent the entire formation to General Quarters, and dispatched two of the nearest chasers to make a search and prosecute an attack. To everyone's relief as well as to their later amusement, the apparent U-boat turned out to be a whale, reason and deduction finally reducing her supposed periscope to whatever she'd thrown up through her blow hole.

"I wonder how long it will take the lookouts and the deck watch over there to live that one down?" Terry laughed when the mystery was solved.

"I can't imagine that it will be soon," Ben said, "and I shudder to think what nicknames will be coined to commemorate the event."

Ponta Delgada—when they finally arrived, entered, and tied up in a nest alongside the *Mulgrew*—provided more than a breath of fresh air. With the chaser's tanks once more supplied with enough fresh water from a tender so that they had plenty to spare, the men were able to bathe, shave, and do their laundry. Then, with the greenish-blue mountains rising behind the city, a sight that Bermuda could never have afforded, and with a clean breeze blowing down from the heights, the liberty sections raced ashore to indulge in whatever local beers and pleasures the island provided, including Portuguese food, which was new to them, and the fresh pineapple which seemed to overflow the island with an abundant crop.

Later, in the mess, Ben issued a word of caution.

"I had some of that pineapple last night," he said, "but go easy, gents, or you will be lined up at the head with a bad case of the Los Angeles high-step, the Tennessee frisky, or whatever else you'd like to call it. Very unpleasant, that. Downright inconvenient, if you see what I mean."

With a laugh they all saw what he meant, and pointed to Light as their example.

"Roach Man, him already give us a demonstration." Scarlatti grinned.

"All right," Ben laughed, "I'll assume you've all taken note."

On the beach, Ben, Terry, Horn, and Feller found themselves a comfortable haven at Machado's on Rua de Cruz, a moderately priced restaurant which started them with a generous bowl of cabbage-based *Caldo verde* followed on their first night by grilled sardines and on their second visit with an octopus dish that failed with Feller but which Ben, Terry, and Horn consumed with gusto. The third and last time that the men ate at Machado's, the restaurant served them a heavy portion of lamb stew that everyone could applaud, even Speck and Hyde, who had managed to join their company. Afterward, still sipping the light red wine that came with the meal and while waiting for the coffee that Machado's brewed only to order, Feller posed the questions that all of them had started thinking about.

"I wonder how we're going to like England?" he said, speaking flatly without expressing an opinion one way or another.

"Think the English will be like the Canadians?" Horn said, turning to Ben. "You must have had some dealings with the Canadians. How did you find them?"

"Congenial," Ben said, after a few seconds of silence. "Different in some ways, most of them small, but not unpleasant. However, there's this for what it's worth. The Canadians seem to think that the English look on them as 'colonials,' and from what little I've heard from them, that suggests 'as untutored inferiors of some kind.'"

"Ha," Speck laughed. "If that's the case, wait until we get up there. They'll probably think of us as a pack of benighted rebels who didn't have the good sense to remain a colony."

"Could be," Ben laughed, "but to be dead honest about it, I don't think we ought to form a negative opinion before we've met the English and the Royal Navy in their lair and had a chance to see for ourselves."

"Ben's right," Horn said at once. "Look at it like this. In one way or another, each of us has met more than a few jackasses on our side of the pond, so human nature being what it is, we are sure to meet a few more wherever we're going. Let's just hope they're few and far between."

"My uncle did a turn at Cambridge," Terry ventured, "studying physics. He said their beer is warmer than ours but a great deal better once you get used to it."

"Now that," Hyde said, "is encouraging. If we begin by telling them that we appreciate their beer, I can't see how we can go wrong."

"On the other hand," Terry said, a grin spreading across his face, "My uncle said that he found their cooking unimaginative, lukewarm, and bland."

"Good grief," Ben said. "If an American said that, it must really be bad."

"Here now," Horn joked, "does that mean that you're casting aspersions on good old American cooking?"

"Far be it from me to criticize," Ben said, "but in my humble opinion, compared to French, Italian, Chinese, and Indian food, not to mention Greek, Indonesian, Spanish, Mexican, and Dutch cuisine, and with the exception of a good hamburger, American food is about as bland as unsalted, un-peppered, un-buttered mashed potatoes served cold and after a day's delay."

"What a way you're developing with words," Horn laughed. "How is it, I wonder, that you've assembled this vast array of culinary experiences?"

"The ship used to put into Chicago," Ben said quickly. "That gave me the chance to try them all."

"Pity," Hyde said, "that we haven't had the same opportunity. However, if Machado's can serve as a preliminary, I'd say that these Portuguese dishes have something going for them.

Two days later, the *Mulgrew*, escorted by the six chasers in Division AA, departed Ponta Delgada and headed northeast in order to make the nearly 1,300-mile voyage to Brest. Below decks, aside from the lazaret which seemed to be stacked to overflowing with them, cases of pineapples appeared to be tucked into every spare cubbyhole.

"At what point," Terry asked as he took up a watch on the flying bridge with Ben, "will the troops become tired of eating pineapples and begin to chuck them over the side?"

"I think you might be missing out on their capitalistic tendencies," Ben laughed. "My guess, although I might be wrong and you might be right, is that they will hoard those things like gold and then try to sell them in Brest or in Weymouth, or wherever they're sending us, with a profit margin that will top five hundred percent."

"I hadn't thought of that," Terry said. "Shame on me for missing the obvious."

"For men who have tried and actually made money by racing cockroaches," Ben said, "the sky's the limit. I wouldn't put anything past them."

The seas on their transit, regardless of the fact that the farther north they went, the colder it became, nevertheless remained what they had been for the voyage from Bermuda to Ponta Delgada: moderate, relatively tranquil in the State 4–5 range, and with skies clear enough at dawn and dusk for both Ben and Terry to once more shoot stars. By the time they were halfway there, Ben thought that Terry had picked up enough celestial navigation so that Ben could trust him to compute the ship's position without supervision and turned him loose to become the chaser's navigator.

Given the distance they had to travel, the necessity for another underway refueling could not be avoided. This time, with Ben standing at his elbow, Ben let Ensign Keel make their approach and take 65X in alongside the *Mulgrew*. When they'd taken on their fuel, passed back the sea painter, and broken away to once more take up their station in the screen, Ben called it a creditable job. "You only bumped twice, and both of those didn't amount to much more than touches."

Terry, wringing wet with sweat, looked at Ben with a straight face and said, "I got off lucky. I don't think I could have done it in heavier weather."

"Not this time," Ben said, "but if you have to do it again, you'll know a whole lot more about doing it before you go into it, and you'll be able to handle it. That's what this experience will have done for you. I don't want to tell you that it's like learning to ride a bicycle because it isn't, but once you've done it, you'll know far more about it and what to watch for on your second time you run alongside."

By midnight that evening, the watch had been forced to change back into foul weather gear, not because a gale had come up but because the temperature had dropped and dropped enough so that everyone aboard had good cause to remember that it was winter. Ben, overseeing O'Neal's watch, remained in his chair in the pilot house, O'Neal standing not far distant, keeping station with regard to the position of the *Mulgrew* as well as he might with only a basic understanding of how to work a maneuvering board. With regard to such things as navigation and the maneuvering boards, the man had proved a much slower learner than Terry. But once O'Neal did learn, what he learned remained with him, and as far as Ben viewed his accomplishments, the things he learned justified the faith that Ben had placed in the man. As a conversationalist, O'Neal didn't prove loquacious, but with regard to seamanship, he could be counted upon to offer up a wealth of knowledge about the sea and seemed a valuable source for judgments about what SC 65X might be able to rig for or perform in a pinch. The man had a wife, somewhere in the States, and about her he remained silent, but he also had a son about to turn two years old, and about the boy he could be more forthcoming than about any other non-service related subject that Ben could mention. The boy, Ben knew, had not only learned to run; he was also learning to talk, and seemed to be spewing out a stream of words that letters from home and forwarded to the ship in the Azores had recorded.

"Tole my ole lady that 'Fire engines is red,'" O'Neal said with pride when Ben asked him about the boy's progress. "Already learnin' his colors!"

Ben tried to imagine how the term "old lady" applied to a woman whom he imagined to be somewhere between the ages of nineteen and twenty-one and gave it up as a mystery that he wouldn't or shouldn't delve into. Whatever it might mean in terms of an endearment, it beat "Ma hog's comin' down, an' I wants ya to meet her, Mr. Snow"—something an able seaman had once said to him aboard his last ship. There was, he realized, no accounting for the language which sometimes leaped from a sailor's mouth, not least the four-letter words that seemed to punctuate their every sentence. Resigned to the fact, Ben let the matter slide.

At midnight, when Terry came up to relieve O'Neal, he quickly observed that if it turned out to be as cold in England as it was at present, the miseries of New London and New York would be with them again.

"Unpleasant down below?" Ben asked.

"That's putting it mildly," Terry said. "Thermometer down in our stateroom's reading all of 35 F. I had a glance into the crew's quarters before I came up. Forward's reading 39 F while back aft, with the galley fires lighted for getting up coffee and mid-rations, things have risen all the way up to a warm 45 F."

"Sounds like they may be sweltering back there," Ben said, sarcasm coming off his tongue before he turned serious. "Pity we can't harness some of the heat coming off the engines to perk up the crew's quarters. I can't help wondering why Swasey didn't think of that when he designed these things."

"Avoidance of gasoline fumes?" Terry ventured.

"Probably," Ben said. "That would certainly explain why there's no direct air flow between the spaces, but you'd think that that watertight steel bulkhead at the rear of the engine room would radiate a little more heat than it has into the crew's space."

"Yes," Terry said, "but that still wouldn't have solved the heating problem up forward."

"Once we get to where we're going," Ben said, "let's see if we can't wrangle a third blanket for each of them. I doubt that will prevent them from having to sleep in their clothes, but it might help to take the chill off."

"I'll hit up the *Mulgrew* and see what can be done," Terry said.

"And if not the *Mulgrew*," Ben said, "it might be worthwhile to see what kind of deal someone on the beach in England might be willing to cut for two or three cases of pineapples."

"Now, there's a thought worth considering," Terry said, his eyes widening suddenly. "Those pineapples may be worth more than anyone has considered. I'll drop a word to both Pack and O'Neal and see what they say."

Two mornings later, finally, with the seas having come up and the temperature having dropped even more, the shivering lookout in the crow's nest sighted land, and not long after, Ben focused his binoculars on a pinnacle that the chart identified as Camaret-sur-Mer. Within the hour, a pilot boat came out, unloaded a pilot up the side of the *Mulgrew*, and with her chasers having fallen into a line astern, the *Mulgrew* led them through the narrows and slowly up the harbor to the American naval base at Brest. There, American sailors standing on the decks of nearby destroyers and at least one American cruiser, pointed, laughed, and cast aspersions announcing that the "splinter fleet" had just made port.

"You'se bums should have it so good!" Ben heard Scarlatti shout back. "You'se ain't nuttin' but a bunch a tin can riders."

"You'se ain't no sailor at all!" Light shouted back, his forehead receding. "We'se iron men on wooden ships! You'se jus' a bunch of Sunday yacht snails."

"Give Scarlatti and Light an extra helping tonight," Ben told Santos when he reached the mess decks that evening. "They've earned it."

7

The *Mulgrew* and Division AA had put into Brest under the mistaken assumption that the new American naval base established there would be able to refuel them and top off all of their tanks. To their surprise and shock, the small oiler that came out to them carried nothing more than Navy crude. The warrant officer in charge of her informed Commander Radford that the tanks ashore were filled with only crude and diesel, and that the only consignments of gasoline anywhere in the vicinity came under the heading of the "petrol" that various Royal Navy air squadrons used to fuel their seaplanes. A quick check of the *Mulgrew*'s tanks showed that she had enough gasoline left to afford each chaser six hundred gallons above and beyond what already remained in their tanks, and with less than three hundred miles left to reach the big Royal Navy base at Portsmouth, the chasers would be in no danger of going dry. As a result, Division AA remained tied up alongside *Mulgrew* for the night, but no one went ashore on liberty, and on the following morning, at first light and with the port authority's permission, the chasers took in their lines, sortied from Brest, and set a course northeast for Portsmouth.

"Just as well," Terry said to Ben as the two of them took SC 65X out. I don't speak a word of French. Do you?"

"I know a few words that I picked up from French Canadian seamen," Ben said, "but I couldn't hold a conversation, and I'm not even sure I could order a meal."

"Best we go on to where we speak a common language," Terry said.

"One hopes," Ben laughed, "although I've also heard it said that we are separated from the English by a common language."

"Lift for elevator, flat for apartment, that kind of thing?"

"Exactly," Ben said.

For the transit across the English Channel—and this was something that Ben checked himself—Commander Radford had sent down a very specific directive. The 3"/23 up forward was to be loaded and manned for the voyage; the machine guns were to be broken out, placed in their housings on the flying bridge, and also loaded and manned. The depth charges on the stern racks were to be set for fifty and one hundred feet, and the Y-Gun was to be loaded and its charges given the same settings. R/T radio phones were to be guarded for communication between the various ships in the formation, and in the event of fog, all of them were to close in to within fifty yards of one another so that contact would not be lost. Radford had told them that he didn't expect to be attacked, but that they were entering waters where an attack could occur at any time. The directives Radford sent down made perfect sense to Ben and backed up to the hilt the commander's parting words to them before they left Brest: "We must be ready *now*." Even so, Ben felt reasonably secure, more secure than he would have felt had he been riding the *Mulgrew* with Commander Radford. The Germans, he surmised, had never seen a subchaser before; they might not even know about them. Given the chaser's shallow draft and what Ben had been led to believe about the depths for which they set their torpedoes, if one or another U-boat did attempt to torpedo a chaser, Ben thought the malicious fish might easily pass right under the chaser's keel and continue toward the open sea. Nevertheless, bending his mind to the issue, he left no precaution unattended and took SC 65X to war with determination.

Save for fog banks which they met in the middle of the Channel, Division AA's voyage to Portsmouth took place without incident. Twice, destroyers exiting toward the broad Atlantic challenged them from a distance, but armed with the appropriate recognition signals, the signalmen on the *Mulgrew* flashed a response which sent the fleet destroyers on their way. During the night, on R/T command, Commander Radford thrice stopped the Division dead in the water so that the C-Tubes could be lowered for the purpose of detecting a U-boat's screw beats should, by chance, one of them be lurking nearby. In each instance, the only sound that the chasers' operators heard was the sound of silence, and as far as Ben could determine, the main point of the exercise was to sharpen the attention of the men on the chasers, give them some practice before they went in, and kill some time so that the ships could enter Portsmouth on the morning tide.

At 0600 on the following morning, with *Mulgrew* leading, Division AA put themselves in a line astern, crossed the mouth of The Solent which marked the entrance to the port of Southampton, and continued north, passing Gosport to port while entering Portsmouth and going into a nest beside *Mulgrew* alongside the sea wall. Thereafter, with very little delay, a yard oiler came alongside, this one carrying "petrol," and topped off every fuel tank in the Division, filling as well the supply tanks aboard *Mulgrew*. Then, in went the work orders, which were handed over to the warrant officers and petty officers aboard the flagship. Within an hour, the specialists aboard *Mulgrew* were crawling all over the chasers correcting whatever problems had developed during the transit up from Ponta Delgada. When summoned by Commander Radford, Ben left Terry to supervise the work and went aboard the flagship with the other chaser captains. There, very quickly and not without a smile on his face, Radford sat them down in the wardroom and told them that they were going up to London.

"Brief your executive officers on their duties," Radford said, "get yourselves into your best blues, and be prepared to leave at 1300 to catch the train. We will be expected to report to the United States Navy Headquarters at 0800 in the morning, all of us together, and I think it best that we don't ruffle Admiral Sims' feathers. He has a reputation for having a sharp bite, and in my book, that is to be avoided. Assemble here with your grips at 1200 sharp."

The train ride up to London showed Ben a clear picture of what he'd hoped to see. Sitting in a window seat beside Horn who sat on the aisle and slept, Ben took in the fields, some of them snow-covered, the rock walls, the towns, the quaint villages where he found thatched roofs in abundance, the occasional great house off in the distance, and what seemed to Ben like a pleasantly rolling countryside, its leafless trees of winter thrusting upward in assorted woods and windbreaks. In the stations where the train made occasional stops, the people on the platforms, bundled in winter coats and scarves against the bitter chill, didn't look exactly seedy but did strike Ben as quietly depressed, somewhat exhausted, and underfed. It was the war, he knew, three long years of it, and the impression that he took from what he observed suggested that determined as the British remained, they were also beginning to look fatigued as though they might slowly be approaching exhaustion.

In London, the impression he'd taken while crossing the countryside struck him more forcefully. London in the winter of 1918 when Ben first saw it looked a light year beyond what he had been led to remember from his readings of Dickens; nevertheless, the city still looked dark beneath a residue of coal smoke, not particularly clean, and cold. And the people he passed in the station and on the street looked slightly gaunt, the probable result of making do with short rations, and if not seedy, at least threadbare, their clothing giving the appearance of having been long worn and often mended. The bright colors invariably apparent on American streets and in American stores seemed altogether absent, the general appearance running more to browns, grays, and blacks in keeping with what Ben sensed to be the nation's mood.

"These folks look like the war is beginning to wear them down," Horn said, as he and Ben pushed into the cab of a taxi behind Feller.

"Stands to reason," Feller said. "From reading the papers, given the carnage in the trenches, there probably isn't more than one in three who hasn't lost somebody over there."

"Over there covering everything from France to Sinai to East Africa," Ben said. "So far, I suppose, our people have been lucky, very lucky, to have kept out of it."

"Ain't that the truth," Horn said. "I wonder what we'll say about that a year from now?"

"I could be wrong," Feller said, "but just offhand, I'd say that it doesn't bear thinking about."

"Or even trying to imagine," Ben said.

The two taxis in which Commander Radford and his captains were riding stopped at Billingsly's, the inexpensive hotel that naval headquarters had arranged for them. If the outside of the hotel gave the appearance of being covered with coal soot, the interior told Ben that it had seen its prime during the middle of Queen Victoria's reign. The carpets were shabby, the faded walls looked like they'd been papered around 1865, and the furniture had that massive, horsehair look that reminded Ben of portraits he'd seen in which men and women sat or stood for photographs during the American Civil War. Behind the desk, an elderly woman wearing a lace collar below a pinched expression attended to them, handed them their keys, and directed them to their rooms.

"Gentlemen," Commander Radford said, speaking before he went up, "for tonight, you're on your own. I have work to do, so I will not be going out. I'm told that the pubs serve hearty meals at reasonable prices. Restaurants are more costly, and given the rationing that's in effect, I'm not sure whether they will be able to give you what you'd like, but I'll let you find out for yourselves. Let's assemble here in the foyer at 0700, and don't be late."

The room into which Ben and Horn walked resembled the rest of the hotel. Long and narrow, it contained a single plain unimpressive stand of drawers, hooks upon which they might hang their uniforms, a china basin with a pottery pitcher, and two cast iron beds, both of them as narrow as their bunks on the chaser. The bathroom and toilet, mentioned on a printed card which rested on the top of the dresser and referred to as the Water Closet, appeared to be down the hall. And there were no chairs.

"Comfort does not appear to have been the Navy's object," Horn laughed.

"One might almost imagine Admiral Sims and his minions to be Spartans," Ben said, scowling as he glanced around. "I shouldn't think we should want to do more than sleep here. Let's collect the others and go find a pub."

The pub they found when they went out, The Bishop's Mitre, not far from Victoria Station, turned out to fit them finally into the England that they'd hoped to discover, with its low ceilings, old oak beams decorated with horse brass, snugs, glazed glass partitions, and a warm fire burning in a grate at the back of the room. The publican greeted them with a smile, served them topping pints of bitter beer, and took their orders for a meal with a broad grin.

"Yanks, are ya?" he said, looking them up and down with apparent pleasure. "Well, lads, welcome to ya, and glad we are to have ya.

Better late than never, and I mean that with warmth. Make yourselves at home. Crowds don't collect before the nightingales begin to sing."

With the three officers in Group AA1 sitting back to back with the officers from Group AA2 in two small snugs, the men sipped their beer, found it much to their liking, and had no trouble experiencing a moment of genuine relaxation after the rigors of their voyage and their train trip up to the metropolis.

"So," Feller asked, "what did the two of you put your orders in for?"

"Ploughman's lunch," Horn said at once. "One of my fraternity brothers who spent some time over here told me about them. Lots of cheese with bread and pickles to make the cheese go down and prevent it from blocking the plumbing."

Feller smiled. "Yes," he said, "that would be a goal to shoot for, wouldn't it now. What about you, Ben?"

"Toad in the Hole," Ben said. "Sausage and maybe a bit of sirloin baked up in bread dough. Had it once in Thunder Bay, up in Canada. Filling meal, and good, if it's cooked right, and it goes very well with beer. And you, what did you put in for?"

"Fish and chips," Feller said. "Call me a tourist if you like, but I want to be able to say that I've indulged myself at least once while we're over here."

"You'll get no argument from me," Horn said. "If the English swear by fish and chips, I see no reason we shouldn't. Came close to ordering the same thing myself."

"So what's your verdict on the beer?" Feller wanted to know.

"For my money, it's a sight better than lager," Ben said.

"That's my opinion too," Horn said. "It could be a couple of degrees colder, I suppose, but if you ask me, the trouble with most American beer is that it's served so damn cold that you can hardly taste it. This stuff's got flavor."

When the food came, Ben returned to the bar and brought back three more pints, so by the time that they'd plowed through their evening meal which had been brought out to them hot from the kitchen, each of them was ready for a third brimming pint. Within less than an hour, given the number of men who had come in, the officers from both ships found themselves locked in conversation, one of the men with whom they spoke telling them that they were only a block or two from Belgravia, which he described as both "posh and fashionable."

"Without intending to," Ben said, "we seem to have stumbled into the high rent district."

"So it would seem," Feller said. "No navvies here. The guy I was talking to said that he was something called a chartered accountant, and the man with him, very nice, appeared to be a retired major."

Regardless, within another hour and after one of the flock had set both a bowler hat and an umbrella on the top of the piano before sitting down to it, the entire room seemed to be singing, and the officers of Division AA, feeling both warm and welcome, did their best to keep up and sing with them. Past their third pint, they never had to buy another, the hospitality with which the pub greeted them bringing them new pints before they could rise to go and fetch more for themselves.

"Damn decent of them," Horn said, at 2230 when the publican finally rang the bell to announce closing.

"If this is any indication of how we're going to be received," Ben said, "I think I'm going to like it here."

"I concur," Feller said, as they looked for a taxi along the darkened street. "If I start to wobble, straighten me, won't you, and whatever you do, make sure that I roll out on time in the morning."

The captain of one of the chasers in Group AA2 managed to get Feller up and down into the foyer in time the following morning.

Nevertheless, once into the taxi alongside Ben and Horn, he complained of a head—a head which he forgot about when the taxi finally pulled up in front of the American Naval Headquarters and disgorged the lot of them onto the sidewalk beside Commander Radford. There, with snap, a Marine sentry presented arms before asking to see their credentials.

Inside, they were not kept waiting. After signing in and showing their orders at a reception desk, very swiftly, following a yeoman, they were led up a flight of broad marble stairs, down a hall, and shown the door to an office marked Chief of Staff.

"All right, Gentlemen," Radford said, straightening his tie, "this is it, so let's take a strain. The admiral is thought to be supportive of chasers, so let's not disappoint him."

And with that, he knocked once, opened the door, and walked inside followed by the six officers in Division AA.

The U.S. Navy captain who met them inside as they entered the room, reported themselves, and stood to attention couldn't have been called effusive, but neither did he show them a scowling face.

"Welcome aboard," he said to them, stepping from behind his desk to shake their hands. "If you will follow me, I will take you right in. The admiral is waiting." And with that, after a tap on the adjoining door, he opened it and walked straight through to announce them.

Vice Admiral Sims, Commander United States Naval Forces in Europe, had, as Ben knew, considerable diplomatic experience, had put forward proposals that had greatly improved naval gunnery, had been the President of the Naval War College, and had held command of the USS *Nevada*, the largest and most deadly American battleship of her day.

From what Ben could see, the admiral was an imposing figure—tall, thin, adorned with thinning gray hair and a pointed beard—and to Ben, he looked like a perfect distillation of the rank to which he had so recently been elevated. Like the captain who served him,

Sims was not an effusive man, but in greeting each of them, he showed them a smile of welcome, told them that he was glad to see them, and gave them a brief lecture on the importance of the work they would be doing to put down and squelch the German submarine menace. Then, without further detail, he turned them back over to the chief of staff who showed them out and took them immediately to the headquarters' operations room. There, a pack of senior officers—some from the U.S. Navy, some from the Royal Navy, and one or two from the French Navy—would, the chief said, "show them the ropes," and spend the next two days acquainting them with the operational picture for the war front into which they were about to be plunged.

The centerpiece of the operations room was patently obvious to all of them the moment they walked into it and stood on a landing where they could overlook it. Below them, on the room's lower deck, nearly the whole of Western Europe and her bordering seas was laid out on massive charts extending from well out into the Atlantic, to the North and Irish Seas, the English Channel, and on south to the Bay of Biscay. Counters showing the position of every vessel or force at sea were being moved as necessary by naval ratings, pushers, who stood surrounding the table holding long rods with which to move the markers so that they would present an up-to-the-moment indication of where every Allied unit was located and where it was headed. Minefields—American, British, and German—were marked on the charts with grease pencils while, on the surrounding bulkheads, blackboards and a series of clipboards on hooks held additional operational information.

Regardless of the importance of the work in this nerve center, nothing of an atmosphere of crisis penetrated the calm exhibited by the people who worked there. From what Ben could see, the prevailing attitude was neither formal nor so relaxed as to seem slack. Instead, as each new bit of information came in from the communications center, quiet discussions were held, information was passed, and decisions were made with minimal fuss, and a general air of competence prevailed. It was, he thought, a sight to behold, the war in the Atlantic and its contiguous seas being prosecuted with committed determination but without fanfare or unwarranted alarm. For the officers of Division AA, it set a tone that made them pull themselves up and think about their mission in a whole new way.

During the two days that followed, the exchange of information that went on between the headquarters staff and the captains of Division AA seemed to take place nonstop. Starting at 0800 each morning, Ben and his fellows sat for briefings on everything from mines, depth charges, and gunnery to the procedures which Admiral Sims sought to establish and the procedures which both the Royal Navy and the French Navy employed in hunting and doing battle with submarines. The rules of engagement were covered, diplomatic niceties were discussed, communications procedures were explained, and in at least two of the lectures, behavior both afloat and ashore received emphasis, with particular attention to how the captains and their crews were to interact with the citizens of the United Kingdom.

The information passed in these sessions did not go all one way. From the beginning, it became abundantly clear to Ben that most of the officers at headquarters had never seen a subchaser or a blueprint for one, and hadn't the slightest idea about what the chasers could or could not do. That is not to say that they were not keen to learn because they were, with the result that in addition to drawing diagrams, simple plans, and an explanation of capabilities, Ben, Horn, and the others were grilled incessantly to provide the information that the staff was seeking about the little vessels. Some of those senior officers hadn't realized that the vessels' cruising range was limited in the way that it always was; others gasped when they realized how lightly armed the chasers were, while still others seemed astonished to learn about the degrees of roll and pitch they were wont to take and about their sea-keeping capabilities. In the end, the headquarters staff declared that it had learned as much from the chaser captains as Commander Radford's captains admitted to learning from the staff—something which Admiral Sims, upon the conclusion of their talks, declared with some satisfaction, to have been a "frank exchange of views and information."

And the admiral had said something else that made an impression and left them in no doubt about what he intended.

"Gentleman," the admiral had said as they prepared to take their departure, "let me leave you with a single order: *Close with the enemy and defeat him.*"

Then, as swiftly as all of them had come up to London, Ben and his fellows along with Commander Radford found themselves back on a train for the return journey to Portsmouth. Sitting side by side, muffled in their greatcoats against the chill which had seeped into their compartment, Ben and Horn studied the Thames as they crossed the river, took note of the ice that had formed along the edges, and made observations about the ice they'd dealt with along the particular Thames river which flowed through New London. As they began to speed southwest, leaving swaths of South London on both sides of the tracks, Horn changed the subject.

"So," Horn said, "if I've got this right—and stop me, if I take a wrong turn—we're returning to Portsmouth but going ultimately to Plymouth where our base, Base 27, is to be built."

"Eventually," Ben said skeptically, "and if you ask me, *eventually* probably means in six months or more which, since that prolonged period hasn't yet occurred, means that we are going to Weymouth instead."

"Because the Royal Navy bases their fast and nasty MLs—which I take to be very quick torpedo boats—in that place and because those launches carry the same gasoline-driven engines we use and can therefore supply us with an abundance of spare parts whenever we need them."

"That seems to be the thinking," Ben said, "and because Portland dockyard can supply us with all of the ammunition and depth charges that we are ever likely to need."

"Neat, don't you think?"

"Sounds like it," Ben said. "Proof will come in the pudding."

"Yes, well," Horn said. "Know anything about Weymouth?"

"I think," Ben said, "that Thomas Hardy lived there for a time."

"*Return of the Native* Hardy? *Tess of the d'Urbervilles* Hardy?"

"That's the one," Ben said. "Dorchester is only a few miles north, and I think that place was the prototype for *Casterbridge*, as in *The Mayor of.*"

"Well, do tell," Horn said, registering mild surprise. "But what I mean is, what kind of a place is it?"

"I'd guess it must have a fairly good harbor," Ben said, "but about the rest of it, I don't know a thing. I don't see how it could be a very big place, unless the war has built it up, so I'd suppose it probably has a population of somewhere between ten or twenty thousand."

"Big enough for a couple of good pubs, then?"

Ben laughed. "From what I know," Ben said, "an English village of five people is big enough to support one pub while a village of fifty could probably support at least two. My guess, and I'm only guessing, is that we can count on at least one home away from home, and probably several more."

"We must talk to Radford and suggest that he make the move at once," Horn said, his eyes lighting up.

But in this, as Ben and Horn discovered once they returned to Portsmouth, Commander Radford had been way ahead of them, the commander and the staff having signaled from London to alert both Captain Kettle on the *Mulgrew* and the waiting executive officers on the chasers to begin preparing their vessels for sea because they would sortie from Portsmouth early on the following morning in order to make Weymouth before the sun set in the early afternoon.

"That means we'll be going out in the dark," Ben said to Terry once he returned to SC 65X and heard the news.

"Winter days are short at this latitude," Terry said.

"Well," Ben said, "we made it in here without any problems, so I guess we can make it back out the same way we came in, and I have to hand it to Radford, getting west to Weymouth while we still have light to see by is a good idea. It'll give us a chance to take our bearings and at least get a feel for the lay of the land before the sun sets."

"I checked a guidebook," Terry said, his eyes narrowing to mere slits. "Made a list of at least five pubs that look promising. Prepared a map."

"Did you?" Ben grinned. "You must convey your information to Mr. Horn. On the way down here, he registered deep concern about the very issue you seem to have researched."

"Since leaving New London, I'm finding it best to survey the cultural amenities of any port we are likely to visit," Terry said.

"As a naval officer, you're showing surprising promise and growth," Ben said.

Weymouth—when they reached the seaport the following day, followed *Mulgrew* into harbor, and nested alongside of her adjacent to what passed for a pier—seemed a picturesque town, not quite a grand city on the order of London, Portsmouth, or Manchester but hardly a village. Along the waterfront which seemed to overlook a beach, red brick three- and four-story facades seemed interspersed with others which had been painted white, and occasionally, Ben saw even one or another painted in the same pastel colors that he remembered from Bermuda. Traffic seemed neither sparse nor dense, and along the walks where occasional shoppers and business people could be seen making their way, Ben noticed that they bent themselves to the wind which had begun blowing in from the Channel at something in excess of 15 knots and carrying with it an unpleasantly humid chill.

"What about the extra blankets for the crew?" Ben asked Terry.

"Those are items which *Mulgrew* isn't prepared to supply," Terry said. "I checked yesterday, before you came down from London."

"All right," Ben said, "when or if we get some time off, head over to the beach and see what can be scared up. What did Pack and O'Neal have to say about doing barter with the pineapples?"

"They thought it a very good idea," Terry said, "and we've still got at least ten crates of the things stashed about the ship in various places."

"Christ," Ben said, "I don't know how they found the space."

"Pack said pretty much the same thing," Terry said.

But before they could exchange another word, *Mulgrew*'s messenger came aboard and summoned them both to a meeting on the tender.

As before, Commander Radford assembled them all in the *Mulgrew*'s wardroom and then began putting out the word without a preamble.

"Each of you officers has an op-order before you on the table," Radford began. "It isn't a long one, so I will expect each man to read it tonight because I intend to launch operations in the morning and keep them going until we've driven the Kaiser from Germany. New code books—and you have those before you as well and will be expected to sign for them before you leave here—go into effect immediately. You'll also find a list of daily recognition signals. The charts before you, divided into search squares, cover the Channel from The Lizard in Cornwall to Portsmouth and all the way south to France. This time, our patrol area stretches from here to Guernsey, a stretch of a little over one hundred nautical miles, but we won't be patrolling all of that, not now and not all at one time. The schedule I'm setting sends Group AA1 out tomorrow morning, and the plan is to send each group out, AA1 and AA2, on a rotating routine of four days out and four days in port to follow with the intention of keeping that up until we win this war. As more chasers join us from the States, we will, of course, be able to patrol more of the Channel with the ultimate intention of throwing up a chaser barrage all the way to France. Tomorrow, at 0800, Captain Horn will lead Group AA1 directly to the square marked 001. The squares, as you will notice, are ten miles on a side, so after an eight-hour search in 001, Captain Horn will then move south to square 002, and after eight hours of searching there, he will go on south to 003. Search squares will eventually be chosen at random so that we don't set up a recognizable pattern that the Huns might detect, but the object is to cover ten to twelve squares during each four-day period before one Group is relieved by the other. In the event that extreme weather develops in the Channel that prevents the use of the C-Tube hydrophones or threatens the safety of your ships, you are to discontinue the search and come in. Otherwise, you are to commit yourselves to the hunt in the hope that we can do the Hun as much damage as possible or hold him down in order to prevent him from doing damage to others. Have you any questions?"

For more than an hour, the chaser officers remained sitting, all of them bombarding Commander Radford with questions, but by the time they finally rose to leave, most of their questions had been answered, succinctly and without quibbles. Radford was determined, and his determination turned out to be something he conveyed to his captains and their officers in no uncertain terms.

Ben and Terry went back to their stateroom, sat across from each other, and read the commander's operations order, and then, they read it for a second time, making notes in the margins.

"Seems pretty thorough, doesn't it?" Terry said, finally looking up at Ben.

"I'd say he's covered just about everything including the galley sink," Ben said. "Find any surprises?"

"One," Terry said. "I thought the Channel was deeper. One hundred and twenty meters on average seems shallow."

"It is," Ben said, "but during the Ice Age, I'm told, this island was joined to France and a man could walk right across what amounted to a land bridge. Whatever the case, shallow though it may be, four hundred feet plus is deep enough to hide a U-boat."

"Right," Terry said. "Going ashore tonight?"

"I think not," Ben said. "I'm guessing that the next four days are going to put us through the mill, that I'm going to have to be awake a lot, and that the time we're forced to be on our feet is going to test our limits in the same way that that storm between New London and Bermuda strung us out. So I think I'll read for an hour or two and then turn in."

"Makes sense," Terry said. "You've been around to see for yourself, but I think the crew has us ready. All that's left is the going."

"Yes," Ben said.

In the morning, with the sun not yet risen but beneath lowering clouds, they went.

8

By noon the following day, with the sun still hidden behind a bank of black clouds and with the seas churning up to at least a State 6 according to Ben's reckoning, Townsend, Ben, and Terry had gone over to computing and plotting their position by dead reckoning. Searching square 002 twenty miles south of Weymouth, with England disappeared over the northern horizon and with all landmarks dropped out of sight, they had no choice. Their last firm fix had been made in the morning when both Terry and Townsend had still been able to take bearings from the tops of the lighthouses ashore, but not long after that, the course south that they followed took all three of the chasers beyond the range of visual piloting and they were left to dead reckon. Horn had reoriented the axis of their search east; the apex of the imaginary search triangle they were following pointed ahead at 090, with SC 56X off Ben's port beam by two thousand yards and SC 71X off Horn's port beam by another two thousand. As the chaser rolled and pitched with her engines stopped and her C-Tube lowered, each man in the pilot house waited for word from the magazine where, bent over the tube with his earphones pressed to the sides of his head, Crim listened for the sound of screw beats—for something, anything, that might indicate a U-boat in their area.

Above decks, although the 3″/23 was loaded and ready, Ben had allowed the three-man gun crew to take shelter in the pilot house. They were crammed together there like so many fish in a barrel, each of them huddled in his duffle, trying to keep warm, ready to race back to the gun mount should the enemy be detected or sighted. Above, on the flying bridge, Paxton—the man Farris had decided to bring up as a striker for a gunner's rating—stood his watch wearing a Sou'wester over his duffle, standing ready to jerk the canvas covering from one of the machine guns should Ben call for its immediate use. Elsewhere, sleeping in their clothes or sheltering on the mess decks, those not actually on watch stood by to man the depth charges and their damage control stations if Ben set General Quarters. In the galley, even so early in the afternoon, Santos, unmoved by either the anticipation or the tension which had developed among his shipmates, had already started making preparations for the evening meal.

"Anything?" Ben shouted down the speaking tube which led below to the magazine.

"Nothing," Grange, the storekeeper shouted back, being the other man that Ben and Terry had assigned to help Crim with the manipulation of the C-Tube.

A minute later, almost on a mark by which a man could set his watch, the R/T sounded as Horn gave the order to up-tubes, start engines, and cruise ahead. As soon as Ben passed the word down to Lithgow, who for that watch happened to be ramrodding things in the engine room, the big engines on the chaser kicked to life, and SC 65X once more got underway, moving slowly forward at a cruising speed of 6 knots.

"It strikes me," Terry said, turning back to check the chart, "that this is going to be a lot like fishing, fishing for trout along a stream, where you make a cast into a hole or under a log, don't get a bite, and move on."

"And where patience becomes the supreme virtue," Ben said, "because skill can only take you so far and no further."

By suppertime, Group AA1 had worked once all the way across square 002, turned north for a distance of what dead reckoning told them was four nautical miles, and reversed course, once more moving toward the open Atlantic on a course of 270. All told, Ben counted six attempts to hear the screw beats of a U-boat, all of them coming up negative, all of them taking up ten to fifteen minutes of patient searching before the Group once more moved forward to a new listening position. Throughout, the seas had remained steady. They were by no means comfortable, but when measured beside what the chasers had experienced on the transit to Bermuda, the crew seemed to judge them to be moderate with a few trifling bumps and twists.

"They're becoming seamen," Ben said to Terry as the two of them left O'Neal with the watch and made their way aft to the hatch that led down to the mess deck. "Before we left Staten Island, I'm guessing that they would have called this a minor gale."

"I think you're right," Terry laughed. "Obviously, we're breaking in. So, what's for supper tonight?"

"Something with bully beef," Ben said. "From what Santos said, according to the Brits on the beach from whom he drew supplies, bully beef is one of their favorites. They also sent along plenty of hardtack to go with it. So what does that tell you?"

"That tells me that Santos got sold a pig in a poke," Terry said. "That tells me that bully beef is what you eat in a moment of last resort."

"Exactly," Ben grinned. "Wonder how the troops will like it? Apparently it's going to be a whole new substance to them."

It was, and regardless of the fact that Santos had spent more than an hour pounding the hardtack into tiny pieces so that he could break it up and cook it with the bully beef, only Scarlatti and Light delved into the mess with gusto and asked for a second helping.

"I think it figures," Ben said, grinning broadly as he and Terry once more climbed onto the main deck and started forward toward Officer's Country. "I shudder to think what those two grew up eating."

"If or when they did eat," Terry said. "I'm guessing that they must have thought they'd died and gone to heaven when they joined up and found they were going to be fed three times a day."

"You're probably right," Ben said. "Virtually no education to speak of, although we can be grateful that they can both read, but in each of their cases, I'm guessing that what you and I call childhood must have been pretty grim for them."

Suddenly, before either Ben or Terry could say another word, the General Quarters gong began to sound, and without hesitating, Ben and Terry broke into a run as they raced for the pilot house, the gun crew bursting from the space to man their weapon even before the two officers could approach the hatch leading into it.

"What have you got?" Ben shouted to O'Neal as he leaped through the door and up to the windscreen.

"I'd be thinkin' a mine, Cap'n. An' by the grace of the Holy Mother, I'll be jiggered if there ain't two."

"Where?" Ben barked at once, Terry swiftly handing him a set of binoculars.

"Ta starboard, Cap'n, 060 not forty yards distant. A feller can spot 'em by they's spikes as they tops da crests."

Snatching the glasses from Terry's hands, Ben scanned the wave crests in the direction that O'Neal had indicated while O'Neal rang the engine room to order all stop. Meanwhile, reacting to Ben's prompt, Terry snatched up the R/T in order to report their sighting to Horn, SC 56X and SC 71X also taking off turns and sliding to a stop upon receiving Terry's report.

"All right," Ben said, after another minute's search in which he scanned back and forth until he finally spotted the first mine where it bobbed to the top of a crest. "I've got one, but we're going to have to back off. All astern one third, O'Neal, but warn Lithgow to be prepared to stop again the second I give the order. Find it yet, Terry?"

"Yes Sir," Terry replied. "Close, isn't it?"

"That's why we're backing away," Ben said. "If we'd blown it where we first saw it, the concussion alone might have done us some damage, and who's to know what kind of shrapnel it might throw out? Get up there on the flying bridge, put Paxton onto it, and when I give you the command, let him cut loose on it with the machine gun."

Terry was out the door and up the ladder before five seconds had passed, and it didn't take five more until he had Paxton's eyes fixed on the target and reported him ready. By that time, Lithgow had managed to reverse the middle engine, and then, moving slowly astern, Ben backed SC 65X away from what he considered the line of danger.

"All stop!" Ben barked, O'Neal immediately relaying the word to the engine room. "Charged and ready?" Ben then called up the speaking tube to Terry.

"Charged and ready, Captain," Terry called back.

"Battery released!" Ben roared up the tube, and in the same second, with Terry repeating the order topside, Paxton pulled the trigger on the Browning, and the Browning responded like the spanking new machine gun that Farris had known it would be when he had lifted it from the Section Pier armory on Staten Island.

Given the rolling and pitching motion of the chaser as she took off sternway, Paxton had to walk his rapid fire onto his target, one round or another having apparently struck a horn. The mine went up spewing a dark spreading geyser of the English Channel's salt water in all directions.

"Holy Mother of God!" O'Neal exclaimed.

"See what you saved us from?" Ben said to his bosun. "We were very lucky you spotted that rascal before nightfall or we might have run into it, and I don't want to think what it could have done to us if we'd hit it. Well done, O'Neal! You've a good eye that's saved us all."

"And may the saints preserve us ever," O'Neal replied.

"Amen to that," Ben said. "Now, everyone, let's start looking for the other one."

The second mine was farther away, at least a hundred yards farther away, but when Ben finally worked SC 65X over close enough to give Paxton what he believed to be a clear shot at it, the five or ten rounds that Paxton threw out merely penetrated the air chamber that held the mine up, sinking it without fanfare and without an explosion.

For what it was worth, upon receiving Ben's report over the R/T, Horn issued an immediate BRAVO ZULU with a special commendation for whoever spotted the mine first. Ben immediately passed word to O'Neal and the rest of the crew that both he and Terry thought to be a nice lift to their morale.

"Not a U-boat, but the next best thing," Terry said when he came down from the flying bridge.

"Right," Ben said, "but it's evidence that a U-boat has been through here recently because those were German mines, and there can be no doubt about it."

"From a Hun minelayer?" Terry asked.

"Judging from the size, the shape, and the configuration of the horns that Sims' staff showed us when we were up in London, I don't have a single doubt," Ben said. "Suppose you go below and start writing up an after-action report. Once you've got one drafted, I'll look it over, add whatever I need to, and we'll have it ready to submit once we're back alongside."

"Mentioning both O'Neal and Paxton by name?"

"Absolutely," Ben said, "giving credit where credit is due."

On the following day, as Group AA1 swept into area 005 under only slightly better weather conditions, Horn's chaser spotted and exploded a mine. Two hours later, SC 71X spotted one and sank it. Then, with Terry spotting another and Horn finding and sinking his second, the number of mines that the Group accounted for had swelled to six. Even as the day made its final passage from afternoon to dusk, the lookout standing next to Paxton on the flying bridge alerted Ben to an object in the water. When Ben had taken the chaser alongside so that O'Neal could lower a boat hook and lift it from the sea, the object turned out to be a lifejacket, or most of one, with the name of a ship, the *Tucker Hanson* stenciled on the side.

"I wonder if one of those German mines sunk a ship here?" Terry mused when he and Ben finally had a chance to inspect the lifejacket.

"No way to know," Ben said. "Doesn't look to me like this has been in the water for very long, but it might well have been one of those mines that got her, and then, too, it might not."

"What will we do with it?"

"Hold it. Turn it in when we return to port. Intelligence will make the necessary connections, and where we found it may be an indication of where the ship went down," Ben said. "On the other hand, this bit of debris could just as easily drifted in here from somewhere else, given the currents that are running through the Channel."

"Not pretty to think about," Terry said.

"No," Ben said.

Throughout the remainder of that day and the next, stopping, listening with the C-Tube before starting up and moving on again, the Group worked its way south in the direction of Guernsey, the weather and the seas remaining essentially what they had been since the chasers had first come out and started their patrol. On their fourth morning, while Ben sat in his chair with his eyelids drooping with fatigue, somewhere in mid-Channel, Terry, standing an alert watch, spotted another mine—this one clearly British, judging from what Ben could see through his binoculars of its size and configuration.

"Shit!" he hissed as he stood beside Terry with his glasses raised. "As if we didn't have enough to worry about from the Germans. This one must have broken off somewhere to the north of us and drifted all the way down here."

"Kind of adds insult to injury, doesn't it?" Terry said with disgust.

"That it does," Ben said. "Paxton's had his fun with the first three. I'll get on the R/T and see if Horn won't allow me to turn the gun crew loose on this one."

Horn gave permission, and when Ben turned and passed the word to Farris, the gunner's eyes suddenly brightened with the dazzling intensity of a carnival midway. Seconds later, after Ben had shouted the order for "Batteries Released!" Farris' 3″/23 slammed out its first round, which went out sounding like a sharp clap of thunder. Making the shot from a one-hundred-yard distance, success could never be assured. After two overs and three unders, Ben felt no confidence in Farris being able to hit the mine at all. The sixth round—either striking the mine direct or throwing up enough of a concussion to break one of the horns—produced an explosion and spreading plume of water that absolutely dwarfed what the Hun mines had produced when they'd been blown.

The cheers that went up fore and aft across SC 65X's decks made Ben and Terry smile.

"Destructive lot, aren't they?" Terry laughed.

"Like a bunch of kids with a sack of firecrackers," Ben said, shaking his head with a smile. "I suppose there's no accounting for some people's delight in destruction."

Over the R/T, Horn sent them a lighthearted suggestion that they save the next one for the Fourth of July. Then, following another

BRAVO ZULU, Horn put out an order for a turn to the north where, at a point on the chart designated Point Baker, they were to meet and turn over to Group AA2, their relief.

Prior to the evening meal, in port but still wearing their seagoing togs, Ben, Horn, and Feller sat down in Commander Radford's office aboard the *Mulgrew* while the commander swiftly read through their after-action reports, which each captain had prepared for final submission during his return to Weymouth.

"Yes," Radford said, looking over the final paragraphs of Ben's report, "the *Tucker Hanson*. We had a message about her. She was a coaster, coming down from Liverpool and making for Portsmouth with a cargo of coal. Operations lost track of her three days ago. From what this tells me, she must have struck one of those mines the Huns laid. Pity. Still, let me commend you for a job well done. You may not have sighted or attacked any U-boats, but in my estimation, you've had a very successful patrol, and I rather imagine that Admiral Sims' staff will come to the same conclusion. Now, while you're in and while you see to your upkeep, officers are granted shore leave as the spirit moves them but only after you've checked out with me, and I'd like to suggest that you give your crews port and starboard liberty." Radford grinned. "That will give them a day in which to hit the pubs and drink their beer," he said, "and a day in which to recover, although a word from you on the virtues of moderation would not be out of order."

Ben tried to imagine Light and Scarlatti practicing moderation and found that he couldn't. And then he wondered if they even knew the meaning of the word.

"All right, gentlemen," Radford said, "well done, all of you. Get some rest, and then go out there yourselves and discover what you will of Weymouth and England."

Neither Ben nor Terry wanted to discover anything other than their bunks on their first night in from the Channel. Without making any apologies, immediately following the evening meal, they piled into bed and tried to catch up on the hours of sleep that they'd been unable to collect during their four-day patrol.

The following morning, like the remainder of the crew, save for the duty section, Ben and Terry slept in, only rising in time for quarters, discovering when they did so that Horn, Feller, Speck, and Hyde had taken off for a day's jaunt to Salisbury, riding a bus that had been arranged by the officer in charge of recreation for the crew aboard the *Mulgrew*.

"Nice of them to have invited us along," Terry said, sarcasm dripping from his every word.

"Actually," Ben said, "Carson had the deck this morning, and I think they did stop, at around 0600, to see if we wanted to go. Carson told them we were still sacked out."

"Remind me to thank him for the intelligence of his response," Terry said. "Salisbury will still be there when we eventually go to find it, and I doubt that the cathedral will be moving anywhere either. If those guys were up at 0600 this morning, they must be out of their minds. And I can hardly imagine Horn spending his time making brass rubbings. More like, he'll settle into the first pub that opens and make himself comfortable there."

"I'd put money on it," Ben said. "I'm more in favor of a gentle stroll into Weymouth."

"I think I may need some more sleep," Terry said.

Regardless of what Terry intended, they did stroll, the two of them, but not into Weymouth. Instead, summoned by messenger, their stroll took them straight back to Commander Radford's office.

"Glad to find you two still aboard," Radford said, showing them a smile. "How is it that you didn't head for Salisbury with the rest of your group?"

"I'm afraid, Sir," Ben said with a trace of a sheepish grin, "that we were resting on our laurels."

"Quite wise," said the commander, "and lucky for me that I found you still here. I have an assignment for you which might also be a bit of a plum."

Ben's senses became alert. The Navy, as far as Ben knew it, did not hand out plums. What the Navy was notorious for handing out were what the men referred to as "shit details" disguised as "plums."

"Three miles north and just off the road to Dorchester is the lovely estate of Trincombe Abbey owned by Colonel and Lady Fitzhugh. The Colonel, I believe, led his regiment with Kitchener in the Sudan. Lancer, if I'm not mistaken. Baronet apparently. Lady Felicia grew up at Trincombe Abbey, and she's a few years younger than the Colonel. I've been out there twice for social gatherings since we arrived, semi-official welcomings to the area, if you see what I mean, and I've found the couple most congenial. Lady Felicia telephoned last night after all of you had returned to your ships. She's holding a dinner party this evening, 1900 sharp, and she's short two gentlemen for her table. So, my lads, you're elected. No arguments. Anglo-American relations must be kept tidy, and all of that, so I'll make a vehicle available to you at 1800 this evening, and the uniform will be service dress blue. Any questions?"

Ben had anticipated what was coming from the moment the commander had named Trincombe Abbey. He'd never seen the place, and he didn't know the first thing about it, but he did know that there wasn't any way that he and Terry were going to be able to get out of it.

Back aboard SC 65X, Terry turned to Ben and said, "Well, what do you suggest?"

"Probably," Ben said with a laugh, "what we ought to do is go straight out in town and get dead drunk, and if we're lucky, we could hope that the bitter and the buzz would carry us through the evening."

"But we're not going to do that."

"No," Ben said. "Instead, I think we'd better remain as sober as judges because I have a nasty feeling that when we do sit down to eat tonight, we're going to be sitting down with humorless, reserved elders who won't hesitate to ask why we've come to the war so late and what, as *amateurs*, we think we have to contribute."

"Prim spinsters with lace collars and pinched lips, denizens of the civil service gifted with acerbic wit, all of it directed against us, that kind of thing?"

"You've read my mind," Ben said.

"I think," Terry said, "that if you don't mind, I will once more take to my bed for the morning in order to fortify myself for our adventure."

"Go right ahead," Ben said. "O'Neal and Pack have things well in hand, the work orders are in, and the folks from the *Mulgrew* are already over here tending to them. I'd join in your endeavor, but the truth is that I'm slept out. I think I'll go for a walk along the sea wall and try to find out what it's like to stand on stable land once more."

Ben's walk, his stroll really, took him north up the Esplanade fronting Weymouth Beach. Snow had apparently fallen the night before, but whatever had reached the ground, save for a patch here and there, had melted, leaving the walks clear but still wet. The temperature, however, remained cold; it was above freezing, but the humidity in the air lent it an extra bite, which left Ben feeling pleased that he was able to muffle his body inside both his greatcoat and his scarf.

Here and there, he stopped to look at the goods in some of the shop windows, and on occasion he actually went inside the shops themselves, once to buy a packet of pipe tobacco, and twice to examine some Toby mugs on display. Toby mugs were not items that Ben had been used to seeing in the States, and aside from the amusement they afforded him, he found that he liked the warm, glowing faces that he saw on most of them.

Emerging from one such shop, Ben looked up to see a young woman wearing a dark tartan Scottish tam pass on a bicycle, and then, not twenty yards beyond where Ben stood, the bicycle's chain suddenly jumped from its sprockets, causing the woman to lower her foot instantly to the pavement and make an awkward series of rather jarring and hopping motions as she tried to bring the unwieldy two-wheeler to a stop.

"Pardon me," Ben said, carefully approaching the young woman from the direction of her left shoulder, "but may I be of help?"

Spoken to unexpectedly and with an accent that she didn't recognize, the young woman turned, still fuming over her misadventure, and glanced in Ben's direction, showing him a pair of blazing blue eyes surrounded by a flip of saucy copper-colored hair framing a face and pouting lips that Ben instantly knew that he would very much like to kiss. Suddenly, England began looking better than Ben had imagined it ever might. But even as Ben realized that he been touched by the young woman's appearance, he also knew, seeing the expression on the woman's face, that anything other than restrained behavior on his part would not be met with welcome.

"Drat," the young woman said hotly, "it will have to be mended."

"If I may help you to dismount," Ben said, offering his hand but keeping his distance, "I may be able to repair it."

Merely by placing her own small left hand atop Ben's for a moment, the woman succeeded in removing herself from her bicycle without making a stumble, and then her hand was instantly gone, given over to holding the bicycle upright by the left side of the handlebars.

"American Navy, are you?" she asked, without charging her words with a smile.

"Yes," Ben said. "If you will allow me to take the bicycle, Miss, I think I might be able to put the chain back on for you."

"You won't risk damaging it, will you?" the woman said, showing an instant concern about what Ben was offering to do.

"I wouldn't dream of it," Ben said. "No risk whatsoever, I promise you."

The woman let him take the handlebars, and then, acting swiftly but with firm control, Ben lifted the bicycle, turned it over, resting it on its seat and its handlebars, and quickly restored the chain to its sprockets. Then, he just as quickly set the vehicle upright and wiped off both the seat and the hand grips with his handkerchief.

"Rather adroit, that," the young woman said, for the first time showing him something resembling warmth. "Thank you."

"My pleasure," Ben said, standing back while holding the bike upright so that the woman could once more take it from him. "If I may, I should introduce myself. My name is Ben Snow."

"Benjamin or Benedict?" the woman asked.

"Benedict," Ben said.

"Welcome to Weymouth," the woman said, her smile widening, "I'm Nicola Dewar-Strang, and I'm afraid that I'm late for an appointment, so I must go. Thank you for your help. Most welcome that. I will hope we meet again. Ta, now."

And with that, she mounted her bicycle and went, before giving Ben time to invite her to take tea with him or even so much as contact her again, a sudden development which Ben considered a disappointment in every way.

Well, he thought to himself with a slight shake of his head, *that's the beauty who got away, but such is life. I'm no better for it, not by a sight, but buck up, lad, tomorrow will be another day.*

Around noon, wandering into a pub called The Green Oak, Ben finally sat down to a pint, lunched on a generous serving of fish and chips, and read a newspaper. In the Middle East, Allenby had apparently captured Jericho. On the Eastern Front, the Germans seemed to be making such deep penetrations into Russia that Ben wondered if the Russians might surrender or sign a separate peace, and if they did so, he couldn't imagine what that might mean while the multitude of German divisions fighting there were suddenly transferred to the Western Front. Then, too, he found an article suggesting that the Royal Flying Corps and the Royal Naval Air Service were soon to be combined into something new called the Royal Air Force. What, he wondered, might that mean, particularly where the Royal Navy was concerned? Ben went on reading, thumbing quickly through the political pages and the sports news until, finally, just as he was finishing his last pint and preparing to drop the newspaper, he stumbled onto a tiny squib of less than a column inch in which he read that "Miss Nicola Dewar-Strang, having returned from Edinburgh where she has attended her uncle's funeral, will be reopening The Infant's School at 27 Dorchester Road on Monday, 4 March."

Now there, Ben, said to himself, *is news worth reading.* Rather than go in person, Ben resolved to buy and send a handwritten invitation, inviting the pretty redhead to a Saturday tea, believing in that way that she could accept or decline without feeling that he had put her under any pressure that she didn't wish to receive. And then, with the hint of a smile curling at his mouth, Ben rose and returned to the chaser where he found Terry just crawling once more out of his bunk.

9

Going up on deck in the middle of the afternoon to take a look at the work that the duty section had in progress, Ben was astonished to see a rooster racing up the starboard side of the ship, dropping a trail of little truffles in its wake, while Light and Scarlatti raced to catch it. Forward of the pilot house and not far from the hatch leading down into Officer's Country, the rooster stopped, once more deposited a truffle, tested the air with an upraised beak, and made a beeline for where Ben was standing. It stopped in front of him, glancing up as though expecting to be fed tidbits of some kind and then dropping its head to peck at the deck as though expecting it to be spread with feed. There, finally, Light and Scarlatti caught up with it, Light scooping the bird into his hands.

"Ship's mascot," Light said, showing Ben a begging sort of smile.

"Neme 'im Zeek," said Scarlatti, his eyebrows rising in a search for approval.

"No," Ben said firmly.

"Good for merele?" Scarlatti ventured.

"NO," Ben said with even more firmness. "And you, Light, get that bird back onto the beach and get rid of it right now while you, Scarlatti, get a swab and a bucket and start cleaning up the mess that your bird has made. No animals allowed, and that's my rule.

They're too much of a health hazard, and we are not going to risk disease here. Now, *march!*"

"What's all the hubbub?" Terry asked, coming up on deck after Light and Scarlatti had disappeared down the side. And then, "*Shit!*" as he unwittingly put his foot down on one of the rooster's little truffles.

"And there you have it," Ben said, "literally. Chicken shit! Light and Scarlatti seemed to think it would be a good idea to bring a rooster aboard as a mascot."

"You sent them packing?"

"In a heartbeat," Ben laughed.

"Those two are going to have to be watched," Terry said.

"You'd better believe it," Ben said. "I can't begin to imagine what they were up to before they enlisted, but whatever it was, it's bound to have been a menace to vast swaths of the public and not a few commercial establishments. One can only imagine the police records they must have accumulated."

"For stupidity rather than malignant intent."

"You can bet on it," Ben said.

At 1800 that evening, wearing their carefully brushed service dress blues beneath their greatcoats and muffled up to their chins in their white scarves, Lieutenant (j.g.) Snow and Ensign Keel walked out to the head of the pier, started the engine of a gray-painted Ford Model T with the block letters USN painted on the side, and drove off to find Trincombe Abbey. Beneath the vehicle's canvas top and behind the wind screen they'd put up, even with the cold, the drive wasn't half bad. Eventually, high stone pillars flanking open iron gates showed them the entrance to the estate, and after threading their way through those and driving on up a well-kept tree-lined gravel lane, they reached the great house, something that looked to Ben like it had been cobbled together by joining a Georgian wing to the restored remains of an abbey church that must have been originally erected sometime in the thirteenth or fourteenth century.

"Impressive, isn't it?" Terry said as they rounded the circular drive leading to the front of the house where they found other automobiles parked and parked their own.

"Not as big as some, I'd venture," Ben said, "but larger than most and larger, certainly, than anything in my experience."

A butler greeted them at the door, showing them the right amount of deference without becoming obsequious and just the right amount of reserve to protect his dignity. After disposing of their coats and hats, the butler then led them toward nearby sliding doors, opened the doors for them, and announced, "Lieutenant Snow and Ensign Keel," and with a slight motion of his hand, ushered them inside.

Immediately, a lovely lady with bright green eyes and skin tones that belied her years came forward to greet them with her hand raised, introduced herself as Lady Felicia, took Ben by the arm, and began to lead the two of them around. She introduced them first to a scowling vicar and his wife, then to Major and Mrs. Roberts, local landowners, then to the Colonel who stood by the fireplace sipping a whiskey, and finally to the Harold Pattersons, a young couple who had recently come into the neighborhood, the wife showing herself to be very attractive and pert, the husband, slightly more reserved, walking with a cane, a clear indication that he had been wounded earlier in the war, survived, and been invalided back to England. For a few moments, for the time that it took for a footman to bring the both of them whiskeys of their own, Ben and Terry stood talking to the Colonel and the Pattersons while Lady Felicia sought to entertain the Vicar and his wife as well as the Roberts. The Colonel, whom Ben judged to be approaching eighty years or more, nevertheless kept up a lively line of questioning, asking all sorts of technical questions about the chasers and the kind of duty in which Ben and Terry were engaged—questions which, within the barriers of security, they answered readily and with interest while becoming aware of the fact that in spite of his age, the Colonel seemed to be quite well briefed and up to date with regard to both the war and the means by which the Allies intended to win it.

In the midst of their discussions, Ben chanced to glance once more around the room, and when he did, it occurred to him that the party seemed complete; that, contrary to expectation, Lady Felicia's table seemed to promise no spinsters, no tweed-clad sporting matrons, and no pinched-lipped doyennes for them to "take in" as dinner partners. When the revelation broke over him, Ben felt a wave of relief and wondered if Terry might not be feeling the same sense of deliverance. And then, as the doors to the drawing room once more slid open, the butler announced, "Miss Lettice Mayfield and Miss Dewar-Strang," and Ben's solar plexus took a jump. What kind of parents, he first asked himself, would name a daughter after a salad? Discarding the thought almost immediately, he couldn't stop himself from wondering whether he ought to thank the gods of war, the saints, or simply Lady Felicia for a benefaction about which she could have had no prior idea.

Formally attired in keeping with the other guests, Lettice Mayfield, a lively little blonde wearing a low-cut frock in pale blue, proceeded into the room with a rosebud mouth that seemed filled with apologies for being late owing to some "misplaced turn" she had taken in leaving Weymouth. Nicola Dewar-Strang, exhibiting more reserve but showing a pleasant smile, came smoothly in a yard or two behind her and then stood quietly, listening and watching as her vivacious friend seemed to cover the amenities for them both. Clad in dark green velvet which Ben thought the perfect complement to her copper-colored hair, Nicola seemed a picture to him, something he might have seen in a book or presented on the cover of a fashionable magazine. So struck by the sight of her that he might have wanted to stand back and heave a sigh, Ben nevertheless steeled himself to maintain his reserve and simply let his eyes and mind take in the sight of her. And then, with Lettice moving swiftly from the Roberts to the Vicar and his wife professing effusions of despondency for her mistake, Lady Felicia took Nicola by the arm and brought her forward to introduce her to Ben and Terry.

"By this morning's good fortune, my good fortune," Ben said, following Lady Felicia's introduction and while making Lady Felicia and Nicola a slight bow, "Miss Dewar-Strang and I have already met."

"I have Lieutenant Snow to thank for mending my bicycle for me," Nicola said, showing Ben a smile and extending her hand to him before she repeated the motion to Terry and asked him how he did.

"Ah," Lady Felicia said, slightly raising one eyebrow, her bright eyes smiling. "Perhaps Lieutenant Snow will consent to take you in to dinner then?"

"Lieutenant Snow will be delighted," Ben said.

"Ben and Terry then made the acquaintance of the vivacious Lettice who didn't require two minutes of fluttering talk before she drew Terry aside and began to regale him with tales about her numerous adventures with "her motor." And minutes later, upon Lady Felicia's urging, Ben offered Nicola Dewar-Strang his arm and took her in to dinner.

"You reached your appointment without arriving late?" Ben asked as they passed into the dining room.

"I did," Nicola said, "thanks to your expertise."

Reading the place cards from a distance, Ben pulled back Nicola's chair and saw her seated. And then, he sat down beside her.

"My condolences regarding your uncle," Ben said. "I understand you've only just returned to Weymouth."

"Only just. How did you know?"

"The announcement in this morning's paper, about the reopening of your school," Ben said. "I happened to stumble onto it while taking my lunch."

"Ah, yes, the announcement," Nicola said. "My little charmers will be once more filing through the door soon, and I shall be delighted to see them."

"You are a teacher then?" Ben said.

"Of early learning only," Nicola said. "I have thirty, ages five to seven. I teach them to read, if they haven't already learned, to do small sums, a bit of geography, a few notable historical events, and some art. It's nothing very demanding, mind you, the learning that is. Deportment and discipline are the greater challenge, as you might imagine for their age."

Ben grinned. "I can well imagine," he said, his mind recollecting his afternoon meeting with Light and Scarlatti. "I sometimes experience a similar challenge. Let me tell you a quick tale about a rooster."

The soup—something which combined tiny dumplings with a tasty chicken broth—struck Ben as delicious, all of it being punctuated by the musical sounds emitted by Lettice and Terry who seemed to be vastly enjoying themselves immediately across the table. The main course, "harvested," Lady Felicia said, from the Abbey's park, consisted of a joint of venison accompanied by a helping of creamed potatoes and a serving of marvelously pickled beets.

"So much," Ben said, "for the negative propaganda about English cooking."

"How so?" Nicola asked, setting down her fork with a delicate hand.

"Stateside rumor," Ben said, "implied that it would be bland, cold, and tasteless. This generous meal has proved anything but."

"Mandy, she is the treasure who cooks for Lady Felicia," Nicola said, "seems to have been handed down by the gods. I shouldn't like to think that you might find the same quality at many of the establishments in Weymouth."

"You've known Lady Felicia for a long time?" Ben asked

"She was a particular friend of my mother's," Nicola said, "and she's been a particular friend to me. When my mother died some years ago, Lady Felicia asked me to come here and start The Infant School. She said that there was a need. At the time, I happened to be completing my degree at Somerville, and afterward, the change of venue seemed like an opportunity."

"And has it been?" Ben asked.

"Oh, quite," Nicola said, as the footman removed her plate and set a helping of chocolate mousse before her. "Lady Felicia chairs my board. That, perhaps, explains my rush this morning; I didn't wish to be late for a board meeting."

"Ah," Ben said, but before he could say anything else, the Vicar spoke up and asked the two officers at the table some rather pointed questions about how soon the American army might show up and how many of them would be coming over, and how soon they could be expected to join in combat.

"If I may," Terry said diplomatically, "I think I shall defer to my superior."

"Oh, thanks very much," Ben said, grinning at Terry from across the table. "I shall try to remember you for this the next time I fill out your fitness report"—a remark which drew gentle laughter from the remainder of the table. But then, Ben turned to the Vicar, a man who seemed wholly supportive of the war, and spoke seriously. "Reverend Smythe," Ben said, "speaking frankly, I cannot answer your questions, not with any degree of expertise. That the United States are enlisting, drafting, and training an immense army, I can assure you. That the American army will commit itself to action as soon as it can make ready, I can also assure you. And that Americans will fight like tigers when they do take the field, I can guarantee.

But with regard to specific dates and a timetable, our masters, Mr. Keel's and mine, have not felt it necessary to inform us. Instead, they have given us a specific job to do by sending us to curtail the German submarine threat, and we are now trying to do that to the very best of our ability."

"Hear, hear," the Colonel said heartily from the head of the table, "and glad we are to have you, young Sir. Very glad indeed," to which Major Roberts and Mr. Patterson threw in a pair of "hear, hears" as well.

"Oh, you brought that off very nicely," Nicola whispered as the guests returned to their desserts. "The Vicar is a bit of a war horse and a staunch supporter of Lloyd George. Much too old to go, he beats the drum endlessly in support of the troops, and even to the point of mentioning my Freddy in far too many of his sermons. Oh, how I do wish he would stop."

"Your Freddy?" Ben said.

"Sorry," Nicola said. "I shouldn't have mentioned him. Freddy Littlejohn, the Mayor's son. The Vicar believes we were engaged. We weren't, but we knew each other before the war, and for the Vicar and his wife, that seemed to put some kind of community seal on a relationship which didn't extend beyond friendship. Freddy was killed near Mons in 1914, but the Vicar, who confirmed him as a boy, can't seem to let him go."

"No real attachment, then?"

"No," Nicola said.

"Any real attachments now?" Ben said. "I ask because I had it in mind to invite you to take tea with me on Saturday at some place of your choosing."

Without answering the first of Ben's questions, Nicola Dewar-Strang placed her dessert spoon on the plate holding her unfinished portion of mousse, and turned her face to Ben. "Might your invitation include the option of substituting a coffee or an Italian espresso for tea?" she asked brightly.

"The answer is an unqualified 'yes,'" Ben said, his face breaking into a broad smile. "But you are going to have to enlighten me about what an Italian espresso might be. As far as I know, whatever it might be has not yet reached any place in the States where I have ever been."

"Better, I think, to let you try the experience for yourself, and then let you make up your mind from there," Nicola said. "Saturday morning, ten o'clock?"

"Twenty-seven Dorchester Road?" Ben asked.

"Very astute, aren't you?" she said. "Yes, I live in a flat over the school."

"I'm afraid we'll have to walk," Ben said. "The Navy does not release its vehicles on the whim of a lieutenant junior grade."

"Ha," Nicola laughed, "in Weymouth, everyone walks, or nearly so, save for Lettice whose father is a doctor and receives a special ration. The Colonel and Lady Felicia also receive a special ration because they live in the country and own a tractor. Agricultural allowance, don't you see. The rest, those who still have cars, have to husband their fuel coupons."

Nicola might have said more, but at that moment, Lady Felicia rose from the table, and the other ladies in the room, all of them apparently trained to the tradition, rose with her and made their exit. Then, a footman opened a sideboard, drew out the port, and placed it on the table before the Colonel before making his own exit from the room.

"So," Mr. Patterson asked, "now that the ladies are gone, gentlemen, have you seen any action in the short time since you've arrived?"

Keeping his silence, Terry once more deferred to Ben.

"Across the past week," Ben said, speaking without emotion, "we've destroyed several Hun mines and one which we determined to be British."

"British, you say!" exclaimed the Vicar, appearing to deny and be outraged at the very idea.

"Mines, Vicar," Major Roberts said as though as to set the matter at rest, "are apt to break loose and sometimes go astray. Given the numbers we've sowed in our multitude of barrages, I'm quite surprised that our American friends didn't encounter more."

"Reprehensible, that's what I call it!" the Vicar said. "To think that our brave men risk being blown to smithereens by our own contrivances. Why, it is absolutely unthinkable. What proof, young man, do you have for the aspersion you have cast?"

But Ben never had the chance to answer.

"Vicar," Mr. Patterson said, speaking flatly and forthrightly so that he couldn't be misunderstood, "in 1915 at Ypres, just as I was about to take my platoon over the top, I was blown up by a round fired by an English gun. That round did for me and no fewer than seven of my men. Killed every one of them and wounded two more. War is a very imperfect business, Sir. We don't kill as many of our own people as the Hun does, but we account for far more men by friendly fire than you and the average British citizen realize."

"He's right, old fellow," the Colonel said, giving the Vicar a friendly pat on the arm as the port came around. "Alas, he's right."

They talked on for another hour, but at the end of the hour, almost on cue, the Colonel rose, and they joined the ladies for coffee in the drawing room. There after coffee and some small talk, the Colonel and Lady Fitzhugh sat down to bridge with the Vicar and his wife while the Roberts and the Pattersons sat down to whist.

"Do you play?" Ben asked Nicola.

"I do not," she said. "My father and mother were not exactly ardent Scotch Presbyterians, but they considered cards and the wagers that went with them to be rather a waste of their time."

"What about Lettice?" Ben asked.

Very quickly, Nicola put her hand to her lips to suppress a laugh. "I love her to pieces," Nicola said, "but I doubt that she could sit still long enough to draw a hand, much less do a shuffle and deal. If you will observe the degree of animation with which she is speaking to Mr. Keel, I believe you may take my point."

Ben glanced across the room to where the vivacious Lettice seemed so deeply engaged with his executive officer and saw that her hands seemed to be going everywhere.

"Lettice's mother is French," Nicola said, "so rather than go up to Somerville or Girton, her mother sent her to the Sorbonne for two years, with the result that you see."

"And how did that go?" Ben asked.

"You would be mistaken to judge her by her hands or her manner," Nicola said. "She may drive like a bird on the fly, but she has the mind of a trap snapping down on the neck of a rat, particularly when it comes to solving mathematical problems. Twice last year, she made calculations for the Ministry of Transport, and in one case that I know about she was asked to apply her talents to something having to do with diplomatic ciphers."

"And are you also a mathematician?" Ben wanted to know.

"Hardly," Nicola said. "I read for a degree in modern literature."

"Quite wise," Ben said.

"And most enjoyable," Nicola said.

While the card games continued at the table, Ben and Nicola, Terry and Lettice talked on, each of them absorbed by the other, each of them blissfully unaware of the time. Nicola's father, Ben learned, acted as a Professor of Classical Literature at the University of Edinburgh. Her mother had been an accomplished painter, one of whose still lifes remained on a wall in the National Gallery. Of brothers and sisters, she had none, although she remained close to a cousin—the son of the uncle who had passed away—and that individual, a captain in a Scottish regiment, was serving in France and had remained there, commanding a company, for some time. When asked if she eventually intended to return to Scotland, Nicola hedged, saying that she loved her home but that she'd established both a new home and friends in Weymouth and preferred the weather near the Channel to what she described as the sometimes bitterly cold winters in Edinburgh. Perhaps, she told him, if she were a true Highlander, she might feel differently, but given the economic climate that prevailed in Scotland, she felt much better able to make her way in England.

"Our family may have an old name," Nicola mused, "but whatever money may once have attended it must have disappeared with the last of the Stuarts. My grandfather was a schoolmaster, and according to my father, my great grandfather held a post as a steward on one of the estates in the vicinity of Falkirk. Nothing very grand, you see, about any of those posts. And you?"

"Prior to their death," Ben said, "my parents had a machine business in New York; it was driven nearly into bankruptcy by the downturn of 1909, so like you, I must fend for myself, and thus far, I can't say that I've been disappointed."

When Lady Felicia's guests finally stood up from the card tables, Ben felt stunned to look at his watch and see that the evening had extended all the way to 2330.

"You will follow your ladies," Lady Felicia said, "placing her hand on Ben's arm, "to make sure they arrive back in Weymouth safely?"

"Most assuredly," Ben said, "and thank you, Lady Felicia, for a most lovely evening."

"We will hope to entertain you again," Lady Felicia said, flashing Ben the warmest of smiles, "both the Colonel and me. And if I should also ask the two of you to accompany Nicola and Lettice, I hope that you won't feel put out."

"Lady Felicia," Ben said, "your wit becomes you."

On the way back into Weymouth, Ben found himself hard pressed to keep up with Lettice. Lettice, he and Terry discovered, happened to be driving a Rolls-Royce Silver Ghost and driving it with what both Ben and Terry considered to be abandon.

"The wonder to me is that Nicola feels safe to get in the car with her," Ben said.

"If she ever asks me to drive anywhere, and she's going to," Terry said, "and you better believe that I'm going to accept, I think I'm going to deserve at least a Navy Cross for taking the risk."

After they saw Nicola to her door, which opened to the side of the school onto stairs that led up to her flat, they then tried to follow the Rolls as it shot through the streets heading toward wherever it was that Lettice lived. They succeeded but barely, and when they did arrive and saw her turn into another curved drive toward a house that rose like a small castle at least a hundred yards from the gate, both of them looked on the pile and felt stunned.

"Not as big as Trincombe Abbey, but moving in the same direction," Terry said.

"My lad," Ben laughed, "you seem to have fallen into the chips. If that girl's father isn't landed money, he is, beside being a medical man, a captain of industry on no small scale."

"Seems like we haven't done half bad for ourselves," Terry said with a wide grin.

"I don't want to overdo it," Ben said, "but right about now, I could almost get down on the deck and kiss Commander Radford's feet for this one."

"And all because we missed the bus to Salisbury," Terry said.

On the following morning, a Friday, Chief Pack informed Ben that one of the pumps in the engine room required an overhaul, and after determining that the job could be done within twenty-four hours and that the *Mulgrew* had the spare parts required to complete the job, Ben gave Pack permission to tear the pump down. Terry, meanwhile, put his head together with Grange, the two of them going over the crew's pay accounts. Then, together, they both sought out the dispersing officer aboard the *Mulgrew*, drew the men's pay for the month, returned to the ship, and lined the crew up on one side of the ship, running them individually through the pilot house, and paying them while using the chart table as the repository for their accounting arrangements. Later, summoned once more to meet with Commander Radford, Ben and Terry found him with a smile on his face.

"I gather," Radford said, "that you weren't lassoed at Lady Felicia's by two hundred pounds of lard spouting gibberish about drains, fox hunting, and a paucity of servants."

"No Sir," both said at once.

"Your visit was less than arduous, then?"

"Much less, Sir," Ben said.

"Such was Lady Felicia's report when she telephoned me this morning to offer her thanks. I gather that you acquitted yourselves with honors, did right by your country, and found yourselves suitably rewarded for your courage in meeting the locals. Lady Felicia did not exactly say that you had *embraced* the locals, but if I do not mistake her words, I gather that you may intend to."

"Only if fortune continues to smile upon us," Ben said.

"Yes," Commander Radford smiled, "well, carry on, the both of you, and well done for showing the colors."

Collected before noon by Horn, Feller, Speck, and Hyde, Ben and Terry joined them in a jaunt into Weymouth, Horn leading them on an almost direct path to an establishment named The Crown and Binnacle where the publican immediately pulled pints for them and took their orders for the bar food that was to comprise their lunch.

"And Salisbury was a success?" Terry asked as the six of them sat down around a table near the end of the room.

"The air was crisp, the cathedral was magnificent, and the pints were refreshing," Feller said.

"And we met some girls," Speck added, "shop girls, but lively."

"And pretty," Horn added.

"Very," Hyde said. "We're meeting them again on Saturday, in Dorchester for what they call a *walkabout*."

"That sounds almost Australian," Ben said. "Were these girls English or Australian?"

"We didn't ask," Hyde said.

"Absolutely not," Horn said.

"We judged them merely on looks," Feller said.

"And willingness," Horn added.

"And willingness to be sure," Horn said. "What about you two lay-a-beds? Rumor has it that Radford forced the two of you to endure some kind of social evening with paragons of society. Meet any lovelies?"

"Lovelies of the two-hundred-pound variety," Terry said quickly. "You know the type, tweed suits, hunting horns in their purses, talk about the hounds, that sort of thing."

"Stop," Speck said, "you're making me ill."

"Really," Horn asked, "it was that bad?"

"Ours but to do and die," Ben said. "Let it be sufficient to say that we went, we endured, and we survived."

"You poor sods," Feller said. "You should have been with us—wine, women, and song, and then more wine. As it turns out, your punishment for not going with us was to have slept late."

"Yes," Terry said, feigning misery, "we shouldn't have been so remiss."

"Sorry we can't scare up two more girls for the jaunt to Dorchester," Horn said, "but I'm afraid you've missed out and will have to fend for yourselves."

"We'll try to scare up a little something," Ben said, speaking in his most reserved tones.

On Saturday morning when he got up on deck, Ben found the day to be crisp and relatively clear. To his shock, only a light breeze blew in from the Channel, and the sea, while not as smooth as glass, nevertheless failed to show a ruffle. With all things considered, at least with regard to weather, the day looked appealing.

Moments later, Terry stepped up on deck showing the evidence of a clean shave.

"And so," Ben said, "with the rest of the bunch off to Dorchester, what might you have on tap for today?"

Terry's face broadened into a smile. "The lovely Lettice has informed me that she will be *collecting* me at 1100 hours so that she and I may *join* her mother for *luncheon*. I don't know about you, but I find that I am wholly enjoying the English formalities of speech. I gather that I'm to be exhibited to the mother as a sort of prize pig brought home from the fair."

"It does sound as though you are making very rapid progress," Ben said.

"Try to imagine Lettice doing anything at a moderate pace or slow," Terry said. "It won't compute. Having seen the way she drives, I can only wish that Rolls-Royce might have installed seatbelts in their automobiles so that I can avoid being hurled asunder should she collide with a hay wagon or the corner of a building somewhere." He paused. "And you," Terry said, "what are you and your Miss Dewar-Strang getting up to?"

"Ever hear of something called espresso?" Ben said.

"Yes," Terry said. "Some kind of Italian coffee concoction, isn't it? Supposed to be bitter, and when it comes, there isn't very much of it in the cup. But I'm not sure about that; I've never tried it."

"Neither have I," Ben said, "but apparently I'm about to. Miss Dewar-Strang and I appear to be 'walking out together' this morning, if I have the English terms right, although what that might actually mean is a little beyond me. I'm to meet her at her 'digs' at 1000 hours, and from there, we will boldly set forth."

"In greatcoats?"

"Let there be no doubt," Ben said. "and carrying *brollies*. I've heard that you can't trust English weather for a minute. From all reports, the skies can be clear for five minutes and raining cats and dogs ten minutes later."

So as not to be late, Ben left the ship at 0930 that morning, walked slowly up the Esplanade, turned north up the Dorchester Road, and reached the pavement before Number 27 with a good five minutes to spare. Glancing at his watch, Ben thought to stroll up and down for the time remaining, but before he could make a move, the door to Nicola's stairs opened, and she stepped out before him, showing him a warm smile and a pair of lips that he once again wished that he could kiss.

"I thought you might be a mite early," she said, stepping forward to greet him wearing the same Tartan tam as before and a sleek black coat that he'd never laid eyes on. "I feared that you had a shorter distance to come than you perhaps realized and might arrive early. Shall we walk?"

"Let's," Ben said. "But I think we should rely on your knowledge of local establishments for our choice. I don't know the first thing about Weymouth or where we might go."

"You may leave that to me," she said with assurance. "The Bristol Tea Room, I think. I believe you might like the atmosphere."

The Bristol Tea Room turned out to be located on a quiet street two blocks west of the Esplanade, and once they reached it, entered, and were shown to a table, Ben found that he liked the place very much and appreciated the well-polished oak with which the wainscoting had been constructed. On the walls, rather than the pastel prints of flowers which he had expected, he saw caricatures, of lords and ladies, barristers, military men, hunters in pink riding coats, and a bevy of navvies wearing their cloth caps and smoking pipes. And on the tables, rather than the empty surface that he would have expected to find in a coffee shop at home, he saw that places had been laid with attractive silver as well as a plethora of cork-backed table mats for everything from cups and saucers to dessert plates and sugar bowls, all of them depicting what Ben imagined to be nautical scenes from Bristol harbor.

"Not quite what you expected?" Nicola asked, a smile bringing a twinkle to her eyes.

"Not quite," Ben said, returning her smile, "but altogether enchanting, if you take my meaning."

"I just love this place," Nicola said. "I think you might almost say that I'm a regular here."

As if on cue, glancing out through the window, Ben saw that it had started to rain.

"Good lord," he said, "where did that come from?"

"Our weather has a habit of doing that," Nicola said, "particularly in the winter. Not to worry; it will pass, but because I think it may keep us confined for a time, let me suggest that we forego the espressos for this morning—they are rather small if you see what I mean—and opt for coffee or tea instead. They'll bring us full pots, and those will allow us to linger until the rain stops."

"You're on." Ben said.

"On what, exactly?"

"I mean that I agree," Ben said.

"Ah," Nicola said, suddenly enjoying the turn of phrase. "*You're on*. I must remember that. I wonder if Lettice knows it?"

Before Ben could answer, a rather plump young waitress wearing a clean white apron over a black dress appeared beside their table. "Good morning, Miss," the young woman said, "may I take your custom?"

"Good morning, Isla," Nicola said, looking up and showing the girl a smile. "I will take a coffee, if you please, and Lieutenant Snow will choose for himself."

"Coffee for me, too," Ben said.

"With scones, Miss?" Isla asked, directing her question to Nicola.

Nicola Dewar-Strang hesitated, leaving Ben with the instant impression that she didn't want to put Ben out for what he imagined to be a trifling expense.

"Does Miss usually take scones?" he asked the girl pleasantly.

"Oh, yes, Sir," she replied. "Our scones is very good, Sir."

"Then we'll have scones," Ben said.

"With clotted cream and jam, Sir?"

"With clotted cream and jam, to be sure," Ben said.

"You needn't have done that," Nicola said when the girl went away. "I shouldn't like to leave you with the impression that I'm expensive company."

"In the first place, I didn't have breakfast this morning," Ben said, "and in the second, I'm not buying us the Albert Memorial. And if you will put a third item on your list, I'd like for you to think of a place where, later, the two of us can have a very good lunch without a word of caution about the expense. I have months of unused pay sitting in the bank, and I've already had fish and chips, so that's out. A nice restaurant is where I'd like to take you."

"Truthfully," Nicola said, "we've been on short rations for so long that I'm afraid I've rather lost touch."

"Surely," Ben said, "with all of the Royal Naval officers in this port, you have been wined and dined almost nightly."

"I'm afraid not," Nicola said firmly. "I'm afraid the Vicar, his wife, and their Freddy fixation have seen to that. They put it about that I'm supposed to be in mourning, so aside from a few evenings at Lady Felicia's, your invitation to tea is my first outing in months."

"You're kidding," Ben said, his jaw dropping slightly.

"I'm not," Nicola said, pursing her lips to show her displeasure.

"There appear to be some English customs," Ben observed, "which wouldn't in the States receive a moment of grace."

"And perhaps you're better off for it," Nicola said, "but let's avoid that subject. Tell me, Ben, what are your plans for the future?"

"You mean after the war ends and we send the Kaiser packing?" Ben said, making a swift mental note to put the Vicar in his place if the man ever overstepped and approached him regarding Nicola.

"I think that's the general idea," Nicola said, her face breaking into a most fetching grin.

"I hold a third mate's certificate in the American Merchant Marine," Ben said, "so I think that I could get a ship almost anywhere, as long as we keep the U-boats from sinking the most of them. If it turns out that I like the Navy—and so far, I do—it might be possible for me to augment and apply for a regular commission in order to stay with it. And then, too, from time to time, I've given some thought to going ashore and establishing some kind of business in support of maritime trade. My father's business manufactured parts for marine machinery, and there is always ship chandlery as well. I can't say that I am much attracted by maritime insurance or maritime law, but those are options that I may also want to consider. But first, of course, we've got to get through this thing, defeat the Huns, and establish a peace that will hold and keep a war like this one from ever happening again. What about you? Will you continue to teach and run your school?"

At that moment, Isla returned with their tray, placing beautifully crafted china cups, saucers, and a full coffee service before them followed by plates, little pots of jam and clotted cream, and a tiny sugar bowl.

"Good heavens," Ben laughed, surveying the spread with disbelief. "In the States, someone would have dropped a heavy mug on the table, filled it with weak coffee, and that would have been the limit!"

"We do have our ways," Nicola said, "and some of them are rather nice."

"Yes," Ben said, "and you were saying?"

Nicola poured for both of them, and then replaced the pot on its table mat.

"What with the war and the nation's finances, Ben, the United Kingdom is approaching bankruptcy. I shudder to think about the debt we owe to New York banks, not to mention American banks in Boston, Chicago, San Francisco, Philadelphia, and the farther reaches of South Dakota—and as the nation goes, so go the rest of us. We will be years, perhaps decades, recovering. My school is a private one, so it survives on the tuition that Weymouth's parents are willing or able to pay and on a generous contribution which Lady Felicia and the Colonel chose to make in order to keep up its support. Once the war concludes, the parents of my children may find that they are either unwilling or unable to go on supporting the school, and if so, I will simply have to close. Even now, finances are tight and becoming more so. For the past three months, I've been carrying two of my pupils, bright ones, on credit, but that cannot continue for much longer. My own income is a pittance, but still, I must eat. And both upkeep and maintenance on the building sometimes seem staggering. I think that gives you the picture, so I won't belabor it, but to put things in what you Americans call 'a nutshell,' I regret to say that the Empire is in decline, and the decline is having an effect on all of us."

"Not a pretty picture, is it?" Ben mused.

"No," Nicola said. "In Edinburgh, even my father's salary has been reduced, and he's a university professor without independent means. If my school closes, I shall have to go to work elsewhere, of course, but I have teaching credentials, and I have been offered other opportunities as well, so I don't face starvation, but the prospects are nevertheless something other than bright."

They talked on through the remainder of the morning, consuming their coffee and scones, discussing elements of the war, telling stories from their youth, and gradually getting to know one another more thoroughly. Later, with the rain stopped, they walked along the Esplanade, braving the chill, and when, finally, Nicola said that she felt too filled with scones even to consider luncheon, they went to the pictures, took yet another stroll, and made a seven o'clock date for taking their supper together. Ben then returned her to her apartment so that she could rest, bathe, and change for dinner, while he returned to the ship for his own bit of rest.

Once back aboard, he found Terry sitting in their stateroom, his eyes glazed, his feet propped up upon their fold-down table.

"Nice 'luncheon'?" Ben asked.

"The mother is the fourth daughter of an earl with estates in the Midlands and coal mines west of Newcastle," Terry said. "French mother of her own, originally."

"Pleasant was she?" Ben wanted to know.

"And beautiful, and gracious, and the food was both plentiful and incredibly good," Terry said.

"You really have fallen into it, haven't you?" Ben said.

"I have," Terry said with a cat-that-swallowed-a-canary smile. "And what about you, good Sir? Viscount's daughter, perhaps? Heiress to the Laird of Mull? Honorary colonel to a Scottish regiment?"

"Nothing so grand," Ben laughed. "Nicola is beautiful, mature, and forthright, and I'm happy to settle for that. We had a really nice afternoon, and I'm meeting her later for dinner. What about you? What do you and the lovely Lettice have on tap?"

"We're going to the pictures," Terry said. "My hope is that we can leave the Silver Fox parked somewhere near the head of the pier and walk. She scared the hell out of me horsing that chariot of hers around these narrow streets, and my guess is that they all know her for her driving because I saw one mother snatching her children into front doors and old men running for cover when she turned down their lanes."

"Motorcyclists appear to wear crash helmets," Ben said. "I've seen one or two wearing them. Perhaps you should consider buying one yourself."

"I would, but I'm afraid I might risk showing the white feather to Lettice, and that might be worse than a crash, if you see what I mean," Terry said.

"So, for the time being, you are willing to risk your life instead?" Ben said.

"I'm considering it a sort of test that she's putting me to," Terry said. "Once I pass it, there are going to be some changes."

Later that evening, with the streets dry, the sky clear, and the stars shining, Ben walked Nicola to an inn named The Ploughman's Retreat, and there, starting with mushroom caps, they dined on Dover sole with boiled potatoes, followed by a serving of trifle which came to them in a cut glass cup. Their wine, a house white, they ordered in a carafe for economy at Nicola's insistence.

"With the war, I'm afraid I've rather gotten out of the habit of wines," she said, "so I shouldn't like to put you out for something that I'm not up to enjoying fully." Later, she told Ben that aside from the meals she'd taken at Lady Felicia's table, the dinner they'd shared that evening had been the best she'd had out in three years.

As Ben walked her back to 27 Dorchester Road beneath the stars, without either his urging or his resistance, she'd taken his arm.

"Thank you," she said, "for a perfectly lovely evening."

"It's been more than nice for me," Ben said, giving her hand a squeeze where she held him by the arm. "May we have another next Saturday?"

"Will you be going out again soon?" she asked, her voice quickening.

"Yes," Ben said, "tomorrow."

"And you think you'll be back again by Friday?"

"Yes," Ben said, "if all goes well and we aren't sunk."

"Don't say that," she said sharply, drawing closer to him. "Don't ever say that to me, Ben. Promise."

"All right," he said. "I won't. Sorry, I didn't mean to upset you. I meant it as a joke."

"I know," she said, "but I've seen too many lost already, and I couldn't bear to think of you being one of them."

At her door, as Ben waited for her to find her latch key, she said, "I would have you up, but given the times in which we live, it would be the end of me, of the school, of my reputation, and of everything that I've built. The Puritan strain in the English character remains Cromwellian, and I'm sorry to say that there is nothing that I can do about it."

"I know," Ben laughed. "I won't hold it against you."

And then, without further preamble, she leaned up and kissed Ben, sending something like a charge of electricity straight down through his body to the tip of his toes.

"Be careful, Love," she said quickly, and in the next second, she was through the door and up the stairs, leaving Ben all but quivering on the walk below.

10

At 0537 on Sunday morning, as Horn's engineering ratings prepared SC 56X to get underway in order to lead SC 65X and SC 71X to sea, someone in the engine room made a mistake regarding the auxiliary engine, touched off a spark, and set the engine room and the auxiliary engine on fire. The fire was quickly put out, and damage to the engine room did not appear to be extensive, but the auxiliary engine proved to be a loss until it had been either removed from the vessel and replaced or until it had been completely taken down, overhauled, and a number of its parts replaced. Horn was furious; the man who'd made the mistake, having shown himself to be negligent, was disciplined, but that didn't solve Group AA1's problem. In a nutshell, Horn would not be leading AA1 to sea; he wouldn't even be going.

"Well, then," Commander Radford said, after surveying the damage. "Everyone in Group AA2 will be thoroughly exhausted after their time on station, their chasers will need maintenance, and I can see no virtue in trying to send one of them straight back to sea with you. So this will be a two-chaser patrol with Lieutenant Snow in charge. Two chasers acting in concert will be better than none. I suggest reacting on a baseline of three thousand yards since there are only two of you going, and while it seems clear that you can't develop a perfect fix on a contact with only two lines of bearing, you can still most certainly put yourselves in the picture to close and prosecute an attack. So, Lieutenants Snow and Feller, proceed to sea, transit from here to Search Area 019, and begin your search there, and let me wish good hunting to the both of you."

Ben and Feller both saluted, turned on their heels, went to their chasers, and got them underway, the disappointed sailors standing above decks on the stricken SC 56X saluting them as they sortied.

Given the distance they had to go, cruising at 8 knots, they were five hours reaching their start point. Once there, with Terry on watch as officer of the deck and with Ben sitting in the pilot house chair next to him, Ben got onto the R/T with Feller, oriented their search base on an east/west axis with a three-thousand-yard interval between them, and began a search sweep to the south on a course of 180, moving ahead at 5 knots while stopping every twenty minutes for a ten-minute listen on the C-Tube. For hour after hour through the afternoon and on into the early evening, the search proved unproductive, an eventuality which led Ben to move the search south into Search Area 020 and later that night into Search Area 021. Reckoning his position from the star fix that he'd worked out at dusk, Ben had charted the position of both chasers to be some thirty-five miles to the northeast of Guernsey with the intention of closing the coast more nearly only after sunrise the following morning. For the time being, while the seas carried a chop, conditions did not seem to be unruly, and Ben imagined that if he plowed areas 021 and 022 through the night, he and Feller would be able to account for the areas closer to Guernsey during daylight the following morning before stretching their search to the west and starting to patrol back north toward the English coast.

Santos gave them pasta and ground meat for their evening meal that night, so after O'Neal ate at 1600, he came up to relieve Terry for supper, and Ben also went down at the same time, conversing genially with Pack, Terry, and Crim at one end of the table, while Garcia, the oiler Bates, and Grange finished their meals at the other end. Terry, wishing to catch some sleep before rising for the mid-watch, went immediately to their stateroom following the meal. Ben, expecting to stand the evening watch and after checking with Crim in radio about any communications from the beach, returned to the pilot house, hauled himself into his chair, and dozed for a while in advance of his own watch.

Around 1930 that evening, Ben woke to find that regardless of the moonlight which seemed to filter through it, fog had come up, cutting visibility to less than one hundred yards. Feller, over the R/T, assured Ben that the fog was as thick where he cruised. Immediately Ben warned his junior to cut his speed to 4 knots, take care that his lookouts kept watch with the eyes of eagles, and gave instructions for dead reckoning through the night with the added warning to make sure that his helmsman made no mistakes because he didn't want the two vessels closing together and risking a collision. Fortunately, the seas remained calm, Ben's own helmsman reporting that he could easily keep the chaser on course by means of rudder corrections to no more than 2 degrees of the base course Ben had given him to steer.

At midnight, Terry came up to relieve Ben as officer of the deck, and very rapidly the crews standing port and starboard watches on the gun mount and on the depth charges changed, their fellows once relieved dropping straight below into their racks. Because they were stopping to listen on their C-Tubes and then restarting to move forward on a set time schedule, although he could not see Feller through the fog, Ben felt reasonably assured that the two of them were running parallel and knew he had no choice but to take that assumption on faith. And so SC 65X stopped, listened for ten minutes, started, and moved on through the night only occasionally doing a radio check with SC 71X to be sure their equipment operated properly. Throughout the whole of that time, their search didn't produce a sound, leaving Ben to assume that there wasn't a German U-boat anywhere within twenty miles of them and possibly nowhere in the entire English Channel.

With Terry standing a more than competent watch, Ben didn't so much as bother to consider going down to his bunk. Instead, wrapped in his duffle, slumped comfortably in his chair, he allowed himself to drift off and slept soundly until 0400 when O'Neal came up to relieve. Once he found that the fog remained socked in around them and that no one on the C-Tube had heard a screw beat anywhere, Ben permitted himself to go back to sleep and slept soundly until 0600 when the enlisted watches changed in the pilot house. Finally, once more waking to find the fog as thick as ever and with a sunrise which might finally burn it off still some two hours away, he hauled himself to his feet, told O'Neal that he was going down for coffee and breakfast, and went below.

Santos' coffee was good, and its strength forced Ben quickly awake. The breakfast that morning, oatmeal with raisins, was at least hot, but even Ben had to admit that it was nothing that the men might have written home to rave about to their wives or sweethearts. Nevertheless, when Ben finally climbed back to the pilot house and resumed his place, standing beside O'Neal while leaning on his chair, he felt reasonably rested, renewed after a fashion, and hopeful that the fog would clear and allow him to reunite with Feller and SC 71X without delay.

At 0800 that morning, Ben relieved O'Neal and sent him below for his own breakfast with a strong recommendation about the coffee and little said about the oatmeal. A swift check over the sound-powered phones with the crews on the forward mount and on the depth charges alerted them to the fact that their captain had the watch, which invariably came to them as a warning against skylarking. Then, stopping on the dot at the appropriate time, Ben found that Crim, the best of the instrument's operators, was on the C-Tube and felt reassured that if a Hun put in an appearance, Crim would pick it up.

Outside around 0830 that morning, Ben could see that a gray, fog-ridden dawn was barely beginning to lighten the atmosphere. Twenty minutes later with visibility still no greater than one hundred yards, Ben detected a certain change. Leaning against the wind screen with his glasses raised to his eyes as he sought to penetrate the fog, he felt the hair on the back of his neck suddenly stand on end. Before he knew what was happening, he shouted through the open wind screen to the gun crew: "Gun crew on your feet! Target two points off the starboard bow, one hundred yards! Batteries released. OPEN FIRE!"

Ben did not need to order the gong for General Quarters to be sounded. The first of the 3″/23's rounds going out and the clatter of the ship's manned machine gun took care of that. Ben watched the first of his chaser's rounds strike the conning tower of the U-boat, doing damage that even through the fog Ben could detect. Twice more, Ben believed his gunners struck the U-boat's conning tower; with their fourth three-inch round, he believed that they might have struck and, he hoped, holed the boat's hull. But before a fifth round could be thrown out, the U-boat had disappeared, dived, and gone underwater. Ben immediately took the chaser up to as much speed as Chief Pack could give him. Seconds later, over the position where he judged the U-boat to have advanced, he loosed four depth charges, two flying out from the Y-Gun, two more rolling from the chaser's stern racks. Then, with the chaser barely running clear, the seas behind them heaved, erupting in giant plumes of sea water that could be clearly detected even through the fog. Rather than turn to port and risk colliding with Feller, Ben turned to starboard and away from the potential danger of a collision. In the moment he had fully reversed course, he stopped in order to give Crim a chance to listen for the U-boat's screw beats. The sound Crim reported, almost instantly, was the sound of silence.

Meanwhile, with Terry back in the pilot house, Terry had leaped to the R/T and gotten on the horn with Feller. Feller's C-Tube operator reported cracks that sounded to the operator like wood or metal being snapped or breaking up. Prior to Terry coming up on the R/T, consternation was rife on SC 71X, everyone having heard the sounds of action and assuming that SC 65X had either struck a mine or been torpedoed, the crew going half mad trying to prepare to recover survivors.

"*Shit!*" Ben exclaimed when he'd heard from Crim. "Crim isn't hearing what Feller is hearing. Our C-Tube's gone on the fritz!"

And in the next second, he was on the R/T with Feller, ordering him to close along the bearing that his operator had given him, searching for the U-boat or any debris he might be able to find.

"We can't know that we've sunk him," Ben said over the R/T, "but we hit him with gunfire, and our depth charges might have finished him off. And if he's merely damaged, he might be forced to surface once more where we can get at him. I'll do my best to keep clear of you and give you a free hand, but warn your lookouts to watch for us, and I'll do the same. We don't want a collision in this soup."

With Ben standing off to the south from the position where he expected Feller to be searching, Feller took SC 71X in to prosecute the hunt. Across the hour that followed, as the fog slowly dissipated and lifted as the sun burned through, Feller's C-Tube operator reported no sounds beyond what he had heard when he first reported the breaking-up noises. Finally, with the fog having lifted enough to permit them to make visual contact, Ben and Terry caught sight of SC 71X no more than one thousand yards to the north. Both vessels then resumed their hunt together, recrossing the area where Ben believed that he had made initial contact with the U-boat. There, finally, they ran through an oil slick that seemed to be spreading over an expanding area. But throughout the remaining hour that they spent plodding back and forth through the sheen, they found no debris and no firm indication of any kind to show that a U-boat had been sunk.

"This slick is large," Terry said, hopefully. "I think we got him, Ben."

"I'd like to think so too," Ben said, "but without some debris to prove it, I don't think we'll ever know. Those things carry canisters of oil for the sole purpose of deceiving us after attacks like ours, and that's all that this oil slick may be. The Navy will credit us for making an attack, and they'll appreciate that we've forced a U-boat down, but they'll never give us credit for a sinking, and you can be sure of that."

"I still think we got him," Terry said. "I saw that last round hit myself, and I'd be willing to bet money that we holed him and that the depth charges ruptured his hull."

"I'll keep that in mind," Ben said, surveying the seas with a grim expression on his face, "but the staff in London will remain skeptical, and that's about the best we can hope for."

When Ben broke off the search at around 1100 that morning, he knew absolutely from Crim that SC 65X's C-Tube was dysfunctional. Why it had failed when it was so desperately needed was something that none of them could explain. Back in Weymouth, the chaser would have to be hauled onto a trolley, pulled up onto the beach, and the C-Tube lowered so that *Mulgrew's* technicians could inspect the instrument and make whatever repairs were found necessary. In view of this unwelcome development, SC 65X had almost become a liability for the patrol rather than a contributing asset— but not quite. Once back in company with Feller and SC 71X, Ben acted so as to make the best of things, directing Feller to search ahead while Ben stood slightly back off his starboard quarter at no more than three hundred yards and followed like a trained dog, standing ready to lend both gunfire and additional depth charges to an attack should Feller's search turn up anything.

In the afternoon, finally, the two chasers closed Guernsey to within visual range. From there, after something like a six-hour search that didn't produce the slightest indication of a U-boat anywhere in the vicinity, they turned east, moved slowly into Search Area 029, and began to work back to the north toward the coast of England.

With regard to keeping their relative station on SC 71X, Ben and Terry, more confident about what they were doing, relied largely on that nautical proclivity called "seaman's eye." O'Neal, less confident about his sea-keeping and station-keeping abilities, chose to make frequent use of the stadimeter, which allowed him to measure his range to their sister ship down almost to the yard. As far as Ben was concerned, all three of their arrangements satisfied their needs, and with nothing in their continued operations being dependent on keeping an exact distance between the chasers, their mutual arrangements worked well enough to keep everyone happy and in a good hunting position. In the end, as all of them were sorry to realize, it didn't much matter because, throughout the night and the following day, nothing was heard over SC 71X's C-Tube and nothing turned up to inhibit the relative calm with which they prosecuted their search.

"Fairly quiet up there?" Pack asked, when Ben dropped onto the mess deck and sat down beside him for the taking of his evening meal.

"Dead silence," Ben said, wondering what Santos might be serving up.

"But we got one, nevertheless," Pack said, putting a best face on what he thought they'd accomplished. "And that's a sight more than most of the escorts out here have ever accomplished."

"Well," Ben said, "we might have got one, that's true. That we got some rounds into one and probably did her some damage with the depth charges . . . well, I think that's true too, but I don't think we'll ever be able to say we sank her, Chief. No direct evidence."

"I see your point," Pack said quietly, "but this crew is convinced, Captain, and their morale is shooting through the roof."

"So let's not dampen that?" Ben asked.

"Right Sir." Pack said. "The brass ashore can think what they like, but these lads ain't interested in the kinds of quibbles those folks will get into. They's convinced they sunk a U-boat, and while I think we have too, I intend to let 'em go on thinkin' what they're thinkin'."

"Good enough," Ben said, "but with this stipulation. They aren't to say a word about it when they go ashore. Whatever we did yesterday is considered TOP SECRET. Those folks ashore you were talking about don't want any word of it getting back to the Huns. If they have indeed lost a U-boat, our people want it to stay lost, at least as far as the Germans are concerned, so that they'll keep worrying about it in hopes that it will finally show up. I suppose the object is to keep them in the dark as much as possible, and that fact needs to be conveyed to the crew."

"I'll see to it," Pack said, as Santos placed a steaming serving of canned salmon and noodles before them.

Back in the pilot house following his evening meal, Ben found the seas picking up, a chop developing, and some rain falling. Once more, he brought the gun crew inside to avoid the spray that had started whipping back from the bow each time they plunged down from a crest into the trough. With equal speed, he made sure that the machine gunner on the flying bridge and the depth-charge crew had donned foul weather gear in preparation for what might be coming.

Ben's initial worry was that a gale of considerable force might develop, but one did not. Instead, for the following twelve hours, the chasers endured a blow that left them rolling and pitching to the point of discomfort.

"Standard Channel weather, do you think?" Terry asked when he came up to stand his watch.

"From what I've been told," Ben said, "I think you've hit it spot on."

"I gather that Lettice and her mother have traveled to New York and back a time or two," Terry said, "but according to what she told me, three or four of her trips back and forth between Dover and Calais were far worse with everyone on the packet boat becoming seasick."

"Tell her about our voyage to Bermuda, did you?"

"I did. And she told me that I was exaggerating," Terry said.

"And you said?"

"I told her that she would have to learn to trust me if she expected to get anywhere in life."

"And that produced?"

"Laughter," Terry said, "peals and peals of laughter."

"I believe, my friend, that you have gotten hold of a live wire."

"Oh, you don't know the half of it," Terry said. "On the way home from the pictures the other night—she took me there again, in the evening, for coffee with her mother—she told me that she thought I might adjust rather well to things *as soon as she got me organized*. Now, how's that for showing your hand?"

Ben couldn't help but laugh. "I suspect that much depends upon what she might mean by *things* and *organized*," he said.

"And whether or not I'm soon to find out," Terry said.

"I'm told," Ben said, "that young women of virtuous mien and perspicacious training can be subtle beyond a man's knowing."

"That's very philosophical of you," Terry smiled. "I take it you're suggesting that I go armed?"

"That would be my advice."

"And your beautiful vanilla?"

"Nicola seems a more straightforward companion," Ben said. "She and Lettice seem to be thick as thieves, but one imagines that opposites make close friends."

"If not partners in crime?"

"Well," Ben said, "there's that too. We'd best be mindful."

"Yes, we'd best," Terry said. "I can't help finding a touch of discomfort in the word *organized*."

On Wednesday afternoon—the day before they were to go in—cruising northwest of the island of St. Anne, Feller's lookouts spotted a mine whereupon both chasers immediately hove to in order to examine it through their binoculars.

"I hate to sound stupid," Terry said, looking at the mine through the upraised windscreen in front of him, "but what the hell is it? As far as I can tell, it doesn't resemble those German mines that we sank, and it doesn't seem to be as big as the British mine we blew up."

"Be it Rooshun?" O'Neal said, remaining in front of the helmsman where he'd been standing his watch when the mine was sighted.

"I wonder," Ben said, "if it could be Austrian? Seems unlikely that an Austrian U-boat would make the trip up here, but I suppose it might for some unfathomed reason. But then, too, one or another German U-boat might be putting out Austrian mines."

The mine presented a mystery that none of them could solve. Aside from the fact that it was dangerous and a hazard, they had no idea how to interpret its presence, where it came from, or what country might ultimately be responsible for its manufacture. With a pencil and a sheet of paper, Ben drew as good a reproduction of the mine's appearance as he could, consulting both Terry and O'Neal about points of detail. Then, with the drawing tucked away to go in with his after-action report, Ben turned Feller and his crew loose to destroy the threatening mine—something the machine gunner aboard SC 71X did with a single burst when the mine, rather than exploding, sank out of sight.

Throughout the remainder of that day and the following night, conforming to the pattern that Ben had established for the two chasers in the moment that he knew that his C-Tube could no longer function, the two boats cruised, stopped, listened, and moved on, moving north at a slow pace, meandering through two southern search areas as they headed north in the direction of Weymouth and an exchange of duty with Group AA2. Ben, still wrapped in his duffle and with his scarf tied around his watch cap and over his ears, continued to remain in the pilot house, sleeping in his chair. At 0400 on Thursday morning he rose, went down for coffee and an early breakfast, and then went back up to relieve O'Neal and stand the watch which would return them to port.

To Ben and Terry's surprise, and to the shock of the remainder of the crew, they found their normal nesting spot beside the *Mulgrew* already filled when they returned. Subchaser Groups AA3 and AA4, six additional chasers, had come up from the Azores by way of Gibraltar one day before SC 65X and SC 71X returned from sea.

"Will this mean more days off between patrols?" Terry asked.

"I doubt it," Ben said. "What it will mean, I think, is that we'll be putting double the number of patrols out and covering a much wider search area."

Indeed, when they finally tied up outboard alongside SC 56X near the head of the pier, a nesting position from which they could easily extract themselves when it came time to beach in order to repair the C-Tube, they learned the truth of Ben's assumption when they reported themselves in to Commander Radford and handed in their after-action reports.

"By the end of May," Radford said, seated behind his desk, "I expect to have an additional twelve chasers in here, bringing our numbers up to twenty-four, and with that number of vessels, we should be able to throw out a bit of a chaser barrage of our own, something that should give the Hun fits and, one hopes, drive him into bouts of apoplexy. Now, take a seat while I read through what you've brought me. And you may smoke if you like."

Feller, who did not smoke, declined. Ben produced his pipe, filled it, and lighted it with a match.

"Yes," Commander Radford said when he'd finished reading, "this backs up the limited details that your radio message contained. Splendid job, the both of you, Mr. Feller for finding and sinking that mine before you came in, and Mr. Snow for his timely and effective attack on the U-boat. Without evidence, direct evidence, it seems unlikely that Staff in London will credit you for having sunk the vessel, Mr. Snow, but between the two of us, I think you got it, and if the two of you will indulge me for a few moments, I believe I can reveal some intelligence that ought to interest you because it has certainly interested me."

For a moment, Radford paused, whetting their anticipation.

"The drawings of the mine that both of you have submitted with your reports accord well with what we know about a mine of Austrian design, a mine we have designated AUS27B, if that fact is of any interest. Now, that is one thing to keep in mind, and here is the next—and this is where it becomes particularly interesting in regard to Mr. Snow's action with the U-boat. Naval Intelligence at Admiral Sims' headquarters, probably as a result of some very astute work by his cipher clerks, seems to have knowledge that an Austrian submarine passed through the Straits of Gibraltar some five days before you attacked your U-boat in the Channel. Possibly, and I only mention this as a possibility, the Austrian boat, if she had headed north rather than out into the Atlantic, might have reached a position near where you attacked your U-boat by the time that attack occurred. Apparently, the Huns in Berlin had expected that boat to report to them by radio transmission three nights back. For the past two days, they have been moving heaven and hell to make contact with her and have, in each instance, failed. It seems to us, speaking for myself and the staff, that if the Austrian had gone out into the Atlantic, they would have had little reason to contact her whereas, if she had been transiting up the Channel with the hope of reaching Wilhelmshaven or Bremerhaven, she would have been right in the position where you found your target and attacked it."

Once again, Commander Radford paused, looked at both of their faces, and continued.

"Speaking only for myself," Radford said, "the Austrian mine suggests the presence somewhere in the vicinity of an Austrian U-boat, and the fact that you attacked one in the area and that the Germans seem to be having fits because it hasn't turned up suggests that you sunk it. I suspect that we will only know the truth after the war, if we ever get our hands on the Imperial Navy's archives, and possibly not even then, but I congratulate you, the both of you, on doing a splendid job under very difficult and harrowing conditions. Your actions have gone far to justify our presence here and the value of submarine chasers to both the Navy and the war effort, and on behalf of our country, I thank you both. Mr. Snow, before I dismiss you, let me just tell you that the *Mulgrew* will have SC 65X out of the water tomorrow with the intention of seeing to repairs on your C-Tube and having your chaser once more afloat by Saturday or Sunday. You and Mr. Keel need not remain aboard; your leading petty officers are perfectly capable of supervising the little that your crew will have to do. All right, gentlemen, well done, and you are dismissed."

To Ben's surprise, before he could even go to the bathhouse to bathe, shave, or change, he found himself summoned to the head of the pier, a note from the gate guard acquainting him with the fact that an unidentified civilian happened to be waiting to see him. Worried that the message might have come from Nicola and that she might be in some kind of difficulty, Ben did not bother to change; instead, still wearing his duffle, sea boots, and watch cap, he made a beeline for the gate only to discover that the person who had caught him in the throes of lingering fatigue after a four-day patrol turned out to be none other than Reverend Smythe, the Vicar. Impatiently pacing back and forth in front of the gate house, he was obviously miffed about having been kept waiting while not being allowed into the base. From the moment that Ben had seen the man, he'd sensed the reason for his coming. It angered him not a little, and he set his jaw as if ready to grind steel with his teeth. But before passing through the gate, Ben resolved to change his demeanor and let the man speak his piece.

"Good morning, Vicar," Ben said, showing the man a good-natured smiling face as he passed through the gate to greet him. "You wished to see me?"

The Vicar, visibly shocked by Ben's appearance, failed to hide his disdain for what he happened to be wearing. He drew his lips tightly together, exhibiting a degree of revulsion indicating to Ben that the man would have expected better from an officer of the Royal Navy. When he finally brought himself to speak, he said, "Yes, young man, if you will walk with me for a moment."

"All right," Ben said, "lead on."

Turning on his heel, the Vicar began to walk with determined steps along the breakwater as Ben fell in beside him.

"I am aware," the Vicar said stiffly, "that as an American you may not be aware of the customs and traditions that govern our lives here in England, so I have come this morning to see if I can't help you adjust to them by putting you straight about one or two things."

"Oh, thank you," Ben said, doing his best to muffle the irony with which he spoke.

"Regarding Miss Dewar-Strang," the Vicar began, "I think you may be about to put a foot wrong, thereby endangering her reputation, your reputation, and indeed, young Sir, the reputation of the entire United States naval establishment in Weymouth." And from there, without the least fellow-feeling that Ben could detect, the Vicar launched into a lecture "informing" Ben, as he so generously put it, that Miss Dewar-Strang had been very much in love with and engaged to Lieutenant Fredrick Littlejohn before that officer had been killed; that her bereavement and eternal mourning sustained her soul; that the blessed memory of her dearly departed fiancé depended upon the lasting nature of the faith they had placed in one another; and that Miss Dewar-Strang's reputation and the protection of her livelihood depended upon the spotless purity of the memory she'd kept so carefully preserved through the long years in which she, Lieutenant Littlejohn's family, and the Smythes continued to lament his passing. "You will therefore, I'm sure young man, wish to leave Miss Dewar-Strang to her thoughts and in a state of graceful, peaceful repose," the Vicar concluded firmly. "It simply won't do, young man, to disturb what the Almighty in his wisdom has already established."

"If I may speak a word, Sir?" Ben said pleasantly, stopping suddenly and standing in place.

Stopping abruptly, the Vicar turned and faced him. "As you wish," he said, showing Ben a suddenly benevolent and condescending expression in confirmation of his sense that he had done his duty and was about to be rewarded for it by hearing Ben intone his compliance.

For a moment, Ben continued to look at the Vicar with a level gaze, and then, quite suddenly, his eyes bored straight through the man.

"Vicar," Ben said firmly, "the presumption you have shown in attempting to deliver this sermon is almost enough to force a confirmed Anglican to covert to Roman Catholicism. It will not do, Sir, to attempt diminutives when speaking to an educated person on your own social level, and with regard to my life and Miss Dewar-Strang's, it will not do for you to meddle, particularly when you appear to be so grossly ignorant of the actual facts involved. Young men and young women, Sir, are perfectly capable of arranging their lives for themselves. So let there be an end to the matter, now and for the future. Good day to you, Sir." And with that, Ben turned on his heel and left the Vicar standing in the wind.

Later, in the bathhouse, as Ben shaved and Terry came in to shower, Terry saw him at once and asked, "Where'd you disappear to this morning? Missed you over coffee. Thought you'd come up here earlier."

"I had a louse that I had to crush," Ben said.

"A real one?" Terry asked with shock.

"No," Ben laughed. "Metaphorical. The Vicar thought it his duty to warn me off Nicola. I sent him packing with the louse in his ear."

"Lettice has absolutely no use for him," Terry said. "She seems to think he's an officious bastard, and from what she said about him after dinner at the Fitzhughs, I gather that she's told him where to get off more than once. She says he's so imperious that his congregation has shrunk to the size of a small Sunday school class."

"I wonder how it is that the Colonel and Lady Felicia tolerate him?" Ben said.

"From what Lettice said, I think the wife is distantly related, through marriage, to Lady Felicia's sister," Terry observed. "I gather that the 'toleration' doesn't carry beyond a dinner or two at distant intervals."

"Figures," Ben said. "Sour doesn't go down well at anyone's table."

"Heading for town, are you?" Terry put in, as he entered a stall and turned on the shower tap.

"No," Ben said. "I have to send Nicola a note, about tomorrow, but after I do that, I intend to crash. The last four days have pretty much done for me. I need some sleep."

Ben got off his note to Nicola, a simple one: "*I've returned. Saturday, 10:00 am?*" and deposited it in the mail in time to be sure that it would reach her in the afternoon post. But crash, he did not because in contravention of his expectations, dockyard workers showed up, forcing Ben and Terry to clear the crew from the chaser so that it could be run over to the trolley and hauled up the rails onto the beach. By noon, with the chaser elevated and the C-Tube lowered, the *Mulgrew*'s ratings who tended to the connections and mechanics of the offending tube had found that electrical connections inside the tube had parted, made the necessary repairs, and seen the C-Tube withdrawn back into the hull. So by 1600 that afternoon, with enough of a crew still available to help, Ben and Terry found the chaser back in the water, where they could move her alongside the nest and tie her up outboard. It was then that Horn and Speck rushed aboard.

"Come on," Horn said, his eyes bright, his enthusiasm igniting the atmosphere with a burst of energy, "Speck and I are buying! We want to hear chapter and verse about this sub you guys sunk."

"That is an issue which remains very much in doubt," Ben said straightforwardly, "and to be perfectly honest, I'm bushed. I need some sleep."

"I'm afraid that I have a date," Terry said. "The lovely Lettice has already promised to come and collect me, in less than an hour."

"Is that one of those spinsters the two of you coughed up when you didn't go to Dorchester with us?" Speck wanted to know.

"Exactly," said Terry. "Long in the lip, broad in the waist, flat in the chest. You know the type. Drives a tractor for recreating, and goes everywhere with a pack of hunting hounds."

"With a Pinocchio report like that, we probably ought to stick around, take a look at her, and bathe in her aura," Speck said.

"Can't," Horn said. "Pubs are open, and we're taking Ben to supper. Two pints, a pub supper, a full report on the sub, and we'll let you go," Horn said, looking at Ben. "A couple of pints will do for you nicely, put you right to sleep when you get back, and I promise we won't keep you past 1900."

"All right," Ben said. "But I'll hold you to it, the hour I mean, and you won't have to spring for my dinner; I'll cover that myself, so lead on MacDuff."

Leaving Terry to wait for Lettice, they strolled up the pier, passed through the gate, and walked out into Weymouth, finding a cozy snug inside a pub called The Burning Bush. With pints of bitter sitting on mats in front of them, they put in their orders for lamb stew and waited patiently for their meal to be delivered while, in quiet tones so as not to be overheard, Ben once more narrated the details of SC 65X encounter with the submarine.

"And Radford really thinks it was Austrian?" Horn said *sotto voce*.

"Apparently so," Ben said, taking a sip of his beer.

"What the hell would an Austrian sub be doing up here?" Speck said, also lowering his voice. "I thought those things confined themselves to the Med or were bottled up in the Adriatic by the Otranto Barrage."

"Sorry," Ben said, "but I don't have a clue. In the first place, the fog was so thick out there that I never saw anything that could clearly identify that boat as Austrian or German, and the assumption that it was Austrian is merely that—an assumption drawn vaguely from cipher intelligence. And, of course, there's the fact that Feller spotted that Austrian mine as well. But some mysteries are never solved, and this may well be one of them. Personally, I'm done with it. We may have sunk the thing, but the chances appear to be equally good that we didn't, and I don't know if we'll ever learn the truth."

They talked on then, Horn going over the details that governed his and Speck's extra time in port while they removed and overhauled their chaser's auxiliary engine.

"No replacement for that beggar," Horn said, "but *Mulgrew* supplied every part we needed, and we did the job ourselves within two days. Then, while you remained out, we repainted our hull because some of it had already started to peel. If you ask me, that trip down to Bermuda didn't do us any favors. The wonder to me is that it didn't strip the paint off every vessel in the Division."

"I intend to set my crew to the task while we're in," Ben said.

The lamb stew when it arrived put a smile on their faces, and afterward, Ben downed one more pint while the three of them talked; then, glancing at his watch, he looked up and said, "That's it. It's 1900. Sorry to leave you guys, but I'm dead beat, and I've got to have some sleep. I've got big things on for tomorrow, or so, let me say, I hope."

"Ha," Speck laughed. "That means you've got one of those doyennes of your own stashed somewhere out there. Flapping ears, nose like a puffin, bifocals?"

"Oh, you cagey rascal," Ben laughed, "you've already seen her, haven't you?"

Half an hour later, when Ben returned to the chaser, he found a small vellum envelope that had been placed by the mail orderly on the surface of his and Terry's fold-down table.

"*I'll be waiting,*" the note said, and it was signed "*Nicola.*"

11

When Ben went to collect Nicola the following morning, he could sense the first hints that spring might be in the air. The chill seemed to have diminished, if only slightly, and the skies remained clear, and here and there, in a front garden on his way to 27 Dorchester Road, he thought he saw daffodils beginning to appear. Nicola, when she came down, still wore the same Tartan tam and the same fitted black coat which he had seen before, but her face seemed to carry a bloom that Ben had not previously seen, and when she reached up and gave him an unexpected peck on the cheek, he thought he felt a bloom of his own coming on.

"Welcome back," she said, as she took his arm. "I'm rather delighted to see you home safe, if I may use the word *home* to describe Weymouth for you. And how was your cruise?"

"Quiet," Ben lied in order to preserve security. "Not much doing in the Channel, I'm afraid."

"And let's the both of us hope that it remains so," Nicola said. "Shall we do The Bristol again, or would you like to try some place different?"

"Let's try the espressos at The Bristol," Ben said, "as long as they'll give us scones to go with them."

"Oh yes," Nicola said with pleasure. And then, after a second or two of silence as Ben enjoyed the pressure of her hand around his arm, "I've had a visit, I must tell you."

"Oh?" Ben said.

"Yes," Nicola said, "two days ago. Mrs. Smythe took it upon herself to drop by . . . to enlighten me about my responsibilities, while I am still thought to be in mourning and pining for he whom she apparently believes to have been the sainted Freddy."

"You jest," Ben laughed.

"Alas, no." Nicola said. "I informed her that I was very sorry that Freddy had been killed, and then I also informed her that Freddy and I had never been more than friends and never entered into an arrangement of any kind, and then, I quite bluntly told her that she would do well to mind her own business and sent her packing."

"Good for you," Ben said. "I dealt with the Vicar pretty much in the same way yesterday morning, not more than an hour after we'd returned from sea and while I was still in my seagoing togs."

"Oh, the gall of the man!" Nicola said, her eyes blazing fire.

"Not to worry," Ben said. "Henceforth, I doubt that the Vicar and his wife will bother us again."

"And I will greet that development with the utmost pleasure," Nicola said, her voice sounding less incensed. After a moment's hesitation, she squeezed his arm more closely and said, "I found, Ben, while you were at sea, that I didn't very much like having you away."

"Could that mean that we are now 'walking out together'?" Ben asked with a smile.

"Yes, it could," Nicola said, "if you will have it so?"

"I will have it so," Ben said. "But I shouldn't like for you to feel that I'm rushing you in any way."

For eight or ten more steps, Nicola Dewar-Strang remained silent, but then, finally, she spoke. "I began my twenty-sixth year while you were away, Ben, and . . ."

"Well, Happy Birthday," Ben said at once. "We must celebrate!"

"Not yet, Love." Nicola stopped him before he could say more. "I want to finish what I'm trying to say before you try to launch a party."

"Sorry," Ben said, going quickly silent.

"As I prepared myself to say," Nicola sent on, "I turned twenty-six two days ago. I have not yet reached middle age, and I do not fear becoming a spinster or an old maid. I warn you that I am very much my own woman with a mind of my own as well, and if you do not find me stepping out with a young man, it is not entirely owing to the Vicar's interference, although there has certainly been that and one or two who have not had the courage you appear to have shown by putting him in his place. But leaving that aside, I'm afraid that with the war on and the young men in Weymouth having mostly gone to fight it, I simply haven't met a man who excited my interest. Not until I met you at Lady Felicia's. Tell me, am I making myself clear?"

"Abundantly," Ben said.

"Then what about you, my handsome American naval officer—do you have some young and lovely creature stashed way in the States upon whose toes I should very much like to tread?"

"No," Ben said, dropping all hints of humor. "Prior to coming over here, I was four years at sea, nearly without a break, and prior to that, I was four years at the Massachusetts Nautical School where the atmosphere was not only monastic but spartan, so I am wholly unattached and uncommitted."

"That's incorrect, Love. You are walking out with me, and while I doubt that the English phrase carries much the same meaning in the States as it does here, it means a great deal here and a great deal to me."

"And from now on," Ben said, "it will mean a great deal to me."

Stopping without warning right there on Dorchester Road, Nicola Dewar-Strang stood on her tiptoes and gave Ben a sudden passionate kiss, and then, after leaving him slightly breathless, she turned back to the street, gave him a slight tug where her hand clutched his arm, and once more started the two of them walking toward The Bristol with a glow showing on her face.

"Let me ask you," Ben said, "since I should like to understand the inner workings of your terms thoroughly, might this also suggest that my lad, Terence, and Miss Lettice are also walking out together?"

Instantly, Nicola let out a shriek. "Oh, good God, NO!" she laughed. "In the first place, I doubt that those two have taken three steps anywhere that Lettice hasn't driven them, and that's if they haven't run into something along the way. Lettice doesn't walk, Love, she proceeds, by motor. In the second place, although you probably do not know, Mrs. Mayfield has . . . well, let us call them 'elevated connections,' which means that Lettice is somewhat constricted when it comes to forming social relationships. It is true that she has had Terence to her home to meet her mother, but beyond what Mrs. Mayfield considers acceptable social outings, one imagines that what we normally mean by 'walking out together' exceeds their limit. Light luncheons, dancing parties, social suppers in private homes, the pictures, group picnics in good weather—those sorts of things will probably fall under the heading of what Mrs. Mayfield finds acceptable. Anything more significant probably means that she will invite Lettice to have something called 'a serious talk' with her."

"Terry will be too busy to be heartbroken," Ben said.

"That, I rather imagine, is the general idea," Nicola said. "On the other hand, beneath what appears to be her light and flighty demeanor, Lettice sometimes demonstrates a will of iron and an independent streak a mile wide, so please, Ben, do not cast a damp towel over Mr. Keel's head because we have no idea what might develop in the future, and this war, wretched as it is, seems to be changing things faster than any of us can measure. Only last week, for example, I saw a Royal Navy officer calling upon Isla's sister. The sister is a rare beauty by anyone's measure, but the apparent social distance between the two is something that would have prevented their so much as speaking even so recently as three years ago."

"Point taken," Ben said. "In the States, some girls are even beginning to bob their hair. Barriers of one sort or another are bound to come down. But enough of that. Do we celebrate by doubling our espressos, or will you wait until I can buy you the biggest dessert that is offered in whatever establishment it is in which we dine tonight?"

"Tell me," Nicola asked as the two of them sat in The Bristol enjoying their espressos and scones, "are you familiar with Thomas Hardy, the author?"

"I've read *The Mayor of Casterbridge*," Ben said.

"Did you enjoy it?"

"According to what I know of tragedy," Ben said slowly, "I thought the novel to be a more than fair tragedy in prose."

"Yes," Nicola said, "I would certainly call it that. Something almost bordering on the organization of *King Lear* or *Macbeth*, perhaps. Are you aware that Casterbridge is supposedly modeled on Dorchester?"

"In a vague way, yes," Ben said.

"Would you like to see it—Dorchester, I mean? We could take the omnibus. It's not far, and this looks like a lovely day for an outing."

An hour later, they boarded what appeared to be a ramshackle omnibus, seated themselves comfortably side by side not far behind the driver, and departed for Dorchester. Once beyond the confines of Weymouth, Ben began to see even more pronounced hints of the coming spring than he'd seen in the town. Here and there, brown fields were tinged with green, some of the trees seemed to be trying to bud, and along the edges of the road, the hedges were coming into leaf while only tiny patches of ice remained in the crevices of the rock walls.

"And this is Hardy's Wessex?" Ben asked.

"A part of it, I think," Nicola said. "I believe he lives at a place called Max Gate which is outside and somewhat to the east of Dorchester, but I have never seen him and cannot attest to that. Oh, and there's another place that you must see one day, off to the west on our way to Dorchester."

"Oh, and what might that be?" Ben asked, responding at once to the moment of suspense that Nicola had seen to provide him."

"Maiden Castle," Nicola said with genuine enthusiasm.

"I'm afraid I don't know what that is," Ben said.

"It is a massive hill fort," Nicola said, "and beautifully constructed with concentric rings of mounded fortifications. Bronze Age, if I'm not mistaken, supposedly dating back several thousand years. Celtic, and covering more than forty acres. We must go there in the spring when the weather is fine and the wind won't sweep us off the hill. Perhaps we can convince Lettice and Terence to go with us and provide transport, and then we could take a picnic."

"I shouldn't like to disturb your rapture," Ben laughed, "but do you think that the lovely Lettice could get us there and back without striking a vehicle or running us into a ditch?"

"I shall sit in front beside her and dispense restraint," Nicola laughed, "while you and Mr. Terence cower in the back seat."

"Oh, thanks very much," Ben said. "I certainly hope that you don't expect us to hold hands."

In Dorchester, they went to look at the Corn Exchange, the Shire Hall, the County Museum, and eventually, they wandered out to the Maumbury Rings, which had played such an important role in Hardy's novel, and strolled inside.

"Local fortress, like your Maiden Castle, do you think?" Ben asked.

"I think," Nicola laughed, "that one might place forty of these inside Maiden Castle, as you will notice at once when you finally see the place, but a local fortress? Possibly, or merely a Celtic cattle enclosure. I don't believe that anyone knows."

"But impressive nevertheless," Ben said. "I wonder how the Romans found it when they swept through here?"

"I should think that they were not greatly impressed," Nicola said. "They are thought to have swept through rather swiftly. Maiden Castle presented them with much more of a challenge. Their effort in reducing it was thought to have been grievous."

"Are Roman ruins often found in the neighborhood?" Ben asked.

"Oh yes," Nicola said. "Villas, baths, the occasional mosaic. This part of England became very Roman and stayed that way for much longer than some of the other places on the island."

Rather than return to Weymouth for their supper, Ben and Nicola shopped the windows along the high street for the remainder of their day but stopped for an early supper in an inviting establishment called The Cloisters. There, under the high beams of a restored church, they dined on salmon which had been baked in pastry shells and shared a bottle of hock. At Ben's urging, Nicola agreed to indulge in a slice of five-layer cake in a delayed celebration of her birthday, a treat which nearly caused them to miss the last omnibus departing for Weymouth. Having run to board it, when it finally pulled away from the curb and made its departure, it seemed to be blissfully empty of passengers save for one elderly man sitting by the driver with his West Highland Terrier perched in the seat beside him.

With the evening chill descending and without heat, the bus was cold, and in recognition of the fact, Ben raised his arm and put it around Nicola. She moved next to him and rested her head upon his shoulder.

"I hope you've liked our outing," Ben said.

"Oh, I have," she said, "but this is the best part of it. Dorchester is nice, and our supper was lovely, but I like having your arm around me and being next to you like this. You make me feel more secure, Ben. You make me think this war will end and that the way we are now, sitting beside one another like this, will become our norm."

"May I kiss you for saying that?" Ben whispered.

"Oh yes," she whispered back. "Oh yes, most certainly."

And there in the darkened omnibus, for the first time, Ben kissed Miss Nicola Dewar-Strang with all of the previously restrained feeling that he could convey.

On Sunday morning, awakened early by Chief Pack who happened to be standing the early morning watch as Officer of the Deck, In Port, Ben suddenly found that he was faced with a problem—the first of its kind that he had been called to deal with. On the beach on the previous evening, Scarlatti and Light had gotten into a fracas with two sailors from one of the recently arrived chasers in Group AA4. Words had been exchanged in one of the pubs, a few blows had been struck, and the publican had called the police. The police, to Ben's relief, had not arrested the men involved; instead, showing remarkable restraint from what Chief Pack recounted, the police had merely returned the men to their respective ships, turning them over to the gate guards at the entrance to the base. Commander Radford, however, upon receiving the news early on the following morning, had dispatched notes—one to Ben and one to the commander of the other chaser involved—directing the men's commanding officers in terms that could not be mistaken to "*Take Action and Put a Stop to this At Once.*"

"Pisser, isn't it?" Terry said, crawling out of his bunk and starting to get dressed. "Do you plan to hold a Captain's Mast?"

"I could," Ben said, "but I have a better idea. You hold the fort. I'm going over to see my opposite number in Group AA4. Scarlatti and Light are to remain on board, confined to the mess deck until my return."

Throwing on his uniform and his greatcoat, Ben left the ship, walked aft down the pier to the *Mulgrew*, crossed her brow, and went to find the captain of the chaser whose sailors had been in the fight with Scarlatti and Light. The business they had to conduct didn't take long, so by 0900 that Sunday morning, Ben was back aboard, standing on the fantail, with Scarlatti and Light braced up and standing at rigid attention in front of him. As the chief master at arms, Chief Pack had brought them up to punishment, with one or two men in the duty section standing at a distance with their ears wide open in order to hear what their captain meant to do.

"All right," Ben said, directing a hard gaze onto both of the men before him. "Let's hear it. What happened in that pub? You first, Scarlatti."

"Dem bums say weze ain't done nuttin' since we gets here but sit on our ass. Deys said weze two bits an couldna tell a U-boat from a fish."

"And you, Light?" Ben said, realizing that Scarlatti had already used up his fund of words.

"Dem was unkind to us," Light said. "Dey call us creeps an' no-accounts."

Ben's response to Light's use of the word "unkind"—one of the most quietly delivered understatements that he thought he'd ever heard—nearly caused him to break out in a roar of laughter, but by merely grinding his teeth, he managed to keep himself in check.

"I see," he said. "Well, if it's going to take a fight to settle this, Captain Emmett and I are going to see that you get one, one hour from now, in the sandpit in front of the Esplanade. Each of you is going to put on the gloves and go three one-minute rounds with the men you tried to fight last night. I'm going to referee the first match, and Captain Emmett is going to referee the second, and if each of you doesn't get in there and fight to your limit, Captain Emmett and I are going to put on the gloves and mix it up with the four of you, all in the interest of good sport, and I must tell you beforehand that both of us have boxed in college and will be looking forward to the exercise."

It was not what Scarlatti and Light had expected. Neither man was very large, and as it turned out neither man off the other chaser turned out to be much more than a lightweight either. Allowing none of the four to wear more than a sweatshirt against the chill, at 1000 hours precisely, Captains Snow and Emmett matched the first pair. And with Ben acting as referee for the first match, and with more than one hundred men collected from several crews having assembled to watch the match, Scarlatti heard the bell and went in swinging.

As a boxing demonstration, the matches not only left much to be desired; they produced enough ridiculous comedy to humiliate the participants owing to the laughter that emerged from the crowd. But at the same time, given the degree of tension that the two unprofessional amateur fighters felt, three one-minute rounds so exhausted each of them that they could barely keep on their feet by the time the last bell sounded.

And then, the various captains of all of the vessels tied up in the nest and alongside the *Mulgrew* gathered before the assembled crews and allowed Ben to speak for the lot of them.

"I will say this only once," Ben said, "so listen up! As far as we know, there isn't a trained boxer anywhere in the chaser division, so this has been a demonstration merely, and as you can see, these exhausted men have fought for only a total of three minutes. If there is another disturbance ashore, the opponents will meet again, here, for three three-minute rounds, and if an additional disturbance occurs, the rounds will be extended to four minutes. You wouldn't like that, any of you, and I doubt that there is a man among you who could last the fight, so remember, we are all in this together.

So, get along together, and let this be an end to any trouble between you. Dismissed!"

Later that morning and once back aboard, both Scarlatti and Light took to their bunks. Both of them, according to Chief Pack when he delivered a report, were so thoroughly exhausted that he wouldn't find himself surprised to see them sleep for the remainder of the day.

"You seem to have handled that rather adroitly," Terry said, as he and Ben once more sat in their stateroom waiting for the hour in which they would meet Lettice and Nicola for afternoon refreshment. "Did you really box in college?"

"Yes," Ben said, "during my first and second years. Lost the first regimental championship on points but won the match during my second year."

"Think you could last three four-minute rounds?" Terry asked.

"No," Ben said. "I went three three-minute rounds in both of those championships, and it took me days to recover. And I was in training at the time. I doubt that most of our men could go three two-minute matches, not serious ones, and still stand by the end of them. Doesn't look too difficult if you're a spectator, but if you are in the ring, throwing and trying to avoid punches or actually taking them, those minutes seem like hours, and they leave the body shaking from nothing more than the mere tension that one is under."

"So, did you have a boxing team or something with which to compete?"

"We boxed in physical education classes," Ben said. "Merchant crews carry some rough hands, so it seems to have been thought best to teach us to be able to handle ourselves in case one or another able seaman went off his head and tried to throw a punch at us somewhere aboard."

"I suspect that makes sense," Terry said. "Ever run into anything like that?"

"Once," Ben said, "two days before we got into Chicago. An ordinary seaman got drunk on duty and took it into his head to come at me with a Marlin spike. I had to deck him. The old man had him arrested once we got to Chicago, and I don't know what happened to him after that. Never saw him again."

"Good lord," Terry said. "The most I've ever had to contend with was some pushing with one of the bullies in the hall while I was in high school."

"I think all of us have to hope that that is the most any of us will ever have to confront," Ben said. "Certain kinds of men tend to get their juice up and throw a punch without thinking, never realizing how easy it is to kill another man if they hit him the wrong way and wind up doing prison time for what they didn't know. Our problem is that the same kind of loutish thinking also leads to wars, and then all hell breaks loose. Well, ready to go fetch the girls?"

"What an excellent idea," Terry said, his face lighting up. "Let's."

For once, having parked the Rolls in front of 27 Dorchester Road, Lettice appeared content to walk. So, when the two young women came down the stairs from Nicola's flat, chattering like magpies, they joined their partners and stepped out without complaint, making a lively foursome as they worked their way toward the High and a place called The Pheasant's Nest, where they could not only be served tea or coffee but also buy ice cream individually dished up with nuts and chocolate sauce in elevated cups.

"So what have you lads been doing this morning?" Lettice asked as the four of them seated themselves around a tiny marble-topped table and prepared to await their server. "Neither of you looks the worse for wear, so I don't suppose you've had to box a rudder or straighten your compass, or anything too arduous in the nautical category?"

"We have been attending a sporting competition," Terry said.

"Not cricket, certainly," Lettice snapped back. "This isn't the time of year for it, and I don't suppose you've been following a hunt either. Those usually take place in the fall, after the harvest."

"I'll let Ben tell you about it," Terry said quickly. "He organized it, and a compelling event it was too."

At Nicola's urging, Ben told.

"Most astute," Nicola said.

"And that, you believe, solves your problem?" Lettice asked.

"I can only hope so," Ben said. "Boys will be boys, but there's a limit on what Commander Radford or the remainder of the captains will tolerate, and fighting ashore exceeds that limit. Our good fortune is that none of our people have fallen into a scuffle with sailors from the Royal Navy. That could create sticky problems for everyone and leave a bitter aftertaste."

"We do not often see them in town," Lettice said. "The torpedo boats, as I've heard them called, seem to conduct raids abroad, and the ratings seem to be kept very busy servicing their motors. For a while, one of the shop girls with whom we do business walked out with a stoker, but her father did not like the man and put a stop to her going to the pictures with him."

"The 'walking outs' are kept under a tight rein?" Ben asked.

"Very," Lettice said. "The girls are testing the air for freedom, but their mummies and daddies are only quite slowly loosing such ties as bind them. As soon as we are permitted to vote, I dare say that things will alter rapidly, and we are going to get the vote, as I believe my companion will tell you."

"By the war's end, we will have the vote," Nicola said firmly. "I believe wagers could be placed on it. Owing to the shortage of manpower, women have been doing all sorts of work that men formerly did, and I would very much be surprised if our sisters in gender were content to return to their ovens in order to bake biscuits in future."

"And have the two of you been active in this movement?" Ben asked.

"Yes," they both said in unison.

"My father holds different views," Lettice said, "but my mother and I have formed an alliance against him, so over the course of time, he has found that a minority position is not conducive to his comfort."

"I must say at the outset," Terry said, his eyes twinkling, "that I, for one, have *always* been so progressive as to believe that the fair se . . . sisters in gender should have the vote."

"And most fortunate it is for you that you reached that wise conclusion," Lettice said, raising one well-sculptured eyebrow in Terry's direction, "otherwise you might have the misfortune to find yourself alone and walking everywhere."

"And you, Ben?" Nicola said, showing Ben a serious face.

"I will support the Nineteenth Amendment," Ben said, flatly and without qualification.

"And that will give women the right to vote in the United States?" Lettice asked, inquiring with intensity.

"It will," Ben said, "when it is ratified."

"And when do you think that might be?" Nicola asked.

"My guess," Ben said, "is that you will have the right to vote here before the women in the States, but I doubt that they'll be far behind you. Once the war is settled, I would guess that things will move forward on the issue, but I'm no expert. Nevertheless, I think their vote is coming, and soon."

After another hour spent over their ice cream and coffee, the four emerged from The Pheasant's Nest and went to see Jack Pickford in the film production of *Great Expectations*.

"Oh my," Lettice said, as they emerged from the cinema, "Louise Huff made such a beautiful Estella!"

"Difficult girl, Estella," Terry said.

"Why, because she maintains her independence?" Lettice snapped.

"I was thinking about the way Miss Haversham conditioned her," Terry said, reaching for a diplomatic solution to the issue he'd so dangerously raised. "Environmental determinism, that sort of thing."

"Ah," Lettice said, accepting his explanation, while behind them as they walked, Nicola and Ben looked at each other and smiled.

Supper that evening they took at The Maid's Cross, a modest establishment two blocks back from the Esplanade that didn't quite rise to the level of a restaurant but which didn't quite descend to the atmosphere of a tea room. A man from Cornwall and his wife who had once served in the Mayfield household owned and ran the eatery, and at Nicola's bidding, they prepared omelets and chips for the foursome, something they set off with cheese and fruit in a way that more than satisfied their desires.

"There are times," Lettice said pertly, "when one foregoes one's eggs for breakfast but looks forward to them for the evening's repast."

"This does go down well," Ben said.

"Yes," Nicola said. "After one glance at Miss Haversham's wedding cake in the film, I don't think I could have stood the bread pudding that someone mentioned earlier."

"And after our supper?" Terry asked.

"I am afraid," Lettice said, "that I must disappoint you, oh expectant one. Mummy chairs a committee tomorrow, for Belgian relief, and has asked me to help her organize her statistics."

"Alas," Nicola said, giving Ben's hand a squeeze beneath the table, "I, too, must be home before the coach becomes a pumpkin. I must teach on the morrow, and little darlings though they may be, they still require more than an ounce of preparation before I greet them. So when, may we ask, should we expect your return from your next seagoing adventure?"

"If all goes well," Ben said, quickly adding after a glance at Nicola, "and I can see no reason that it should not, I think we should make port by Thursday afternoon or evening. Might we arrange a date for supper on Friday evening?"

"We might," Nicola said.

"One finds a country pub just this side of Portesham which serves a splendid meal," Lettice said. "Nicola and I shall come and collect the two of you on Friday. Shall we say at 5 pm?"

Terry looked at Ben. "Let's," they both said.

The following morning, with Group AA1 taking the lead and with Group AA3, following astern, the chasers of Division AA once more went to sea, each group altering course outside the breakwater toward its own distant search area.

12

Between the remainder of March and the middle of August, through the warm and then the occasionally hot months, with Horn still leading them, Group AA1 patrolled north and south, east and west over broad swaths of the English Channel, extending all the way from Land's End to the seas south of the Isle of Wight. From the States, additional chasers arrived, twelve in the first group and then twelve more of them, and those Commander Radford based with their own tender at Plymouth. It was an arrangement which allowed him to keep eighteen of the vessels at sea at one time and cover multiple areas during any given patrol.

The schedule that Group AA1 followed normally sent them to sea on Sunday evening or early on Monday morning and returned them to port on Thursday evening or Friday morning after they had turned over their patrol areas to whatever Group or Groups had come out to relieve them. To the Group's disgust, between the middle of March and the end of June, they didn't turn up a mine, a trace of debris, or a single contact on the C-Tube that they could pursue and attack. It was, they later called it, their "long dry spell," and without having to take extreme measures of any kind, Ben did discover that he had to attend more to the crew's morale than he had ever had to do in the past. In plain point of fact, the men became bored with the duty, and that worried him. Men who'd become bored could also become inattentive, or careless, or downright despondent, and that, Ben knew, he couldn't have. In consequence, setting Terry to the task, he had his exec organize a cribbage tournament and followed that with a poker tournament. Later, having acquired them cheap ashore, he started the off-duty sections playing chess and found, to his disbelief, that the game consumed them. Then, to spice up the action, when the chasers were in, he convinced some of the other captains to give chess a try and set SC 65X to challenge some of them to playoff matches during their time in port. And as the weather warmed, there was also baseball when the vessels were in port.

"How in the hell, if I might ask," Terry said to Ben, "did you ever imagine that chess would become a consuming passion with them?"

"I didn't," Ben said. "I'm as bowled over by their response as you are. I turned to it out of sheer desperation. I thought it might attract only two or three, and now, it seems to have caught on with nearly the whole bunch. I even saw Light playing. I wouldn't have thought he had the intelligence to move a pawn, much less a knight or a bishop!"

When the chasers were in port, Ben and Terry made good use of their time keeping company with Nicola and Lettice—Lettice driving, Nicola sitting in the front seat to "restrain" her, and both Ben and Terry sitting in back, sometimes with their hearts in their mouths and doubt that they would survive the maneuvers that Lettice put the big Rolls through. They generally used their Friday evenings to venture into what Lettice took to calling "the Outback" in order to find and sample the culinary fare put up by a variety of country pubs. As a result, they variously dined on venison, pheasant, jugged hare, or some other game that came to them off ration and, in Ben and Terry's case, returned to Weymouth with a growing appreciation for English country ales. On Saturdays, they ventured farther, doing at least two picnics at Maiden Castle while studying the site, going twice into Dorchester for walks and meals, and finally making it all the way to Salisbury for an examination of the cathedral and what Nicola called the "lovely town center" as well as the shaded walks that flanked the River Avon.

Ben did not inquire or pry into the relationship that he saw to be developing between Terry and Lettice. Nicola had warned him about possible hurdles in their arrangements, and those he meant to leave to the two of them. Theirs was none of his business. With regard to his own relationship with Nicola, Ben knew that it had passed beyond affection, beyond merely walking out together, into something deeper and more lasting. Sensing that the war might be winding down, that the Germans were approaching the time when he expected them to be on their last legs, he found himself wondering what he was going to do about it. If the Hun surrendered, what might that mean? Would he be demobilized in Britain, in the States, immediately, or later? Would he be offered a chance to augment? Would the chasers be sold to France, or Italy, or Greece, or to the Royal Navy, and if so, what might that mean? Would they be given the chance to remain in England? Would they be required to go home? And how would they get there? Would they take their vessels back with them or be shipped home aboard a fast transport, or even a cattle boat? Ben didn't know, and for the time being, he didn't want to think about it; yet, he found that he had no choice.

Meanwhile, the war continued. During the second week in July, on a hot day in the Channel with the temperature rising and a merciless sun pounding them from above where he and Terry stood on the flying bridge in the midst of Terry's watch, Crim, bent over the C-Tube in the magazine, suddenly reported hearing screw beats. With that, Ben immediately sounded the gong for General Quarters.

The hunt that Group AA1 prosecuted that day lasted for eight hours. As soon as Ben reported his contact over the R/T, Horn acted with dispatch, reorienting the search to the northeast in the direction of a Channel area south of Portsmouth while setting the three chasers in a formation from which they could triangulate their target. For once, with all three of them gaining contact, hearing what they all believed to be a U-boat's screw beats, they were able to conduct the kind of search that the Navy had trained them to conduct—stopping their engines for three or four minutes to listen, triangulating their bearings in order to estimate the submarine's apparent position, and moving swiftly forward to advance their proximity to the underwater boat. Within three soundings, having raced ahead into a promising position, Horn went in to make the chasers' first attack. In quick succession he expended four depth charges, the seas erupting into high gray mountains of foam and spray. The other two chasers stood off in order to try to hold or regain contact once the attack had been made.

Twice during the afternoon and late into the evening, they believed that the U-boat had reversed course to shake them off. Once, for more than an hour, they believed that it had gone deep and gone silent to trick them into thinking that they'd sunk it by releasing first one and then a second canister of oil, the sheen spreading across the relatively calm surface of the channel in all directions. But when the U-boat went silent, Horn also had the chasers cut their engines, stop where they were, and wait. Finally, after an hour and seventeen minutes by Ben's watch, the boat began to move, ever so slowly, heading once more northeast, its screw turning just enough so that Crim could detect it. They knew that it was still intact, that they hadn't sunk it, and resumed their hunt. In the end, with most of their depth charges expended but without the sub ever broaching or coming to the surface, it managed to elude them. This left them without so much as a smidgen of satisfaction for having damaged it, prevented it from making headway, or doing any more than merely keeping it down where it could not rise and make an attack on Allied shipping.

Horn might have prosecuted the attack even farther up the Channel had his standing orders allowed him to do so. But in keeping with what Commander Radford had established as their set procedure, south of Portsmouth, in order not to interfere with Royal Navy operations, Horn turned over their search and pursuit to a Royal Navy destroyer and two trawlers, all three of them armed with listening devices and depth charges of their own. After reversing course, he left the three to continue the hunt as best they could.

"Well, *shit*," Terry said. "I don't know how else to put it. I thought we had him."

"So did I," Ben said, with a shake of his head to register his disgust, "so did I, but they're cagey, the bastards, and this one was more so than our first. And to be totally honest about it, they're stronger and more difficult to sink than we can imagine. I don't know how that thing stood up under the pounding we gave it, and how it got away from us is the biggest mystery of all."

"Hun, do you guess, rather than Austrian?" Terry said.

"That would be my guess," Ben said, "but who can say? There's no telling what might have come up the Channel. Let's hope the Royal Navy catches up with it somewhere before or around the Straits."

Hours later, they learned that the Royal Navy had caught up with a U-boat that night, depth charged it long into the early hours of the morning, and caused it to broach. The destroyer had taken it under fire with a four-inch gun, apparently sinking it, and debris had been discovered when the sun came up, allowing them to take credit for the sinking. Nevertheless, Commander Radford had received a BRAVO ZULU from the Royal Navy and Admiral Sims' staff in London commending the chasers for having detected and attacked the sub in the first place and, when they reached the eastern limit of their search zone, for having passed the hunt they'd been conducting on to the Royal Navy for its continued prosecution of the contact.

"Well, I suppose that's something," Terry said, standing by Ben and O'Neal who happened to be taking SC 65X back into port that morning.

"Yes," Ben said, "it's something. At least we didn't blot our copybook, as the Brits like to say. At least we can hold our heads up, but probably not very high."

Back alongside the *Mulgrew*, Farris and his depth-charge crew took on and struck down to the after magazine a fresh new supply of depth charges, while Terry completed the finishing touches on their after-action report before handing it over to Ben for any comments he might want to add or changes he might want to make. Meanwhile, Ben got off one of his brief notes to Nicola—"*Home again. Friday, 1600?*"—and dispatched it with the morning post, only to find when the afternoon mail arrived that no reply was included.

Terry had somehow alerted Lettice that the chaser was back in one day early, and Lettice had sent him word that she would collect him later in the afternoon for a Thursday evening trip to the pictures. When Terry went out to the head of the pier to meet her, he soon came rushing back to fetch Ben.

"You'd better come with me and hear what Lettice has to say," Terry said, a pained expression showing on his face. "Nicola's gone to Edinburgh. I gather that her father's had a sudden stroke and died."

Ben felt the weight of it at once. Not for Nicola's father whom he'd never met, but for Nicola. He imagined that she would be crushed by what had happened, longed to be able to comfort her, and felt helpless and miserable because he knew that there wasn't a thing he could do for her beyond send a telegram of condolence.

Outside the gate, at the head of the pier, bending over the open window of the Rolls, Ben heard the whole of it.

"Professor Dewar-Strang apparently died two days ago, in the morning, on the day after you went to sea," Lettice said, speaking for a change without the flighty tone of conversation that usually seemed to be her norm. "I gather that his housekeeper discovered him almost at once when she prepared his morning coffee and took it in to him. He appears to have been sitting in his chair and must have had a stroke and gone instantly. She contacted Nicola that afternoon, and because her school is closed for the summer, Nicola packed and went at once. I took her to the station, and she sent a wire to tell me she'd arrived safely. She asked me to tell you that she'd be away for at least a month. She'll have to see to the funeral, of course, meet with her father's solicitor, close his flat, and see to the disposition of whatever estate he's left. I don't envy her the work, but it is something that all of us will have to do one day, and I do not look forward to it."

"I'd like to be able to help," Ben said, feeling more helpless than ever, "but I'm caught here and have no choice."

"She knows that," Lettice said. "I spoke with her on the telephone this morning. How she managed to get a call through, I don't know, but she did, and she wanted me to tell you that she sends her love and that you are not to worry about her."

"Fat chance," Ben said.

"Don't," Lettice said flatly. "Nicola is strong woman, Ben. She went through this with her uncle, and now, much too soon, she has to go through it again with her father, but she will come through this with flying colors, I assure you. Your task, like the task of this scamp who attends you, is to look after yourself and see that you both get back here in one piece after your adventures."

And with that, she handed Ben a slip of paper showing Nicola's address as an indication of how to be in touch with her.

"I'll write tonight," Ben said, "and every day that we're in port."

"Do," Lettice said. "It will help, Ben, it really will."

As Terry finally got into the Rolls beside Lettice, and Lettice popped the clutch and bolted away from the pier, Ben wondered if a letter would really be of much comfort to Nicola—if comfort of any kind could actually relieve another person's emotional distress. He didn't know, but because it was the best—the only—attempt he could make, he returned to SC 65X, saw to the work that Pack, O'Neal, and Farris had underway, dropped down into his and Terry's quarters, and began writing Nicola the letter that he intended to send her that night. This time, before appending his signature, he wrote a single, final sentence and told her that he loved her, wondering whether that might mean to her what he hoped it would.

Two weeks later, out in the Channel north of Guernsey, SC 65X spotted and exploded two mines, both of them German—a clear indication to Ben that a U-boat had passed through the area. At the time, Ben happened to be commanding Group AA1. Horn, following their several months of joint operations together, had been summoned to London in what turned out to be a permanent transfer. The staff, wanting an experienced chaser captain to help advise them, had sent an order for one to Radford, and Radford had sent Horn, elevating Speck to command SC 56X and assigning a new ensign, Ensign Tip Chester, a fresh-faced kid from Hoboken, to act as his exec. And that was when Radford had Ben up to his office and told him that henceforth he would be commanding Group AA1, and that he, Commander Radford, had every confidence that Ben would achieve results.

Having three rather than only one chaser under his direct command did not present Ben with an unwarranted burden. His navigation had always been the best in the Group, and indeed, in the Division. About the only thing that changed was that he was now officially charged with triangulating the bearings on any contacts they detected and ordering both their halts to listen and their advances in pursuit, and judging when to order those, he found, in no way taxed his abilities.

Nicola remained away, seeing to the closing of her father's affairs, and in her absence, Ben wrote to her daily, even when he had a moment at sea, and sent her a running account of what he could tell her about what he was doing without breaking the restrictions imposed on him by security. Something he did not tell her about occurred on August 5, 1918, thirty miles south of Weymouth, when Feller's sound operator suddenly gained contact and Ben quickly reoriented AA1 for a search which headed them southeast toward the coast of France. Within minutes, Crim picked up the screw beats, and finally, Speck's operator also acquired their sound through his C-Tube. Then, very swiftly, with sound bearings from three chasers, Ben triangulated a fix on the contact, discovered it to be only about four hundred yards distant, and went immediately over to the attack, racing forward with all the power that Pack in the engine room could give him—running smooth, running hard, the chaser's bow slicing through the water like the blade of a hunting knife. "Depth Charge Release!" he shouted, and Farris fired the Y-Gun, while back aft Paxton and Scarlatti rolled two of the big ash cans from their racks and dropped them over the stern. As SC 65X scooted forward with all the power in her plant, the seas astern lifted toward the skies, hurling clouds of water in all directions.

On the way out from the blast, putting the chaser into a tight turn to starboard so that he could round the area and fall back in with the two chasers supporting him, Ben called over the R/T for bearings on the target from his two fellows. It was then that he learned from Speck that Speck's sound operator had made a blunder:

he'd left his C-Tube extended during the attack, the horrendous explosion caused by Ben's depth charges temporarily deafening the man. His C-Tube, when the second operator got onto it, had gone silent owing to damage caused by the strength of the four depth-charge explosions.

Very swiftly, Ben brought all three chasers to a halt so that Crim as well as Feller's operators could listen and try to regain contact. When they did, quickly marking the point where their bearings on the U-boat's propeller sound intersected, Ben ordered Speck to attack, vectoring him to the point of intersection, while providing ranges until Ben finally ordered him to launch his depth charges.

The point of the attack as indicated by where the two bearings crossed, as Ben well knew, could be distant from the actual position of the U-boat by more than one or two or even three hundred yards. While he and Feller continued to hold the contact, he had no guarantee that Speck could drop his charges anywhere within killing distance of the submarine—and that submarine was doing everything it could to slip their grasp.

Twice more within a span of forty minutes, Ben ordered Speck in for an attack along a bearing that Ben sent over to him via the R/T; twice more, nothing, not even a patch of oil, showed up to indicate that Speck's attack had been successful. Then, as quickly as the contact had showed up, it disappeared entirely. Ben could only assume that it had finally eluded them, the U-boat's skipper having thrown them a tactic by which to make his escape that they couldn't even begin to fathom.

In the event that the U-boat's captain had taken his boat deep in order to sit on the bottom and thereby escape detection, Ben kept Group AA1 searching the same area for six more hours without results.

"If he were there," Terry said, "I think he would have tried to move by now."

"Yes," Ben said.

"You think he's gotten away then?"

"I do," Ben said. "How, I can't say, but I think he may have reversed course while Speck was racing in to make that last attack and run right back beneath us, heading for the Atlantic."

"What's needed," Terry mused, "is some kind of device that would throw out a sound that could strike the U-boat and bounce straight back here to us—something active, let us call it, rather than passive."

"Yes," Ben said, "I do hope you'll let me know as soon as you invent something along that line. Radford, I'm sure, would greet it with a degree of euphoria heretofore unseen, and I wouldn't mind having something like that myself."

"I wonder if we'll ever see anything like that?" Terry laughed.

"Who knows?" Ben said, laughing a little himself. "Not more than five or six years ago, airplanes were largely given over to circus stunts, but look where we are now. Some of those birds we've got flying up there can get up to 20,000 feet and hit speeds over one hundred miles per hour, and they've even got machine guns that can fire through their props without shattering them to pieces!"

"The modern world moves at a rapid pace," Terry observed.

"Yes," Ben said, "almost too rapid to contemplate."

What did not move at a rapid pace appeared to be the closure of Professor Dewar-Strang's estate. Originally, Nicola had thought she would be away for three to four weeks, but by the time she finally returned to Weymouth, those weeks had stretched into six and nearly seven by Ben's count—time enough for Ben and his Group to sortie for seven complete patrols which turned up in total only the one U-boat contact they'd unsuccessfully prosecuted as well as two more Hun mines which they'd sunk on their fifth time out. Three chasers out of Plymouth calling themselves Group CC1 had managed to sight a U-boat on the surface south of Land's End, force it down, depth charge it, and keep it down for four hours until it escaped them. As far as Ben knew, those were the only encounters that the chasers had experienced while Nicola had been away, although he'd heard a rumor that another Plymouth chaser had sighted and fired on a U-boat the morning she returned. Ben felt most fortunate to learn that Group AA1 remained in port, having only returned to Weymouth the day before and having put both Speck's and Feller's vessels onto the ways in order to pull them from the water and scrape their bottoms.

Upon receiving a note from Nicola telling him that she had returned and wished to see him, Ben left Terry to oversee to the day's work and set off immediately to 27 Dorchester Road in order to sound Nicola's door pull. When she came down, Ben was mildly surprised to see that she had left both her tam and her coat in her flat, and when she opened the door and looked at him for the first time in weeks, three seconds didn't pass before she was in his arms.

"Come up," she said, after holding him close for more than a minute.

Ben hesitated. "Nicola," he said, "what about the neighbors? There could be talk."

"To be honest, Love," she said, turning back to him and showing him a slight smile, "I don't really care. In a manner of speaking, I think I'm through with all of that. Like I told you at some point in the past, I'm my own woman, and more so now than ever before."

Closing the door behind him, Ben followed her upstairs, walked into her flat, and found it beautifully but inexpensively appointed, one large room furnished with a comfortable sofa, upon which they immediately seated themselves, and two wing-backed chairs, with a tiny kitchen off to one side and what Ben imagined to be a single small bedroom beyond a walled door on the north side of the room opposite the stairs. Behind the wing-backed chairs, two immense bookcases held Nicola's books, and between the bedroom and the little kitchen, a small table and four straight-backed chairs seemed to serve a multiple purpose—for dining and as Nicola's desk.

"This is lovely," Ben said, his enthusiasm for the room genuine.

"Thank you," she said. "Nothing elegant, I'm afraid, but it's cozy, and I make do here. I hope I'll be able to keep it."

"How so?" Ben asked, the tenor of her remark having instantly caught his attention.

"Lady Felicia and I have decided to close my school," Nicola said, steeling herself not to make a display of emotion. "I've had letters from six of my parents while I've been away," she went on. "Regretfully, they can no longer afford to pay the tuition we need from them in order to keep the school going. Lady Felicia is as generous to me as she has always been, but the agricultural economy upon which the well-being of Trincombe Abbey depends is suffering the same downturn that the rest of the economy is experiencing, so she is unable to increase my stipend. For a while, I had hoped that the settlement of my father's estate might leave me enough to tide things over, but it did not. I find that if I live frugally, I will have enough to pay my rent, buy my groceries, and keep up a less than modest appearance, but nothing more, and I will not have nearly enough to keep my school open. I've written to the parents to let them know that I'm closing, and tomorrow, I intend to begin searching for employment. Lady Felicia seems to have had a word with your Commander Radford, and I have an interview which might offer me a clerical place in your shore establishment. Office management, I believe, in the building which governs your overhauls and upkeep."

"That," Ben said, trying to sound cheerful, "sounds like uplifting news."

"It is," Nicola said, "with the added blessing that it seems to have developed swiftly."

"You've been hit hard," Ben said, "and all at once, and I am sorry for it, Nicola. I wish things had turned out otherwise."

"I shouldn't like to sound dramatic," she said quickly, "but if I've learned anything while I've been away, I think I've learned that one must endure what one must endure and continue to hold one's head up."

"Yes," Ben said, and then, for the space of a moment or two, he hesitated before once more speaking. "I want to say something," he said finally, "something that I intended to say weeks ago and never did because when I finally came in, I found you gone to Edinburgh. In the first place, as I hope I managed to convey on paper, I have missed you hugely. In the second place, I love you, Nicola. I may have seemed to you a little slow off the mark, but your absence has felt crushing to me. I don't want to be without you, Nicola, so I'm asking you to be my wife."

Nicola's eyes blazed and she stood. "I will not have charity, Ben! I will not have it!"

"I am not offering you charity," Ben said forcefully, also standing. "Not in the least. This war will end soon, and the thought of going back to the States without you, or even staying here without you, tears my soul. I love you; I want you to be my wife, Nicola. I want us to live together for the rest of our lives."

"You're sincere, aren't you?" she said, her anger beginning to dissolve and be replaced by wonder as though Ben's sudden profession had taken her by surprise.

"I've never been more so," Ben said in the most matter of fact tone that he believed he had ever used.

"When?" Nicola said.

"Right now," Ben said, "tomorrow, or whenever you'd like. I've heard that the registry office is very convenient for performing the marriage ceremony. If it is a ring that you will need before you're convinced, I'm sure that we can go out and find one."

"How long will you wait before I give you an answer?" she said, a warm, teasing expression beginning to suffuse her face.

"Till doomsday, if necessary," Ben laughed.

"Then I accept," she said, throwing herself into his arms. "Let's do it now, Ben. Oh, I've so missed you, and I've never needed you more. Lettice told me you would propose, but I didn't believe her. I thought you might leave me when the war ends, and I don't know how I could have borne it."

"You would never have had to," Ben said, kissing her long and fervently. "Let's go and find the registry office."

"No need," Nicola said, giving her copper hair a sudden flip, her face shining, "I know exactly where it is and the fastest way to get there."

At 1500 that afternoon, having obtained a license from the appropriate clerk at the Weymouth Registry Office, and after hastily summoning Lettice and Terry to act as witnesses and stand up with them, Ben and Nicola exchanged vows before the officiant and were pronounced married. No one had dressed for the occasion, and the only ring produced turned out to have belonged to Nicola's mother—a small but solid gold wedding band which Ben had easily slipped over Nicola's finger.

Following the ceremony, with a late afternoon sun shining brightly, the quartet went to Lettice's Rolls where, this time, leaving Ben and Nicola to sit together in the back seat, Terry pronounced himself prepared to sit in front where he could "exercise restraints" upon Lettice as she drove them east out of the town.

"If I hear a single word bordering on what you seem to be referring to as *restraints* with regard to my motoring habits," Lettice said following Terry's announced intentions, "I believe that you will find the boot most uncomfortable when I force you to travel inside of it."

"I assure you, I was only speaking metaphorically," Terry protested. "I wouldn't dream of interfering with your freedoms in motoring. I would simply like to avoid the sorts of disasters that often accompanied the enthusiasms of the inimitable Mr. Toad."

"Watch it," Lettice snapped. "You are treading a very precarious path at the moment."

And with Ben and Nicola grinning in the rear seat, the Rolls bolted away from the curb, shot swiftly between a lorry and a beer wagon, and sent a small dust bin spinning before Lettice finally got control of it and aimed for the open road. Fortunately, Ben thought, they didn't have far to go.

The wedding supper, what passed for one, took place at The Smuggler's Chest, a country pub in the village of Osmington, not many miles distant from Weymouth. Their entrée for the evening consisted of a generous serving of roasted duck cooked up in a profusion of Morello cherries, which they polished off with a snifter of brandy and a small coffee. Afterward, with the sun still bright and only hinting that it might later set, they strolled along a country path which afforded them shade on one side and a distant view of the Osmington White Horse figure of King George III, which had been cut into limestone across the slope of the far-away hillside. The massive white display stood out brilliantly against the surrounding summer green.

"Are there many of those in the country?" Terry asked.

"A few," Nicola replied. "The Uffington White Horse in Oxfordshire is, I think, the oldest; it goes back to nearly 1000 BC according to the scholars who are supposed to know about such things. All others are more recent, although I believe one or two can be dated to the seventeenth century."

They walked on, the four of them, chatting and laughing for perhaps another hour, and then, once more braving the Rolls and Lettice's skills behind its wheel, they returned to Weymouth where Lettice and Terry deposited them on the walk in front of 27 Dorchester Road, said their goodbyes, and bolted away. Then, with the two of them feeling a trifle strange, Nicola unlocked her door, and they ascended into the flat and for what Nicola later whispered into Ben's ear turned out to be a night of perfect bliss.

Ben did not go into the ship the following morning for quarters. Instead, with Nicola snuggled next to him in bed after the few hours of sleep that they had allowed one another, they simply remained lying there, their warm bodies never breaking contact, giving themselves over to what Nicola continued to call "more bliss" and what Ben reported back to her to be "wonderful beyond anything I'd ever imagined." Ben knew, if anything pressing came up, Terry would either handle it without disturbing him or know where to find him.

On their second married morning, they were up early, Nicola serving Ben fried bread and an egg for breakfast before kissing him goodbye and sending him off to his chaser so that he could check on the condition of his ship and his crew, attend to whatever paperwork had come his way during his absence, and order whatever preparations had to be made before SC 65X departed for patrol the following Monday morning. There, in the midst of his quarters while reading the message file that Terry had brought him, Ben found himself summoned aboard the *Mulgrew* for an interview with Commander Radford.

"Good morning," Radford said, showing Ben a smile when he reported. "From the note you sent me, I gather that congratulations are in order. I met your young lady briefly on the first night I took supper at Trincombe Abbey, so I have no hesitation about congratulating you on your good fortune. A most lovely young woman, and both I and the Navy wish you the best of marriages."

"Thank you Sir, on my wife's behalf and on my own," Ben said, trying to sound appreciative without sounding stiff.

"And with that said," Commander Radford went on, "I have a brief story to tell you which I hope you may find amusing."

"Yes Sir," Ben said, feeling primed but wholly ignorant about what might follow.

"Yes," Radford said, his face breaking into a broad grin. "Well, Sir, at 0800 this morning, while I was still down in the wardroom having breakfast, the Reverend Smythe apparently barged onto the quarterdeck and demanded to see me."

And from that instant, Ben felt he knew what Commander Radford was about to tell him.

"At the time," Radford went on, "I had barely finished with breakfast and not yet had my coffee, but nevertheless, I returned to my stateroom and had him shown up, and there, the good Vicar strode straight in and began to deliver a diatribe about the scandalous and immoral behavior of American naval officers, my duty as their senior to "keep them in line" in order to raise them to the standards of the Royal Navy, and deliver his demand that I arrest you at once for breaking discipline by—and I am quoting his own words here—*living in sin while debauching a local woman of previously unquestionable virtue.*"

Ben suddenly felt his color rising and his face burning. "If you will pardon me, Commander," he blurted out, "that objectionable man has shown himself to be a perfectly officious bastard!"

Commander Radford broke out laughing. "You may not believe me, Mr. Snow, but that is exactly what I told him. And then I explained that if he were a chaplain in the United States Navy, I would have him before a court-martial for libel, and then I told him that you and the former Miss Dewar-Strang had been married for the past two days, and I rather think it struck him as though I had kicked him between the legs. And finally, showing the man as much of a smile as I could muster, I told him that if I ever saw him aboard the *Mulgrew* again, I would have him thrown in to irons with the greatest pleasure, a remark which virtually caused him to race for the pier."

"Thank you Sir," Ben said. "I am in your debt."

"Finding married life agreeable, are you?" Radford said.

"Very, Sir," Ben replied.

"I sincerely wish you and your lady every happiness," Commander Radford said. "Sorry to have taken you from your duties to hear this story, but I thought it might be one which you and your wife will come to appreciate in your years ahead. You depart on Monday morning, I think?"

"Yes Sir," Ben said.

"Then good hunting, Mr. Snow."

"Thank you, Sir," Ben said, coming back to attention, doing an about face, and leaving the commander's quarters. And by the time he returned to his stateroom, he found that he couldn't stop himself from laughing.

Later that evening, when Ben recounted the story for her, Nicola did not laugh. But then, after a moment or two of shocked anger, she did begin to laugh, expressing her belief that she would have paid money to see the look on the Vicar's face when Radford revealed their marriage and then threw the meddling puritan off the *Mulgrew*.

13

By late September, the weather in the Channel had already started to become unpleasant. Gray clouds often blotted out the sun, the chop had picked up, and the summer calms had virtually disappeared, leaving SC 65X to roll and pitch in ways that sometimes brought back distant memories of their initial voyage down to Bermuda. The last of the summer heat had disappeared, and while the full chill of a late fall had not yet rolled over them, Ben, Terry, O'Neal, and the remainder of the crew stood their watches wearing foul weather gear against the spray which the winds and the ship's pitching bow frequently threw back to them. In the mornings, with the arrival of the dawn, fogs rose to disturb and obstruct their vision, forcing the watch officers in the pilot house to continuously caution the lookouts to remain vigilant so as to avoid surprises.

"It wouldn't do to run onto a mine in this soup," Terry said, justifying to Ben the fact that he had reduced the chaser's speed to 5 knots following a brief listening period.

"No," Ben said, "it wouldn't do at all, and if you ask me, these are just the conditions that a mine laying U-boat's skipper would be looking for in which to drop off his eggs."

They were cruising north of Guernsey at the time, running northeast so as to thread the needle between the island of St. Anne and the western tip of the Cherbourg peninsula. They were running slow, with SC 56X two thousand yards to port while Feller's SC 71X was stationed two thousand yards to starboard, and for the two days that they'd been out, no one on the C-Tubes had heard so much as a single screw beat.

The dawn—what little they detected of it through the fog and the low cloud—seemed to show dim that morning, diffusing what little light they could pick up, imbuing the moment with the same suspended quality that a dwindling dusk might have carried. For ten minutes, Ben lost contact with both Feller and Speck, their vessels hidden by the mist, their tracks, he hoped, continuing to parallel his own; then, finally, with the light only slightly improved, he once more caught sight of Feller off to the east. Scanning slowly back to port to look for Speck, Ben froze. There, no more than five or six hundred yards out in front of them, was a U-boat, its gun crew turning from the submarine's stern where they had been trailing something and running to man their after deck gun.

"U-boat, one point off the port bow!" Ben roared. "Open fire, all batteries!"

As SC 65X's machine gun started to chatter, the ship's main battery barked out a round. Owing to the chop, it exploded ten yards short of its target. As Paxton took the sub's gun crew under fire, Ben could see the machine gun Paxton manned on the flying bridge raising sparks up the U-boat's after deck. The impact of Paxton's rounds saw men being blown back from their deck gun.

But if Paxton had been fast in getting onto his target, he hadn't been quite fast enough to prevent the German gun crew from loosing at least one round. With deadly accuracy, it slammed into the chaser's wherry while slicing a crease through the overhead to the engine room and driving a hail of splinters in all directions. Topside, one of those splinters drove itself into Paxton's thigh, Pack received cuts across his arms from three of them, even as both Garcia and the oiler, Willis, fell to the deck with splinters driven down into their shoulders. Back aft, a sizable chuck from one of the wherry's oars struck Light with enough force to drive him against the ship's depth-charge rack and break two of his ribs, while Scarlatti, knocked from his feet by yet more debris, temporarily lost consciousness. But of these wounds and injuries, Ben knew nothing; while they were occurring, he had focused his whole attention on trying to direct Farris and his forward gun crew onto their target. In the second before the Germans not felled by Paxton could load and cut loose with a second four-inch round, Farris finally exploded a round of his own against the conning tower, sweeping the last remaining Huns from the U-boat's deck, and the skipper of the boat had started her down.

By that time, too, Feller's SC 71X had gotten into the act. Feller's gun, after a round thrown long, struck the U-boat's conning tower with a high-capacity round long enough before she disappeared from sight for Ben to believe that Feller had done damage. Speck emerged from the fog only after the other two chasers, arriving on scene in the last moment before the U-boat went under. Ben ordered him over the R/T to stand by after the attack that he was about to make to listen for screw beats while Feller followed Ben at five hundred yards to make a second depth-charge drop to starboard, in case the Hun made for the direction of France in order to hug the coast.

Seamen Kaine and Osborn, two of the men in Ben's depth-charge crew, got off the Y-Gun on Ben's order. But owing to the fact that both Light and Scarlatti were down, the charges in the racks were released slightly later, giving Ben's attack a less than perfect spread when Kaine and Osborn had to race back to release the two additional ash cans. Feller fared better, his depth-charge attack going off well. Five minutes after it had been delivered, and after the giant plumes that both attacks had raised in the water settled, Speck reported hearing screw beats on a bearing which indicated that the U-boat was still underway. It had turned directly north to escape the depth charges which had been dropped on her, and seemed to be heading for the open Channel. Once more on the R/T, estimating how far she could have progressed at her much lower underwater speed, Ben reoriented Group AA1 and went in pursuit.

By this time, Ben had started receiving damage reports. When he knew how many men had been injured and wounded—in view of the fact that he didn't have either a doctor or a pharmacist's mate aboard—he pulled Terry from plotting the trace, turned that task over to Townsend, the quartermaster, and sent Terry to doctor the wounded as best he could.

Meanwhile, Ben focused his attention on the pursuit and the attack which he began attempting to conduct. Running up toward the position for which he imagined the U-boat to be heading, he gave the command to halt over the R/T, lower the C-Tubes, and listen. Within two minutes he had collected three bearings which he quickly triangulated; then, ordering each chaser to fire its engine, he raced them ahead, taking SC 65X itself in for the first drop, O'Neal and Treemont dropping from the stern racks even as Kaine and Osborn let fly from the Y-Gun.

This time the pattern was right, and Ben knew it. In the seconds that followed, with tension mounting, he ordered both SC 56X and SC 71X to close on his flanks and drop their own patterns approximately four hundred yards ahead of where he'd made his own drop. Ben hoped to catch the sub turning one way or another as it attempted to elude him by swinging 90 degrees away from the track that the U-boat's skipper might have expected him to follow.

This time, to the shock of every officer and sailor in the Group, they succeeded. As Ben prepared to send out the order to once more halt and listen, not three hundred yards from where Speck had dropped his pattern, the greenish-looking U-boat—a huge black Imperial Cross painted on its conning tower—broached and came to the surface streaming sea water. At once Ben rounded the three chasers on it, their forward mounts spitting out three-inch rounds with thunder, plastering the conning tower and the pressure hull with one explosion after another. Fore and aft, from the sub's hatches, her crew poured up on deck and leaped over the side into the cold waters of the English Channel.

She sank without fanfare, leaving only a few bubbles from her damaged air tanks floating to the surface. Then, as the oil slick she left behind her began to spread, all three chasers rushed in to rescue the remnants of her crew. Speck picked up four, Feller five, and Ben seven, including a single Leutnant zur See who didn't look old enough to Ben to have been long out of secondary school. From the young Leutnant, who had a smattering of English, Ben learned that fourteen or fifteen more men, including the boat's skipper and his executive officer, had apparently gone down with their ship. Those who survived—wet, cold, and looking nothing remotely like the fearsome Huns in newspaper reports and common propaganda—huddled together behind the undamaged shelter of the engine room's housing where the crew brought them blankets. After a delay in which to fire up the galley stoves, Santos produced coffee for them and some of the bread he'd baked before the chaser left port.

If SC 56X and SC 71X remained untouched by the fury of the fight, SC 65X did not. She had wounded men aboard, Garcia and Paxton being the worst, all of them needing the attention of a doctor. Given the damage to the engine room's housing, Ben reckoned that it wouldn't do to risk a gale which might bring on enough flooding to kill their engines and short out their electrical system leaving them dead in the Channel.

Once they'd retrieved all of the surviving Germans, Ben didn't hesitate. Within minutes of picking the last German up and getting him aboard, he got onto the R/T, ordering Speck and Feller to lash brooms to their masts, and to turn and head north for Weymouth at 15 knots. In the meantime, calling

O'Neal to the bridge to take the watch for him, Ben went to see his wounded and injured men. He was satisfied that Terry had done a commendable job in patching them up in a temporary way, even having closed the wound in Garcia's shoulder with five well-placed stitches. A doctor might not leave them in, but for the time being, until they could get the man proper medical attention, the wound was closed in a spot where a mere bandage might not have done the job sufficiently.

Swiftly and with few words, Ben drafted a preliminary after-action report, detailing the sinking of the U-boat and requesting medical personnel as well as military police to be standing by when the Group reached port. This Crim he sent out using the simple code that the chasers sometimes employed for quick and easy operational messages.

Finally, once more relieving O'Neal in the pilot house and having surveyed the damage to his ship, Ben set Terry to writing both requisitions and work orders for replacement equipment damaged in the action and repairs that would have to be completed before SC 65X could once more go to sea. At last, rather than stand on his feet for the remainder of their voyage home, Ben climbed into his chair, picked up his glasses, and scanned the seas ahead. As he did so, he also began to feel his body responding as the waves of tension he'd been operating under slowly seeped away from him.

With SC 65X leading, Group AA1 returned to Weymouth that afternoon shortly after the hour of 1500. As they came in, sailors from the crew of the *Mulgrew* and from some of the chasers in port lined up along their sides to cheer them.

"Radford must have already made an announcement and released the news," Terry said, standing beside Ben as Ben conned the chaser into a berth next to the pier.

"Yes," Ben said, "that appears to be the case. I just hope the medical people are on the job. Why don't you head out onto the pier and urge them on their way if you see any faint hearts among them?"

Ben needn't have bothered. Even as the first lines from the chaser went over and a pier crew fixed them to the bollards, a plethora of medical ratings came aboard with stretchers and quickly removed Paxton, Garcia, Light, and the oiler Willis. Scarlatti walked ashore, ordered to go so that he could be checked for concussion. Pack, after telling Terry that he had taken care of himself with nothing more than iodine and sticking plaster, only went when Terry ordered him to go with a stern warning about the dangers of infection.

The Germans were the next to go, British Military Police—Redcaps—showing up to take charge of them. The entire contingent of fifteen bedraggled Hun seamen and one Leutnant assembled on the pier in two ranks before the Redcaps marched them off toward three paddy wagons waiting at the head of the pier to take them for interrogation and to whatever prisoner-of-war camp that would be waiting to receive them.

Then, finally, as Ben stood outside the pilot house watching the prisoners go, Commander Radford stepped aboard and came threading his way forward to where Ben happened to be standing.

"Have anything like a cup of coffee aboard this vessel?" Radford asked, after Ben had saluted and greeted him.

"If you will step down to our wardroom," Ben said, "I believe that our steward can be induced to bring some up to us."

Jammed into what passed for Ben and Terry's stateroom, sitting across from one another on either side of the space's tiny, fold-down table, Radford looked Ben in the eye and said, "Good job, Mr. Snow. Very good job indeed. Let's hear the facts."

Ben recounted the action for him, trying as hard as he might not to overlook the details.

"It was a group effort, Sir," Ben said. "I think we got a round or two into her when we first sighted her, Feller and I, and I think we did her some damage with our depth bombs, but the attack that brought her to the surface was Speck's, and then all three of us plastered her until she went down."

"And that," Radford said, "is how I shall put it in my report, appending mine to the ones you three will be submitting just as soon as you can write them out in long hand and give them to me."

Ben's was ready. Terry had drafted a three-page rough before the Group had sighted land, and on the way in, Ben had corrected and edited the draft, and that was the report that he handed Commander Radford.

"Excellent," Radford said. "You're paragons of virtue, you and your exec both. Working on requisitions and work orders, are you?"

"Those are also ready," Ben said. "Would you like to take them now, Sir?"

"I'll take the requisitions," Radford said, "but the particular work orders you have, given the considerable damage this vessel has incurred, need to be delivered to the Office of the Bureau of Ships which has been set up in what is passing for an administration building over by the ways. That office has recently developed a reputation for being a stickler for efficiency and detail, and I rather imagine that when you get over there you might be grilled about what you've been through in ways that you can hardly begin to imagine."

"Well," Ben said, rolling his eyes with disgust as he anticipated the ordeal, "Better to get it over with now, I imagine, rather than later. Nicola doesn't know I'm back early, and I'd very much like to get home before she goes out with Miss Mayfield somewhere."

"Quite right," Radford said. "Take the whole batch with you and drop them like a bomb. The BUSHIPS Office is bound to be thrilled, and if you drop your things quickly enough, you may be able to get away early. Good luck."

And with that, taking Ben's stack of requisitions, Radford stood and departed, leaving Ben to put on his blues, pick up the work orders that Terry had prepared for the restoration of the engine room housing as well as a number of other battle scars, and set off down the pier, leaving Terry and O'Neal to attempt to begin putting the ship in order.

On the reception desk inside the ramshackle wooden building that served to house any number of administrative offices for the oversight of functions that, six months before, had been left entirely to Commander Radford, Ben came face to face with a huffy second-class yeoman. Gruffly he asked, nearly demanded, that Ben show him his identification, and then, in an equally demanding tone just short of insolence, demanded to know what Ben wanted.

"What I want," Ben said, his voice hardening slightly, "is the Office of the Bureau of Ships."

"Another one," the yeoman said, speaking with a smirk out of the side of his mouth to his fellow on the desk.

"Another one, what?" Ben barked, his anger showing as he charged his voice with a bite.

"Sir," the first yeoman said, instantly dropping his offensive tone.

"It's the new babe in BUSHIPS, Sir," the second man said. "We've had officers parading in and out of here all day, just to take a look at her."

"Fine," Ben said. "That's just fine. What I've got here are a stack of work orders for a vessel that took battle damage in a fight with a German sub this morning, so you, sailor," he said, speaking to the insolent yeoman, "get off your ass and show me the way."

The man needed no more prompting. In a flash, he was on his feet "yes Sir-ing" Ben all the way to a distant door where he stopped, turned, came to something resembling attention, and said "Bureau of Ships, Sir."

"Right," Ben said, "thank you, and henceforth, sailor, that's the tone you'll want to keep on the desk when you're out there on watch."

"Yes Sir," the man said, his face reddening, his body all but quaking.

Ben knocked and opened the door, and then, as a broad grin stretched across his lips, he stopped dead in his tracks. From behind her desk, Mrs. Dewar-Strang Snow looked back at him, expressions of surprise, and then mild shock, and finally considerable joy spreading quickly across her face.

"I heard that this office harbored a babe," Ben said quickly. "I came to see if she might be free for supper tonight."

"Oh, Ben, where did you come from? What are you doing back?" Nicola said, her voice registering her delighted disbelief as she rose and hurried around her desk to kiss him and welcome him home.

The two of them still remained entwined when a door to their left suddenly opened, and Ben, through his left eye, spotted a lieutenant commander entering the room.

"Here now!" the man said, registering an affront and reacting in a protective way.

"My husband," Nicola said, with a bright smile. "Commander Trilling, it pleases me to present Lieutenant Snow, the commanding officer of SC 65X and Group AA1."

"Ah," Trilling smiled, "you're the officer who sunk the U-boat this morning. Congratulations, Sir! You are a credit to the service. Indeed, I congratulate you both. Mrs. Snow has been with us for only two days, Sir, but you can be proud of your wife. She is a most efficient office manager, and we are pleased to have her."

"Thank you, Sir. I'm very pleased to have her myself," Ben said.

From Nicola's reaction, he knew at once that news of their action had been kept from her because Lieutenant Commander Trilling's announcement seemed to be the first word she'd heard of it.

"I understand," Trilling went on, "that you'll have a number of work orders for us. Radford said that you'd taken damage, so if you will turn those over to your wife, we'll get cracking on them as quickly as possible so as to get you back out there with the least delay."

At some point, Trilling realized that Nicola had been totally unprepared for the news, that what he'd set forth had given her a shock, and that she was visibly shaken by what she'd heard.

"Oh Lord," he said. "I thought you knew. I'm so sorry to have broken it to you in this way. Bull in a china shop. Tactless and stupid. *Mea culpa*. Really, Mrs. Snow, I apologize."

"Not to worry," Nicola said, pulling herself quickly together. "I was bound to hear about it sooner or later, and much better to have heard it here, with my husband standing directly beside me where I can see that he is whole and obviously unharmed."

"The two of you must let me make a recompense," Commander Trilling said quickly. "Suppose you allow me to treat the two of you to a supper this evening at my expense."

"Really, Sir, you need not," Nicola said.

"Really, Mrs. Snow, I insist," Trilling said, as though the matter were settled. "I have no intention of imposing myself upon the two of you, but I want you to go to The Sheffield where the service is excellent and the food a delight. Please think of it as my wedding present and as a sincere apology for my so precipitous blunder."

Nicola looked at Ben, and Ben looked back at Nicola.

"Thank you, we accept," Nicola said, "and we will do our best not to break your bank."

"Thank you, Sir," Ben said. "You're very generous."

"Not at all," Commander Trilling said, "and I promise you, Mr. Snow, that we will have your chaser up on the ways before the sun shines fully tomorrow."

One of the better hotels along the Esplanade, The Sheffield was modest in size but exquisite in its appointments and the care with which it treated its guests. The staff treated the Snows with the same degree of attention that the hotel's regulars received, giving them oysters for their starter, a pleasing cut of roast beef for their main course along with a side of steamed cauliflower, and a small but admirable soufflé for their dessert.

"With the rationing," Nicola said, "I don't know how they manage such a meal."

"Do we dare to try to walk home after this?" Ben joked as they finished their coffee.

"I think we must," Nicola said, "so that I don't have to let out the waistband on any of my skirts. Oh my, such a lovely dinner for such a small charge. I must write the commander a thank-you, for the both of us."

"I think he felt genuinely upset when he realized he'd unsettled you," Ben said.

"I know he did," Nicola said. "I felt bad for him; it was the last thing he intended. That's why I accepted."

"So," Ben said, pushing back his chair and preparing to rise. "Home again, then?"

"Home again," said Nicola, her face shining, "and to a night of bliss, one hopes."

"Let's not delay," Ben said.

"No," Nicola said, rising and squeezing his hand, "let's not."

SC 65X remained on the ways with a bevy of ship's carpenters hovering over her for more than a week, the crew bunking in a receiving barracks for the duration. The barracks instantly became a place in which the men were none too comfortable, and they became such an object of Ben's sympathy that he finally approached Commander Radford about a spot of leave for the men. Radford agreed, with the result that all of them—half going in one draft and half in another after the first group returned—spent four days in London, living it up on the pay they'd accumulated during their long months afloat. Without anticipating it, and added to the successful sinking of the U-boat, Ben found their leave to have given them the biggest lift in their morale that he'd ever seen. And when they managed to return without a single case of VD showing up among them, Ben knew his and SC 65X's luck remained intact.

Terry, left to his own devices during the time that he'd been expelled from his quarters aboard, put up in a guest house—a quiet little place with a garden just off the Esplanade, from where Lettice picked him up each day in the Rolls. Twice, in the evenings, the two couples went out together, motoring through the countryside west of Weymouth to continue their inspection of country pubs in the region. Once, on a Sunday, through connections that Lettice had, they visited what Lettice called one of England's "stately homes," a baronial estate that had been handed down through one family across at least four centuries.

"It rather looks back to the days when land was everything," Nicola observed as the two of them strolled through the house, the home, the establishment, goggle-eyed over the lavish nature of the décor and the furnishings.

"But those times are changing, are they not?" Ben said.

"Most assuredly," Nicola said, "and have been for nearly the past hundred years. Owning a factory or a textile mill in Manchester, a shipyard in Liverpool, or a brokerage in London seems to be where the money is sourced today. Land has almost become a liability rather than an asset, and my guess—and it is only a guess—is that establishments like this one are going to begin disappearing at a rather rapid rate following the war because the landlords and the old aristocracy won't be able to afford them. Theirs seems to be a dying way of life."

"But it was apparently very good while it lasted," Ben said.

"Very," Nicola said.

Each morning, Ben walked Nicola to her office, left her there to contend with whatever projects the engineers of BUSHIPS had going on the base, and went to see for himself how the work happened to be proceeding aboard SC 65X. Once, in company with Commander Radford, he took his lunch in the wardroom on the *Mulgrew*. Then, after five days ashore and after talking the matter over for three nights in succession with Nicola, Ben dropped into the base office of the Bureau of Personnel, filled out the appropriate paperwork, and requested permission from the Navy to augment and become a regular.

"You are aware," said the officer with whom Ben spoke, "that this will take time. Your papers must go to Washington and be examined there before any decision is to be reached."

"Yes," Ben said. "I'm prepared to exercise patience."

At much the same time and much to his surprise, Ben received a packet one afternoon which, upon opening, he found to contain papers indicating he'd been unexpectedly promoted from lieutenant, junior grade, to full lieutenant in the United States Naval Reserve—a development which necessitated his having to call upon a tailor to re-stripe his uniforms. That evening, as he stopped at Nicola's office to collect her, he let the new enlarged stripes on his sleeve make the announcement for him.

"Does this mean that we celebrate?" Nicola asked, the twinkle in her eye showing her pleasure in his promotion.

"It does," Ben said. "Given the sudden rise in my pay, if we were in the States, I would treat you to a hot dog and a sarsaparilla, but since we are here in the United Kingdom where the food is reputed to be so horribly bad, I think we must settle for something mundane like oysters on the half shell, Dover sole perhaps, and a generous helping of Banoffee Pie."

"I think, Love," Nicola said quickly, "that the bananas for the Banoffee Pie are in rather short supply and that we will be fortunate if we can coax a dish of ice cream from wherever we go."

"Then we will make a quick revision according to the vicissitudes of life," Ben said. "Where would Madam like to go?"

"Why don't we go home for a few episodes of bliss before we make our decision," Nicola said, tweeking him on the hand before taking his arm.

"Why Madam," Ben said, his face spreading into a smile, "you surprise me."

"Oh," Nicola said, emitting a little giggle, "I certainly hope so."

When SC 65X came off the ways, she'd been fully restored to fighting trim, something the yard foreman told Ben before he could even go aboard and inspect her following the work that had been completed. But even then, he was delayed when he found himself summoned to an interview with Commander Radford.

"Congratulations on your promotion," Radford said when Ben knocked and entered the man's stateroom aboard the *Mulgrew*. "Been back aboard your chaser yet?"

"No Sir," Ben said. "I was about to go aboard when I received word that you wanted to see me."

"Sit," Radford said, as a wardroom steward appeared and delivered them two mugs of coffee. "There are to be some changes, and I need to tell you about them. In the first place, when you do get down to that cubbyhole stateroom or wardroom of yours, you are going to find that a third bunk has been installed."

Ben's eyebrows rose a tad, but in response, he said nothing, waiting for whatever revelation Commander Radford was about to drop on him.

"With a rise in rank goes an increase in responsibility," Radford said quickly. "Henceforth, you will be commanding the whole of Division AA, not merely Group AA1, and the six of you will be operating together when you go to sea. In a nutshell, that will make you a sort of squadron commander, if you see what I mean, and that is going to mean an increase in the amount of oversight you will have to exercise and in the amount of R/T communications that you will have to involve yourself with in order to retain command of your vessels. I am therefore giving you one additional officer to take some of the burden from your shoulders. My suggestion is that you leave normal watch keeping duties to Mr. Keel and that petty officer, O'Neal, who you've trained up, and once this third officer reports, you can train him and feed him into your watch sections."

"Yes Sir," Ben said.

"That should give you a bit more freedom to oversee your chaser division and a little less to worry about aboard your own craft."

"When might this new man arrive?" Ben asked.

"Oh, I think you'll find him waiting on the pier the minute you leave here," Radford said. "But just another word or two about your operations before you go because you will be taking your division to sea on Monday, and you'll need to confer with your captains before you take them out."

"Yes Sir," Ben said, alert to what Radford was about to tell him.

"In the past, with three of you sweeping an area, your C-Tubes were able to search a lateral distance which extended from about one thousand yards to either side of your flanking chasers; that extended the width of your search to about six thousand yards or three nautical miles, whichever you prefer. By adding three more vessels to the work, my hope is that you will be able to stretch what you are doing to twelve or fourteen thousand yards, six or seven nautical miles, and sweep your assigned search areas in half the time. As it is, I'm already sending chasers from the Plymouth groups all the way out beyond Land's End and some have even moved up into the Irish Sea for modest sweeps. The objective is to make maximum use of our resources, now that we have the majority of them over here with us. This particular approach is experimental, so I'll want to hear from you in writing about how it is working as soon as you return."

"Yes Sir," Ben said. And then, he broached another question that had been on his mind. "If I may ask, Sir, how much longer do you think the war will continue?"

Commander Radford heaved a sign. "Not long, I think," he said, "although I merely speculate. In the Middle East, Allenby has taken Damascus. In the Balkans and on the Italian front, the Austrians appear to be weakening appreciably, and according to what I hear about France and Belgium, the Allies have a major offensive underway, and the Germans, even though they are fighting to hold the Hindenburg line, nevertheless appear to be folding and dropping back. These divisional sweeps that I have in mind for you may never reach the point where they actually bear fruit. We're into October now, and from what London tells me, the war could conclude any day or drag on for only a few more months. I think we've pretty much exhausted Germany and squeezed off her supplies."

Thanking Radford for his candor, Ben rose and took his departure. As he left the *Mulgrew* and walked down the pier to where the yard people had tied up SC 65X, he spotted what he could only imagine to be a green ensign wearing a spanking new uniform looking somewhat dejectedly in all directions as though he didn't know where he was, what he was to do, or where he ought to be.

As Ben approached and the ensign spotted him, the man suddenly came to attention, saluted, and after Ben returned his salute, asked, "Might you be Captain Snow, Sir?"

"I am," Ben said. "And you are?"

"Ensign Porter Maxwell, Sir. Personnel told me that I was to report to you for duty aboard your submarine chaser."

For a moment, Ben studied the man. In the first place, unlike Ben and Terry, he couldn't have stood more than five feet five inches in height, and in looking him over, Ben estimated his weight not to exceed 120 pounds. Blue of eye with dark hair showing beneath his cap, the young man's ears stuck out slightly behind high cheekbones which tended to shade a rather thin and pointed nose over a slightly narrow mouth through which, nevertheless, the voice had sounded strong and in no way wilting.

"By what name do you go among your friends?" Ben asked.

"Port, Sir," the man replied.

"Then welcome aboard, Port," Ben said, showing the ensign a smile and extending his hand. "You have not seen Mr. Keel yet?"

"No Sir," Port Maxwell said. "The yard foreman told me that Mr. Keel was over at BUSHIPS, seeing to some paperwork, so I'd resolved to wait for him."

"Well, your waiting is over," Ben said, stepping toward the brow. "Follow me, and I will show you where to stow your gear while we have a chat."

Ben could see that the confined space in the chaser's officer's quarters gave Port a start as the man tried to scoot his duffle round Ben and onto the top bunk which Ben himself was seeing for the first time.

"When Mr. Keel and I first came aboard, there were only two bunks in here," Ben said, "so this is the first I've seen of the new configuration. It's tight, but we'll make do. So, Port, what's your background. Where do you come from, and so forth?"

"I grew up in Lakewood, Washington, Sir, on the Sound. It's a little south of Tacoma, if you know where that is. I took a degree in business at Washington State in Pullman in 1916, enlisted not long after, went through boot camp at Great Lakes, and then applied for a commission, and after a few weeks' schooling, I was commissioned and sent here. Given where I grew up, I'd imagined I would be placed on the West Coast somewhere, but the Navy sent me here. It's a real plum assignment for me."

"Ever been to sea on a chaser before?" Ben asked, with a slight sense of amusement. "After a time or two in the Channel, you might think differently."

"No Sir," Port said, "but I've been out on my father's boat. He's a commercial fisherman, so I fished the Alaskan coast during my college summers, to pay for my tuition. I know how to pilot, Sir, and I think I've got a fair pair of sea legs."

"Good for you," Ben said, his appreciation for his new ensign growing. If Port Maxwell thought he'd been assigned a plum by coming to SC 65X, Ben thought Radford and the Bureau of Naval Personnel had dropped him a plum of his own by sending him the man. "What kind of catch did you go for?"

"Salmon, Sir," Port said, breaking open his duffle and beginning to store his gear in the spaces that Ben showed him.

"They're better eating than most," Ben said, "although I find that I'm developing a taste for Dover sole. Stand watches on your father's boat, did you?"

"Yes Sir," Port said. "On Dad's boat, as a lookout in the beginning, and later, as his mate inside the pilot house. I've never stood a deck watch on a Navy ship yet, but I'm ready to learn."

"Good," Ben said. "If you know how to pilot and keep clear of other vessels afloat, you're already partway there. Mr. Keel and I as well as O'Neal, our bosun, will be instructing you, and we'll qualify you for your own watch as quickly as we can. That seems to be why you've joined us, in order to relieve me of some watch standing so that I can exercise a firmer hand over the Division when we take it out."

Before he could say anything more, Terry returned, carrying an op-order and a sheaf of papers whereupon Ben introduced him to Port and the two of them shook hands.

"He's had some experience, horsing his father's fishing boat off the coast of Alaska," Ben said.

"That's good news to the ear," Terry said. "So you are not as green as we ensigns usually look," Terry said.

"Well," Port said, "at least I hope not. I don't think I'd know how to handle a destroyer, but the chasers don't seem to be a great deal larger than my father's boat, so I hope that I won't be wholly at a loss."

"Why don't you take him out and show him around," Ben said to Terry. "I'll sit here and tackle this op-order that you've so generously brought me, and when the two of you get back, you can brief me on what you've found—like if the yard has added another bunk or two anywhere else. And while we're on the subject, when's the crew coming back aboard?"

"Pack is marching them back over here right now, or in a few minutes," Terry said. "I stopped at the receiving barracks and gave him the word as I was coming back, and at the moment, that is one happy bunch that he is bringing with him. I don't think they liked the receiving barracks much."

"No," Ben said, "I don't think they did. Home, or what passes for home, is always a sight more comfortable."

The following Monday morning, with SC 65X leading them out, Division AA with Lieutenant Snow commanding went to sea. Port Maxwell, Ben and Terry quickly found out, had, without intending to, concealed something of his light under a bushel. His experience aboard his father's fishing boat had apparently extended even beyond what Port himself had been able to imagine. The happy result was that after only their second week at sea, and after teaching him a few things about watching over his forward gun mount and his depth-charge crews, and the intricacies of the C-Tube searches that they needed to triangulate, Terry reported to Ben that Port was ready to stand deck watches by himself, and Ben put a letter in his personnel file declaring him to be so.

Between the beginning of October and November 11, 1918, Ben took Division AA to sea a total of six times—enough to make him realize that he could exercise complete and tight control over the six chasers under his command, enough to prove Commander Radford's assumption that he would be able to search double the area in half the time previously devoted to the duty, and enough to make every man aboard every chaser in the Division understand thoroughly the new job they were trying to do. But if the tactical situation showed the level of expertise that Radford and Ben hoped that it would, the final results—aside from turning up three mines on one trip and two on another—produced no contacts with a U-boat anywhere in the areas they searched. Somewhere in the Irish Sea, according to rumors that they heard, a Royal Navy destroyer had sunk or damaged one U-boat; there were also rumors that more than one, apparently severely damaged, had been scuttled off the coast of Flanders. With regard to active combat, however, none of the chasers in Division AA ever again came close. Then, even as the Division was returning to port on the morning of November 11, 1918, the Armistice went into effect and the war ended. For Ben, Terry, and Port the news was met not with a bang but with a whimper, and when they finally put into Weymouth that afternoon and tied up, the celebrations had already started. Ben found Nicola waiting for him on the pier, let in at last to what had formerly been considered a secure area.

"Oh, Ben," she said as he stepped up onto the pier and gave her a kiss and a hug, "it's over, and you've survived! Isn't it wonderful?"

"Wonderful, it is," Ben said, holding her close. "Wonderful indeed."

But as Ben discovered the following day when Commander Radford called him in, it was not over, not by a long way, and neither he nor the remainder of the chasers in the Division were about to be demobilized.

14

On the day after the war ended and after he dropped Nicola at the door to her office, Ben stepped a lively pace to the brow of his chaser, went aboard, and found a note from Commander Radford summoning him to a meeting on the *Mulgrew*. With Terry and Port barely on their feet and dressed, Ben left the two of them to see to morning quarters with the crew, stepped back onto the pier, walked to the brow of the *Mulgrew*, and went aboard.

Commander Radford, when Ben was shown up to his stateroom, already sat at his desk, and as swiftly as Ben could enter and sit down, the commander's steward set two mugs and a pot of coffee in front of them and left them to their interview.

"Well," Radford said, "it has been a long haul, but the war is won, so now begins the hard part. At some point in the coming weeks or months, the politicians and the diplomats are going to have to gather and try to cobble together a peace, and I shudder to think what a hash they might make of it. We can be hopeful, of course, and I am, but as a realist, I must remain skeptical. Still, I suppose, we'd do well to hope for the best, and we will. Meanwhile, I wonder if you were expecting to be demobilized?"

"I doubt that I have a man on board who hasn't wondered about the question, Sir," Ben said.

"Yes," Radford said, "that's pretty much what I'd imagined. Well, young Sir, you may go back, when I turn you loose, and tell them not to get their hopes up. The doughboys might be going home, some of them, those who are not required for the occupation, but we are not. Apparently, a contingent of our chasers—and I intend to draw them from the divisions we have stationed at Plymouth—are to go north, all the way to Murmansk, where we seem to be offering some kind of support to the Russians who are attempting to throw back the Bolsheviks. A tender will go with them. How long they might be up there is something I have not been told. The remaining chasers in Plymouth will apparently be split into two groups. Some are destined to return to the States; others will come here and join my entourage on the spot for further operations as directed."

"Any indication about what those might be?" Ben asked.

"Yes," Radford said, letting loose a sigh. "Tell me, Mr. Snow, what do you know about mines?"

"Not much," Ben said quickly. "My only experience with them was with the Hun and Austrian mines that we sank in the Channel and that one British mine that showed up near the beginning of our tour of duty."

"Right," Radford said, reaching across his desk and handing Ben a thick Navy manual. "That publication is classified SECRET, so handle it with care, and be sure that it is locked in your safe each minute that you are not reading it. My best suggestion for you is that you study it thoroughly because what we will be doing in the coming year will have a great deal to do with mines, and in order to protect yourself, you are going to want to know everything about them that you can find out."

Commander Radford needed to see nothing more than the expression on Ben's face to induce him to continue.

"Here's the long and the short of it," Radford began. "In order to bottle up the U-boats and keep them from getting into harbors and even parts of the Channel, the Brits have laid minefields all around these islands—minefields they will take the initiative in clearing, leaving us to other work entirely. The minefield we will probably concern ourselves with is the North Sea Barrage. In total, according to the figures I've been given, the U.S. Navy and the Royal Navy have laid at least 70,000 mines—50,000 American made—across the North Sea in an attempt to keep Hun U-boats bottled up in the Baltic. In order for commerce to resume so that every economy in Northern Europe can begin to recover, those mines have to be cleared and cleared fairly quickly. The target date for completing the job is November 11, 1919, one year from now. The wag who came up with that date apparently selected it so as to commemorate the Armistice. That same man probably doesn't have the slightest idea of what he is asking, but that's no matter because, applying the usual Navy *Can Do* spirit to the job, we will do it or heads will roll. Following me so far, are you?"

"Yes Sir," Ben said.

"Our job will be further complicated by the weather," Radford continued. "North Sea weather during the winter months will probably make minesweeping downright impossible. The waves up there sometimes rise to a height of forty feet or more, so for now—and this is something my so-called 'wag' probably doesn't know a thing about either—the minesweeping operation is on hold and will remain that way until, probably, April at the earliest. Still with me?"

"Yes Sir," Ben said once more.

"So, in late March or April when we do go up there, this is what we'll be doing. The mines that are to be swept are, most of them, American Mark VI mines, and I'll explain about those in a moment. But my point is that they've been set at various depths: 45 feet, 80 feet, 160 feet, and some as deep as 240 feet. Our intention is to send our minesweepers in—and we are presently assembling a small fleet of them—and let them sweep parallel to the track of the mine fields for which we have very good, very accurate charts showing the individual placement of each mine. Some of those mines will explode on contact with the sweep cables, and our hope is that one explosion may set off others through sympathetic vibration. It seems inevitable that in many cases the sweep cables will merely cut the cables holding the mines to the bottom and cause them to rise to the surface, and that is where the chasers will come into their own. The chasers will be stationed behind the minesweepers and set to follow them; so, when a mine does pop to the surface, the crews on the chasers may then sink the offending mines with rifle fire as soon as they are spotted. You've already done the job with German mines, so you know what's involved. Your crewmen, if they are good shots, may need to get as many as five or ten rounds into a mine in order to sink it, if they don't hit a horn and explode it outright. So, in the weeks to come, we are arranging for all of the crews on the chasers involved to pass a rifle course in hopes of making them into better marksmen than some of them may already be."

Upon hearing what Radford had just delivered to him, Ben found himself instantly aware of the dangers. In the first place, there were the mines, each of them capable of blowing SC 65X straight out of the water and into splinters if he approached the mine too close. In the second place, regardless of the course the men were to go through, thinking of men like Light and Scarlatti, Ben registered multiple degrees of apprehension about whether one man or another might start horsing around while armed with a loaded weapon and wind up blowing off his toes or some appendage on the man standing next to him. Tight control would have to be exercised, and for Ben's money, O'Neal was going to have to be on deck to exercise it.

"Now," Radford said, "regarding the mines themselves. I have given you the manual on them, and I urge you to read and study it. But in a nutshell, here's the drill. Most of the mines in the North

Sea Barrage are of the nasty Mark VI type which our very own scientific and engineering experts have so insidiously developed. That is, rather than being contact mines that a ship could detect by sight in advance and must run into to activate the trigger and cause an explosion, they are magnetic mines which react to a ship's magnetic field when it passes over them. Once activated by an electro-magnetic impulse, the mines swiftly rise to the surface and blow the bottom out of a vessel before it can safely pass beyond the mine's danger zone. So, right now, we have 70,000 of those rascals waiting on the bottom of the North Sea. If no ship goes near them, the mines remain inactive, but if one of them is activated, all hell breaks loose."

"If you don't mind me asking," Ben said, "how are the sweeps to avoid being blown up?"

"That is also in the manual I've given you," Radford said, "and it's complicated. In short, we will run an electrical cable inside and around each minesweeper's hull and charge it with a current that will neutralize the minesweeper's magnetic field, leaving it safe to make its sweeps. If it works as designed and if the ratings who are to keep it working do their jobs properly, the sweepers will not activate the mines over which they pass. Your chasers being built of wood will have far less to worry about, and in addition, you will be moving well behind the minesweepers."

"Clearly," Ben said, "if we are to remain safe, I need to find out all I can about these mines. I had no idea we had anything that complicated in the arsenal."

Radford took a sip of his coffee. "Here's the short course," he said, his eyes narrowing. "A minelayer launches its mines on a small weighted trolley that slides into the sea from a rack. When that trolley touches bottom, a trigger releases a spherical mine which then rises to a set height above the trolley but remains anchored to it by a cable. And from there a small float carrying the antenna, a thin copper wire, rises from the mine toward the surface although it remains below the surface so as to remain unseen. It is that antenna coupled to a very complicated and sophisticated sensor inside the mine which detects the magnetic field of a ship passing overhead and triggers both the release of the mine from its anchor and the explosion once the mine rises to whatever height it has been set for."

"One can hardly imagine it," Ben said, after absorbing what Radford had told him.

"This sort of thing has advanced a light year since the Civil War, when a man had to conceal himself on the bank somewhere and then touch off what we then called a 'torpedo' with the wires he held in his hands," Radford said.

"It's a little staggering to try to come to grips with the means modern men have developed for trying to kill each other," Ben said.

"Let's be thankful that we didn't have to contend with mustard gas out here," Radford said.

"Yes," Ben said. "So, when we do begin this operation, from where might we operate, Sir?"

"That's still unspecified," Radford said quickly, "but if I had to guess, I would imagine that it will be somewhere like Lerwick in the Shetlands or Kirkwall in the Orkneys. I regret to tell you, Mr. Snow, that wives will not accompany us for this deployment, but you need not worry about Mrs. Snow. At least twenty of the chasers will remain here, pending either their return to the States or their ultimate sale to Allied navies, so Mrs. Snow's job will remain secure until we return and a disposition is made of your own division."

"May I inform her about what's in store for us?" Ben asked.

"You may," Commander Radford said, "but tell her to keep the news to herself when you do so, and with regard to your own officers and crew, you may inform them with the same restrictions on any loose talk they might contemplate."

"Yes Sir," Ben said, sensing that the interview had ended and rising from his chair.

"One more thing," Radford said, as Ben prepared to go. "For the next two weeks, I intend to keep all vessels in port. I suggest that you divide your crew into port and starboard sections and grant each section a week's leave. It won't be a great reward for their part in winning the war, but I rather imagine that it will be a welcome one."

"That it will be," Ben said, showing Radford a grin to match his own. "Most assuredly."

When Ben picked Nicola up that evening and began walking her home, he noticed at once that she seemed particularly quiet and withdrawn.

"A penny for your thoughts?" Ben said finally, the near silence of his question matching her apparent mood.

"I saw a photo today," she said, "in the newspaper. It was an annual school photo taken at Eton, showing the massed faces of nearly eleven hundred boys."

"Yes," Ben said.

"And then in the caption," Nicola continued, "I found a notation indicating that more than 1,150 Etonians had fallen in the war and will never be coming back. Oh Ben, that's an entire generation," she said, her fist going suddenly to her mouth to stifle a sob.

"I know," Ben said. And within the second, he put his arm around her shoulder and gave her a hug as they walked side by side toward the flat. "I heard somewhere today that we Americans have lost between two and three hundred thousand, dead and wounded combined. It seems a lot, but it appears to be slight alongside what Britain, France, Russia, Italy, and Germany have lost. I shudder to think what the world has given up, and I can only wonder about the need. I think the old men, the ones who were supposed to know better, sold us down the river on this one."

"I can only wonder how our friend, the Vicar, will feel when he finally sees the statistics," Nicola said.

"Considering the man," Ben said, "probably justified, without ever stopping to count the costs."

"Oh Ben," Nicola said, "I'm so glad that it's over and that you are out of it and whole."

"Yes," Ben said. "We can be forever thankful, truly thankful."

Ben did not broach the subject of mine clearance with Nicola that night. Instead, he waited until the following afternoon when an air of euphoria had spread itself across the base, as this or that section of the chaser crews and no inconsiderable element in the shore establishment went on leave in recognition of the war's end.

That evening, as the two of them walked home together, Ben waited for an appropriate moment and told her what he had heard from Commander Radford about the security of her job for the following months. Then, as though observing no more than a gentle breeze pass, he said, "Oh, and there's a possibility that we might have to endure a brief separation this summer," and went on to tell her what he believed the U.S. Navy had in store for his division.

"And for how long do you think, really think, that your Navy will force you to desert me?" Nicola asked, fuming, less than amused, but determined to accept what she had no choice but to accept.

"That," Ben said, "I do not know, but considering the numbers of mines we will have to clear, it seems just possible that we might be up there from May until August."

"Well now," Nicola said, her eyes flashing, "isn't that just peachy. Lettice and I will have to form a sewing or knitting circle."

Ben broke out laughing.

"And what's so funny about that, Mr. Smarty?" Nicola said in a huff.

"I can well imagine that you've been taught to ply your needle," Ben said, "but the idea that Lettice might be acquainted with a knitting needle exceeds belief. I can hardly wait to ask Terry if she knows what knitting needles are."

A second or two passed in utter silence before Nicola began to chuckle. "I believe," she said, "that I once heard her say that she had seen her nanny do a bit of knitting rather in the same way that she might have mentioned seeing a comet pass overhead or an eagle collide with a tree. She appeared to find the activity to be a complete mystery to her, one that required explanation."

"That is rather as I had imagined," Ben said, adding, "Surely young ladies of Lettice's background spend most of their time waiting for their maids to do their hair or help them change costumes for the various times of the day."

"Now, now," Nicola cautioned. "What might have been true for Lettice's mother in her youth is not quite so common for Lettice. Her family may be wealthy, but she has a practical streak and applies herself very adroitly when hired to employ her mathematical talents. If you didn't know, the War Office has asked her to do something with numbers relating to war wounds and the future of veterans' remunerations."

"No, I didn't know," Ben said. "Terry has said nothing about it."

"Perhaps he doesn't know," Nicola said. "Aside from a select few, Lettice normally fails to mention any work she has going for the government."

"But you are one of the select few?"

"Of course," Nicola said. "As a result of long association."

"Like a pair of criminals," Ben laughed.

"Now stop that," Nicola said, "or you might find yourself doing without bliss tonight."

"What, am I to be disciplined?" Ben protested.

"For withholding this news about your impending summer away from me, I shouldn't wonder," Nicola said.

"Not to worry," Ben said, "I'm sure that I'll hurry things along just as swiftly as I can."

"But not so swiftly that you take chances and run risks," Nicola commanded.

"Of course not," Ben said. "That much, I can promise."

The following Friday evening, Lettice picked up Terry from the boarding house where he'd elected to remain living when away from the ship, collected Nicola and Ben from their flat, and then drove to the head of the pier where Mr. Port Maxwell fitted himself into the rear seat alongside Ben and Nicola.

"I'm afraid," Nicola said to Port after greeting him, "that Lettice and I do not know with whom Lady Felicia will match you as a dinner partner this evening. If it is one of the doyennes of her acquaintance, they are usually lovely women with a knowledge of the locale, even if they do have gray hair, and I rather think you will enjoy dining at Trincombe Abbey where the food is not only delightful but the atmosphere is nearly regal."

"At least," Lettice said, speaking from behind the wheel as she raced up Dorchester Road, "you will be spared having to sit beside the Vicar's wife. Owing to the Vicar's recent social lapse, he appears no longer to be welcome at Lady Felicia and the Colonel's table."

"Let the heavens be praised," Terry intoned, as Ben let go with a laugh, leaving Port to wonder what they were all talking about.

"You've read *The Scarlet Letter*?" Nicola asked.

"In high school," Port said, "under duress."

"The Vicar and his wife apparently attended the same school as Roger Chillingworth," Nicola suggested. "One rather imagines the three of them enjoying a high good time dunking a witch or scourging a Quaker from their village, if you see what I mean."

"I think I grasp your point," Port said.

"I told you he was swift on the uptake," Ben said to Nicola.

"I am gratified to know," Nicola said, "that you are surrounded by such competent young men—men who will keep you out of trouble and return you safely to the fold once your impending operations are complete."

"You are speaking in favor of Mr. Maxwell, of course," Lettice swiftly put in, lurching the Rolls into a threatening position in relation to the verge and the ditch. "I should be fearful if you had to rely on the scapegrace sitting next to me."

"Now is that any way to thank a man whose timely warnings and well-timed suggestions have saved you from more automobile accidents than we can count?" Terry asked.

Port Maxwell, as Ben and Terry were pleased to see, did not have to sit at table that evening beside a spinster, doyenne, or harridan of the pinched and graying kind. Instead, after Lady Felicia's gracious welcome to her drawing room when the butler showed them in, she and the Colonel almost as swiftly produced a Miss Willow Finch, who happened to be just down from Oxford following the Trinity term and employed as an estate agent in what the Colonel called her father's very reputable firm in Weymouth.

"Willow has the cutest little motor," Lettice said. "It's a two-seater Templar, and it goes like the wind."

"Willow is pretty cute herself," Ben whispered to Nicola. "Where did you find her?"

"We made up a list of all the girls we know in Weymouth," Nicola whispered back, "and then we tried to estimate their heights so as not to leave Mr. Maxwell standing in a shadow."

"Very adroit," Ben said.

"Yes," Nicola said, looking on with satisfaction. "I can see that we didn't misfire by the glazed look on your Port's face."

"I understand," the Colonel said later over the joint of beef that Mandy had served up for their supper that evening, "that your

President Wilson has announced that he intends to promote his Fourteen Points during whatever peace conference eventually takes place."

"I have heard much the same thing," Ben said, "but I'm afraid, Colonel, that I have not had the time to study his proposals or much consider what they may involve."

"Two or three of his points might prove knotty," the Colonel continued. "Colonial issues never seem to leave us without a considerable tearing of hair. I suspect that Middle Eastern oil concessions will give the negotiators fits, and the question of disarmament is bound to become a sticking point. Our army might be willing to reduce itself appreciably, but the Royal Navy will never give up its ships in any way that proves willing."

"No Sir," Ben said. "And with good reason, I think. Some of our chasers will go home; some will be sold, and some, those no longer able to hold together, will probably be broken up. But after what the country has been through in preparing our own fleet, I doubt that we will want to give up any capital ships and imagine that our plethora of new destroyers will go into what I have heard called 'mothballs' so as to store and preserve them for future need, should the need ever arise."

"That," the Colonel said with emphasis, "is what I hope a just peace may preclude. If Clemenceau and French volatility exercise too heavy a hand over Germany, I think we will face going through something like this or something worse in the future, and that is an eventuality that none of us wish to face."

"Absolutely," Ben said. "Once should be enough for any man with a head on his shoulders."

"My dear," Lady Felicia said, with a lilting tone, "I think, perhaps, that we should leave politics and turn our attention to something like the departure of rationing and the good things that will surely follow from that benign development."

"Yes, yes, of course, my dear," the Colonel said quickly, "restoring a bit of peace to your table, what?"

"Exactly," said Lady Felicia, exhibiting the grace of a swan while inviting Willow to expatiate upon what she knew about the sale of some beach properties that had been rumored to be coming onto the market in the neighborhood.

Ben listened as Miss Willow Finch gave a brief, detailed, and utterly precise explanation of the beach properties that Lady Felicia had mentioned. Then, as Lettice brought up the subject of South American fruit imports which were expected to improve radically with the disappearance of the U-boat menace, Ben happened to glance once more in Miss Willow and Port's direction. He saw her turn, flash Port the warmest of smiles, and suddenly say to him, "Oh, Mr. Maxwell, I do so hope that you are not one of the 'macho hearties' that has dropped our way from the United States."

"Macho hearties?" Port said, after a slight hesitation. "I regret to say that I am not acquainted with the term."

"I'm sorry," Willow said at once. "I'm afraid that's Oxford slang for young men who become absorbed by games worship and bore their lady friends to tears with stories about their rugby and cricket exploits."

"*Ah*," Port said, showing her an amused but understanding smile. "I believe I can relieve you of that worry at once with a firm promise not to make any attempt to explain baseball, and to gild the lily for you, I will also refrain from any talk about salmon fishing."

"Oh, *super*," said Miss Finch. "I can see that you are to be a friend indeed."

"Yes," Port said, "I certainly hope so."

"Your Ensign Maxwell and our Miss Finch seem to be getting along very well," Nicola once more whispered to Ben.

"Your self-satisfaction becomes you," Ben said, reaching over beneath the table and giving his wife's hand a squeeze. "While we're away, perhaps you, Lettice, and Lady Felicia could establish some sort of brokerage with which to arrange romances and marriages for visiting members of the American contingent in the Peace Delegation. Thus far, your track record seems unparalleled."

"I rather think," Nicola said, suddenly straightening her back, "that Lettice and I, while you and your vessel disport yourselves in northern waters, will concentrate all of our mental faculties on remaining alluring enough so that our young men never give a thought to going astray in places like Kirkwall or Lerwick."

"Why, whatever can you be thinking?" Ben said.

"Reports from the distant north describe blonde beauties, descended from Vikings, and therefore given to such unwholesome activities as raiding for plunder," Nicola said smoothly.

"I shall warn my crew," Ben laughed, "so that they may stand by to repel borders."

"Yes," Nicola said, "see that you do."

Following an evening of light conversation in Lady Felicia and the Colonel's drawing room, when the guests rose to say their goodbyes and depart, Port, with a somewhat sly smile on his face, informed the others that he would not be returning to Weymouth with them. He went on to say that Miss Willow had offered him transportation in her two-seater Templar and seemed anxious to put the little car through its paces for him.

"Do not," Terry said, "let her take you over the jumps in that vehicle. Lettice has twice taken me over a series of them, and I warn you that it can be most disconcerting. Hunting the fox in a motor is not to be recommended."

"Perhaps the master hunter would like to walk," Lettice said without hesitating.

"If I did," Terry rejoined, "I could never forgive myself for abandoning Ben and Nicola to an uncertain fate. You very much need me along to moderate your enthusiasms."

On the following weekend, beginning with a train trip on Friday afternoon when Commander Trilling closed the BUSHIPS office before lunch, Ben and Nicola went up to London. There, relying on Lady Felicia's advice and the budget they had established for themselves, they put up in a small hotel on Ebury Street, not far from Buckingham Palace, an establishment that catered without embellishments to established families who had been guests of longstanding. In the evening, they treated themselves to a show at the relatively new Victoria Palace Theatre, which was in easy walking distance of their hotel. Then, after celebrating with a bottle of bubbly in the hotel bar, the went up to their room for an evening of bliss.

The next morning, they did not rise for breakfast, indulged themselves instead with more bliss, and later dressed and went out to enjoy a filling pub lunch. But then, because neither had ever been there before, they took themselves to the British Museum and made a leisurely afternoon tour through the halls that were open. Emerging from the museum near the hour of 1600 that afternoon, Ben was quick to notice that the evening was already coming on. "Winter approaches. It will be dark again in minutes," he said.

"Which explains, perhaps, why so many in this country prefer to spend their winters in the south of France or on the beaches in the sunny Caribbean," Nicola said. "They haven't been able to do that for the past few years, so if the nation were not broke, one might expect a mass exodus."

"Most of our winter evenings don't come on until nearly five-thirty or six," Ben said.

"With summer nights that are appreciably longer than ours, I suspect," Nicola replied.

"That's true," Ben said. "The sun usually sets around eight or eight-thirty in a Great Lakes summer."

"As you know by now, our summer sun sometimes lasts as late as 11:00 pm and tends to rise again by as early as 3:00 am," Nicola laughed.

"Hardly seems the same world, does it?" Ben said.

"I can't imagine what it must be like to live in Australia or New Zealand where even the seasons are twisted about," Nicola said.

"I suppose it would take some getting used to," Ben said. "And speaking of getting used to things, I think I might be able to get used to a pint about now. What say we find ourselves a nice pub with a cozy fire where I can give you a little something that might refresh you after our immersion into foreign cultures and centuries?"

"I think some bliss might be very refreshing," Nicola said, squeezing his arm, "after a pint and glass of wine perhaps and as an appetizer in advance of a late supper."

"Why, you lovely girl," Ben said. "How *do* you come up with these ideas?"

On Sunday, in a London without wind, with a late morning sun showing through a clear sky, the two of them once more rose late and treated themselves to a long walk through Kensington Gardens. Here and there, they saw riders on the path, walking their horses at a steady pace. Families emerged from the surrounding homes, and nannies with prams, and a few older people wrapped in coats and scarves—all of them out for a stroll in weather that for the moment, at least, seemed conducive to taking exercise.

"So how does the city strike you?" Ben asked, "compared to other times you've visited?"

"I was here several times during my breaks from school," Nicola said. "End of term visits with friends. That sort of thing. I might be wrong, but I think London shows the effects of the war. The people look thinner. They are happy to be out, but their faces have that gaunt look that suggests that they haven't been eating enough. The streets don't seem as clean as they were when I was here in 1913, the windows don't look washed, the railings, doors, and window frames seem to need paint, and wherever I look I can see a film of grime from the coal that we've burned. Things aren't exactly Dickensian, but the Belgravia we just walked through didn't look like it had been lifted from what Trollope envisioned in *The Palliser* novels either."

"I've only read one of those," Ben said, "*Phineas Finn*, but I'd say you're right. Weymouth looks none so hard used."

"And just a touch closer to Barsetshire," Nicola said, "but with the downturn, the decline may soon set in even there. We will survive it, I'm sure, but I don't like to think what the near future is to be like."

"No," Ben said, "nor do I."

They took the late afternoon train back to Weymouth, arriving several hours after dark, walked with their valises to their flat, ate cheese on toast for a late supper, and turned in, happy, contented with their time in London, and weary. The following morning, Ben once more walked Nicola to her place of work and then reported to his ship.

15

Two days after his return from London, Ben mustered the off duty section of SC 65X's crew on the pier in dungarees. There, rather than turning them loose for liberty, he caused them to board a bus and took them to the rifle range for a course of marksmanship. The instructor for their session turned out to be an American Marine sergeant named Foss, a barrel-chested fire plug of a man in his late thirties who brought two of his corporals with him, all three of them doing duty with the Marine unit detailed for service aboard the *Mulgrew*. Each of them came to the range—a facility borrowed from the British Army—armed with a homemade swagger stick, a used cartridge case fixed to the butt end. Following eight hours of practice with the M1903 Springfield infantry rifle using its five-round clip of .30-06 ammunition, each of Ben's sailors qualified at least for a sharpshooter when he didn't qualify as an expert.

Sergeant Foss and his corporals went about their instruction methodically and brooked no inattention. If one or another of the sailors drifted momentarily, he was brought quickly back into concentration when Foss or a corporal tapped him sharply on the head with the butt end of the swagger stick that he carried, inflicting enough pain so that minds were not allowed to wander. Ben, in the midst of supervising the training, also elected to participate in it; he found that he liked firing the Springfield and came away believing it to be highly accurate.

On the following day, Terry and Port took the chaser's other section to the range. Several of the men qualified as expert, including, to Ben's later surprise, Santos, who was declared to be a dead shot, and who Foss said could have shot the eye from a mosquito at two hundred yards.

"One imagines," Ben said when he heard the news, "that with these guys, the wonders will never cease."

"Honest to Pete," Terry said, when he gave Ben the news, "I don't think the guy ever once missed the bullseye. It was the darndest thing you ever saw."

"And you two?" Ben asked.

"Port did well," Terry said. "I think I qualified as a sharpshooter because Foss felt sorry for me."

"More's the reason to leave you manning the R/T when it comes time to start sinking mines," Ben said. "Make up a list of your most likely candidates for rifle duty, and I'll add it to my own. Santos sounds like a good bet, but we can't have his rifle work interfering with his cooking or we'll all starve out there."

The following day, not long after he walked Nicola to her office and reached the chaser, Radford called for him. When Ben arrived aboard the *Mulgrew*, he learned that Division AA would once more be putting to sea.

"Yesterday, at precisely 1619," Radford said, as though the time were important, "a vessel approaching Cherbourg ran into a mine not thirty miles out in the Channel. The ship didn't sink; the crew managed to put out fires and secure the damaged hold, but a good bit of cargo had to be written off, and the owners are in a tremendous flit. My point is that we still have loose mines in the Channel. So, tomorrow morning, we are going to start to hunt for them. Sweeps will be sent out from Plymouth, and Division AA will follow them to pot whatever they turn up. Think of this as practice for the work you are to eventually do in the North Sea. Sweeps will also go out from Portsmouth and Falmouth, and Divisions CC and BB are detailed to follow them. Frankly, I doubt that you'll turn up much. Here and there, you might snag a Hun mine that has been drifting and that we haven't spotted, but if there are others out there, I would imagine that they're British mines that have broken loose and drifted toward the French coast. You are to take a strain, of course; this is duty that must be performed properly, and be sure to brief your captains in a way that makes that point stick with them. It will not do to make a mistake with this work."

"Yes Sir, understood," Ben said.

"The commander of the leading sweep will be in charge," Radford continued. "I suspect that you will be out for at least four days at a time, and when you are close to the French coast, you may be putting in to French ports to harbor for the evenings. If so, see to it that our crews behave themselves."

"Yes Sir," Ben said.

Across the six weeks that followed, as the minesweepers and their various divisions of chasers once more swept every area formerly marked off on the charts for the U-boat hunt, Division AA spent four days at sea, handed off to another chaser division, and spent the following four days in port. In some ways, it felt like old times, the old times that went with the war. The Channel, all of them were sorry to find, did not cooperate. Instead, time after time in December and January, it kicked up gales that left them tossing like the cork that they were, upending every man who tried to cling to his bunk and leaving the men on watch weak in the legs following four or more hours of attempting to keep their footing as the seas worked against them and tried to throw them to the deck.

"Still not as bad as the trip to Bermuda," Terry said to Ben.

"Yes, there's that," Ben said. "I seriously doubt that anything could ever top that voyage for misery, but if you ask me, the stuff out here is giving it a run for its money. How's Port holding up?"

"Ha," Terry laughed. "According to Port, this is exactly what he used to see during his summers in the Bering Sea."

"Perish the thought," Ben said, "and let's hope we never have to take up commercial fishing for a living."

The take, after so many weeks, didn't amount to much. In Division AA's areas of search, they sank one mine that they could identify as definitely German, one of indeterminate origin, and four of apparent British manufacture. Thrice during that time, they put into Cherbourg for overnight harbor, having swept in close enough to the French coast to make the in-port periods feasible. The quartermaster, Townsend, for reasons that Ben was never able to fathom, apparently had a smattering of French at his command. So, in a unique arrangement for the crew, Ben detailed the man to remain on liberty for every night the vessel spent in the French port to accompany the liberty section, help them with such things as food and drink orders, and keep them from getting into any untoward difficulties with the locals. Ben, Terry, and Port also went ashore, stuffed themselves with the best omelets they had ever tasted in bistros not far from the harbor, took in some of the sights, and returned to the chaser after each outing with enough good food inside them to keep them happy, and just enough French wine to help along their digestion. French beer, after months of drinking English bitter, they declared to be an utter failure, but once or twice, having gotten their hands on bottles of imported Italian beer, they found that they were able to register a mild degree of acceptance if not satisfaction.

"Makes one long for an English pub, doesn't it?" Terry said one evening as the three of them sat inside one of the bistros they'd discovered and shared a pitcher of draft.

"Decidedly," said Port.

Back in Weymouth during their periods in their home port, life as they'd come to know it resumed. They were back in Weymouth for Christmas that year, Lady Felicia and the Colonel treating them to a sumptuous Christmas dinner in the middle of a cold December afternoon. Ben, Terry, and Port attended in company with Nicola, Lettice, and Willow, and a fourth couple, the Herberts, he a solicitor, Mrs. Herbert a committee woman with whom Lady Felicia had arranged one or two relief activities during the later years of the war.

The meal that Mandy served the company exceeded everyone's expectations—a leg of lamb served with a beautifully prepared joint of venison, not to mention a well-roasted breast of goose, and topped off with a genuine plum pudding as well as individual servings of Mandy's figgy pudding, all of it accompanied with crackers and paper hats. Ben imagined that it seemed traditional fare for the majority, but he was right to assume that he, Terry, and Port had never experienced anything quite like it. Later, after the port, assembling in the hall, the servants were invited to join the celebration. After Lady Felicia handed presents around to them, the entire entourage joined in singing carols and sharing a cup of mulled wine which had been carried out from the kitchen by members of the staff.

Following the festivities, as Lettice only twice ran off the road on their way back to Weymouth, Ben told Nicola that he thought they'd just celebrated the nicest Christmas dinner that he'd ever attended.

"You don't do this sort of thing in the States?" Nicola asked.

"We celebrate Christmas, certainly," Ben said, "but according to my recollection, presents usually come from under the tree in the morning, and while our dinners are good, they never came close to what Lady Felicia served up. Turkey is the normal fare, and I don't remember seeing a servant anywhere at any Christmas dinner I ever attended. Few of the families around which I grew up could afford them. Once I'd been sent off to school, Christmas dinner at a place like Massachusetts Nautical seemed rather a stiff affair to be enjoyed if the food allowed it and terminated on something like a holiday schedule without any subsequent celebration. This was a warmer event by far, and I'm pleased that we were included."

"I'm glad," Nicola said. "Lady Felicia and the Colonel are dears."

"Here!" Terry said from the front seat, speaking to Lettice in what sounded to Ben like an authoritative tone. "I think you really ought to watch it, Lettice, or you're liable to crawl right up the tail of that little Templar!"

"Not to worry," Lettice said smoothly. "Willow has been letting things drag, and I'd merely hoped to offer her some encouragement to go faster."

"On a road like this and at this time of night," Terry fumed, "thirty-five miles an hour is quite fast enough, don't you think?"

"No," Lettice said, "the road into Weymouth simply begs for a moderate forty, so let's hear no more about it, or Father Christmas will not be forthcoming with your present."

Ben wondered about what present Father Christmas might have in store for his exec but didn't ask and felt relieved when Lettice dropped them at the door to their flat still in one piece.

With Division AA having handed over to FF out of Plymouth and back into Weymouth for New Year's, Ben expected that he and

Nicola might spend the evening at home, in quiet celebration. To his surprise, upon his arrival back in port, Radford informed him that the officers on the base along with the officers from the chasers had been invited to a formal ball to be held in what passed for Weymouth's assembly rooms—something the mayor and the council had decided to put on in celebration of the war's end and to honor both the United States Navy and the Royal Navy establishments in the area. Radford told Ben that he expected him to reappear on the *Mulgrew*'s fantail at 1500 that afternoon along with the captains of the other chasers in Group AA, and when Ben asked him why, Radford demurred and told Ben that there would be time enough for explanations when the three of them arrived.

When Ben and his fellows arrived that afternoon, they found themselves somewhat surprised to find a round of officers from the *Mulgrew* standing at rest along with the chaser officers from Division AA, and even more surprised to find Nicola standing on deck beside Commander Radford. Very swiftly, calling the entire assembly to attention, Radford called first Ben and then Feller and Speck forward and, after a brief speech and the reading of a citation from Admiral Sims, decorated each with the Navy Cross for their successful sinking of the German U-boat.

Coffee and light refreshment in the *Mulgrew*'s wardroom followed, and it was there that Radford gathered all three of his captains together and told them that their medals were to be worn for the ball they would be attending.

"The United States Navy is not encumbered by many decorations, and my hope is that each of your executive officers will be awarded a commendation for their contributions during the engagement, but those have not yet been approved. Your Navy Crosses have been approved, and this seems an instance in which it would be best for you to show them, as a testament to the fact that we've been in the fight and proof that we've contributed to the victory."

"I'm so proud of you," Nicola said to him on their way home that afternoon. "I think it is absolutely reprehensible that you kept the details of your engagement to yourself, Ben. I would very much like to have shared more fully in your success and told our friends about it."

"And that is precisely why so much of it was kept from you and the primary reason for doing so," Ben said. "Security was paramount at the time; we didn't want the Germans to know that we'd sunk one of their boats. And be honest, Love, after we had come in and you learned of the battle damage we'd taken, I don't think you had a restful night's sleep until this war ended as it did."

"No," she said quietly, "I didn't. All right, Love, I'll let it go."

"That would be best," Ben said. "It's all behind us now, and we don't have to ever again remain awake worrying about another U-boat rising from the sea to disturb us."

When Nicola emerged from dressing that evening, Ben felt stunned. "You look absolutely beautiful!" he said in honor of a new frock that he'd never seen before.

"Lettice and I picked it out," she said, turning a whirl for him, "all the better to excite your . . . interest."

"What clever girls you are," Ben said. "And you have no idea with what success you've brought it off."

"I shall, I hope, later," she said, once more tweaking him on the arm in a way that he'd come to recognize as invitational.

"I will try to restrain myself, until later," Ben said.

"Yes, that would be best," Nicola laughed. "I don't think it would do for you to try to shag me behind one of the aspidistras."

Ben broke out laughing. "Where, under the sun, did a young lady of such refinement and demure features ever learn the word *shag*?" he wanted to know.

"Lady graduates attending this nation's universities acquire all sorts of linguistic attainments that most young men never hear about," Nicola said pertly. "You simply can't imagine the words our sisters used to bring back from London after their jaunts there."

"Always the surprise, aren't you?" Ben said,

"And always hope to be, Love. And always will hope to be," Nicola said coyly, giving him yet another tweak.

The ball in the assembly rooms went off as Ben and Nicola imagined it would and as Commander Radford had hoped that it might. Nicola, Lettice, and Willow, along with a bevy of their attractive female friends, attracted considerable attention, enough to insure that dance cards remained filled and the dance floor remained lively. The Navy Crosses that Ben, Speck, and Feller wore drew the interest that Radford had intended them to, first in the receiving line where a rear admiral in the Royal Navy raised an eyebrow when told what they were for, and later on the ballroom floor where Royal Naval officers asked about the meaning of the gongs. Although news of the sunken U-boat seemed widespread around the base, their Royal Navy counterparts in the area knew nothing about it. Once informed, Ben could see that the sinking had made an impression and that in some inexplicable way they were suddenly treated less as country or colonial cousins and were admitted to the fold. Harboring a degree of undemonstrated amusement, Ben imagined that the United States Navy had taken a slight step forward in the Royal Navy's opinion and surmised that it was the effect that Radford had sought from the start.

Here and there during the evening, Ben and Nicola spoke with this officer and his wife or the lady he happened to be escorting for the evening, and exchanged words with some of Weymouth's leading citizens who had helped to sponsor the event. At other times, they danced pleasantly together, the orchestra for the evening providing an array of lively tunes, and twice, they helped themselves to selections from the considerable buffet which had been set out in an adjoining room. New Year's itself, when it came, came with cheers and fireworks over the harbor. After at least two glasses of fortifying champagne, Nicola finally stood on her tiptoes and whispered in Ben's ear that she thought she was ready to go home, that she'd like to show him a bit of bliss in celebration of this particular New Year that might give them substantial cause to continue remembering the evening for the remainder of their lives.

Leaving Terry, Lettice, Port, and Willow to disport themselves as well they might, Ben and Nicola retrieved their coats and slipped out, folding up their collars and tightening up their scarves around their necks. They walked easily home together before falling into bed the moment they passed through the door and making the clocks stop with a celebration that seemed to have no end.

By the end of January, having swept the Channel twice over and after having sunk or destroyed every mine that they could find, Admiral Sims finally secured the operation, returning all minesweepers and all submarine chasers to their ports. The crews moved ashore into the receiving barracks. Ben, when he wasn't at the base overseeing the work, and Terry and Port sharing a room ashore when they weren't doing the same, changed their routine radically, while each chaser in Division AA was hauled up onto the ways, scraped down to clean her hull, and given a thorough overhaul in preparation for the vicissitudes of the North Sea. During the day, Ben, Terry, and Port worked crammed together in a tiny office in the basement of the administration building, seeing to work orders, casualty reports on equipment, final reports having to do with their logs and their war diary, and a host of incidentals which required their attention before they could launch themselves once more for the trip north.

In the evenings, depending upon what the ladies had planned, they sometimes went off together, doing trips to the cinema, inspections of Dorchester, and dinners at more country pubs that Lettice and Willow had been able to turn up. Once, cramming themselves into Nicola and Ben's flat, they shared a rather tasty lamb pie that Nicola had managed to put together over a weekend. In the middle of February, Lady Felicia and the Colonel once more had them all out to Trincombe Abbey for a Valentine's Day celebration. Treated to a cold buffet and an enormous spread of cakes and pastries, they were also treated—along with several other young couples invited in from the neighborhood—to an evening of dancing, some of it dependent upon a collection of new jazz records which had been received from the States.

"Is this the sort of music that is always played in the United States?" Nicola wanted to know.

"Jazz has its place," Ben said, in a reassuring way, "but I suspect that our musical tastes range as widely in the States as they do all over the rest of the world. So depending upon where you go, you are just as likely to hear a chamber group doing Bach as you are to hear a fiddler sawing away at some Appalachian hill number, and nearly everyone seems to be humming one Broadway show tune or another."

"So jazz does not provide your steady musical diet?"

"Not by a long shot," Ben said. "It's popular; it has its place, but then, so do all other types of music. I don't play an instrument myself, but gobs of people do, which means that entertainments of one kind or another seem to be going on everywhere."

Nicola seemed glad to hear it. "More so than here, do you think?" she asked.

"Save for the almost nightly sing-songs in the pubs," Ben said, "I would think so. Walk down an American street on a summer evening, and while you will find dozens of people chatting on their front porches, somewhere along the way you are just as apt to find three, four, or more of them making music together. However, the wireless seems to be coming into fashion in the States, so I can only wonder if that may not eventually come to fill the same need."

"Oh, I do hope not," Nicola said.

Following the evening's festivities that Lady Felicia had been so gracious to provide, the three couples returned to Weymouth, climbed the stairs to Ben and Nicola's flat, and shared a celebratory bottle of champagne.

"No danger of upsetting the people down below," Lettice asked as the three of them laughed loudly together over something that Port had said.

"Once I closed the school," Nicola said, "a stationer moved in, but he and his wife do not live on the premises, so we need have no worry about making a disturbance."

But after the dancing and the food and the lively exchanges at Lady Felicia's, a disturbance was the last thing that entered their minds. Instead, after a glass of champagne shared together, the two visiting couples rose and made their departure, leaving Ben and Nicola to share the remainder of their evening together, which they blissfully did.

When the chasers came off the ways at the end of February, Ben, Terry, and Port found that they were more than pleased to get the crew back aboard and out of the receiving barracks. The men, while in barracks, had been given another refresher course at the range to keep them up to the mark, put through a day's schooling on some of the changes that had been made to Navy Regulations regarding their behavior and the subject of general discipline, and been given exams for promotions in their various ratings. At least six of them—including Bates, the oiler, Carson, Farris, Crim, Townsend, and Grange—were able to sew on their new crows while O'Neal was promoted to Chief Petty Officer and required to buy an entire new uniform in keeping with his sudden elevation.

Down in the engine room, Chief Pack gave Ben a quick tour to show him what had been done there with regard to reducing fire hazards and overhauling the engines. According to Pack, the plant was in tip top condition and prepared for whatever the North Sea could throw at them.

"Foresee any changes down here with Bates' promotion?" Ben asked.

"No Sir," Pack said. "As it is and by now, we have every man doing ever other man's job, so the watch sections, in my opinion, are so well qualified that any man down here could run a watch as well as I can."

"That's always good to hear," Ben said. "Both the Navy and I appreciate the way you've trained them up to that level, Chief."

Twice in early March, because a tug and a target were available, Radford sent them to sea for practice gun shoots, not because any of them expected to see hostile action but merely as a matter of routine training. In the event, given the chop that the Channel happened to be churning up on the days they made their practices, marksmanship with the 3"/23 proved less than stellar but good enough to satisfy Ben that they could strike a U-boat should one ever crop up again and take to piracy. Once, a delegation of three French officers came aboard to inspect the chaser, all of whom could speak enough English to make themselves understood. As a result of that visit, Ben, Terry, and Port reached the tentative conclusion that the French were considering a purchase of chasers, with SC 65X possibly included, as soon as the North Sea Barrage had been cleared.

"Has Radford said anything to you about the Frogs buying these vessels?" Terry wanted to know.

"No," Ben said.

257

"Think they might want to acquire them, do you?"

"I certainly think it's possible," Ben said. "Given what they've spent on the war, they must be in hock up to their eyebrows to the New York banks, and for my money, that means that they have precious little to spend on building ships. For coastal duty and as revenue cutters, the chasers would be the perfect thing, and I'm guessing that we would sell them cheap in order not to have to take them back to the States."

"And where, I wonder, might that leave us?" Port said.

"That's the big question, isn't it?" Ben said. "If I'm allowed to augment, I will have to make arrangements for Nicola to move to the States. If I find that I'm shut out, we'll have to decide whether or not I'll want to try to find a ship out of Southampton or some other port like Liverpool, leave Nicola in the flat, and commute between voyages."

"What about you guys? Anything on the burner for either of you?"

"With Lettice," Terry said, "things are complicated. I haven't proposed or anything like that, and while we've had a grand time, I don't think Lettice is ready to consider a proposal either. Given her background and family connections, I'm not convinced that she would be happy in the States, and given the way the economy is going down the tubes over here, I'm not sure that if I elected to stay I could expect much of a future. Without ever talking things over in detail, I think the two of us have more or less decided to give ourselves some breathing space when or if they send us home, with the resolve to come together again after a period if we find that we can't live without each other."

"And you, Port?" Ben said.

"Well," Port said, "I'm having a great time with Willow as the two of you can see, but I'd have to say that I seem to be pretty much on the same footing as Terry. I think the two of us are enjoying each other's company while we can and committed to letting things develop as they will. Willow won't be held back by the constraints Lettice faces. She's said more than once that she's anxious to visit the States, so if push comes to shove, I'll get her over so she can see how she likes it, and we'll let things develop from there."

"Not like the days when the crossing took longer than a month with only about a fifty-fifty chance of surviving it in a wooden ship, is it?" Ben laughed.

"Thankfully," Terry said, "unless you happen to be on a subchaser, that is."

"If we do take these chasers back with us," Port asked, "how do you think we'll go? Will we run for New England direct, or will we go back via the Azores, Bermuda, and then the States?"

"Frankly," Ben said, "I don't have a clue. I'm not even sure if we would run under our own power or if they wouldn't take the whole lot of us in tow."

"Good Lord," Terry said, "that would be hell and humiliating as well."

"Yes," Ben said, "it would."

Finally, at the end of March, early one morning, stake trucks showed up on the pier and began offloading supplies onto the chasers, including food stocks, medical supplies, and spare parts. To Ben's shock, a third class pharmacist's mate named Deacon carrying not only a duffle but also a hammock and a bulging medical kit was also sent aboard to report to Ben.

"That commander of yours," Deacon told Ben when he reported himself aboard, "tole me that you might find it handy to have a guy like me around where we're going. From what he tole me 'fore he sent me over here, I think he's detailed me to you to farm out to whatever chaser may need me somewheres down the road."

"Fair enough," Ben said. "Forward crew's quarters is cramped as hell, but if you play your cards right, I think you can just about swing that hammock of yours somewhere from the overhead."

Later that morning, Radford summoned the chaser captains for a conference aboard the *Mulgrew*. After laying out a track on the charts for them to examine, he also presented them with an op-order and informed them that they would put to sea the following Monday morning in route to Kirkwall in the Orkney Islands.

"Foul weather gear will be mandatory," Radford said. "I expect the winter to be more than a trifle miserable when we arrive there, and there's no telling what we may meet on the way up, so secure for heavy weather even if we can expect better where the Gulf Stream hits the western coast of Scotland. I won't tell you that Kirkwall is like London because it isn't, but it is supposed to be a cozy little place with pubs enough in which your crews may take refreshment, and if that turns out to be the case, I doubt that we'll hear many complaints from them. I'm afraid that I can't tell you a thing about the Scots, but my best advice—the same as I gave when we put in here—is don't rile them. We've been greatly welcomed in Weymouth, and that is the way I want things to be in Kirkwall."

For another hour, Radford answered questions and went over the details of his steaming instructions, and then he dismissed his officers. They returned to their chasers, gathering their own officers and crews together to pass along what they had heard.

On Saturday, leaving Terry and Port to make SC 65X's final preparations, Ben took Nicola up to Salisbury for a night away, treated her to quarters in a posh hotel, and fed her in the dining room. Following a unique and delicious meal which centered on pheasant and sole, the two sat late over snifters of cognac listening to the dining room's string quartet, which played just enough Vivaldi to lighten the mood and just enough in the way of show tunes to put a lilt on the evening. Then, finally, they went up and remained awake long enough almost to satisfy the hunger they felt for one another.

They didn't return to Weymouth until Sunday afternoon, taking the bus down and walking to the flat from the station, each carrying a valise, Nicola's other arm clutching her husband's. Without fanfare and still feeling sated from the meal they'd had the night before, they once more dined on cheese on toast, content to sit together on the sofa following their meal and making small talk until the time arrived for them to go to bed.

In the morning, at the door to the administration building, Ben gave Nicola a lingering kiss before he dropped her off to work. He also left her with the hope that their separation wouldn't last long. Beating a swift path to his ship, he went aboard to find that Terry had seen to everything in preparation for going to sea, that the crew was standing by to take in all lines, and that all he had left to do, upon sighting the appropriate flag hoist from the *Mulgrew*, was to give the men his command. Within minutes, following astern of the *Mulgrew*, leading his Division, they sortied and went to sea.

16

While making good 12 knots for their speed of advance, the *Mulgrew* and her charges were nearly eighteen hours in transit from Weymouth to Milford Haven in Wales. Once moored, everyone save for the watch standers took instantly to their bunks. Ben, having remained largely seated in his chair in the pilot house throughout the day, felt that he was among those who led the charge. The Channel, when they'd sortied out to it, had been rough. SC 65X had rolled and pitched enough to exhaust even the most hearty of men, and once around the Lizard and into the lower reaches of the Celtic Sea beyond Penzance, things had not improved, the tiny vessels merely caught in the trough from a different direction when they virtually reversed course in order to steer to the northeast on their way toward Wales.

In accordance with Commander Radford's op-order—something which demonstrated his obvious foresight about the voyage—the little task group did not sortie on the following morning. Instead, without going ashore, the day was given over to rest and recovery as the crew of this or that chaser saw to upkeep on a fitting here or a fixture there, items which had worked themselves loose during the pounding that they had taken.

Somewhat rested from what they'd had to endure, the vessels sortied at 0400 the next morning. By starting at that early hour and owing to the fact that the seas had calmed slightly overnight, the next leg of their voyage took them through the St. George's Channel and up into the still more sheltered waters of the Irish Sea. They arrived in Liverpool in time to allow a part of the crew ashore for a pint or two before the publicans rang their bells and announced their closing. No one registered great enthusiasm for Liverpool, and Ben, Terry, and Port didn't even bother to leave the ship. Those who did returned in relatively good condition, time and the atmosphere having dampened any of the more hearty activities in which they might have involved themselves.

Once more departing early the following morning, the *Mulgrew* led them into Belfast following the shortest leg of the trip—a voyage which required slightly less than eleven hours. There, the section of the crew which had not gone over in Liverpool left the ship in a pack, found temporary quarters in a place called The Irish Drum, and carried on a frolic inside until the closing bell sounded. Joined with Speck and Feller and their executive officers, Ben, Terry, and Port also went ashore, found a pub which seemed to offer something other than boiled potatoes, and shared enough of a meal together so that, added to the pints of ale that they put down, they came away feeling stuffed to the gills and happily satisfied.

With the intention of permitting each crew to do ongoing upkeep as the voyage continued, Radford kept everyone in port for yet another night, thereby giving each crew a complete liberty in Belfast. Ben, Terry, and Port, having done so well for themselves the night before, seemed content to remain aboard, dining on a stew which Santos put together, and returning to their bunks for nothing more than reading following their meal.

"We have a long leg on for tomorrow, I take it?" Terry said.

"Departure at 0400 once more," Ben said, "and according to the chart, I'd guess it will take us as long as the first leg from Weymouth to Milford Haven."

"So," Port asked, "what's Portree?"

"Scotland proper," Terry said. "Isle of Skye. I wonder if anyone will be wearing a kilt."

"The thing to wonder," Ben said, "is how cold it will be that far north."

Portree, when they finally reached there late the following night, felt cold but not exceptionally cold, leading Ben to assume that they had finally made contact with the Gulf Stream which tended to warm western Scotland.

"And are we now into what is called the Highlands?" Port wanted to know.

"I think that's the general idea," Ben said, "although what that might actually mean is a bit of a mystery to me."

"And there are really palm trees growing up here along the coast?"

"So we've been told," Terry said. "I expected it to be colder than hell up here, but really, it isn't so bad. And that's got to be the effects of the Gulf Stream getting all the way up here."

"Which appears to mean," Ben said, "that around in the North Sea where the Gulf Stream doesn't *git*, it's liable to be colder than hell with the winds coming down off Lapland and Norway."

"I'm sorry you had to mention that," Terry said, glancing in the direction of his foul weather gear.

"I'm sorry that I even had to think it," Ben said. "Fellow I met told me he spent two April weeks in St. Andrews once—that's on the east coast where the Scottish university and the famous golf course are located—and he said that the wind coming off the North Sea was cold enough to freeze rain in the air while coating his mustache with ice."

"We had enough of that in New London last year," Terry said. "Oh, say it isn't so. And how, I ask, can we sweep mines in that kind of weather?"

"Perhaps we won't have to," Ben said. "Perhaps the Navy is just sending us up to Kirkwall so that we'll be in position when the thaw finally sets in."

"Well," Port said as he turned off his bunk light, "at least we can hope."

The voyage to Portree came off without a hitch, although it proved to be a long one which left them sheltering off the east coast of Skye, riding at anchor in the immediate hours after dark. Owing to the rise and fall of the tide, they did not try to enter the tiny harbor there, fearing that the *Mulgrew* certainly and the chasers possibly might be left sitting on their keels damaging them irrevocably when the tide did go out. Instead, a miniature tanker, no larger than a small trawler, came out to them where they'd anchored and tied up, and there the chasers were refueled before getting underway.

Steaming through the North Minch while leaving Lewis and Harris in the Outer Hebrides well to the west, the *Mulgrew* increased the Task Group's speed to 13 knots. After a week in transit, they finally reached the Orkneys and put into Kirkwall after fifteen hours underway from Portree. Given the length of the quay and the depth of the harbor, the *Mulgrew* tied up alongside the quay, the chasers nesting beside her in two three-chaser groups. As before, when they had tied up after dark, no one went ashore, and no one felt sorry for it. North of the Scottish mainland, the seas had given all of them a rougher ride. All of the crews were only too pleased to put down a late supper and once more take to their bunks in the undisturbed waters of the harbor.

"Well," Terry said, crawling into his bunk and pulling both his blankets and his greatcoat up over him, "we're here at last, and it is just about as cold as we thought it would be."

"Yes," Ben said, crawling into his bunk for warmth still fully dressed in his working uniform, "but at least at rest."

"And tomorrow?" Port said.

"None of us, aside from possibly Commander Radford, has the slightest idea what tomorrow may bring," Ben said. "But that it will bring something, you can be sure."

Early the following morning, Commander Radford sent word that he would expect his chaser captains and their officers to assemble in the *Mulgrew's* wardroom at 1300 that afternoon but not before. So, with upkeep from the voyage well underway, Ben gathered Terry and Port, took them ashore, and started them walking.

"Where are we off to?" Terry wanted to know.

"Patience," Ben cautioned, "but I think there's something we've got to see."

Kirkwall, at least the parts of it they walked south through near the harbor, seemed a compact, tightly built little town, most of it fashioned from gray island stone. The ends of the houses rose two or more stories to form pitched angles to match the steep pitch of the roofs, the angles at both ends concluding in narrower upright chimney blocks which formed the base for two, three, or four gray chimney pots.

"I've seen photos of houses like these in Brittany," Port said, "only in Brittany, they all appeared to be painted white."

"Outside of places like this and Edinburgh, I think a majority of Scottish cottages are also painted white," Ben said. "And for that matter, I think the custom continues in places like Wales and Ireland. Whether it takes its origin from Celtic architecture or not, I couldn't say."

"There seem to be an uncommon lot of pubs," Terry said, "far more than Weymouth, if you see what I mean."

"I think what we're going to see will explain that," Ben said.

"But you're not yet telling us what that might be," Port teased.

"Be patient," Ben said with a smile, "and the surprise will be all the better."

Beyond the town and up a well-paved road, they finally topped a rise, and there with the wind blowing from behind, Ben stopped, looked to the south, and said, "Behold."

"Good God!" Terry exclaimed, suddenly going rigid as he surveyed the sight before him.

To the south, with the sun just breaking over it from the east, the entire Home Fleet of the Royal Navy—battleships, cruisers, battle cruisers, light cruisers, destroyers of every type, and auxiliaries of all kinds—lay anchored before them looking like so many gray towers against the backdrop of Scapa Flow.

"This is the fleet that engaged at Jutland, isn't it?" Port asked, his mouth hanging half open as the moment struck him with wonder.

"I think so," Ben said. "Something of a step up from our chasers, don't you think?"

"My God," Terry said, "that fleet is huge! Look at the guns on those battleships! A single round, even a near miss, would pulverize us."

Ben laughed. "I'm afraid," he said, "that a single round from a destroyer would pulverize us. And if that round from the U-boat had caught us any lower, I'm not sure that it wouldn't have done for us as well."

"And what about the fleet that's farther back?" Port said, lifting his hand and pointing beyond the ships that they saw to their immediate front. "Is that a second squadron?"

For a moment, Ben studied the distant ships that Port alluded to, and then, with a voice that sounded more subdued, he spoke. "I'd say that those ships are the ships that these before us fought at Jutland," he said quietly. "I think that's the German Imperial Fleet that surrendered here in November. This is probably the biggest assembly of fighting ships that the world has ever seen in one place."

"What will be done with them, do you suppose?" Terry said. "Wouldn't be a good idea to give them back to Germany, I don't think."

"No," Ben said. "I know very little about it, but I believe that some kind of final disposition is to be decided by negotiation. It's only a guess, but I'd hazard that the Imperial Fleet will be broken up and parceled out to the Royal Navy, the French Navy, the Italian Navy, and some to us. But I don't know. I suppose that it's possible a few will be returned to the Germans for self-defense."

"Sort of hits you like a bolt," Terry said.

"Yes," Ben said, "that's why I thought we ought to see it."

"I guess this explains all the pubs in Kirkwall," Port laughed.

"Come again?" Terry said, still distracted by the sight before him.

"I understand that Royal Navy tars aren't granted the same amount of liberty as we give our people," Port said, "but I don't see any other liberty ports anywhere around, so Kirkwall has got to be the one place that the British lads can go when they do get ashore here."

"I think you've hit it," Ben said. "And that makes me think, too, that we'd better caution our own people to keep their relations with the Royal Navy amicable. The last thing we're going to want up here is a ruckus of any kind. Ready to go back, are you?"

Tightening the collar of his greatcoat and tucking his chin down inside it against the wind, Terry facetiously suggested that they might jog in order to increase body heat and fight off the chill.

They did not jog back, but with an icy wind blowing in toward them from the North Sea, they didn't linger and stopped for coffee in the first pub they found open on their way down from the hill—an establishment called The Viking Inn. The publican claimed to be descended from Ketil Flat-nose, the patriarch of one of the families mentioned in the Icelandic Sagas. Having never read them, Ben, Terry, and Port didn't know the first thing about the Icelandic Sagas, other than that they existed. Given the height and the girth of Ketil

Flat-nose's supposed descendant and because he brewed a good cup of coffee, they were content to accept him at his word and, later, recommended The Viking Inn to the crew as a pleasant place in which to shelter once the Viking battle axe nailed to the bulkhead behind the bar had been discounted.

"We will be in port, doing upkeep, for the remainder of this week," Commander Radford told his assembled officers when he met them in the *Mulgrew*'s wardroom that afternoon. "On Saturday, I expect an additional division of chasers to arrive, Division BB, and later in the summer, two more groups are supposed to join us as they make their way back from Murmansk where they are presently supposed to be fighting the Bolsheviks. And at some point in the next two weeks, I expect the USS *Black Hawk* to arrive. She will act as flagship for the minesweeping fleet, and supposedly, the USS *Panther* will be coming with her as tender for the sweeps. These will be bird class minesweepers with names like *Seagull, Robin, Thrush, Falcon, Osprey*, and there are to be additional repair craft and trawlers coming with them. So by the time all vessels are assembled, we're going to be packed in here like sardines, which means that ship handling is going to have to be of the highest priority if collisions are to be avoided."

It took the combined vessels of the minesweeping detachment longer to assemble than anyone had imagined. The vessels coming up from the south had experienced the normal number of equipment failures and breakdowns that one expected from small ships, each setting this or that group of sweeps or auxiliaries back a day or two in places like Liverpool and Belfast while repairs were carried out. Other delays were experienced when a vessel had to cut its speed owing to engine problems on the voyage north. And finally, off the west coast of Scotland, regardless of the Gulf Stream, gales had kicked up which had kept at least two of the sweeper groups in port for several days as they sheltered from the storms.

Aboard the chasers during this delay, with the crews enjoying port and starboard liberty on successive days, a sense of general joy prevailed. With each chaser having been brought to a tip-top material condition in preparation for operations—a fact which meant that beyond housekeeping and minimal maintenance, there was little work to do—the crew rapidly turned Kirkwall into as much a home away from home as they had enjoyed when they transformed Weymouth in the same way several months before. Adopting The Viking Inn as their own special place, Chiefs Pack and O'Neal swiftly became chummy with the descendant of Ketil Flat-nose with benefits that suited everyone. The crew, having discovered the port to be gifted with a bevy of local lovelies, also came to grips with the fact that those same lovelies could in no way be called "loose." But given the fact that they were on home ground, where everyone knew everyone else and didn't feel constricted by rigid Scotch-Presbyterian mores, the crew also found that the girls they met did not believe that sharing a beer in the pub was something surpassing original sin. This, everyone admitted, did a great deal to smooth and warm the social atmosphere. In short, ranging from the coxswain, Carson, to men like Scarlatti, Light, and Redfern, the crews of SC 65X and the rest of the chasers in Ben's division didn't care very much whether they ever went to sea again or not.

By the middle of April, finally, with the weather only beginning to warm slightly, the sweeper fleet and its auxiliaries at last assembled in the Kirkwall harbor. With the arrival of Captain Edward Patterson, USN, command of the Task Group quickly shifted from Radford to Patterson, who had been sent north by Admiral Sims to oversee the entire operation. The shift in command, as far as Ben could see, seemed seamless. It turned out that Patterson and Radford had known each other during their days at the Naval Academy, and indeed, Patterson only appeared to be two or three years senior to Radford in the Navy's pecking order. Radford would remain in command of his chasers, while Patterson would ramrod the minesweepers and auxiliaries, and the entire operation would be under his overall direction. These were the arrangements he made and handed down when the captains of all of his combined vessels first met as a group, one of Kirkwall's assembly rooms having been hired for the purpose. There Ben, like the other captains, received detailed charts showing the borders of the various North Sea mine fields, including the precise position of each mine when it had been originally laid. What none of the men could account for—something all of them knew from the start—was how the currents might have shifted some of those mines, how various kinds of damage might have distorted them, or how much the simple action of the waves might have unsettled them.

Captain Patterson, balding though he might have been, carrying at least twenty pounds in excess of what his doctors might have believed to be healthy, and looking at them through closely set black eyes, lectured them on the operations they were to conduct with a voice that poured over them like a tempest in staccato. The man knew his business, and in the course of a two-hour pre-operational conference, he left none of them in doubt about it. Then, very swiftly, parts of the Task Group went to sea and began the operation.

Early the following Monday, the crew of SC 65X found they would be leaving harbor at 0800 to follow in the wake of three sweepers which would begin a sweep to the northeast to drop buoys marking the boundary of the nearest minefield that would have to be cleared. The news was met soberly by the men, several of whom found that they were to be plucked from the warmth of The Viking Inn and from the more than pleasant company they'd been keeping with some of Kirkwall's lovelies.

From the moment they left Kirkwall harbor, Ben knew and felt that conditions in the North Sea were not yet what he would have called conducive to sweeping mines. In the first place, the chop was considerably higher than what he would have believed safe for the operation. In the second, the wind was blowing back spray against the wind screens that made it more than difficult to see what the sweeps might be turning up. Finally, given the size of the waves they were climbing up and over, the chaser was rolling and pitching enough beneath their feet that all of them struggled for balance. That SC 65X offered a less than stable platform from which to shoot and sink mines struck Ben as an understatement of considerable proportion. Nevertheless, bobbing up and down one thousand yards behind the minesweepers, they went, Ben and Terry attempting to remain upright in the pilot house while Port supervised Paxton and Scarlatti, the two riflemen who, with their unloaded Springfields slung over their shoulders, clung to the rails of the flying bridge.

"This ain't going to be pretty," Terry said.

"No," Ben said, "it ain't. And if our Dead Eye Dicks can hit anything in this, even a mine, it will be by an unparalleled stroke of luck."

Half an hour later, the *Grosbeak*, the sweep that SC 65X attempted to follow, streamed her cables and began to sweep for mines. In short order, much to everyone's joy, she didn't have to wait ten minutes before she set off the first one—a monstrous explosion some two hundred yards out which quickly set off two more explosions farther out by sympathetic vibration. A dangerous glitch quickly developed when it became clear that the kite or paravane at the end of the cable—the device which kept the cable submerged at the proper depth for sweeping mines—had been blown off by the third and final explosion. The sweep was forced to haul the remains of the cable aboard to splice or replace it while replacing the kite at the same time. When they did, they generated new complications.

In the first place, merely hauling in the cable cut another mine loose without exploding it. When that information was transmitted to Ben over the R/T, he first had to search for the bobbing sphere with considerable care and then, when he and Terry finally sighted it, direct Port and his rifle team onto it.

"Don't go any closer than forty yards," Ben told Terry, who retained the con. "I don't want that little bastard getting thrown down toward us by one of these waves." Then, shouting up the speaking tube to Port on the flying bridge, he told him to issue Paxton and Scarlatti their ammunition clips and turn them loose to sink the mine.

With SC 65X bouncing up and down in the chop like a badly dribbled basketball, rather than the five or ten rounds that Ben had imagined his sharpshooters would need to sink the mine at the distance, they needed a full five minutes and the expenditure of twenty-three rounds before they hit and holed the beast enough times to cause it to sink and disappear.

"What would you guess?" Terry asked. "They hit it with one shot in three?"

"Probably more like one in five," Ben said. "I'm just glad the damn thing sank rather than exploding. For my money, even at between thirty and forty yards, we're still closer than I'd like for us to be."

Unfortunately, once they were back underway, the *Grosbeak*, having dragged in a mine that had become fouled in the damaged cable, pulled it well inside what Ben had set as a forty-yard limit for SC 65X. Without warning, the mine—unstable to begin with after its long time underwater—exploded not twenty yards from the sweeper, nearly lifting the small ship out of the water. The blast sent rivets popping inside the sweep's engine room that ricocheted around the space and off the bulkheads like a series of machine gun rounds, wounding three men, damaging more than a few pieces of equipment, and forcing the sweep's chief engineer to run the bilge pumps without stopping to keep minor flooding in check.

Within five minutes, the captain of the *Grosbeak* came up on the R/T with a request to speak directly to Ben, asking him, "Do you have a pharmacist's mate aboard?" Ben responded that he did. Less than a minute later, he'd put on turns to go alongside the stricken sweeper where, by means of a boom and a sling extended out over the side, Deacon was lifted aboard to render assistance to the wounded men. Even before this operation had been started, both the *Grosbeak* and SC 65X following as escort had turned and started back toward Kirkwall. Their joint operations interrupted and concluded for the day, Ben remained close by as escort in case *Grosbeak* required additional assistance in making port.

"Not a good beginning," Port said when he finally secured his riflemen and came down from the flying bridge.

"No," Ben said, "but be sure you commend Paxton and Scarlatti. They may have expended more ammunition than we anticipated, but you have to give them credit for sinking that rascal."

"I already gave them each a pat on the back," Port said, "but I'll do it again and tell them it's from you."

"Do that," Ben said.

"So," Terry said, "what's that make it? Five down, and only 69,995 to go?"

"Something like that," Ben said. "But I don't think I'm going to tell Nicola about that because, if I do, she'll begin to imagine that we'll be up here until 1925."

"Right," Port said. "Mum's the word. It simply won't do to tell the ladies, or they're liable to leave us in the lurch and protest that we've deserted them."

How long, Ben wondered, would it really take?

Given what *Grosbeak* and Group AA1 had met when they'd gone out to mark the boundaries, Captain Patterson and Commander Radford determined that the time for extensive sweeping had not yet arrived. Both the sweepers and the chasers were accorded yet another ten days of idle dalliance in port. Meanwhile, with *Grosbeak's* wounded taken ashore to hospital, Deacon returned to SC 65X while the sweeper was hauled into a floating dry dock to be given an extensive repair.

For Ben, Terry, and Port, although they often ate ashore and tipped more than a few pints with the crew of SC 65X inside the warm confines of The Viking Inn, time nevertheless seemed to hang heavy on their hands. Daily, they inspected and supervised the work that the duty section had been set to complete aboard. Then, if not required to write a report of some kind, they read, or slept, or devoured the newspapers, or wrote letters to Nicola, Lettice, and Willow who, with each passing day, seemed farther and farther away. Following lunch, something they invariably took aboard, they dressed and strolled into Kirkwall. They walked the streets until they knew them like the backs of their hands, visited the shops where they were on a friendly and first name basis with many of the keepers, and finally, settled themselves into The Viking Inn, where the relative of Ketil Flat-nose set pints of ale before them of a type that they were particularly beginning to enjoy. From time to time, to provide themselves with a treat, they sampled a shot of this or that locally distilled whiskey and never found one that they didn't like. They were careful about it, knowing they could not linger over shots the way they could linger over pints and that their pints didn't carry the kick that a single shot of malt whiskey invariably carried.

"We'll never get this quality in the States," Terry said one evening as the three of them sat together.

"With the Eighteenth Amendment ratified and set to go into effect at the start of the coming year," Port said, "I don't think we're even going to be able to get a good glass of beer anywhere."

"That seems to be the intention," Ben said, "but if you ask me, I'd be willing to bet that the illegal import of spirits, not to mention the illegal brewing of beer, is going to spring up everywhere, and someone or several someones, probably the wrong types, are going to make a great deal of money from it."

"Like with heroin and cocaine?" Port said.

"Exactly," Ben said.

"What the hell do you suppose ever prompted the country to pass such an idiotic law?" Terry said.

"I'd trace it back to the Puritans," Port laughed.

"I think you're more right than you imagine," Ben said. "I don't know what it is about our country, but the professionally virtuous among us, the do-gooders, and the religious fanatics always seem to want the rest of us walking in lockstep with them. If they find we're unwilling, they then try to force their beliefs down our throats as though all of them spoke for the Almighty Himself and carried Moses' tablets around as though delivered directly to themselves."

"The self-righteousness of the thing sort of boggles the mind, doesn't it?" Terry said.

"Yes," Ben said. "And beyond that, it always leaves me thinking that the Almighty must be enjoying considerable laughter at human presumption."

"Not a believer, are you?" Port asked.

"No," Ben said, "I am a believer in some kind of supreme intelligence governing things, but I've always found that I'm pretty much out of sorts with people who try to put words in His mouth or put themselves forward as experts about what He might be thinking. I had a sailor once aboard my first ship who had the gall to tell me that he'd spoken to God that very morning, and that God had told him to tell me that I was supposed to do something in direct contravention to what the captain had ordered. I took the time to explain to him that his mere assumption of such authority demonstrated the same kind of vainglorious pride that Satan was supposed to have gotten into trouble for, but I don't think he ever saw the point."

"My guess," Terry said, "is that this prohibition thing is not going to produce good results. So the question is, will any of the birds that came up with the idea ever see the vainglorious motivation behind it?"

"Beyond mere speculation," Ben said, "I frankly don't know. But just off the top of my head, I don't see how it's going to lead to good things or produce the outbreak of virtue that those folks seek. Talk to me in another year or two, and perhaps I'll have a better idea."

During the first week in May, with the North Sea somewhat calmed down and with the gales that had so recently blown over it having passed, the U.S. Navy's efforts to sweep the mines from its depths finally began in earnest. Groups of three to six minesweepers, followed by at least three chasers, went out together and committed themselves to the duty. Following four sweepers during their first four days out, the three chasers in Group AA1 which Ben led to sea watched with wonder as the sweepers themselves seemed to explode as many as eight hundred mines, while SC 65X alone accounted for another twenty-two mines on the first day, thirty-seven on the second day, fourteen on the third day, and finally a record forty-six on their last day before returning to port. Yet again, however, one of the sweepers, the *Junco*, had her rudder damaged and one of her screws bent when a mine fouled in her cable drew in too close to the ship before it exploded—an accident that prolonged their return to port by four hours as the *Junco*'s speed was reduced even as she labored mightily to maintain the course she was trying to steer.

Back in Kirkwall, Ben and his officers supervised a number of tasks that were required after the days spent at sea, designed to bring SC 65X back up to perfection before she was ordered out for her next stint of duty. Once again, the crew was granted port and starboard liberty. As before, most of the men spent their time in The Viking Inn or immediately outside of it, sitting at tables which the landlord had set up adjacent to the facade so that patrons could avail themselves of beams from the misted orb that the Scots of the islands were wont to refer to as the sun. On one of those evenings, Ben, Terry, and Port, anticipating what they might be letting themselves in for, nevertheless went ahead and ordered Haggis, neeps, and tatties, something which the relative of Ketil Flat-nose took great delight in serving them while announcing that it was his "special" for the day.

"Well?" Ben said, surveying his fellows after each of them had taken the first few bites.

"I think I'm going to be able to get it down," Terry said, "but I don't think I'm going to make a habit of it."

"Not bad," Port said, "not bad at all, but to go with the haggis, I think I'd prefer a second helping of the tatties rather than the turnips, if you see what I mean. What about you, Ben?"

"I intend to write Nicola and give her orders to put it on our menu at least once a week," Ben said, causing the other two to break out in laughter.

"No, really, it's not so bad," Ben said. "I like food with a taste, and the haggis certainly provides one."

Two weeks later while they were out and with June approaching, Santos blew a mine that had worked to within thirty yards of the chaser. Later, when he had time to think about it, Ben imagined that

Santos, without intending to, had fired a round from his Springfield which had triggered one of the horns on the mine, causing it to explode instantly and without warning. At least that was what Ben hoped Santos had done, because whether anyone intended it or not, that particular mine, their twenty-seventh of the day, had done damage, lifting SC 65X almost all the way out of the water and opening two seams in the bow forward of the head and another near the stern which had allowed sea water into the lazaret. Topside, a sizable piece of shrapnel had embedded itself into the wall of the crow's nest, while a much smaller piece had cut Kaine, the man standing watch there, across his forearm. Once they'd got him down from the crow's nest, Deacon had patched Kaine up swiftly enough. But after another day's running and another sixteen mines accounted for, Chief Pack had told Ben that the opened seams were beginning to get ahead of what the pumps could comfortably handle and that he recommended a return to port where damage repair could be seen to by the experts.

"We're not likely to sink going in by ourselves?" Ben quickly asked.

"No Sir," Patch said, his brow knit, "but if we don't go now, we'll risk flooding the bilges, and if it begins to rise above the deck plates, there's always the risk that we could flood the oil sumps under the engines, and that would leave us dead in the water and sinking."

Immediately, Ben turned control of the five other chasers working in the Division that day to Feller, gave orders to reverse course, and headed for Kirkwall, arriving before sundown even as the water below the deck plates had started to slosh up onto them. It wasn't exactly a near thing because the sumps themselves offered another four or five inches of safety before sea water could have gotten into them, but it struck Ben as a nearer thing than he would have liked. Radford, when he knew the reason for their early return, saw things in the same way; so, within the same hour that they came

279

in, they were up on the ways with a repair team from the *Mulgrew* swarming all over them.

Following that trying day, SC 65X remained in port for six more days, two of them spent on the ways. In the meantime, the *Scrub-Jay* working to the south with Chaser Division BB had one of her screws blown completely off and her stern seriously damaged by yet another mine dragged in by a fouled cable and kite. Two of the men on her fantail were killed outright by the explosion while one forward and two others aft were wounded, one of whom suffered a broken leg to go with his wound. The same afternoon, one of the chasers that had followed behind the minesweeping division had a near miss of her own. The blast unseated one of her engines, bent the associated shaft, and broke the coupling between the shaft and the engine. The exploding mine heaved the entire chaser momentarily to a point where the captain of an adjoining chaser said that he could see daylight beneath the victim's keel.

"This duty ain't pretty," Terry said to Ben, as the two of them sat with Port drinking a pint in The Viking Inn that night after the *Scrub-Jay* and the chaser had managed to make their returns without sinking.

"No it ain't," Ben said. "Like it or not, it seems to be a trifle more hazardous than we'd imagined, and the speed with which we're going about it probably isn't helping it become less so."

"I wonder if the commercial shipping industry has any idea what kind of effort is being put into the clearance?" Port said.

"Probably not," Ben said, taking a sip of his beer. "I might be wrong, but my guess is that all they're thinking about is that the war has ended and, therefore—given their probable line of thought—they ought to be able to go wherever they want to go, whenever they want, and that it's our job to open the shipping lanes to them with a snap of our fingers."

"And that, apparently, is what we've been sent to do," Terry said.

"You can bet on it," Ben said. "I remember once hearing about an expression that was supposed to have been common during the Renaissance: *Festina Lente*. I think it means something like 'make haste slowly.' We probably ought to paint that motto on a scrap of board and nail it to the overhead in the pilot house as a warning."

"More encouraging, that, than *Memento Mori*," Terry said.

"Speaking of warnings," Port said, "I suspect that we don't warn the ladies about the hazards associated with this duty."

"Boy, did you ever call that one right," Terry exclaimed. "Lettice would give me hell if she knew what we were doing. Eh, Ben?"

"Not a word will ever pass my lips," Ben said, "or dribble from the point of my pen."

"Yes," Port said, "that would seem best."

On a Saturday afternoon four weeks later, SC 65X and the remainder of the Division limped back into port having accounted for approximately 463 mines by rifle fire, not to mention the much larger number that the minesweepers had destroyed after their sweep through one of the more southerly minefields. They were stunned to learn that the Imperial German Fleet—the fleet that Ben, Terry, and Port had seen in the distance on the morning after they'd first arrived in Kirkwall—had scuttled itself in depths of Scapa Flow.

"I'm afraid there's little to see," Commander Radford told Ben when he first conveyed the news. "Scapa Flow is relatively shallow, so here and there, a bit of this ship or that ship's superstructure is showing above the water. In a few cases, the Royal Navy was able to get aboard and beach a few of the sinking ships, but that's about the limit of what's showing over there. To put it in plain speech, the negotiations went awry. Apparently there had always been the possibility that the ships would be restored to Germany, but the date which the Peace Conference set for the limit of those negotiations was reached without a decision. The German admiral in command did not receive the word that an extension had been granted, so as a result, fearing that his fleet would be broken up and parceled out to the various Allied navies, he ordered it scuttled. Damn shame, if you ask me."

"Good Lord," Ben said, "how did they do it so fast?"

"Apparently," Radford said, "they'd prepared methodically. Any number of the watertight doors and hatches were welded open so that they couldn't be closed, tools for shutting the sea cocks were dropped over the sides, steam turbines and reduction gears were systematically disabled, and just about everything else you can name that would have helped to take those ships to the bottom was given assiduous attention. The Royal Navy did what it could. As I said, they managed to beach a few ships before they sank, but if I have the numbers right, I think that fifty-three or fifty-four ships were a total loss."

Ben found that he could hardly imagine it, and when he returned to SC 65X and told Terry, Port, and the remainder of the crew what had happened, they found it difficult to imagine as well. Nothing like it that Ben knew of had ever happened before.

"In a manner of speaking," Terry said, "I suppose that really is the end of the war. I mean, on the face of it, there's nothing left for us to fight, is there?"

"Aside from our own mines," Ben said, "there doesn't appear to be. The U-boats are gone, and let's hope that's the last that the world will ever see of them."

"Amen," said Port.

In the middle of July of that year, not eight days beyond the celebrations the ships had held in honor of Independence Day, the USS *Richard Bulkeley* unwittingly dragged in a mine which exploded so close aboard that the ship sank, taking her commanding officer and several members of her crew with her. Elsewhere on the same day, the *Eider* suffered serious damage from another mine, and chaser SC 47 fired on a mine which exploded with such force that it seriously damaged the bulkheads of her pilot house and blew out all of her windows.

Sweeping a field to the north of the stricken ships, Division AA managed to remain intact. SC 65X accounted for a total of thirty-one mines between sunrise and sunset, one of which, allowed in to something like thirty-five yards, gave everyone aboard a shaking when it blew.

Later that evening, Port stood the evening watch on the bridge, running astern of the sweepers which had returned to the safety of waters they'd already swept earlier in the day. After taking supper with the crew and returning to officer's quarters, Terry looked up from where he sat and said, flatly and without emotion, "Ben, my hands are beginning to shake."

"That means you've probably held yourself together better than the rest of us," Ben said. "Mine have been shaking for the last three days. Look around you, almost everyone else is in the same boat. It's the tension, I think. It's not knowing when or where one of those bastards is going to pop to the top and do for us when we least expect it and can't do a thing about it. Our sense of mortality is betraying us, and I'd guess that it explains why some men take to the bottle."

"An option we don't have," Terry said.

"An option we don't have," Ben confirmed.

"So our option is?" Terry asked.

"Ride it out as best we can," Ben said. "Keep our eyes glued to the seas behind those sweeps, and hope for the best."

"Not much of a consolation, is it?"

"Absolutely none," Ben said.

On the 20th, twenty-two miles east of the Shetlands, while following the sweeps on a course that might eventually have led them all the way to Bergen in Norway, SC 65X ran as near as she was ever to run in the direction of a disaster. Directly ahead of them the mine that everyone aboard had always feared rose swiftly to the surface and exploded suddenly and probably sympathetically in relation to three additional mines that the sweeper they were following set off ahead of them. SC 65X's bow lifted high out of the water, nearly stood them on their stern, the blast opening at least three of their seams in the bow and two more in the engine room. Above decks, every man standing was thrown from his feet, the riflemen on the flying bridge only barely managing to keep from being thrown into the sea when they painfully straddled the deck railings. Down in the pilot house where Carson was on the wheel, he was thrown with enough force against the chart table to his rear that he cracked a rib, while Port suffered a broken nose when he crashed into the R/T assembly on the bulkhead. Terry and the messenger of the watch, Osborn, were both momentarily knocked unconscious when they collided going down, and Ben, sitting in his chair, took a sharp cut across his cheekbone from a shard of glass that had been blown back past his eye when the window to his side imploded.

Clapping a towel to the side of his face to stop the bleeding, Ben called for damage reports, collected them from Pack and O'Neal, and summoned Deacon to the bridge to see to the injured. When Carson finally managed to get back on his feet and once more exerted control over the steering, Ben ordered him to reverse course and head for Lerwick in the Shetland

Islands, the nearest port into which he could guide his vessel. Then, finally, he got onto the R/T and turned over command of the Division to Feller, while also informing the leader of the sweeper group that he had lost two engines, was taking water, and intended to head for Lerwick in order to avoid sinking. Asked if he required escort, Ben replied in the negative, informing the sweep commander that he could easily make the distance on one engine as long as the pumps could keep up with the leaks they'd suffered when the mine blew. That he would be taking a risk in making the journey alone seemed clear, but Ben knew his ship and knew his crew. Then, with few words and firm, Ben told Pack to open the remaining engine up and make the run with all possible speed.

With Lithgow and Garcia in the engine room to oversee the plant, Ben's two chief petty officers turned to with a vengeance, driving bed sheets into the opened and flooding seams with a combination of hammers and cold chisels, then shoring where they could with mattresses and timber. Owing to their location beneath the deck plates, closing the seams in the engine room turned out to be much more difficult. But with the flooding reduced up forward, the pumps showed themselves just able to keep the water level in the bilges at an acceptable level.

At Ben's direction, Deacon saw first to Carson's rib, which he bound tightly in hopes that it would relieve the man's pain. Once Deacon had seen to him, Ben sent Carson to his bunk while moving Light onto the wheel. Deacon then saw to Port's nose, cleaned him up, and did what he could with sticking plaster to straighten the mess so that it might heal properly.

"You're lucky you didn't split the skin," Deacon said, "but you gonna have two black eyes, thas sure."

"Ain't life wonderful," Port said, the sound of his voice altered owing to the closure of the nasal passage. "For how long?"

"Ten days, two weeks. Not long," Deacon said, turning to Ben.

With Ben, Deacon used butterfly bandages to close the wound, three of them.

"Not too deep, but deep enough to leave a scar if we don't use these," Deacon said. "I could take stitches, but those would leave a scar for sure, so let's see if dese butterflies will work."

"Good enough," Ben said, once more getting back into his chair where he could feel the rush of the wind against his face through the broken window.

SC 65X made Lerwick without sinking in slightly over two hours that afternoon. There, with the *Panther* in port to see to the minesweepers and the chasers that would team with them when they arrived from Murmansk, Ben found immediate succor for his ship. A way had been built so that his chaser was quickly inspected for damage, pulled up on the way, and the work begun by the *Panther*'s carpenters and engineering ratings while the crew was temporarily berthed aboard *Panther*. Ben, Terry, and Port were billeted together in a single room in a chilly local hotel. At first the elderly female desk clerk hesitated to permit Ben and Port entrance until she had satisfied herself that their injuries had resulted from what Ben called "battle damage" rather than what the woman had perceived to be "uncivilized and barbaric behavior" incurred through excessive drink.

If Kirkwall seemed a tidy small town, Lerwick seemed even smaller and more tightly constructed, the gray stone houses rising along even narrower streets. Somewhat groggy from the day's experience, the three didn't walk far when they left the hotel to seek an evening meal. When they discovered the first pub that they turned up, they went in and found most of the remainder of their crew already in residence. Once more, Ben treated himself to haggis while Terry and Port settled for mutton, none of the three leaving hungry or thirsty after settling their food with a pint of the local beer. But one beer was enough that night, and back in the hotel, without even waiting for the clock to strike the hour of 2000, all three of them piled into their beds and slept like rocks.

The *Panther*'s carpenters took three days to put SC 65X back into a condition that they considered to be fit for sea. Had they had other sweeps or chasers in port upon which to work, Ben imagined that they would have accomplished the job in half the time. Without much to do before the Murmansk group joined them, the *Panther*'s petty officers seemed content to work slowly but well, and as far as Ben and the crew were concerned, that suited them perfectly.

Once back afloat, they departed Lerwick almost instantly, and after a three-hour voyage, arrived back in Kirkwall only an hour or two before the sweeps and the remainder of Division AA returned to harbor. It was during that interval that Commander Radford called Ben to come to his office on the *Mulgrew* and report.

Commander Radford waited until Ben had reported fully how SC 65X had been damaged and what the *Panther* had done for her. Then, showing Ben a broad smile, he launched into a short speech of his own.

"Your chaser as well as the others in Division AA will go briefly into dry dock for a few days, and then we're done here," he said. "Divisions DD, EE, and FF are coming up to relieve us, and the chasers from Murmansk will soon arrive. We were first over, and let the gods be praised, we're the first to be going back. Four days from now, we'll all head for Weymouth, so you might want to send your ladies a telegram because we are no longer confined to security for our movements. Your crew, I believe, will be nothing short of euphoric, and I would imagine that all of you will be able to rest easier knowing that your chances of being sunk by a torpedo or blown up by a mine are finally and truly ended."

Even as Radford continued to speak, Ben could feel an immediate loosening of his muscles as the stress he suddenly realized that he'd been under began to sweep away from him like a dam loosing its water or a twisted rubber binding suddenly unwinding and returning to stasis.

"Don't pass out on me," Radford quickly said, once more alerting Ben to his presence.

"No Sir," Ben laughed. "I just didn't realize that it would be coming this soon. You've sort of caught me off guard."

"Ben," Commander Radford said, "I shouldn't like to overstate, but you and your fellows have done well over here, and I commend you for the leadership you've demonstrated and for the job that you've done. If, in the years that come our way, we find that we are able to serve together once more, I shall consider it a pleasure."

"And I too, Commander," Ben said, standing to shake the man's hand.

When the *Mulgrew* and Division AA took their departure from Kirkwall, everyone aboard SC 65X left with a good feeling about the going away celebrations that the landlord of The Viking Inn had staged for them. They spent eight days making their way back to Weymouth, the summer seas between the Hebrides, the Irish, and even the Celtic Sea remaining calm enough to make their voyage something more like a pleasure cruise than a wartime transit. In the Channel, once more, they rolled and pitched, but never to excess. When they finally turned to port late one afternoon and put into Weymouth, Ben, Terry, and Port felt more than a slight bolt of delight to find the three women with whom they'd looked forward to reuniting waiting on the pier for them.

"Oh my," Terry said, "don't they look lovely, and isn't it simply tops to be back?"

"Amen," said Port.

"Yes," Ben said, "it most assuredly is."

17

For days after Ben returned from the North Sea, he and Nicola experienced a period of bliss that went far and beyond anything they had ever experienced before. For his part, Ben felt overjoyed to be home and back in Nicola's company; for hers, she told him that the days and hours they'd been away from one another had seemed like an eternity and had been the most trying of her life. Lovingly, happily, they settled back into their married life together and didn't much think about the immediate future. But not more than a week after Ben returned, they woke one morning and found that the world had not actually come to a stop and that their lives, like the lives of everyone else around them, would continue to move forward.

Ben had walked Nicola to her office that morning, dropped her off to start her day, and gone to his ship where he found a message summoning him to Commander Radford's office on the *Mulgrew*. Two hours later, around the time for morning tea to be sent around in the administration building, Ben had returned there, taken Nicola outside the building for her brief break from the morning routine, and delivered what he imagined to be a piece of striking news.

"I've received word from the Department of the Navy," Ben said, speaking quietly. "I'm to be allowed to augment, and if I do, we'll be going to the States at the end of September, to San Diego where

I'm to be the executive officer on one of the new Eagle Boats—half the size of a destroyer, twice the size of my chaser, five officers and fifty-six men in the crew. It's a promotion, and a nice one for a former Reserve officer. So, my Love, why don't you give me your thoughts?"

"I'm ready when you are," Nicola said, flashing him a smile and giving him a kiss before she threw her arms around him for a hug.

"You won't regret leaving England?" Ben asked. "Leaving your home?"

"Of course I'll regret it," Nicola said. "I love England, and I love England being my home, but I love you more, Ben, and I couldn't bear the thought of being without you. We will make a new home in San Diego, or wherever you take me, and I'm sure we will be as happy there as we would be anywhere. But if we are going, we will have to make preparations, and you will have to guide me through whatever steps are necessary for my immigration and so forth."

Fortunately, the personnel office handled most of the details for them right down to and including the shipment of their few possessions—assistance gratefully accepted—which left the two of them free to concern themselves largely with a series of leave takings and a signature on a document or two.

Meanwhile, the personnel office also began to demobilize the crews associated with the chasers in Division AA, with the result that early one morning in mid-September, Ben mustered his crew on the fantail of SC 65X. There he made them a brief speech, saluting them for the contribution they had made to the winning of the war, shook the hand of each of his men as he thanked them for their support, brought them to attention, and saw them off with their duffles. Chiefs Pack and O'Neal marched them ashore and up the pier to the bus that would take them to Southampton, a transport, and their transit back to the States.

Ben, Terry, and Port, for the time being, remained on board just long enough to complete the paperwork that took SC 65X out of commission and to receive the officers and crew from the Belgian Navy—representatives of the country which had bought SC 65X with the intention of running her up the Channel to Bruges, where she would in future take to the seas under the Belgian flag. With the final amenities performed, all papers signed, and the vessel's change of command having taken place, Ben, Terry, and Port picked up their duffles and went ashore themselves, glancing back only once at the ship which had been their home for so many long months.

"She looks very small from here," Terry said.

"Yes," Ben said, feeling a sudden sense of loss, "yes, she does. I hope the Belgians will take good care of her. So, what's the drill for you two?"

"We're here for another week, doing our best to keep Lettice and Willow happy," Port said, "but according to our orders, we're to be in Southampton on the 27th for muster aboard some transport named the *Portsmouth Castle*, destined apparently for a transit to New York."

"Right," Ben said, "Nicola and I are booked for the same ship, Stateroom 37C. Drinks in the passenger lounge on the first night out?"

"Absolutely," Terry said, "and dinner to follow."

"You're on," Ben said.

Three weeks later, disembarking onto a pier flanking the western side of Manhattan, Ben and Nicola took leave of Terry and Port, Terry announcing his intention to remain in New York and start law school at Columbia, Port telling them that he intended to spend a few days in New York before heading west to Tacoma and a resumption of commercial fishing.

Having seen the two on their way after a flourish of hugs and handshakes, Ben and Nicola took a taxi to Grand Central, boarded a train, and inside their booked compartment, started their journey to San Diego in a state of bliss.